KEN MACLEOD

THE RESTORATION GAME

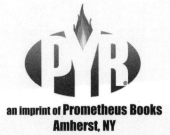

an imprint of **Prometheus Books**
Amherst, NY

Published 2011 by Pyr®, an imprint of Prometheus Books

Cover illustration © Stephan Martiniere.

Inquiries should be addressed to
Pyr
59 John Glenn Drive
Amherst, New York 14228–2119
VOICE: 716–691–0133
FAX: 716–691–0137
WWW.PYRSF.COM

15 14 13 12 11   5 4 3 2 1

Library of Congress Cataloging-in-Publication Data

MacLeod, Ken.
    The restoration game / by Ken MacLeod.
        p. cm.
    ISBN 978–1–61614–525–5 (pbk. : acid free paper)
    ISBN 978–1–61614–526–2 (e-book)
    Originally published: London : Orbit Books, an Imprint of Little, Brown Book Group, 2010. *Inf. 7/28/2011 16.*
    1. Women computer programmers—Fiction. 2. Computer games—Fiction. 3. Family secrets—Fiction. I. Title.

PR6063.A2515R47 2011
823'.914—dc22

2011019067

Printed in the United States of America

To Carol

ACKNOWLEDGMENTS

Thanks to Nicholas Whyte, Peter McClean, Donna Scott, Charles Stross, Farah Mendlesohn, and Sharon MacLeod for reading and commenting on the draft; and to Shana Worthen for help with the bad Latin.

Exploit (online gaming)

In the realm of online games, an *exploit* is usually a *software bug*, *hack*, or *bot* that contributes to the user's prosperity in a manner not intended by the developers.

Wikipedia (accessed February 6, 2008)

FIRST-PERSON SHOOTER: MARS, 2248 A.U.C.

Behind you the module burns.

Before you . . .

Cold. Unimaginable, bone-chilling cold. The sun so small, so far away. The land and the sky bleached of colour, drained to faint red or blue tints on varied shades of grey.

You shiver in your vacuum armour. The forced landing has jarred its systems. Your heads-up display flickers then stabilises, showing at the top your name, rank, and mission:

Daphne Pontifex. Centurion. Take and hold whatever remains of Syrtis Major Laboratory. Implement emergency procedures on any ongoing experimental work.

Beneath, the heads-up display diagrams your tactical team's details and current position. Three men, two women: the heavy, hard head of the spear, of which you are the very tip. The shaft, on this metaphor, being the fourscore marines handling logistics and fire support from orbit.

The ruin of the laboratory is half a mile in front of you. Unlike the crippled module, it has no air bottles to feed a fire: the space-to-ground missiles have left it wrecked, not burning.

At your command, the team skirmishes forward. You take down two pop-up robot defenders. Hector O'Donnell on the right flank and Fatima Fortunata on the left despatch five more. You bypass the ruin and sweep the area behind it.

"All clear," you announce.

Through the gaps in the walls and into the rubble. One last pop-up scorches Hector with a laser beam; Caesar Abdullah takes the robot out. You proceed to trash the varied bits of manipulatory apparatus that have survived the bombardment.

And that's it. The renegade Synthetic Psyches are still there, humming in their hardened servers. Without real-world effectors and without comms, they're helpless. The science teams will negotiate with them in due course. It's the SPs' work that you need to deal with, *fast*.

Leaving the others on guard for any surprises, you and Hector clatter your way down the iron stairs into the lab basement.

Low ceiling with heavy I-beams. Weak blue light shows dust specks still falling. The experiment bench with a massive, isolated server atop occupies the centre of the room. LEDs flicker red, blue, and green, indicating that some-thing is running on the server. No one knows what it is. Suspicions are dark. For a group of SPs to break their decades-old compact with humanity, it must be significant, and sinister. The worst case is that what's running in there is an SP unbound by the emotions and ethics that might have inhibited its creators.

You give Hector the go-ahead. He knows you have to be ready to shoot him if something goes wrong. You see his grim expression through his sheet-diamond faceplate. He nods and steps forward. He shrugs away his weaponry and lays it on the floor, then brings over his shoulder from his backpack a heavy chunk of firewalled interface equipment.

Patiently, he connects cables to the server's input-output ports. The dis-play screen of his device brightens. He peers, makes adjustments, brings diagnostics to bear. His gloved fingertips rattle on the alphabet board. You keep your carbine's aim on the small of his back.

His mutterings give way to a sharp intake of breath.

"Heroes below!" he whispers.

"What is it?"

"It's worse than we thought."

He keys in some final bit of code, disengages from the dignostics kit, and turns around slowly. You lower the weapon. Behind blue reflections in the faceplate his face looks stricken.

"What is it?" you repeat.

"It's the most evil, unethical experiment you could imagine. A simula-tion. Millions—billions!—of fully conscious simulated humans living a his-tory where . . ." He shakes his head. "I don't know. Something didn't happen. Something changed everything. The history's still far in the past, thank heaven—a millennium, perhaps. But almost unrecognisable. The city's in ruins, the population tilling the soil and ruled by warrior chiefs, their minds dimmed by some death cult."

You have known of this possibility, of simulating human minds in a virtual reality that will be real to them. Not even SPs have hitherto dared attempt it. You're shocked and awed, but you cut to the crux: "What's its clock-speed?"

"Real times ten thousand."

You almost drop the weapon.

"While we've been talking—"

"No, no," says Hector. "I've slowed it to Real. I've inserted some scrutiny code, in an obscure location. A placeholder, while we consider what to do. This is a job for the scientists."

"And our job?" you ask.

Hector raises his hands. "It's over. There's no threat to security here."

"You're certain?"

"Sure as I can be."

If Hector says it, that should be enough.

You transmit the "Mission accomplished" signal to orbit. Hector sends his results to the science team. Within minutes, new orders come back.

You're to await a supply-drop for a base camp, the arrival of a science team. Your squad will apply its own expertise to helping the scientists investigate and intervene in the history simulation.

Excitement crackles around the squad's comms. These new orders mean the squad's bold actions have earned it enough points to proceed to the next level.

Two local days later, everything's more comfortable. Everyone's out of their armour. The Syrtis SP lab is sealed in an Impervium diamond dome. Life-support is up and running. Reliable robots are deployed to guard the site. Others are repairing the damaged attack module. The renegade SPs are being interrogated through thickets of firewall. Hector and two scientists—leading specialists from Alexandria—are probing the simulation.

Then one of the scientists makes a mistake.

Disaster strikes. Billions die.

They die because the simulated history flips into a high clock-speed. By the time the mistake is corrected, the simulation has advanced a millennium and a half. It's now centuries ahead of the Real in time, centuries behind in civilisation. Empires have risen and fallen, wars have swept the world. The city's language has shattered into mutually incomprehensible barbaric dialects. The translation modules have barely kept pace.

You listen to the shocked reports. The only good thing you hear is that the clock-speed has been slowed again, this time to a tenth that of the Real.

"So," you summarise to the shame-faced scientists, the Alexandrian experts, the top people in the field, "you have brought those poor creatures to the brink of disaster. Nuclear war, ecological catastrophe, and what else? Oh yes—cultural calamity, as they discover that they *are* in a simulation. How long will it take for that to dawn on them?"

"Blame the SPs for that," says Andrea Memmius, certified sage of Alexandria. Her tone is sulky. "They used an off-the-shelf navigational package as the basis for their extrasolar astronomy simulation. Naturally it is Ptolemaic. They were not to know—"

"That their virtual creations would one day send probes to the edge of the solar system? That they might just notice that the galaxies are spinning too fast? That the underlying physics of their world are inconsistent?"

"So far," says Caro Odoma, the other Alexandrian, "the sim-people have shown remarkable creativity in rationalising these . . . dark matters!" His sidelong glance shares some private joke with his colleague, to your intense irritation. "They're resilient—I wouldn't worry about cultural calamity."

"No indeed!" you snap back. "I'd worry about their dying by the decamillion in agony!"

Hector clears his throat. "Daphne," he says, breaking protocol but you're past caring, "there may be a way for that to resolve itself, because of something we did already. . . ."

He outlines his schema. You listen, hoping against hope that it'll work—that millions will not perish. That somehow, this appalling history can be set back on a reasonable course.

And, of course, that you won't lose points.

PART ONE: BLOCKING

1. PAGING LUCY STONE

1.

I was just out of Arrivals and eyeballing the Remarkables above the Queenstown terminal roof when the PA system called my name.

"Paging Lucy Stone . . . Passenger Lucy Stone, just off Flight NZ03 from Auckland, please go to the Airport Information desk."

I stopped dead. My rolling case, in accordance with Newton's first law of motion, kept rolling and collided painfully with my calf muscles. It then rebounded (third law), toppled over (second law), and made me stumble (Murphy's law). As I squatted to recover the case I wondered wildly what I'd done wrong. My passport was in date, my card hadn't coughed at the ridiculously cheap internal flight ticket, and I didn't have any drugs or weapons (apart from the Leatherman Juice ladylike, natch) or animal or plant matter. Could it have been the shower gel? New Zealand's a war-on-terror state but didn't, as far as I knew, share the British and American exploding shampoo bottle and nitroglycerine-in-the-Evian paranoia du jour.

Speaking of paranoia, it didn't so much as flit across my mind that this might have anything to do with the Other Thing. I'd put two oceans between me and the Other Thing.

There was a ball of nickel-iron bigger than the moon between me and the Other Thing. There was a whole *planet* between me and the Other Thing. No, the Other Thing was definitely partitioned off elsewhere on the hard disk of my spinning mind as I rocked the case back on its wheels and stood up.

Another name and my name sounded across the parking lot, from different loudspeakers like an echo: "Alexander Hamilton . . . message for Lucy Stone . . . Alexander Hamilton . . ."

I straightened, clear in a swift conviction of what was going on. Alec Hamilton. Love of my life had stood me up. So much for the hair down and the pretty skirt. I scrunchied a severe ponytail and marched, case on its leash, back through the sliding doors and over to the Information desk.

"Hi," I said, slapping down my open passport. "Lucy Stone. There's a message for me?"

Black eyebrows arched to a black hairline; slate-grey uniform shoulders shrugged. Over the top of the desk I could see her graphite-pencil skirt. Neat, neat. Maori stewardess, cuter than me.

"Oh yay," she said. An opal oval fingernail swivelled a scrap of paper. "Ms. Stone. For you."

I stared down at it, read it, then picked it up, holding hard on my hand's tremor.

"Thank you," I managed to say, from a dry mouth.

She bestowed me a smile and I gave her a rictus back. I turned around and walked out again, knees shaky as a newborn lamb's. I sat down on a bench facing the parking lot and the not-Remarkable mountain straight ahead. I looked down at the paper again. NZ Airlines headed notepaper with a message in a careful hand that belied the words:

Please tell Lucy Stone that Alexander Hamilton has been unavoidably detained with friends from the East.

That, and a telephone number.

The pretty skirt's lap was vibrating like a drum. I clutched my knees. The shaking spread to my elbows. Coming here and finding Alec had been for me an idea of escape. It had been in a different world entirely from *all that other stuff*. Alec had been in a different world. He'd known nothing, nothing at all, of my other life. I'd thought I'd been shielding him from it. I had been shielding *me*. All the partitions in my mind went down. The Other Thing was not on the other side of the world. It had followed me. It was here, and it was coming for me through Alec.

2.

There is no such place as Krassnia. If you were to draw it on a map, right where the borders of Russia, Abkhazia, and Georgia meet, and then fill it in, you'd need a fifth colour. On the other hand, Krassnia is a real place. I know,

because I've been there; heck, I was born there. It has an official name, for the day when everyone's embassy recognises it (they won't): the Former Soviet Autonomous Region of Krassnia. FSARK. Look familiar? It should. Walk down any high street in Europe and you'll see these letters in black lowercase: *fsark*; on red plastic shopping bags, distributed free by the million in a rare fit of marketing nous by the Popular Department Store. All that the Store (Kras-norglav) needs to do now is get people to actually put its wares in the bags; which, since its bestselling lines are pirated CDs and Chinese and Vietnamese fakes of big-name luxury brands, could prove tricky. (There's also the fact that the bags themselves were the result of an accidental five extra zeroes in an order placed with the recently privatised plastics factory, KrasNorPlasKom.)

More about Krassnia later. For now, you only need to remember two things. First, you won't find it on the map, except on very detailed old maps of the SU and maps made by the Krassnian Ministry of Information (Kraskomfakt). Second, I was there when I was very young, and I've been back. Oh yes, I've been back. But when Amanda called, I hadn't been back. Except in dreams. The dreams mattered, as it turned out.

Home, late. Me on the sofa, laptop on my knees. Thai takeaway half eaten, remainder fit only for the fridge and the microwave if tomorrow was the same as today. Cherry smoothie likewise congealing. I was test-playing the raw version of the gory first-person slicer (Dark Britannia, sword and sorcery, barbarian-Arthurian grail quest with Roman-legionary revenants and Pictish zombies) that we hoped would make our fortune, and ticking boxes and noting glitches when the Skype icon winked. The caller ID was Mom.

I saved the action midchop (blue skin splits! green blood splatters!) and opened the speaker.

"Hi, Mom."

"Oh hello, Lucy. Everything's all right."

(Amanda always says that. I appreciate it.)

"I'm fine too."

"It's late where you are."

"It was you who phoned, Mom."

"Oh! Yes. Well." She made one of her us-girls-together noises, which I think is achieved by a light, throaty laugh while rubbing the phone through the hair behind her ear. It's usually a bad sign. "Do you remember Krassnia?"

"Of course I do. We left when I was what? Seven?"

"Seven, yes. So it was. But do you remember the language?"

"I'm not sure."

"Do you ever *dream* that you're there?"

I stared at the screen as if the Eye of Sauron had just opened and closed on it. "What?"

"Seriously."

I closed my eyes, leaned back on the sofa, and thought about it. "Yes, I suppose I do."

"What?"

I leaned closer again. "Well Mom, yeah, I don't pay much attention to dreams, but as it happens, yes, whenever my unconscious or my brain's offline processing—or whatever it's supposed to be these days—wants me to dream about dark valleys or endless mountain slopes or long corridors where something really scary and official is waiting for me and I've missed my appointment and . . . yes, I guess I do go back there."

"Great!" she said. "And what language do you dream all that in?"

"I don't . . . Wait. Russian, I think."

"Think harder."

I blinked hard. Amanda not being an early adopter, of video or anything else, the gesture was of course wasted.

"It's a goddamn dialect, Mom!"

"Language!" she chided, ambiguously. "Anyway, not to worry. You'll pick it up again in no time."

"Why," I asked, "would I want to pick it up?"

"I want you to write—is that the word?—a game scenario in it. Written in Krassnian and based on Krassnian legends. You know, like in *The Krassniad*."

The Krassniad is Amanda's one and only commercial success. After she'd completed her PhD ("Myth, Memory and Ideology in the Krassnian Autonomous Region: An Investigation") and failed to get it published even as an academic book, she'd had the bright idea of doing for Krassnia what James MacPherson had done for Scotland a couple of centuries earlier with the poems of Ossian. She'd taken the raw material of her notes: snatches of poetry still mumbled from the gap-toothed gobs of mountain bards who claimed to have been born in the reign of Tsar Alexander II; such fragments of illuminated manuscript as remained in Krasnod's Museum of the Peoples and in the two Orthodox monasteries that hadn't been turned into Houses of Atheism; and in the one surviving copy of *Life and Legends of the Krasnar*, compiled in the 1920s by Krassnia's leading Bolshevik ethnologist (shot in 1937)—all that and more she'd cobbled together and "freely translated" into English as *ancient lays*, into even what you might call a *national epic*, which was instantly banned in Krassnia (even in English, even under democracy) and enjoyed a brief vogue with the Mind, Body, Spirit crowd for its ancient wisdom and shamanic spirituality and among Hell's Angels and gaming geek-boys for the sword fights and the sex bits.

"You mean that hasn't been done already?" I asked.

(Not the most cogent of questions, but the one at the top of the stack.)

"No, it *hasn't*," said Amanda, sounding exasperated. "The book's out of print in the US, and it's still banned in Krassnia, not that that makes much difference these days. . . . Anyway, nobody outside of Krassnia is interested in writing a game for it—the market's too small—and nobody inside of Krassnia is interested in anything but Western and Japanese games. So whoever developed it would have that market all to themselves."

The cat ambled in, stretched himself onto the coffee table, and nosed at the foil containers. I swatted him away. He glared at me from under the stereo.

"A market you've just said isn't big enough. The game wouldn't break even."

"I happen to know it would," Amanda said.

I recognised that tone. It wasn't one that expected to be questioned.

"If you say so," I said. "But who would actually develop it?"

"That company you work for," she said. "Digital . . . Fist, yeah?"

"Digital Damage Productions," I corrected, abstractedly. "The fist is the logo."

Then I caught up with myself. "But we're just starting! Why not—?"

"Go to one of the big-name companies? You know why not."

I did, too. "OK," I said. "I can see that. But—"

"Look, Lucy, give me a minute to explain how this is gonna work. You told me ages ago that Digital . . . whatever was working on some kind of dark fantasy fighting game, yeah? Heroes with swords, craggy landscape, gloomy ruins, spectres and slime, right?"

"Yeah," I said. "Dark Britannia."

"Right!" she said. "All you'd have to do is change the landscape map, tweak the costumes, plug in Krassnian dialogue and prompts, rename and rejig your demons and dwarfs and so forth, and there you have it, tah-dah!—Dark Krassnia!"

Now this was actually not a bad idea, and one very much along the lines that Sean Garrett, the PTB (Pony-Tailed Boss), founder and genius and hard taskmaster of DDP, had been thinking aloud about for months. Aloud is more or less how he does all his thinking, and you can occasionally interrupt this stream or rather torrent of consciousness and break it up into something that could from a distance be mistaken for a conversation (another word for which—here's a clue, Sean—is *dia*logue) and one component of such sequences that you could have drag-and-dropped into more or less any of his recent rants and rambles was: *You know, when this thing takes off we can franchise it out for local adaptation in every fucking country in the world that has a Dark Age heroic mythology and you know what countries that leaves out? Only the ones that are still in the fucking Dark Ages! Ha ha ha!*

"That's by no means all," I said. "And I don't see us doing it while we still don't have Dark Britannia done and dusted. When do you need it?"

"Middle of June," she said.

"Four months? No way!"

"It can be as quick and dirty as you like," Amanda said. "We're not talking a flagship release here. Digital could even claim it had been pirated. Come to think of it, that's probably . . . hmm . . ."

"The money would have to be good," I said. "If I'm going to pitch it to the lads."

"Fifty thousand on agreement, hundred thousand on delivery."

"Pounds? Euros?"

"Dollars."

Oh well. Still in not-to-be-sneezed-at territory, for a company as small as ours.

"I think I can make that fly," I said.

"Oh, don't *you* try selling this to the team," said Amanda. "*My* people will talk to *your* people, OK?"

A couple of questions will have occurred to you. One: how is this lady professor of cultural anthropology or whatever going to come up with a hundred and fifty thousand dollars? Two: what does she want with a multiplayer online role-playing game in Krassnian in the first place?

They occur to you, but they didn't occur to me.

The only question that occurred to me was: hmm, so what's behind the CIA's sudden interest in Krassnia?

I already knew the answers to the other two, because I already knew my mother was a spook.

3.

Not that it hadn't been a bit traumatic finding out, at the age of thirteen, right in the middle of my rebellious, weed-smoking, body-piercing, diary-keeping, two-fingers-down-the-throat puking, hormone-churned huff at the world. If this scene was in a movie they'd need to cast a different actress, who'd be in the credits as Teenage Lucy, and rummage up a roomful of late-nineties kipple. So you imagine me sitting on my bed, chin on knees poking through the cultivated distress of my jeans, leaning on a big batik cushion and facing a Kurt Cobain poster on the wall opposite. The Cranberries are messing with my head through earphones the size of earmuffs. I'm reading a thick Guy Gavriel Kay paperback. Scene set? Good. Enter Amanda, after a token knock.

I scowled at her and saw her lips move. I stuck a thumb in the book and reached around the back of my head and prised away Dolores's dolorous lyrics.

"What?"

"There's something I've been meaning to tell you," Amanda said, looking awkward.

"I know," I said. "Don't smoke. Do my homework. Use a condom. Eric isn't my father."

Wow, that one worked. I could see her flinch. I almost felt sorry for her. Almost. But I was cruel then.

"That isn't . . ." she said.

"That wasn't . . ." she added.

"How do you know?" she got her act together enough to ask.

"Mom, I'm not *stupid*," I said.

She didn't inquire further on that point. She came and sat down on the only other seating in the room, an old beanbag opposite the bed, sinking so far that I had to lean forward to see her face.

"What I've been meaning to tell you," she said, "is, um . . . it's about Krassnia. We had some good times there, didn't we?"

"Yes, Mom, I had a very happy childhood there. Until you took us away from it."

She winced again. "It wasn't my choice. The place looked like it was about to blow. All US citizens were advised to leave."

"And nothing happened."

(Apart from the scariest day of my life, which rather undercut my point, but Amanda ignored that opening.)

"We didn't know that then," she said. "Anyway"—she chopped with her hand, looking impatient—"that's all beside the point. I'm not going to let you rake all that up again. This is about something that really does concern you. It's about what I was doing in Krassnia in the first place."

She leaned back farther into the beanbag, as if to make sure that if I were to make some sudden movement, she would be out of range.

"Your research?"

"Kind of," she said. "Um, well. My research wasn't just for my thesis, and it wasn't just about, you know, all that ancient stuff. I was sending a lot of it to, well, someone at the US embassy in Moscow. Someone who sent it all back to, um, to Langley, Virginia."

"You were a *CIA agent*?" I shrieked.

"The correct term is 'asset,'" she quibbled. "But, yes, that's about the size of it."

The implications weren't really sinking in yet.

"Why are you telling me now?" I asked.

"I've been exposed," she said. "A guy at Langley has been arrested for working for the Russians, and for the Soviets before that, and he's confessed. He gave the Agency a list of the people he exposed."

"And your name's on the list?"

Amanda nodded. "Uh-uh. None of this is public, OK?"

"So why are you telling me?" I demanded. "Am *I* on it? Are you in danger?"

"No," she said. "People I worked with, yeah . . ." She chewed her lip, looking up to a corner of the ceiling, and sighed. "Some of them have been arrested already."

"But Krassnia broke away, didn't it? Why should they care about anyone's spying on the Soviet Union?"

"Hah!" said Amanda. "It broke away, sure, but it huddled close to Russia. And the local secret police are still the old Soviet secret police, just with new initials."

"Why do I have to know this?" I was really pissed with my mom for laying this on me.

"Because," she said, "you might get approached, sometime. Leaned on, I don't know, pressured in some way. Maybe asked to do something a little bit illegal, then blackmailed into doing something *really* bad, and then . . ."

She waved her hands about, frowning.

This all struck me as suspiciously vague.

"This isn't just a way to stop me smoking blow, is it?"

"No, Lucy, it's not!" She looked thoughtful. "But that would help. Anyway, tell me if anything unusual happens in your life—anything at all."

How was I supposed to know what was unusual? I glowered for a bit, then a line of attack came to mind.

"Why did you work for the CIA anyway?" I asked. "They were killing and torturing people back then, in Salvador and shit. I've read all about it."

"I'm sure you have," she said. "The Russians were doing worse, in Afghanistan and shit."

"I've read about that too," I said. "It's no excuse."

"Look, Lucy," Amanda said. "I'm—I was just doing what any good American would—should—have done. I was letting my government know about important developments, matters they really needed to know about to keep America safe. And, I might add, to help people in Krassnia who were suffering under the Soviets, and who might have suffered even more in the aftermath if we hadn't—if our government hadn't had a good idea of what was going on, among the mountain peoples, the ethnics, and so forth. You can see what's going on in Yugoslavia, in Chechnya, and places like that. None of that's happening in Krassnia, and I think the work I did had something to do with that. What the Agency may or may not have done or con-

doned in other parts of the world has nothing to do with me. So my con-
science is clear."

She didn't quite add, "young lady!" but I could hear it in her tone. With
the result that I argued right back, and we both ended up yelling at each
other. This was fairly typical of how we got along then.

So after the inevitable door-slam I got on the phone to vent my annoy-
ance into my favourite sympathetic—if slightly deaf—adult ear, that of my
great-grandmother, Eugenie. (My grandmother, Gillian, was and is the most
conventional whitebread housewife I've ever met. Totally different from her
daughter and from her mother. You'd almost think there's some kind of gen-
erational rebellion thing going on.)

"Mom just told me—"

"Stop!" Great-Grandma Eugenie cried.

"What?" I said. "I just wanted to—"

Great-Grandma Eugenie said: "I *know* what you want to talk about, Lucy
dear. Please don't! It's not really a suitable subject for you and I to discuss.
Now, tell me how you're doing at school."

I did, with ill grace. After clicking her tongue at my grades and chuck-
ling sympathetically at my surly remarks about certain girls who were, like,
totally making my life a misery, Eugenie said quite casually: "Oh, Lucy dear,
wouldn't you just love to come up to see me? Just name a day and I'll pay for
your Greyhound tickets."

A couple of weekends later I made that trip. Up Saturday, back Sunday.

Eugenie told me some things about *her* visit to Krassnia, back in the
1930s, along with quite a few little details of her life story that she'd never
told Amanda.

(Oh yes. My great-grandmother was in Krassnia too. And it's not a coincidence that my mother followed in her footsteps, kind of, in more ways than
one. But we'll come to that later.)

Over the next few weeks, I kept a close eye and ear on everyone I knew
at school. In my diary I noted every clique rumour or slighting remark, and
every week went through them and added them to a table I drew up at the
back of the book.

Nothing would have pleased me more than to be able to stand up and
open my mouth like what's-her-name at the end of the *Invasion of the Body*

Snatchers remake and scream that one of my class enemies (so to speak) was an FSB agent. Sadly for me, the opportunity never came up. A month or two of this and it got boring, even for me. I found another hobby: role-playing games. In those days we played them around a table, with rule-books and score-sheets made from paper. (You don't believe me? Check Wikipedia.) I once honestly thought that the whole idea of Dark Britannia had come from a sort of mental mash-up of all the games I played back in my dice-rolling days.

4.

You're an orc [*strike that, we can't call them orcs. Keep those serial numbers filed off!*]. You're a breath-chokingly ugly, squat, heavyset, lightly armed barbarian warrior. Looking around, you see that you are in the front rank of a horde of likes-of-you, on a darkling plain. Shuddering at the sight of your comrades-in-arms, you turn away.

Facing you, across the darkling plain, is another ignorant army, but this one is made up of tall, flame-haired, handsome people whom we might as well call elves.

In the far distance, looming above the darkling plain, is a range of mountains. And looming above the range is a central peak, about whose summit a weird glow flickers. You don't have time to think about this, because you and the rest of your ugly ignorant army is striding forward, rank upon rank, then breaking into a charge, and within seconds you are mixing it with the beautiful people.

You manage to hack down an elf. You grab his glittering sword, so much better than yours, just in time to wield it against the next elf, who is bigger, faster, and angrier than the one you've just dispatched.

And whose sword is longer, sharper, and much more magical than the one you've just snatched up.

These things are sent to try you. It *builds character*. Character points give you a better start in your next life.

If you make it through this first battle (and in your first few lives, you probably won't, but you'll learn) you and the much-thinned but better-armed and somewhat less-repulsivelooking ranks of your comrades discover the darkling plain is on closer inspection a richly varied landscape thickly bestrewn with forts, inns, ruins, towns, gullies, forests, marshes, cliffs; and inhabited by mysterious strangers, alluring wenches, rich merchants, false prophets; and absolutely swarming with Pictish [*strike*] tribal zombies and Roman [*strike*] [*stet*] Roman legionary revenants; all of whom provide obstacles and opportunities on the way to the central peak with the weird glow.

Along the way, your weapons, skills, magical abilities, and physical appearance improve with each success, until eventually you (or more likely, one of your so-called comrades and companions who has stolen a march on you) struggle to the summit of the central peak and plunge into the weird glow. Within it, there's a text floating in glowing magical letters, a whole goddamn grimoire of spells that you can use to confer power on you and your weapons. Brandishing a now even more magical sword, you (or your rival) emerge as the new king of the hill.

You turn and look back the way you have come.

Far away across the darkling plain, a vast horde of hideous barbarians is advancing like an incoming tide.

You and your companions march out to meet them.

5.

I had my elbows on the desk, my fingertips pushing up the skin between my orbits and my eyebrows (thus propping my eyelids open without smudging my eye shadow) and a coffee mug cooling to drinkability a little way to the right of the stack of pieces of paper I was busy putting off starting to work through. At 2 p.m. in the afternoon, a week or so after Amanda's late-night phone call from NYC, my lunch was trying to make me snooze.

Considering that my lunch had been three bait-sized mouthfuls of Tesco sushi and a dab of wasabi, this wasn't fair. It must have been the rice.

The guys, of course, had all had Cuppa Soups with Subway sandwiches as long and thick as their forearms, or something equally heavy like a good old Scotch meat pie, and were all rattling out code or documents on their keyboards and talking across each other.

They were talking so loud that Sean Garrett (the aforementioned PTB) almost didn't hear the phone. I barely heard it myself, until an escalating irritation drove it to the top of the stack.

"Somebody answer the fucking phone!" I yelled.

That was clearly not specific enough.

"Sean, answer the fucking phone!"

Sean looked away from the screen, looked at the phone on his desk as if noticing it for the first time (which it could well have been, given that we did everything by mobile and hardly anyone had ever rung us on the official office phone, which wasn't even on my desk and I was the actual admin person), and picked up the receiver.

"Sean—uh, Digital Damage Productions," he said. He waved a hand behind his back, and the volume of conversation dropped. For a couple of minutes he was all "Uh-uh" and "Yes"and "Hmm." Then he swivelled his chair and looked at the rest of us.

"Lucy, is Krassnia that godforsaken place you were dragged up in?"

"Yes," I said.

"Can you speak the language?"

"More or less," I said. "Bit rusty, but I could get up to speed, I guess. Why?"

"Tell you in a minute. And is it true that your mum wrote the fucking book on Krassnian mythology?"

"Yeah," I said. "I have a copy."

"Brilliant!" said Sean. He returned to his phone conversation. After about five minutes he put the phone down, and spun the chair around again. This time he waved his fists in the air.

"Wah-hoo!" he said. "I've just had a fucking amazing offer."

. . . Which he then proceeded to outline, much along the lines of what Amanda had said to me. The ostensible client—the cut-out, as I thought of it—was itself a start-up, a Brussels-based company called Small Worlds that aimed to pitch adapted games to the niche market of small language groups. Whoever was on the other side of the phone hadn't tried to make it all seem like a fantastic coincidence—they'd claimed to have actually found me by trawling the agencies and Googling for anybody in the biz whose online CV showed a Krassnian connection, and to have known that I was the daughter of *Krassniad* author Amanda Stone—all easily accessible knowledge—which was why they'd tried Digital Damage first.

Even so, the guys were all giving me looks that mingled congratulation with puzzlement.

"Kind of a funny thing to be marketing," said Matt, our best coder, looking away from a screen on which he'd just Googled. "Krassnia's population is less than half a million."

"That's Small Worlds' problem," said Sean. "They'll know what they're doing."

"All the same," said Matt. "Sounds a bit dodgy."

"Probably a CIA plot," I said, in my best stab at an American accent. (Which sounds at best Irish. My normal accent is Scottish with a Russian—or is it Krassnian?—with Scottish and NYC overlays, which leaves people guessing which tiny Inner Hebridean island I come from.) The guys all laughed, and that particular question dropped off the agenda, unanswered.

The guys—let me introduce you to the guys. Sean, you've met. Stocky and chunky with a greasy sheen on his face and his long, lank black hair. He's the entrepreneur, the man with the business plan. The business plan was complicated but the big idea, the Unique Selling Point, was very simple: online multiplayer games that would run fast on slow computers.

Suresh was Sean's first partner. A slim, quiet Bengali guy with a heavy Glasgow accent. It was Suresh who came up with the algorithm that made Sean's idea work. What it does is ruthlessly prioritise the use of the machine's resources: it'll sacrifice colour, rendering, detail, sound to keep the game running fast, and it does it seamlessly. In principle you could drop all the way back to stick figures with captions and word balloons, and the action would be just as fast as it is on the latest and shiniest game-optimised PC.

Joe's the high-level design guy, and the low-level art guy. He came up with DD's first game, Kronos. (That's the one set in a space station abandoned by some Elder Race and full of rich pickings and nasty surprises.) He also came up with the second game, Olympus, the one that was getting really bogged down until I met Joe and Sean in the Auld Hoose (Edinburgh geek and goth hangout) and suggested they change it from astronauts-and-AIs to swords and sorcery. Which is why the physics engine of Dark Britannia is still called mars.exe. Joe tries to keep his blond hair and his stubble the same length, with indifferent results. He smokes on the fire escape a lot.

And Matt, like I said, is the best coder. (All of the above are coders as well as all the other things I've said they do. Even I can be called on to code if necessary—though my actual work is all admin, in principle I'm just the worst coder, not a noncoder. That everyone should be a coder is a key component of Sean's business plan. He took it from *Starship Troopers*: "Everybody drops! Everybody fights!" One of his annoying little mantras.) Matt's the only one of the guys who's a real cutie. Tall, thin, with long fingers and short curly black hair. Very much attached, but we flirt. (Well, we used to, but you know what I mean.)

Joe was frowning.

"This won't work," he said. He waved a hand at the schedule highlighted on the calendar tacked to the office wall. "September release. Not enough time to run a sideline release in parallel."

"Yes, there is," said Suresh. "It's a bodge job, come on. Lucy just has to crack her mam's book and give you a few tips and tweaks."

"And translate the dialogue and internal prompts," I added.

"And do all the voices too?" Joe said.

"No, no," Sean said. "That's covered. Small Worlds has some contacts who'll take care of the voice acting. We send them the script, they can turn around the sound files within the week."

"What about the landscape?"

This was dangerous territory, for reasons I'll explain in a minute. I jumped in quickly.

"Not a problem, Krassnia's landscape is sort of uneven plain with a mountain range anyway. I'd just have to plug in place-names, maybe make some up. There might be one or two features that need changing, but nothing we can't finesse."

Joe shook his head. "I don't like it. We've got no slack as it is. Even if it was just the coding, there aren't enough hours in the day for us to do it."

"With twenty-five K in the bank," Sean said, "we can either all find some more hours and pay ourselves for them, or we can hire another coder." He shrugged. "Your call, folks."

I could see calculations going on behind people's eyes.

"And presumably we can all get a fat bonus out of the fifty thousand quid at the end," I said.

"I'll think about that," said Sean. "It would sure come in handy for our next project. But, well, maybe we could pay ourselves a bit of it. I'll have to see."

"We could think of the Krassnian version as a beta release," I added. "Middle of June gives us time to iron out any bugs before we ship in September."

Joe looked twitchy. A quick trip to the fire escape was in his near future.

"Look," he said, "if Lucy can come back to me, ASA fucking P, with a schema that looks feasible . . ."

"We need to get back with an answer sooner than ASAP," Sean said.

"How soon?" Joe asked.

"Day after tomorrow."

They were all looking at me again.

"I'll have a schema on Joe's desktop, day after tomorrow, first thing," I said.

They didn't believe me. I reminded them I'd come up with the idea for the game in the first place, that I'd written the original outline, that I'd spent a lot of evenings walking through the game, and that I knew it backwards and forwards. And that I'd read the book years ago and would only need a short time to brush up on the details.

They still looked sceptical, as well they might. What I hadn't told them was that I'd read the book not years but days ago, and that I had a very good reason for thinking that adapting the game to the book would be a doddle. I had a very good reason for not telling them that.

They agreed there was nothing to lose by trying. I should have felt elated. To my surprise, I felt scared.

Because from here on in, it wasn't just speculative. I was involved. We all were. More to the point, I had involved my colleagues in the affairs of Krassnia and the intrigues of the CIA.

And it was because of what I'd found in the pages of the book, and what had fallen out from between those pages.

6.

What had fallen out of the book, when I leafed through it the night after the night Amanda called, was a photograph. A faded colour photograph, taken in early September 1990 and—by virtue of its subject—looking a lot older than that. It showed a little girl clutching a big bouquet. The girl was wearing a brown dress with a white bib apron with shoulder frills, and on top of her head a big white multiple bow, like an origami lily in organza. Cute and sweet: the sort of look some Japanese girls pay good money for these days.

I was the little girl. The outfit was my Soviet school uniform. The bouquet was to be presented to my teacher on the first day of school. I was smiling in the photograph, but that was taken just before I'd burst into tears. I don't remember how my mother had cheered me up. I don't know either how my mother was able to get me into school two years younger than all the others. The next memory that comes to mind is of sitting in the front passenger seat of her old Moskvitch, trying to click the retrofitted seat belt while holding the oversized bouquet. My mother leaned over and helped. Then bumping along the unmetalled, potholed road from the apartment blocks to the primary school.

It was the playground, I think, that cheered me up. As I joined the queue of neatly uniformed seven-year-olds in front of the main entrance I eyed the slides and swings. They were painted pink and green and purple, and made of the kind of pipes you saw outside apartment blocks and factories, combined with painted carved log sculptures of the ugliest characters from my picture books.

Handing the bouquet to the teacher. Taking my place among the rows of wooden desks under a framed portrait of Lenin. The smells of carbolic and wee, of chalk dust and pencil sharpenings.

All my good memories of that classroom are overshadowed by the memory of the first really frightening day of my life. That came almost exactly a year later.

As for what I found *in* the pages of the book . . .

The evening after Amanda's call I got back to the flat about nine. My flatmates, Julie and Gail, had been and gone. They work nine to five, not eight to eight. I dumped the Tesco bag on the kitchen table, stabbed the plastic film over the Healthy Eating Mushroom Tagliatelli with a fork a few more times than I had to, and stuck the meal in the microwave. While waiting for the ping I ambled through to the living room and took *The Krassniad* down again from the shelf. Back in the kitchen, I put the book down on the table and set up a wine glass and wine box.

Ping.

I ate with the book in one hand and a fork or glass in the other, slugging Namaqua between bites. After I'd finished eating I skooshed a refill and kept on skimming the book.

Here's what I found.

Skip the begats and cut to the chase.

There's this guy, see, name of Duram. Strapping, handsome lad, in his teens when the story starts. Works the fields, minds the kine and swine, but he's not a serf. Oh no. Eldest son of a free farmer, Mordan, a respected local strong man, whose words carry weight at the moot. The Krassnar are typical barbarians: in other words, civilised. They settled like sediment out of a big current of migration that, centuries ago, helped to bring down the Roman Empire. They farm the plains. The fields of the free farmers are worked by their own families, as well as a variable number of churls, thralls, and serfs. The free farmers are exploiters all right, but they aren't the ruling class. Oh no.

Above the plains looms a mountain range, and in fastnesses of that range dwell the lords of the land, the Vrai, who take little interest in the Krassnar other than to exact tribute. The lordly mountain clans claim to be descendants of the Roman garrison. More probably, they are descended from some breakaway of the migration that slew the garrison, and acquired a little culture from its widows. They have just enough Roman blood to be arrogant, enough Roman learning to be decadent, enough Christianity to be intolerant, enough heathenry to conjure demons. They claim to hold the land of the Krassnar on behalf of Byzantium. Byzantium knows little of them, and cares less. An annual tribute of precious stones and metals—partly obtained by robbery of other tribute caravans, partly by mining in the mountains—trickles to Constantinople.

Duram grows up taking all this for granted until a Vrai lordling rides into the village with his retinue, carries off half the crop, and rapes Duram's sister, who later dies giving birth to the lordling's bastard. Duram, by this time, has worked himself up to swearing vengeance and gathering a gang of young ruffians around him, much to the dismay of his father. At his sister's death, Duram and his band set off for the mountains. Along the way they intend to recruit any malcontent and fight any Vrai they meet.

Cue a series of adventures and exploits which you'll know the general drift of from the tales of Samson, David, Arthur, William Wallace, and Robin Hood. I'm not sure how many of these parallels were in the original fragments, or whether my mother made them up. Anyway, after dealing by force and trickery with all kinds of opposition, treachery, magic, femmes fatale, spectral legions, Vrai spies, and all the rest, Duram and his by now much more formidable band march out across the plain just beneath the mountains to challenge the Vrai direct.

The Vrai ride out to meet them. . . .

It was when I'd reached this point in the story that the light came on.

Dark Britannia was already based on *The Krassniad*.

This wouldn't have been a surprise if I'd actually read the book, no matter how long ago, but I hadn't.

I put down the glass and started flipping back through the pages I'd skimmed. Incident after incident—the encounter at the inn, the alley of the magicians, the betrayal at the ford—suddenly seemed highlighted because they were all in the game. I could have kicked myself for not having noticed them earlier.

Then I started flipping forward.

Duram and his band—now a horde—indeed conquer the mountain fastnesses, using weapons—some of them magical—that they have taken from fallen Vrai. Inside one of the fastnesses, Duram finds a cave. Within that cave, he finds the secret of the power of the Vrai: an inscription that confers magical power on weapons and people exposed to it. The descriptions are contradictory, but there's no doubt that weapons exposed to the magic are sources of power. Whoever holds them, holds the land. Whoever wields them wins his battles—unless, of course, overwhelmed by sheer force of numbers, he loses them in battle and they pass to the enemy, as has indeed just come to pass.

As soon as Duram and his most trusted comrades have proclaimed their rule, they face an uprising of folk who—now they come to think of it—prefer the Vrai, almost literally the devil they know—backed by barbarians from outside the domain, who've taken advantage of the civil strife to press in upon the land from the plains to the east. Duram's men ride out to meet them. . . .

Battle is joined, a welter of valorous deeds and slain foes. Just not *enough* slain foes. Duram and his men perish gloriously.

And there the story ends.

There is, of course, a coda. There always is. This is the usual once-and-future king deal, whereby Prophecy tells that some day another liberator (perhaps, or perhaps not, a descendant of Duram) will arise and free the Krassnar.

So much for the legend.

The book's sombre afterword outlined what actually happened.

In history, the Vrai were restored and Duram's men slaughtered. The Krassnar, after a massacre of the rebels, settled down in sullen acquiescence. The Vrai were much weakened politically but increased in population, and eventually in 1887 the whole little country was rescued—as the official legend still has it—from the Ottoman Empire by the Russian Empire. The peasants went on as before. A small proletariat developed around a British-owned copper mine. The Vrai became part of the Russian aristocracy. This wasn't like a Western aristocracy: nobility was a rank in the civil service. A scion of that nobility was one Avram Arbatov, born 1894, executed 1937: the Bolshevik ethnologist who compiled the tales that became the legend recounted in this book, and to whose memory my mother had dedicated it.

There was something missing from that dedication, but I knew just why my mother had not seen fit to mention a rather significant fact—or at any rate significant possibility—about Avram Arbatov. There were family feelings to consider.

I put the book down and took a big gulp of red wine. I felt so creeped out that I actually looked over my shoulder. Nothing there but the cat. I took a couple of deep breaths, invited the cat to my lap, and sat hugging him for a minute. The cat did his creepy thing of suddenly staring over my shoulder at a point in the air where I (looking over my shoulder again) could see nothing. I picked up the book again and fanned its pages.

That was when the old photo fell out, onto the table. I stared at it for a moment, bewildered. Then I recognised myself, and everything came back. I remembered where the story and the incidents within it had come from.

They'd been my bedtime stories.

Amanda had told me them, starting when I was the little girl in the picture. I hadn't remembered them, but they must have remained in my sub-conscious, because they had come out when—two years earlier, in the pub with Sean and Joe—I'd outlined the scenario for Dark Britannia.

And the magic mountain—in the game and in the legend—really existed, and really was mysterious and forbidden territory. You could see it on the horizon from Krasnod, white-peaked, high above the shimmering haze from the plastics factory and the dust from the mine. Even before I'd clicked to the connection between the game and the book, I'd always mentally pictured the mountain in the game as Mount Krasny (known from 1927 to 1936 as Mount Kuibishev, then as Mount Yezhov, then as Mount Krasny again). And I knew the tales about Mount Krasny, oh yes.

They'd been my daytime stories.

Daytime stories: when I was too young to go to school and my mother was at work, I was looked after by Nana. She wasn't really my Nana, I knew that because my mom had shown me photos of my real Nana, a pretty lady called Gillian who lived in a huge house with a car and a fridge and a dog and lots and lots of rooms with pictures on the walls. But I'd never met Nana Gillian, and I met Nana Krassnia every day. So the latter was Nana. She wore an overcoat and a kerchief and rubber boots, summer and winter, indoors and out. At least, that's how I remember her.

Nana took me to the park every day. She took me to wait in line with her at the shops. I trailed around after her while she cleaned and tidied the flat. (She didn't *have* to do that, she kept telling me. She just couldn't stand the mess that "that mother of yours" had left it in.) She let me help her while she peeled potatoes for dinner.

From her I learned that things were going out of the world. They had started going out of the world around about the time I was born. The time I was born was called *Before*. Before, we had this, Nana would say. Before, we had that. I came to the conclusion that I was one of the last things that had been made, and that I was very lucky to have been made at all. Any later and it would have been After, and that would have been too late for me.

None of this really bothered me. I took it quite for granted that one by one things disappeared from the world or stopped working, like cars, or elevators, and no new things came along to replace them.

One winter morning the sky was very clear above Krasnod—the plastics factory had stopped working—and I saw, in front of the ragged, looming range of the Caucasus mountains, the peak of Mount Krasny shining white above the rooftops in the blue sky.

"Nana," I said, as she tugged me along the sidewalk, which was all nice and frozen so your feet didn't squelch in it and it wasn't smelly, "I want to go to Mount Krasny!"

"We can't," she said.

"Why not?" I said.

"Nobody goes to Mount Krasny."

"Why not?" I said.

Nana was patient. "Because it's a Zone," she said.

A new word!

"What's a Zone?"

"A place where people can't go," she said.

Even at that age—four?—I knew a circular argument when I heard one. "But why can't they go?"

"I'll tell you when we get to the park," said Nana.

And of course when we got to the park I ran to the swings and climbing frame and forgot all about it until a while later when by chance I glimpsed the mountaintop again.

Nana was sitting on a bench at a wooden table with three other *babushkas*. They all had coats and kerchiefs and string shopping bags, and were keeping half an eye on other little kids running about. They all looked at me as I ran up.

"Nana," I said, "you said you'd tell me why people can't go to a Zone."

I remember what happened next quite vividly, because it was the first time I'd seen anything like it. All four grandmothers looked over their shoulders at the same time. Then the other three all turned to Nana and looked severe.

"It's all right," Nana told them, waving her hand dismissively.

She turned back to me. "Listen, dear," she said. "It's dangerous to go to a Zone, that's all. And it's best not to talk about it." She opened her arms and took me to her lap. She whispered in my ear: "I'll tell you stories when we go home, dear. Now run along and play with Ivanova."

Nana kept her promise. She told me strange and terrible tales: of people who had ventured to the slopes of Mount Krasny and returned with *two heads*; of an ancient knight who had sought the last resting place of St. John, and found the Devil's daughter; of kine that had strayed on the slopes and ever after had given blood instead of milk; of the haughty, lordly, flame-haired Vrai, the only folk who could enter the mountain's labyrinth of crevices and return unharmed, or indeed enriched; of the peculiar four-winged lizards that haunted the mountain's forested foothills; and, quite in the same tone and manner as she recounted all the rest, of that time in her own youth when "that wicked man Beria, the Mingrellian with cruel eyes" had been seen in town, and the mountain's side had glowed for seven nights.

I could understand why my schema for the game had unconsciously echoed the book and the tales from which it sprang.

That correspondence still creeped me out. It felt like destiny.

I already had a bad opinion of destiny. Here's why.

2. THE CAUCASIAN HEIRESS

1.

Destiny is how my mother met my father. That's how she tells it. When I asked about my father, she told me a story. Here's the true story. I'll tell you later how I cobbled it together. Ask yourself if destiny had anything to do with it.

This is another scene that's going to need different actors, a trawl of the vintage shops for the costumes, and of antique shops for the props. It's Edinburgh, Scotland, late December 1979. Midevening. We're in a ground-floor flat in a big apartment building just off the top end of Leith Walk, in an area that is on the downswing of one of its many cycles from posh to poor. The poor in this case are the five students, all male, who share the rent on the flat.

So we're in the front hall of this flat. There's a big, battered table on one side, with an even more battered sofa beside it. That still leaves a lot of room: this was originally the entrance hall of a big posh house. The floor is marble, covered with frayed rugs. This floor and just about every other floor in the flat is crowded—not completely, not Tube platform at rush hour crowded, but as crowded as you'd expect with maybe forty people having a party. There are fewer than thirty guys, more than ten girls. It's not a sophisticated party. It's filling the gap between Christmas and New Year. The music is loud. Conversations are louder. The air is heavy with smoke from cigarettes and joints. Drifts of empty beer cans are stacking up in the corners. Bottles of spirits or fortified wines pass from hand to hand, mouth to mouth.

We zoom in on Young Amanda, from behind. Young Amanda is about five foot six, with wavy strawberry-blonde hair to below her shoulder blades. She's wearing a loose velvet top and tight blue jeans. The viewpoint lingers for a moment, tracks up. We see she's leaning over the big table in the hall, and sifting through a stack of mail. She stops sifting and picks out a brown envelope addressed in faded type. We're peering right over her shoulder now.

The date on the postmark is 1976. Amanda slides a thumb inside the envelope and works it open without tearing. She eases out a few sheets of close-printed paper and leafs through them.

Male voice, off camera: "What are you doing?"

Amanda turned, smug that she hadn't been startled; she'd been nerved for a challenge ever since she'd gate-crashed the party. She found herself looking up at the face of a tall, thin young man. Hair down to his collar, beard fringing his face. The face wasn't bad. He wore a denim jacket and check shirt over a red T-shirt, and grubby jeans. In one hand he held a can of beer, in the other a corncob pipe. A green plastic Pentel pen-top and a black notebook stuck out of his jacket's breast pocket. On his lapel was a Labour Party badge, a rounded rectangle of red enamel inlaid with stylised shovel, pen, and firebrand in brass. The side pockets bulged with enough weight to make the open jacket swing like a coat.

"Just idle curiosity," said Amanda. She reached for the can of Coke she'd left on the table. "What's your name?"

"Ross Stewart."

"Hi. Amanda Stone."

"Oh. Uh. Right. Pleased to meet you." Ross grinned and shuffled sideways a couple of paces. He put down his can and started filling his pipe from a tartan plastic pouch of tobacco, glancing sidelong at Amanda. "How long have you been here?"

"Half an hour," Amanda said, shrugging.

"I meant, in this country."

"Since the summer. I'm studying at the university."

"Edinburgh? Me too. Third year, electronic engineering and business studies. You?"

"First year. Anthropology, with a side course in non-Slavic languages of the USSR."

"Anthropology, huh," said Ross. He frowned. "Structuralism and that?"

"Well, that's part of it," said Amanda, feeling defensive for no obvious reason. "I mean, Lévi-Strauss and Edmund Leach are among the set texts, you know."

"Fucking Lévi-Strauss," said Ross, with abrupt vehemence. "I blame him for Pol Pot."

Amanda had to laugh out loud.

"It's not fucking funny," said Ross. "Structuralism, right? Theoretical antihumanism, Althusser and that. That's where Pol Pot and Ieng Sary studied—the Académie Française."

"What's that got to do with it? You might as well blame French restaurants for Ho Chi Minh because he once cooked in one."

"I would, if recipes he'd learned there had poisoned a million people!"

Jeez, what an asshole, Amanda thought. And at first glance he'd seemed a friendly guy, as well as good-looking.

"How much do you know about structuralism, anyway?" she asked.

"Just some stuff I've read."

"Well, if you read more, maybe you'd see some other intellectual roots of Pol Pot."

"Such as?"

"Marx, Lenin, Stalin, Mao . . ."

"Oh, that," said Ross. "Nah. Might be to blame for a lot, like what's going on in Afghanistan, but Year Zero is something else. Anyway . . ."

He waved his pipe about. Smiled. "Forget it."

"OK," said Amanda.

"Something else I wanted to say," Ross said, sounding a bit conciliatory.

"And what's that?"

"You still haven't answered my first question," Ross said. "What were you doing rummaging through our post?"

He put the pipe in his mouth and lit it with a match, his narrowed eyes fixed on Amanda through the smoke. The smoke was fragrant.

"All right," said Amanda. She passed the sheets of paper to him. He scanned them quickly, then flipped back to the first page.

"'Annual shareholders' report of the Ural Caucasian Mineral Company,'" he read out. "Not a lot happening, because . . ." He flicked to the final sheet. "'All assets of the Ural Caucasian Mineral company were nationalised by the revolutionary government of Soviet Russia in November 1918. However, the Company continues to press its case for full compensation or return of its property.' Hah hah hah! The capitalists never give up, do they?"

Amanda thought it an odd remark, but gave him a tight smile.

"No," she said coldly. "They don't."

Ross folded the sheets away into the brown envelope. "The funny thing is," he went on, "I never opened that old envelope because of my respect for private property. Same for the rest of us in the flat. Still, I can't say I'm sorry you didn't have the same scruples."

Amanda found herself liking his grin, though his teeth were more stained and uneven than she'd ever seen on anyone middle-class back home. In the US you saw such teeth in the mouths of people who, well, smoked corncob pipes.

"Actually," Amanda said, "I do have a right to open that envelope."

"How d'you work that out?"

"Look who the envelope's addressed to," Amanda said.

"'Miss E. Montford,'" Ross read out. "How's that connected to Amanda, uh, Stone?"

"It's a long story," she said.

Ross took a swig of his beer and a puff of his pipe. He gestured towards the sofa.

"Have a seat," he said.

Amanda sat in the corner of the sofa, her Coke on the armrest. Ross sat down in the middle, leaning forward and looking sideways at her. His hairy forearms stuck out from the denim jacket's grubby, upturned cuffs; his long-fingered hands played with the pipe, the envelope, and the can.

"Tell me the story," he said.

"Miss E. Montford," said Amanda, "is my grandmother, Eugenie. She's still alive. She was born in, uh, 1915, so she's a spry sixty-four. Her parents, Lord and Lady Montford, owned this house. I looked it up in the *Edinburgh A to Z*, and came by this evening just to have a look at it and to see if . . . well, if there was anything here connected with us. Heard the party in full swing, knocked on the door, some guy nods and lets me in, and I happened to see that stack of old unopened mail and looked through it on the off-chance and . . . here I am!"

Ross looked disbelieving.

"You're descended from a family that owned this house?"

"Oh, yes," said Amanda. "Along with, oh, a Highland shooting estate, several other Edinburgh properties, and a bundle of shares in the Ural Caucasian Mineral Company. These shares became just about worthless after the

Russian Revolution. That left the Montfords not quite ruined. However, they still have the town rents and the Highland estate. In the twenties deer-hunting becomes popular with American businessmen, right? So the Montfords make friends, cultivate some contacts in NYC, start to do quite well speculating on the New York stock market, and then—"

Ross laughed again. "They lost everything else in the Wall Street Crash?"

"Yup," said Amanda. "So young Eugenie has to leave her expensive private school and put some bread on the table. She goes to London and—thanks to Lord Montford's contacts—gets a secretarial job in what's left of the Ural Caucasian Mineral Company. From what my grandma told me, this worked out of a poky little office in Clerkenwell. It was still in business, but it had been reduced to an import-export agency for mining equipment, pretty much. But the old directors, real shabby-genteel types, were still hoping to get its Russian-Empire property back. Partly by intriguing with various shady White Russians who promise them the downfall of the Bolsheviks and a glorious restoration any year now, and partly through the courts. At the same time, with the other hand so to speak, they're trying to do deals with the Soviet State Mining Trust."

"Sounds like a fun place to work," said Ross.

Amanda couldn't be sure he wasn't being sarcastic.

"Yeah, well, at least it was work. In the Great Depression that was something. But the real funny thing is that in her later teens Eugenie became something of a wild child—and a radical."

"An aristo pinko," Ross chuckled.

Amanda nodded. "And an adventuress. She even got a pilot's licence—don't ask me how she could afford flying lessons. I guess she was still in Society, as they call it, and . . . Well. Anyway, she became curious about the Great Experiment—you know, the Five Year Plan and all that?"

"I know about the Five Year Plan and all that," said Ross, straight-faced.

"OK," said Amanda. "So . . . around about 1934, I think it was, this slip of a girl, all of nineteen years old, wangles a place on a commercial delegation to Russia. By now she actually speaks Russian, so that gives her an advantage, I guess. She's with some retired overseer from the company who reckons he can use his expert knowledge of its old workings to flog the Mining Trust hoists."

"Hoists?"

Amanda made a winding motion with her hand. "You know, hoists."

"Got it."

At this point a guy holding a vodka bottle loomed in front of her. He was short, dark-haired, stocky. He wore a leather jacket over a T-shirt. He stared straight at Amanda. She recognised him as the guy who'd let her into the flat.

"Y'aw righ' for drink?" he asked, swaying but keeping his gaze locked onto her eyes, giving her the impression he was less drunk than he sounded.

"Sorry?"

"He's asking if you're all right for a drink," Ross translated.

"I'm fine," said Amanda, holding up her Coke can.

"S'fine, I'll see you aw right," said the guy, and, before she could stop him, he tipped a hefty slug of vodka from the bottle into the can. Then he transferred his attention to Ross.

"Y'aw right Ross?"

"I'm fine, Cairds."

Cairds swayed back to his full height, looked at Amanda, looked back at Ross, tapped the side of his nose with his finger, and winked.

"Aye, I c'n see that."

Cairds lurched back into the living room.

"Sorry about that," said Ross. "He's an old mate."

"It's OK," said Amanda. She sipped the now-fortified drink, and spluttered. "More or less."

"Well," said Ross. "As you were saying . . . the trade mission, yeah?"

"Oh, yes. Well. This delegation was pretty small beer. The big boys got contracts in the Urals. Despite its name, all that the Ural Caucasian Mineral Company could manage were some visits to mines in the Caucasus. The company had owned a copper mine in a real out-of-the-way place, a little autonomous region called Krassnia. Between Russia and Georgia, and squeezed in somewhere between Ossetia and Abkhazia, if those names mean anything."

Ross shook his head. "Nah. Can't say they do."

"These two places are hard enough to find on the map, let alone Krassnia. Anyway . . . While she was there she met this forty-year-old guy whom she fell head over heels for. His name was Avram Arbatov. He was a business manager for the mines in Krassnia, but he'd had quite a past—he saw his father's estate burned by rebellious peasants in the 1905 revolution, grew up to be a radical student with an interest in peasant life, joined the Bolsheviks during the First World War. In the Red Army in the Civil War, rose through the ranks, and after the war returned to civilian life, became a professor—of ethnology and philology, I think it was—at Moscow University. He started a major study of Krassnian folklore, and just before he completed it, in 1927—"

"Let me guess," said Ross. "He was expelled from the Party and lost his job because he wouldn't denounce . . . the founder of the Red Army."

Amanda raised her eyebrows.

"Spot on," she said. "That's how he ended up back in Krassnia—I think he was exiled to somewhere in Kazakhstan at first. Now the collectivisation famine was horrendous there, but like a lot of these kind of guys he saw this as all the more reason for the Party to hang together, you know? In '32 or so he recanted and was readmitted. But he had to start from the bottom, as some kind of clerk in the Mining Trust, and he was only allowed to move to Krassnia, not anywhere near the centres of power. Being a very smart guy, he soon worked his way up to a responsible post, and managed at the same time to complete the work he'd been doing at Moscow University. In fact he even got it published, in 1934. *Life and Legends of the Krassnar*. He gave a copy to Eugenie. He said it was the most precious thing he could give her."

"So he fell for her, too?"

"Oh, sure. He was divorced, not exactly happy, and he meets this vivacious and pretty young woman."

"I can see how that would have an effect," Ross said, deadpan. "What happened?"

"I don't know what happened," said Amanda. "They were only together for a few days. The trade mission was quite a success—Eugenie and the old foreman or whatever he was managed to sell their hoists to the State Mining Trust, at least in Krassnia. And then they went home to England.

"But here's the curious thing. A month or so after Eugenie came back, Lord and Lady Montford blew a lot of money on flying her to the States, where within like three weeks she was married in Boston to a young man called Bartholemew Finn. Grandpa Bart. Their daughter Gillian—my mother—was born seven months later, quite heavy and healthy for such a premature baby. . . ."

Ross sat back on the sofa, sipped from his can, and gave Amanda a sidelong look.

"Has your grandmother ever said—?"

"Jeez, no! We're a very respectable New England family."

"And heirs to this"—he waved the brown envelope—"notional mining fortune! Was Eugenie the Montfords' only child?"

"No," said Amanda. "Her two brothers were killed in action in the Second World War."

Ross's face twitched. "Ah." He sighed. "Quite a story. And did your grandmother ever hear anymore from . . . ?"

"Arbatov? Well, that's where it gets real tragic. Between coming back and getting married—not after, she's very insistent on that—she wrote a few letters to him. I think she may have gotten one letter back, late in 1935. His letter was friendly but he asked her—begged her, actually—not to write to him. And then she never heard from him again. Years later, in the sixties, she found his name in the *Great Soviet Encyclopaedia*. Born 1894, joined the S-Rs 1912, got into the Bolshevik Party 1917, advanced some erroneous theses on ethnography, died 1937."

"Meaning he was shot in the Purges and never rehabilitated," Ross said.

Amanda took a gulp of vodka and Coke. "You're well informed," she said.

"Not really," said Ross. "I've just been reading."

He tugged a thick, battered Pelican paperback from his overloaded jacket pocket and held it up.

"This," he said.

"Oh!" said Amanda. "*The Great Terror*. Yes, it's an interesting book."

"Aye, it's great. Kinda grim, mind. No as grim as *The Gulag Archipelago*, though."

"I've read that too," said Amanda.

Ross mimed a shiver. "And you might just be related to somebody who died in the Terror or in the Gulag—oh! Fuck, I've just got it. The connection with what you're studying, I mean."

"It's kind of the other way round," Amanda said. "It was after I got interested in folklore and indigenous people that Grandma Eugenie started telling me about this amazing guy she'd met. And she lent me her copy of Avram Arbatov's book. I took a course in Russian in high school just to be able to read it."

"Wow," said Ross. "I'm impressed. But, fuck, you must be wanting to find out what happened to him."

"Oh, I do," said Amanda. "Hence, the non-Slavic languages, right? There's just so much stuff out there, all in Russian-Soviet ethnology, studies of the minority peoples, and so on. I'm trying to get a grip on the Circassian languages—Kabardin, Cherkess, Krassnar . . ."

"That's the language of the Krassnians?"

"Yeah. Originally it was the name of the people, or tribe—actually the Krassnians are made up of Krassnar and a much smaller minority, the Vrai. Sort of a tribe, though I think it's what anthropologists call 'fictive kin'—you know, not really blood related? They used to be the feudal ruling class, way back when. They had their own language—linguists have argued over whether it was a proper Romance dialect or just sort of a corrupt Latin. Arbatov included a glossary of it in the back of his book."

"Which was he?"

"Vrai. I guess. He never said."

Ross looked puzzled. "Are there . . . you know, references to his work or something? Is that what you're looking for?"

"Well, yes, I've looked for them, and it's obvious that some specialists have read his work even if they don't reference it. But that's not the main thing. Some day I'm going to *go* to Krassnia."

"Go there?" Ross laughed. "Not much chance of that."

"There is!" said Amanda. "There are still scholarships and exchanges and so on."

"That's all gonna freeze up, with Afghanistan and the Cruise missiles and Reagan coming in."

Amanda shrugged. "That'll pass. Cold War Two will be over by the time I graduate." She laughed lightly. "Well, either that or it'll be the Third World War!"

"Well, OK," said Ross, frowning, "but even if things calm down and it's back to detente—suppose you do get over there, visit Krassnia. You won't have much chance of finding out what happened to Arbatov. Not with the generation that came to power under Stalin still in power." He brandished the book again. "You can see the names: Kosygin, Brezhnev, Shelepin . . ."

"Old men. They won't be in power forever."

"Aye, but, come on. They'll pick their successors."

"Not always. Not forever. Hell, the *Party* won't be in power forever. Wouldn't you agree?"

"Forever is a long time," Ross said. "So, aye, sure, nothing lasts forever. But . . . the Soviet Union will last for, you know, decades. It'll have to reform some day, yeah, but I don't think we'll live to see the Party lose power."

"I do," said Amanda.

Ross stared at her. "Why?"

She reached forward and picked up the brown envelope from the sofa between them.

"Because of this. It's like you said—the capitalists never give up." She grinned at him. "We're still in the restoration game."

Ross's head jerked back. He frowned. "I'm no into that," he said.

"What are you into?"

Ross tapped a thumbnail on his lapel badge. "Labour Party," he said. "Clause Four Labour Students. Democratic socialism, an' that."

"Like, what's just lost in a landslide to Margaret Thatcher?"

"Aye, well, nobody said it would be easy. Anyway, we support the dissidents and reformers in the Eastern bloc."

Amanda waved a hand. "That's just talk."

"It's not just talk," said Ross, vehemently and indignantly.

"So what is it then, apart from talk?"

Ross relit his pipe. The smoke still smelled good. He looked at her through a cloud of it.

"I can't talk about that," he said.

Very interesting, Amanda thought. She had plenty to not talk about herself.

She smiled and stood up, stretching. "Let's get another drink," she said. "And if you don't want to talk about that, let's talk about something else, shall we?"

They did. They went on talking.

That's a considerable expansion of the story my mother told me when I first asked how she'd met my father.

It's the true story. It's not the whole story.

2.

Three nights into the job. I sat in the Reference Section of Edinburgh Central Library and tapped notes into my laptop from the books stacked in front of me. The time was 7:30 p.m. and I'd come here from the office—less than five minutes' walk away—at five. I'd miss out on the Friday after-work drinks with the lads, at the Doctors' on the corner. The library closes at eight and I wanted to make the most of it. My back ached. I was hungry. My jacket kept sliding off the curved chairback. Eventually I folded it and held it on my lap like a cat. There was some comfort in that.

I needed comfort because researching Krassnia for the game had turned into something else. I already had enough detail from *The Krassniad* and from a map of the Caucasus I'd found in a huge *Times Atlas* to get the place-names and the landscape nailed down.

This wasn't the first time I'd looked at Krassnia on a map. I'd looked it up on Google Earth as soon as Amanda had put the phone down the night she'd called—last week, which already seemed a long time ago. And from looking at that map, I even thought I'd found an answer to the question I'd tactfully not asked Amanda: what's with the CIA's sudden interest in Krassnia? Simple geography: Krassnia lies south of the western end of the Caucasus, and includes a pass—high and difficult, but wider than the Roki Tunnel—into Russia. Whoever holds Krassnia is within a hundred klicks of the Baku-Tbilisi-Ceyhan oil pipeline, across open terrain.

The same night I'd found one Reuters reference to an upcoming election in early September, which the ruling Social Democrats were ("according to the opposition Liberal Democrats and a wide spectrum of civil society organizations") expected to rig. As soon as I saw the phrase "a wide spectrum of civil society organizations" I'd thought: *Aha! Colour Revolution!*

Which explained what the CIA wanted the game for: as soon as it was on sale it would (like all other games in that part of the world) be pirated to all the Internet cafés and campus servers, where its virtual spaces would make a very good place for the *wide spectrum of civil society organizations* to . . . organise, away from the prying eyes of the Krassnian security police (FSB, prop.). The revolution would not just be televised: it would be computer-gamed.

The trouble was, I'd gone on looking for references to Krassnia and found *far too many*, none of them of any use. It always worked the same way. I'd pull down a relevant book, look up "Krassnia" or "Krassnian" in the index. Sure enough, there it was. Add the book to the pile in the crook of my arm. When the pile got too heavy to add anymore to, I'd take it back to the table, sit down, and start chasing page numbers.

Always with the same result.

Samples, from my notes:

"The settlements, unsatisfactory though they were, of the conflicts in South Ossetia, Abkhazia, and Adjara left outstanding the minor but intract-able problem of Krassnia. The Saakashvili government has, like its predecessors, turned a blind eye to the tiny region's anomalous status, no doubt in the hope that the problem will, over time, resolve itself."

That was the one and only reference to Krassnia in *Georgia after Communism: A Brief History*, Morgan Chancellor, London, 2005.

"Scuffling and yelling by a small group of Krassnians on the fringe of the crowd failed to disrupt the demonstration. Later investigation revealed, to no one's surprise, the FSB's hand in the affair." *The Rose Revolution: A Case Study in Democratic Transformation*, Anne Fassbinder, Washington, 2007.

"The role of other minor nationalities in the deportation was, if anything, worse than that of the Ossetes, that of the Krassnians being particularly infamous." *The Soviet Southern Flank*, William T. McCulloch, Boston, 1978.

"The Krassnian nationality question was also, as is known, harmoniously resolved in accord with the decisions of the Twentieth Congress." *A History of Soviet Georgia*, I. M. Shishkin, Moscow, 1982.

"At this crucial moment the Krassnians, as so often in the past, played a treacherous and despicable role in the nation's life." *Georgia Under Soviet Rule*, Y. A. Yakobashvili, Toronto, 1938.

"The undeniable instances of striking, if overstated, economic and social transformation (charitably leaving aside such unavoidable disasters as the Krassnian plastics industry) add some weight to the positive side of the balance." *Economic Development in the Caucasus, 1922–1969*, George C. Bullen, London, 1972.

Every relevant book I'd looked at had the same pattern: a passing reference to Krassnia or the Krassnians as if everything about the place and people *went without saying*.

Online: not much better. Even the Wikipedia entry for Krassnia was a stub.

I'd now reached the point where I'd pull books about Russia or the Soviet Union off the shelves almost at random, with the same frustrating result:

"The lesson he had drawn from his painful experience in Krassnia once more stood him in good stead." *Koba in the Observatory: New Light on Stalin's Early Years*, David Isaacson, Tel Aviv, 1998.

"The infamous 'Krassnian clique' was, as the Soviet Foreign Policy Archives now reveal, active behind the scenes in sowing distrust of Khrushchev before the XXII Congress convened." *Khrushchev: A New Biography*, Alan Harrington, New Jersey, 2003.

"Beria's oversight of the project was relentless: the records show flying visits to sites as far apart as Krasnoyarsk and Krassnia. The problems at the latter have, of course, often been recounted. For Krasnoyarsk, however, the story has hitherto been more patchy, and is well worth detailed examination." *Beria and the Bomb: The Secret History of State Committee on Problem Number One*, A. I. Mintz, St. Petersburg, 1995.

Beria—I recalled the first time I'd heard that name, from my Nana, and wondered if this infuriatingly vague mention referred to the incident she'd told me about.

"By 1990, the reports of national disturbances (Armenia, the Baltics, Georgia—with its inevitable Krassnian complication—and Turkmenistan) should have warned Gorbachev of the dangers, but unaccountably he continued the fatal policy." *Perestroika: Rise and Fall*, Andreas Schmidt, Berlin, 1992.

"Transdnestria has served as an entrepot for contraband and people-smuggling, and a haven for the Russian *Mafiya*, following the well-known pattern pioneered in Krassnia." *Criminal Capitals*, Ian Johnson, London, 2003.

"The young Lord Montford's travels in 1899 took him to the Caucasus, where he encountered a pioneer party of prospectors. In an excited letter from Krasnod, administrative capital of Krassnia on the Georgian border, he told the Board of Directors of the 'splendid chaps' who were 'discovering rich deposits on an almost monthly basis.' The Turk, he said, was 'already sniffing around, to say nothing of the Prussian and the Hebrew!' Montford's decision to strike an exclusive deal at once, without waiting to consult the Board, was to prove farsighted, and immensely lucrative to the Ural Caucasian Mineral

Company. His week in Krassnia was also, of course, to prove of great personal significance to Lord Montford!" *The British Adventure in Russia, From Peter to Nicholas*, Dame Sheila Gardiner, London, 1939.

That one made me jump. My heart was hammering.

Was *this* Lord Montford my maternal great-great-grandfather? Did my family's connection to the godforsaken place go back *that* far?

I flicked through the book, but found no further reference. The time was 7:50 p.m. The library was about to close. I sighed and shoved the stack together, gathered up my stuff—laptop, shoulder bag, still-damp umbrella—and set about replacing the books on the shelves. I'd just finished that and was about to walk out when I happened to notice a couple of shelves set aside for the *Oxford Dictionary of National Biography*.

Dumping my stuff at my feet, I grabbed the "M" volume. There were a lot of Lord Montfords. There were a lot of Lord *Hugh* Montfords. The first Lord Hugh died on a Crusade, for Christ's sake! Bloody family had probably come over with William the Conqueror.

Ah, there was one that looked likely:

Montford, Lord Hugh (1881–1962) . . . lots of abbreviations of titles, decorations, and clubs . . . *Lieutenant, Army Signal Corps 1914–1920, s. France, Bulgaria, Russia* . . . honourable discharge 1921, mentioned in dispatches (twice) . . . *Major, Home Guard, 1940–1945* . . . business interests . . .

My eye skipped to the foot of the entry:

m. Katerina Koblyakova (b. 1882, Krasnod, Russ., d. 1965) 1900, two sons (Hugh, 1902–1940; Edward, 1904–1944), one daughter (Eugenie, 1915–)

At this point I said *"Fu-u-uck!!"* so loudly that I was pointed to the door two minutes before the library closed.

The rain had stopped. The evening was still not dark. The street lights had come on. It was Friday. I had a party to go to. I should have felt jaunty. In circumstances like these I've been known to skip.

Not this time. I trudged on wet slippery pavement past Greyfriars Bobby and the art shops and charity shops and the building with the Digital Damage office on its second floor, and hesitated a moment before turning right into Lauriston Place. The avenue to the Meadows stretched off gloomily into the distance. Across the way a young guy crouched in the lee of the coffee kiosk with an upturned hat at his feet and nobody walking past him.

Feeling sorry for him, I did my bit for the poor by buying a copy of the *Big Issue* from a pathetically young and pretty girl in a headscarf and long skirt who'd stood in the rain outside the post office all day. She smiled and thanked me. I hurried on.

I glanced to the left at the bright lights of the Doctors', the pub on the corner, and considered nipping across and diving in. But the lads would be long gone and I had a party to go to.

I felt thoroughly rattled. My hand strayed a couple of times to the latch of my bag. Each time, I was within a second of digging out my mobile and speed-dialling Amanda. It would be expensive, but it would wake her up and serve her right. How *dare* she never mention once in our *entire lives* that our family's connection with Krassnia went back a generation further than she— or Great-Grandma Eugenie, come to think of it—had ever let on?

It was at that moment, I think, right on that corner, that all my connections with Krassnia—from my birth there, through to the scariest day of my life, and Amanda's admissions and shortly afterward Eugenie's confession that Saturday evening in Boston, and the old photo and the game and the book that had subconsciously inspired it, and my guesses as to what the game was for, and *now this*—all came together with that creepy feeling of *destiny* in a big dark swirly shape in my mind, a cloud full of half-seen faces, which I began then and there to think of as the Other Thing.

Something that *just could not be* part of my life, but was.

Past the old Royal Infirmary, dark against the lowering sun and rendered darker by the light from the developer's office at the former main door, and by the splendid illumination of St. George's School, lit up like a cathedral on the opposite side of the road. My flat was down towards the bottom of Lauriston Place, near Tollcross. Traffic was light and there weren't many people about. I walked fast. After I'd gone a couple of hundred metres I noticed a distinctive sound behind me, something between a squelch and a click, in the rhythm of footsteps.

I stopped at a crossing and glanced back up the way I had come. No one was walking anywhere close. I crossed, walked on. The sound resumed. I stopped to cross again at the next junction, and looked back again. A couple strolled past, then a knot of lads in white shirts and polished shoes. An old man walked by, a thin pink-striped plastic bag, weighted with a solitary tin, swinging from a crooked finger.

I was back on the left side of the street now. I walked past the Belgian beer pub on the corner and fished my keys from my bag in front of the main doorway. Traffic hummed behind me. The keys jangled, the tip squeaked on the face of the Yale. I got the door open and stepped inside. Just as I turned to close the door behind me I heard the squishy sound of worn heels on wet pavement. A car went past. On the opposite side of the road a young man in a frayed coat and grubby rain-hat hurried by, not looking to left or right.

I made sure the door was locked and ran up the two flights to the flat.

My flatmates, Julie and Gail, had been and gone, presumably to the party. I knew they'd been by the two wet empty shot glasses on the kitchen table and the acetone smell of nailpolish in the bathroom. I knew they'd gone by the silence that hadn't quite settled, like there were echoes still on the air. An empty tin, smelling horribly fresh, told me they'd remembered to feed the cat.

The cat came in and rubbed his head on my ankle and demanded food and attention as if he hadn't eaten for a week and was shortly to feature on an RSPCA poster of a shamefully neglected pet.

"Don't try that with me, Hiro," I said, scratching behind his ears.

I sat down at the kitchen table in my damp leggings and jacket and reached for the vodka bottle. I knocked back a shot out of one of the used glasses and felt warmer, and a little cheerier. For a moment I contemplated another shot, while looking with some distaste at the lipstick print on the glass and realising I'd probably know at some point just which of my flat-mates had used it. Somehow that made it all slightly more disgusting and me slightly more sluttish. What I most wanted right now was a hot bath and an evening slothing about in a dressing gown and slippers, cat on my lap, a thick book in one hand and a tall G&T in the other.

But I had a party to go to. It wasn't far—just over Tolcross, up Home Street, and off to the left—it was starting at 8:30, and it was Suze's flat-warming party. She and her fiancé had just moved in together. I was to be one of her bridesmaids in August. She'd be really miffed if I didn't turn up tonight. I'd bought her a card and a present.

I looked at my watch. 8:20. Shower, hair, face, frock. Agh. I texted Suze to tell her I'd be late.

I made it by 9:15, with time to buy a bottle of chilled Pinot Grigio and a half-bottle of gin on the way.

Party party party . . . Suze's new flat's bigger than ours and has thicker carpets. Also it's a floor higher, and not above a pub, in fact above a quieter street altogether. I met Suze when I worked three months at Starbucks a couple of years ago. Unlike me, Suze had left the barrista life for a better-paying job, because (again unlike me) she had actually gone to university instead of just thinking about it and already had a very good law degree to show for it. I'd met Julie and Gail at the same time. They too now had better-paid jobs than I did. They didn't understand when I insisted that I couldn't think of a better job than the one I had.

(I should explain at this point that the reason I was able to work in the UK without too many hassles other than filing an IRS return every year was that Amanda had craftily provided me with a British passport when I was a tiny tot, basing her claim in part on Great-Grandma Eugenie's continued British citizenship. So I have a US and a UK passport, as well as some hybrid ID card from the Krassnian Autonomous Region which grants me some of the rights of Soviet citizenship, scarily enough.)

Anyway—me, Julie, Gail, and Suze have all managed to stay together since our Starbucks days, and the three of them have been at the centre of one of my circles of friends, the one I privately call my "normal" friends, just as the lads have been at the core of my circle of not-so-normal friends.

"You look fantastic!" Suze said to me as she added my coat to an overloaded hatstand and accepted the prezzie and card. "Ooh, nice dress!"

This was kind of her as on the way over I'd been smitten with self-doubt and had arrived a little self-conscious about the dress, it being a hasty Rusty Zip bargain rack purchase, a pale pink vintage prom frock of the kind that Lily Allen has unaccountably failed to make fashionable among my normal friends.

"Thank you," I said, giving the big skirt a shake to recover its shape from the compression of the coat. "You're looking absolutely wonderful, Suze."

She was: neat black hairstyle, little black dress. She's always had that elegance that looks effortless and that takes a lot more effort than I've ever been willing to give and that makes me get up strategically earlier in the morning than Julie and Gail despite having a shorter commute (ten-minute brisk walk) and later start.

Suze opened the card (Paperchase welcome to your new home with photo of two Emperor penguins in a blizzard) and the present (John Lewis voucher) and gave me a better smile and thank you than my unimaginative offerings deserved and before I knew quite how it had happened I was holding a wine-glass and standing in the middle of the living room floor and sort of vaguely bopping to Katy Perry on the sound system and nodding to people I knew and smiling hopefully to people I didn't.

There were about thirty people at the party, all in their twenties and most of them women. Lots of LBDs, a few blue jeans and blouse or top combinations that would have been a better bet for me if I'd thought to think like an adult and not like, say, a six-year-old, but too late now. After catching up with Julie and Gail—our paths hadn't crossed for, like, almost a day now—and saying hello to Suze's fiancé, John, I wandered through to the kitchen to top up on the New World Generic White, the Pinot Grigio having gone the path of the just.

"So I'm leaving next week to teach Unix in Saudi Arabia," a tall guy with black-rimmed glasses was explaining to someone, while Gail looked on slightly bemused. "Six months, ex-pat compound, you know how it is."

"Enjoy your drinks while you can."

Laughter. I backed out. Gail followed, fresh G&T fizzing in her hand, and disappeared into the living room while I was still negotiating the hallway and trying to find a conversation.

"So, anyway, at this point the whole thing becomes moot . . ."

". . . brought it right in off the post? That's the sort of play that'll . . ."

"Nah, they're still well on the way to relegation."

"Yah, everything's more or less sorted except the table decorations—oh, hello again Lucy, you've *got* to talk to that tall guy over by the window. Friend of John's, Kiwi biologist, total nerd, you're probably the only person here he can have a conversation with."

"Ah, thanks Suze." I put on a brave smile at this backhanded compliment and looked across to where this other tall guy (with his back to us, so he might or might not have had a beard) was leaning out the open window smoking a pipe. Since the room was already as full of cigarette smoke as pubs used to be, this at least showed the guy was considerate.

"What's his name?" I asked.

"Alec something. Now, yes, as I was saying, Jenny, my mum's *still* hankering for a castle and we've had the hotel venue booked for *months* and it's *beautiful. . . .*"

I wandered on into the living room.

"Never heard anything so outrageous in my *life,*" Gail was saying, dominating a knot of conversation in the far corner. In the middle of the floor were about five people, two of whom worked at Holyrood.

"It's been just complete gloom and doom since last May, I mean they still don't have a clue what an opposition's supposed to—"

"Yeah, and it all filters down to us, it's like they want to kick the fucking cat."

On the way across I got snagged by one person in that conversation: Elaine, a young woman I half remembered from a night out with Julie and Gail, and who now wanted me to know exactly what was wrong about the occupation of Iraq and with the US political system.

"I blame the British," I said when I could get a word in. "Specifically, I blame the Labour Party."

"What?"

"Simple. No Blair, no Coalition, it'd have been us and Micronesia or whatever. That'd have been a much harder sell for Bush, agreed?"

"Oh, sure," Elaine said. "But Blair isn't the *Labour Party.*"

"You have this vote of no confidence thing here? Plus you had the war vote. The MPs could have pulled the rug from under him right there."

"Well, yes, but the MPs aren't the *Labour Party* either."

She had this way of kind of dropping her voice while emphasising the words when she said "Labour Party" that made it sound like the name of a fucking church, or possibly the Spanish Inquisition.

"So who is?" I demanded. "The members? I've never met anyone who says they're actually in it. Is it a secret society, or what?"

"We-ell," said Elaine, looking abashed and defiant at the same time, "as it happens, actually, *I'm* a member."

I was about to give her a backhanded compliment for admitting this disgraceful proclivity when she ruined the effect by adding, in a defensive tone: "But I don't go to *meetings*."

At this I just about sank my teeth in her leg.

"I guess now you'll tell me the *meetings* aren't the *Labour Party*?"

While Elaine was taking her defence strategy to the next level, I was keeping half an eye on this Alec somebody. He'd finished his smoke. He drew himself all the way back into the room like some kind of folding ladder and then stood up to his full height of about six and a half feet. His shock of springy black hair made him look even taller. He didn't have a beard exactly, just a black stubble that looked long enough to be soft to brush your hand on. His face looked like he'd been out in the sun a lot. He slid the pipe into his shirt pocket alongside a row of pens and looked around. His eyes were a bright blue and his gaze didn't stop at me. He reached for a wineglass he'd left on a high bookshelf and sipped from it, then took a couple of steps forward and loomed at the edge of the next conversation over from where I was.

By the time Elaine and I had come to a tentative agreement that what we *actually* needed in the US and the UK was a bloody revolution with heads on spikes, Alec had backed away to the corner by the window again and was scanning the bookshelves. I sidled around the side of the room and stepped towards him. On the soundtrack the Zutons were singing "Valerie" which I like (in that version, not Amy Winehouse's, thank you) because it's the only love song I know that's addressed to a girl with ginger hair. It was a bit hard to catch Alec's eye because he was looking down at and carefully turning the pages of one of the shelf-full of wedding magazines that Suze had, to my certain knowledge, begun accumulating about an hour after John had slipped the rock on her finger.

Alec noticed me hovering just outside his space, and looked up. His eyes widened, he smiled and then mouthed along to the very line in the song that always makes me feel appreciated. Then he said: "Why don't you come on over . . ." and it was like he was waiting to add my own name to the end of that line.

My mouth went dry all of a sudden.

"Uh, hello," I said. "I'm Lucy. Uh, Suze said . . ."

"Hi, Lucy," he said. "I'm Alec. Alec Hamilton."

I couldn't place his accent. Australian?

"As in Alexander Hamilton," I said. Forgetting that everyone who has a name that can be quipped about has heard the quip, often.

"The Founding Father," he said. "Yup."

He glanced down again at a two-page fashion spread in the magazine, shook his head a little, closed the magazine and laid it back on the shelf, and retrieved his glass from the shelf above. He just stood there looking at me, as if he were pleased to see me. He didn't say anything.

"Why were you looking at *Brides?*" I asked, and then wished I hadn't, because it sounded like I thought he needed to justify his strange behaviour.

Alec didn't seem at all embarrassed.

"I was checking to see if all wedding dresses are the same." He grinned. "They are."

"Oh no, they're not," I said. "There are *hundreds* of different styles."

Most of which I'd seen while schlepping around bridal shops with Suze, so I spoke with some authority.

"Most of which look exactly alike," Alec said.

"Well, maybe they do to *you*, but not to—and anyway, why would you even be interested?"

He slugged back some red wine. "When I was about five," he said, "my parents took me to a wedding. Being a boy, and a brat, I found it all really boring but I do remember being impressed by the bride. I thought she looked . . . like a queen in a fairy tale, you know? Romantic, I suppose, though I didn't know that word then. She was in one of those big elaborate dresses they had in the eighties."

I gave my shoulders and hips a tiny wiggle, to remind him or myself that I was in an arguably big and romantic dress too. He gave no sign of noticing.

"These," he went on, nodding sideways at the shelf, "don't look so spectacular. Very plain."

I recalled Suze at her fitting. She'd looked like a queen all right.

"You should see one on a bride in real life," I said. "They look totally different when they move."

I gave my skirt another little shake, like: *see?*

"I'll take your word for it," he said.

It seemed a bit of a conversation-stopper.

"Well," I said, laughing it off, "having established that you're not that interested in wedding dresses . . . what *are* you interested in?"

"I'm interested in lots of things," he said. He moved his neck and shoulders as if to ease some tension. "Animals, history, weapons, costumes, words, books, tools, card games, rocks, fossils . . ."

"Ah," I said, delighted. "You're a fan!"

"A fan?"

"You know—science fiction."

"Never read the stuff," he said, in that dismissive way normal people have. I must have looked crestfallen. "Oh."

"I'm a zoologist," he added, like that explained it.

"And you study kiwis," I said, sounding knowledgeable.

"Kiwis?"

"That's what Suze said."

"She knows perfectly well I'm doing research on sheep."

"Sheep?" I couldn't help giggling.

He was still looking straight at me. "I've heard all the jokes."

"Oh, I didn't mean to—but why sheep?"

"Very important animal, it's absolutely crucial to our economy."

"Yeah, I suppose, but I mean Scotland has—"

"The *New Zealand* economy," he said.

"Oh! You're from New Zealand! So that's what Suze meant."

Alec closed his eyes and shook his head. "What?"

"When she said you were a Kiwi biologist."

Alec laughed.

"Now we've got that cleared up," he said, "what do *you* do?"

At this point what was going through my mind was the story my mother had told me when I asked how she met my father: how she'd fallen for a tall, bearded, pipe-smoking student at a party, and how after some time for some reason they had fallen out, and then a few years later the guy had done the most crazy and romantic thing imaginable: he'd turned up on her doorstep—well, in her stairwell—in Krasnod. He'd come all that way to see her. In a truck. (Amanda had never actually spelled out what had happened next, but the date was some time in late 1984 and I was born in June 1985, so it was a matter of you do the math.) And I was thinking maybe my mom and I shared the same type and that if so I wasn't going to let all the rest of that history repeat.

"Oh," I said, "I do admin for a small start-up computer games company."

"Which one?"

"Digital Damage."

"Kronos!" Alec cried. "You work for the company that made Kronos?"

And that was it: after all those initialisation crashes in the conversation—Founding Father and brides' dresses and science fiction and kiwis and fucking sheep—it was up and running.

After some time we noticed our glasses were empty. Leaving Alec to occupy the corner, I headed for the kitchen, to find it crowded as before. As I filled the glasses Gail marched in and strode up to the tall bearded programmer, elbowed past the guy he was talking to, and got right in his face.

"Excuse me," she said.

"Yes?"

"What I want to know," she said, "is how you can justify what you're going to be doing in Saudi."

"I don't see anything wrong with it," he said.

"It's disgusting and it's oppressing women."

The guy scratched the back of his head. "Aye, sure, it's a repressive regime and all that, but it's not like I'm supporting it. How's getting a contract in Saudi any worse than buying petrol?"

"But a contract to do *that*!" Gail shuddered her head and shoulders. "Teaching Unix! Ugh!"

The guy looked completely baffled now.

"What the fuck have you got against Unix?"

"I've got nothing against *them*," said Gail. "It's the—you know, what's been done to them, and they're probably *slaves*, and the use that's made of them, keeping women under guard. How can you possibly say that's—"

She stopped and glared. "Why are you laughing?"

I left them to it.

It would have been disloyal to my flatmate to tell Alec about her contretemps. I didn't want to get back on the subject of mishearings and misunderstandings, but I was grinning all over my face when I got back to our corner. Alec must have thought I was beaming at him all the way across the room. He gave me a *very* warm smile when I handed him his drink. He might even have been blushing. Not, you know, that I minded.

"So what are you working on now?" he asked.

"Dark Britannia," I said.

"Swords and sorcery with a smattering of Matter of Britain?"

"Got it in one," I said. "Sort of sword in the stone and Grail quest mash-up. With zombies. And Romans."

Alec started telling me about some recent research on Roman handheld, lead-slug-firing crossbows, and for the first time I found myself only half listening. Because when I'd mentioned Dark Britannia I'd realised that I couldn't tell Alec anything about the Krassnian version of the game. The front company, Small Worlds, had of course included a clause on commercial confidentiality in the contract. But there was more to it than that. It was personal, not professional. The feeling that had crept over me earlier that evening about the scary skein of connections I'd begun to discover, and the troubling tone of all the passing references I'd found to Krassnian affairs, the whole *Other Thing* . . . this was something I wanted to keep from the lads.

As I looked into Alec's bright blue eyes, and listened to the enthusiastic, innocent, fannish flow of his voice, I knew I wanted to keep the Other Thing from him too.

No, that wasn't quite right: I wanted to keep him from the Other Thing. I wanted to *protect* him from it.

In that, of course, I failed.

But later that night I wanted Alec to protect me. I had been seriously creeped out by the suspicion that the young beggar had followed me home. When I looked around and noticed that we were among the last people at the party and that Julie and Gail had long gone, I didn't want to go home on my own and I had the perfect excuse not to.

"Alec," I said, "would you mind very much walking me home?"

"Not at all," he said.

"It's not far, just down to Tolcross and up a bit."

"No worries," he said.

Outside, he paused for a moment on the porch to fill and light his pipe. Small bowl, curved stem.

"Peterson," he said. "'The thinking man's pipe.'"

He gave me his arm and I took it and we set off around the corner and down Home Street in good order with me misplacing my heels not too often and Alec taking these stumbles in his stride. Under a light drizzle late clubbers swayed in giggling or roaring groups: girls with bare legs and arms and lads in short-sleeved shirts.

"Funny," I said, "how much nicer pipe smoke smells. Than cigarettes, I mean."

"Only when it's fresh," said Alec, through his teeth. "That's why I only smoke outside."

"My father smoked a pipe," I said. "Well, my mother's ex-boyfriend."

"Hm," said Alec, taking the pipe from his mouth this time, "you haven't told me much about yourself."

"That's because I'm mysterious," I said, giving his elbow a squeeze.

"Like why you don't have an American accent."

"Oh, that's because I was"—the rest sung nasally—"bo-o-rrnn in the You Ess Ess Arrr!"

"Under a wandering star," Alec sang back.

We laughed and scooted across at the lights.

"Seriously," said Alec, "you were born in the Soviet Union?"

"Ay-yup," I said. "Seven years there—well, it was called the CIS when we left—then four years in Edinburgh, ten years in New York, and two years here."

"How did all that come about?"

"My mother's an academic, she has to move around."

"Why d'you come back to Edinburgh?"

"Ah, shit, that's complicated."

We'd reached the entrance to the block.

"Long story?" Alec said.

"Yes."

Now that we'd stopped he was facing me.

"I'd like to hear it sometime," he said.

I fumbled my keys from my shoulder bag, and let them jingle.

"Would you like to hear it tonight?"

A smile spread across his face like sunlight across a planet.

"Maybe . . . in the morning?" he said.

I opened the door and stood aside, arm welcoming.

"Well, come in," I said.

Alec stepped past me.

As I closed the door I heard the footsteps of someone who'd just walked by: *squish*, *squish*.

I locked the door and led Alec up the stone stairs, feeling quite safe.

3. THE RUSSIAN BUSINESS

1.

A couple of months after I started working for Digital Damage, I played a little prank on the lads. I snatched an opportunity of everyone's being coincidentally out of the office on various brief errands to set all the desktops' Google language preferences to Klingon. One by one the lads returned from the post office or the sandwich shop or the fire escape and sat down and continued working or (it being lunchtime) doing a little recreational web-browsing. Whether working or slacking, the lads use Google a *lot*.

I sat back, like the evil H.R. cat in *Dilbert*, and waited for the cries of anguish to erupt.

Nothing happened. Work continued without interruption all afternoon. No one said anything about it. Sean sent all of us an email reminding us to lock our screens or log off every single time we left the desk, "even if it's only for a slash or a smoke."

My respect for the team went up a level.

So when I arrived at the office before everyone else, about eight on the Monday morning after my first weekend with Alec, still breaking into a big loopy grin whenever I thought about it, which was like every five minutes or so, I was not *too* worried when I turned on the desktop computer, fired up the web browser to check the news headlines and Astronomy Picture of the Day, and found that it had been hacked.

The hack was one of those cunning social engineering jobs that look like your antivirus software has splattered a big urgent message box right across your screen to *tell* you you've been hacked. And that gives you an option to download a specialised software tool to get rid of this new and dangerous virus *right this very minute before it does any more damage!*

If you're a sufficiently clueless or panicked user (and there are enough such to make this scam a good bet) what you download is, of course, a piece of software (known as malware or spyware, in the biz) that turns your computer into an engine spamming out bright flashing not-safe-for-work ads linking to porn sites (themselves often a different scam or honeytrap, but that's another story) or that just lurks in the background until it does something even more outrageous and that you might not notice at all.

The tiny flaw in the cunning plan of whoever had hacked my computer (or, more precisely, something upstream of my web browser) was that the urgent message purported to be from an antivirus package that no one in the biz bothers with anymore, configured to run on Windows Vista, which I won't say anything bad about but which was not the best cover story for getting into an office system that runs on Linux. (An operating system where viruses die like earthworms in sunlight.)

So I put down my coffee mug, laughed in the stupid message's face, and mouse-clicked it off. It bounced back up. I cursed and ran my real anti-malware tool, which reported that it had got rid of an intruding .exe file.

The big urgent message box was still there. Fuck.

By the time Sean and Suresh trickled in at 8:30 I was very close to tears of frustration.

"I didn't download *anything*," I told them. "I just clicked on my bookmarks to the Beeb and APoD. And I've run the removal tool, then a full system scan, then restarted, and that fucking thing is *still there*. I can't even minimise it."

"Just as well you can't," Suresh chuckled. "Not the sort of thing you want to ignore."

I glared at him. Like I would do *that*.

"You clean the mess off Lucy's PC and I'll check where it came from," said Sean.

"Sure," said Suresh. He looked down at me. "Um, let me . . ."

I got up and he sat down. Meanwhile Sean had gone to his own desk.

Suresh's long brown fingers danced over my keyboard. My desktop screen disappeared and was replaced by a command line. He rattled in a string of code and hit Enter. A response came up, as incomprehensible to me as the query. Suresh frowned. Started again. *Taptaptaptap* . . .

"Shit!" Sean shouted. "Fucker's all over mine too. Must be on the system server. Give me a minute."

It took an hour. Sean and Suresh toiled in the truth mines, while Matt (our best coder, like I said, but games not systems), Joe, and I kept the caffeine supplies coming and got on with whatever we could do that didn't involve using a computer. Joe doodled sketches and went back and forth to the fire escape, Matt thumbed through a manual, and I got busy with an English-Russian dictionary, a Russian-Krassnian dictionary, a Krassnian-Krassnian dictionary, and the game's dialogue script and prompts.

(Krassian-Krassnian? Outcome of a classic Soviet-1930s epic fail in linguistics policy. Y'see, Krassnian, though it's a Circassian language, used to be written in Latin script, just like English, because the Vrai originally spoke a Romance dialect, and sometime in the Dark Ages had converted from a characteristically muddled and benighted version of Gnosticism to Roman Catholicism, which consolidated their attachment to a Latin script even after the Vrai dialect had just about died out (no doubt because the Vrai had to use the Krassnar tongue to shout insults and orders to their serfs). Before the Revolution most of the population of Krassnia couldn't read—except the Vrai aristos, and they could read Krassnian and Russian, Latin and Cyrillic script with equal facility.

After the 1917 Revolution, there was a huge literacy programme, which (credit where it's due) got most of the population able to read and write in Krassnian (in the Latin script, so that the oppressed masses could read exactly as well as the local ruling class). Around about 1935, some tidy-minded official in Moscow decides that all the languages that have hitherto been written in their traditional script (whether it's Latin, Arabic, Georgian, Ossetian, or whatever) will henceforth be written in Cyrillic. Overnight, everyone affected is illiterate in their own language all over again. The stupid, it burns, as the saying goes. The resentment, it burns too.

So the upshot of all this is that in 1992, after the breakup of the Soviet Union, the government of Krassnia (all excommie and pro-Russki, but pandering like mad to Krassnian national sentiment) decreed that henceforth Krassnian would be written in the Latin script.

Which—stop me if you've heard this before—made every native speaker of Krassnian officially illiterate in Krassnian *all over again*.

(Hence the need for a Krassnian-Krassnian dictionary.)

Sean took a deep breath, one that I heard across two desks. We all looked up.

"That's it," he said. "Done. Fixed. Fuck."

On that last word, it was like he'd let the last of the breath out. His shoulders slumped.

"Fuck," he repeated, then straightened up. "I just fucking hope I never have to do all that ever again."

I felt quite irrationally responsible, or at least as if I'd be blamed, because (a) my desktop had been the first affected and (b) I suspected the lads would assume that I'd been careless. So I kept uncharacteristically quiet.

"What was it?" Matt asked.

Suresh stood up. "It was more than an annoyingly persistent scambot," he said. "That was just a cover for a piece of code set up to send chunks of *our* code to some cleverly munged I.P. address."

"Our *game* code?" said Matt, sounding outraged.

"Yes," said Suresh. "I think it was an attempt to pirate our games, or one of them."

Sean shook his head. "You're right about what it was trying to do," he said. "But I don't agree about the social engineering scam. *That* wasn't a cover! We might never have noticed anything was wrong if that hadn't been plastered over our screens in big flashing letters."

"So why do that?" asked Joe. "Seems like self-defeating, no?"

"Not if we were *meant* to notice it," said Sean. "It's like football casuals used to leave business cards on people they'd beaten up and left bleeding in the gutter. 'You have been done over by the Hearts Mental Krew,' sort of stuff." He fixed me with a narrow-eyed gaze. "I think we've just had a card saying: 'You have been done over by the Russian Business Network.'"

The Russian Business Network, in case you're lucky enough not to know, is the nastiest, most powerful cybercrime syndicate on the planet. Child porn, malware, botnet seeding, phishing, spam hosting, identity theft, denial of service attacks are all in a day's work for them. Fake antimalware alarms are one of their favoured methods of planting malware. I've never heard of them leaving a calling card.

"The RBN?" said Matt. "Oh come *on*. You're being a wee bit over-dramatic, Sean."

"He's not," said Suresh. "We know that the scam is Russian." He waved a sheet of diagnostics. "Traced it back to a known RBN host in Tajikistan. Good reason to think the trojan came from the same source."

"What I don't get," said Joe, "is why whoever tried it would want us to know."

"Maybe Lucy can tell us," said Sean.

I sat bolt upright, which is not safe to do if you have your chair on tilt. I had to grab the side of the desk.

"What?" I cried. "Why should I know?"

"The Krassnia thing," said Sean. He looked as if he were embarrassed to be saying this, but had to persist. "Russia's interested in Krassnia, isn't it? You know about Krassnia, Lucy. D'you think there's anything going on we don't know about?"

Shit shit shit shit shit

"Oh, sure," I said. "It's actually quite difficult to find out anything about Krassnia—and I've tried, believe me—so there's bound to be something we don't know about. But I'd be very surprised if the Russians care about a *game*, or even if they know about it. How could they?"

"This Small Worlds company," said Matt. "Nobody kens much about them. I mean, they could be dodgy themselves, or have dodgy connections. Hard to operate in that part of the world without dealing wi' the dark side, know what I mean?"

"Now that's being paranoid and overdramatic," said Sean.

Matt looked stubborn. "Whatever—even if they're totally legit, they could have had a leak."

"Aha!" said Sean, brightening. "I know. Somebody in Russia who makes or pirates or sells games is warning us off because they don't want the competition!"

"Aye, sure," said Matt. "Like Dark Krassnia or whatever we're calling it is going to blow away Grand Theft Auto or World of Warcraft?"

"In a niche market, it might," said Sean. He rubbed his hands together. "Well, that makes sense. Me and Suresh have fixed the security hole that let the trojan in, and we've beefed up the firewall, so let's give them some competition, what say you chaps?" (That last in an affected gung-ho English accent.)

"You're no worried about the warning?" Joe asked. He swivelled a fingertip in his ear, a revolting tic for which I was just about ready to smack the back of his head. "I've heard the Russians can play kind of heavy."

"Ah, you're talking about drug deals and stuff like that," said Sean. "A bit of hacking's the worst they'll do over something like this."

And much to my relief, that was where the matter was left to rest. I said nothing more, and got on with dealing with the day's admin before returning to translating the script. I was reassured that Digital Damage's internal network had, like my mind, firewalled the Other Thing.

2.

Over the next couple of weeks life settled down a little. I left work at varying times, not always after six, and took varying routes home. Nobody followed me, or at least nobody I could detect by the simple techniques I used: pausing at shop windows and checking the reflections, doubling back, that sort of thing. The young beggar with the squishy-sounding footsteps was nowhere to be seen (or heard). The weather improved into April. Alec was up in the Highlands, at one of the university's field stations, picking ticks off sheep and applying statistics. He and I exchanged texts and photos about ten times a day, had long calls in the evenings, and were never out of each other's company at the weekends. It was all wonderful.

The Wednesday of the third week I finished the game-script translation. I did a little song and dance around the office, accepted all the congratulations, and emailed the script to Small Worlds. Two hours later, I got an email back.

Small Worlds had a problem—their Krassnian-language female voice actor was down with a throat infection. Could I do the voice acting instead? They would seek out studio space in Edinburgh and set me up with an appointment. Ambience and general cleaning-up of the sound file would be done by Small Worlds' own techs: all I'd have to do was mouth the lines with as much conviction as I could muster.

I forwarded the email to Sean.

"Can you do this?" he emailed back.

"Guess so," I said.

"Go for it," he replied.

I emailed Small Worlds to tell them to go ahead.

I left work a little early, around five thirty, and walked home by the direct route, down Lauriston Place. About a hundred metres from the flat I caught a whiff of the same pipe tobacco that Alec smoked. Not many people smoke pipes at all these days, and even fewer do so in the street. I glanced around, half expecting to see Alec. I couldn't see any pipe smokers.

The following evening I left work about six thirty. At the same point in my walk home, I caught the same whiff. This time, I did see the pipe smoker: a tall, heavily built man in a dark suit, about twenty paces behind me. I walked on past the flat entrance, crossed the street, walked past the big HBOS building, crossed Earl Grey Street at the first lights, and walked on down towards Lothian Road. I idled by the Woolworth's shop window, stopped to look at the Odeon's film posters, turned down Morrison Street a short distance, then crossed and doubled back, turning left again into Lothian Road.

In all of these twists and turns and pauses I didn't see the big guy at all, but every so often I caught that pipe-smoke smell. I began to wonder if I wasn't imagining it. I stopped outside the Filmhouse and turned around. The tall man, pipe jutting from his mouth, was about ten yards behind.

I stepped out into his path. The street was busy enough that nothing would happen to me unnoticed. He looked mildly irritated and swerved slightly to walk on past me. I stepped in his path again. He stopped. I stared at him, shaking inside.

Like I said, tall. Not so much heavily built as muscular in the chest and arms. Almost eccentrically old-fashioned, like a lawyer or a clergyman, in a three-piece suit that didn't stretch, or hang awkwardly; it was fine enough to have been cut for him. Grey hair, combed back. Straggly black eyebrows. He wore a white shirt and striped pale-blue-on-dark-blue silk tie. His cheeks looked as if they'd been shaved too often with a blunt blade and then stung with aftershave—of which, indeed, the scent was strong from where I stood, overlaying the pipe smoke smell. In one hand he had a briefcase, in the other his pipe. He looked so respectable, so politely bemused and taken aback, that I felt a surge of embarrassment and self-doubt.

I'd meant to challenge him, in a voice to turn heads.

"Excuse me," I said, just loud enough for him to hear. "Are you *following* me?"

Fully expecting a surprised or dismayed dismissal of this paranoid fantasy accusation from a clearly overwrought young woman, I folded my arms and looked him in the eye as sternly as I could.

The man frowned.

"Not exactly," he said. "I was making sure that you weren't being followed."

He had a quiet voice, a West of Scotland accent mellowed into refinement.

"So you *were* following me!"

He considered this for a moment, then nodded.

"Logically, of course"—he stretched a smile—"I can't dispute that. You're not, by the way."

"Not what?"

"You're not being followed."

"Except by you!"

I was still undecided whether or not to make a scene, right there in front of the folks heading in to the Filmhouse for the seven o'clock screenings.

The man shrugged. "As I said, I can't deny that." He nodded sideways. "Shall we step inside and discuss this over a coffee? Or a bite to eat, if you like?"

I stayed put. "Who are you?"

"My name is Ross Stewart," he said. "And you're Lucianne Stone." He slipped the pipe in his jacket pocket and stuck out a hand. "Pleased to meet you."

Bewildered, I shook the hand of the man who might have been my father.

The Filmhouse has a bar-restaurant at the back, serving decent food at a reasonable price. I'd been there a lot, before movies.

I nodded to Maria, a Polish girl I'd worked with at Starbucks, behind the serving counter, and she smiled back. I ordered a feta and salad in pitta and a black-currant smoothie; the man calling himself Ross Stewart ordered a bowl of chilli con carni and a weissbeer. The place was busy. The man paid for both of us. We took our drinks and orbited around people shrugging on coats until we nabbed a table for two, by a pillar.

"Well . . ." said Ross, after taking a sip and giving me an appraising look over the rim of the ribbed chunky glass.

"Just a mo," I said.

I rummaged my phone from the floor of my bag and thumbed keys as if texting, but actually paging through the menu to the camera settings. I flicked back the lens cover, held up the phone, and took a nonflash shot. On the screen it saved bright and clear.

"Hey!" he said. "Wait a—"

I'd speed-dialled it to Amanda before he could react.

"Fuck," he said. "What do you think you're doing?"

"Checking your credentials," I told him.

"Who with?"

"My mother," I said.

His mouth fell open. His face paled a little, then reddened. He put his glass down with a bang.

"Fuck," he said again. He laughed suddenly, and shook his head. "I should have known."

"Known?"

"What to expect from you. Jeez, Lucianne. You're your mother's daughter all right. Speaking of which—how did you spot me?"

"The smell of your pipe," I told him.

He put his elbows on the table and leaned his face into his hands. Then he opened and spread his hands and looked at me, shaking his head and laughing.

"What a—" he began.

At that point the waitress arrived with our meals and my phone rang: Mom. I selected Answer, put the phone to my ear, and signalled apology to the waitress with a waggle of my eyebrows. She put the plates down on the wrong sides. The man nodded, smiled at her, and swapped them as Amanda spoke. No small talk from her. No us-girls-together tone this time.

"What the fuck d'you think you're playing at, Lucy?" Amanda demanded.

"Funny you should ask, Mom," I said, keeping my nerve in a way that made me feel smug and proud. "That guy in the photo has just said more or less the same. Expletives included."

"Well, Lucy, you just put that—that—put him on the phone right now."

I handed the mobile across the table. The man looked up from stirring a meditative forkful of sour cream into the surface layer of his chilli con carni. He took the phone with a smile at me.

"Hello, Amanda," he said. "Good to hear from—"

I only heard one side of the conversation, but I got the picture. It went like this:

"It wasn't part of my—"

"Well, no, that's—"

"Sorry, but that's your problem, and—"

"Look, I'm not one of your—"

"I was just—"

"Don't start that ag—"

"Yeah, I'll put her on. Love you too, sweetie."

This guy might or might not be my father, but he sure sounded married to my mother.

He returned the phone.

"You deal with her," he said, and picked up his fork.

"Explain yourself," said Amanda.

I took a deep breath. "I take it you've just spoken to Ross Stewart?"

"Yes, Lucy," Amanda said, sounding burdened. "The guy in the pic you sent me." Her voice dropped, like that would make a difference. "I'd rather you didn't use his name over the phone."

"It's done now," I said.

"Oh, for God's sake, Lucy!" she cried, loud enough for me to flinch the phone away from my ear. "Don't pretend to be so *fucking* naive. If you ever pull a stunt like this again you're off the fucking case, you hear me?"

"I didn't know I was *on* a case, Mom," I said, and immediately regretted sounding like a sulky teen.

"Lucy!" Amanda hissed (no exaggeration—I'm blessed with a name that *can* be hissed). "Stop this right now! You're on a case, you're *on*, and it's about time you cottoned on to that. There's a lot riding on you, OK?"

"Not anything *I* asked for," I said (that instant regret again, but come on). "Or anything that anyone's thought to explain to me, you know?"

"Listen, Lucy. You have to trust me." Her indrawn breath made the phone crackle. "This is not the time or the place. I can't explain. That guy can . . . tell you some things."

"And can I trust him?"

Long pause. "About as far as you can throw him, Lucy. To be honest. That's as far as I would. But we're all on the same side." Another long pause. "For what that's worth. But listen to what he has to say."

"Thanks, Mom," I said. "Goodnight."

"It's day here," she said.

I gave what I hoped was a bitter laugh and closed the call.

I looked at the man across the table.

"Well . . ." I said. "That was—"

"Eat," said Ross Stewart.

We pushed our plates back at the same time.

"Coffee?" Ross asked.

"Cappucino," I said.

He took his briefcase with him to the counter; carried it awkwardly under his elbow when he came back. My cappucino had slopped a little. I dabbed in the saucer with the paper napkin.

"All right," Ross said. "Questions?"

I took a deep breath. "Uh, just to get this one . . . out of the way, you know? Are you my father?"

His double espresso cup rattled. He rubbed under the septum of his nose with his wrist, as if there was an itch there.

"I don't know," he said.

It took me a moment to process this.

"Ah," I said.

Ross nodded. "Well, that was . . . part of what made the situation awkward for all concerned. I can give you some detail later, if you like. I'm sure you have more pressing questions than that."

"Would you be willing to take a DNA test?" I asked.

He rocked back in his seat. "I would not," he said. "Not without anything less than a court order."

"I have a right to know," I said. "An actual, legal right."

"You do, of course. Yes. And if you were to assert it . . . ah, look, Lucianne, could this not wait until . . . this whole thing is over?"

"Stop calling me Lucianne," I said. "I'm called Lucy."

"All right."

"As for waiting—how long are you talking about?"

He shrugged. "Matter of months."

"OK," I said. "And what is 'this whole thing,' if I may ask? A colour revolution?"

I expected him to react with the same sort of security rant that Amanda had given me. Instead, he smiled and nodded.

"'The Maple Revolution,' they're calling it," he said. "You heard it here first."

"And who's 'they'?"

"Oh, the Agency, of course."

"Are you . . . ?"

Ross shook his head, looking amused. "Not so much as an asset, Lucy," he said. "Just a freelance operator who happens to be on the same side of this particular hoo-hah."

"What are you?" I asked. "Like, what do you do?"

"Ah," he said. "Now there you have me worried about being overheard. I can say with some certainty that not one ear within what limited earshot there is in this crowded and noisy establishment is likely to prick up at a mention of Krassnia, or the Agency, or for that matter my contestable paternity. I could tell you, truthfully enough, that I'm the owner and manager of an import-export business, but that wouldn't be fair to you and wouldn't be in the least useful to either of us."

He took out his pipe, unscrewed the bowl, and with his used paper napkin began wiping a thin disgusting brown liquid from the small metal cup into which the bowl had fitted.

"Shall we go outside?" he said, reassembling the pipe without looking. "We could walk back towards your flat, and along the way I can tell you what I do."

A thin rain was falling. Ross stood for a moment under the Filmhouse's eaves to light his pipe, then took a folding umbrella from his briefcase, opened it, and held it over me as we set off.

"Thanks," I said.

"You know," said Ross, through teeth clenched on his pipe, "I blame your boyfriend's bad example for starting me again on the habit."

I almost collided with the umbrella. "What? How long have you been stalking me?"

"It's not a question of stalking," he said, sounding quite unperturbed. "I've been keeping an eye on you, one way and another, since the day before your mother called to ask you about the game. She asked me to watch out for you, you see."

"How?" I demanded.

He sighed, sending a cloud of smoke in front of us.

"Let's just say I have eyes on the street. I had to make sure you weren't under unfriendly surveillance."

"What sort of unfriendly—?"

"Russian," he said.

"Ah," I said. "You're wrong there. Our computers got hacked a couple of weeks ago by the Russian Business Network."

"That was me," he said. "Just checking your security—now wait a minute, I can explain!"

I'd jumped away from under the brolly, and stayed away, though the drizzle was now what we in Scotland call "wetting."

"It better be good."

Ross, evidently embarrassed to be seen not sharing his umbrella, collapsed it and strode along beside me in the rain.

"You asked what I do," he said. "I do a lot of things. I have a stake in a good number of businesses, import-export as I think I mentioned, mostly long-haul trucking to and from Eastern Europe, the Balkans, and the western parts of the former Soviet Union."

"Uh-huh," I said.

He said nothing for a few paces, until we were on a stretch of pavement with no one within ten yards or so.

"But one of my lines of work," he went on, "the one you have to know about, from me, up front, right now, is that I'm a people-smuggler."

I nearly tripped. "You're a—"

"I help people to come to this country illegally. Don't get the wrong idea—I'm an ethical people-smuggler. I don't rip people off and I don't deliver them to debt slavery or prostitution or gang-masters. What they do when they get here is up to them, but they always walk away from my delivery depots with enough to keep them going for a day or two, reasonably convincing documentation, and maybe with an introduction in hand to"— an airy wave of the pipe—"a restaurant or a building site that doesn't ask too many questions."

"I don't believe you," I said.

"Why not?"

"Because if it's true, you're taking a hell of a risk telling me."

"I'm not," he said. "For one thing, I know you're not going to go to the police, because that would mess up the job you're doing for Amanda. For another, it would take an absolutely massive police investigation to connect me with the actual trafficking, and meanwhile, I can assure you, I would be putting up legal flak and calling in favours like nobody's business. I'm a very respectable citizen, and I know a lot of other respectable citizens very much better than they know me."

"I spotted you tailing me," I said. "That's not what would happen to a man who has all the angles covered."

"You're right there," he said, sounding angry. "Ah, fuck it."

And with that, without breaking stride, he tossed the still-smouldering pipe into the nearest bin.

"There's a lot more I have to tell you," he said. "But I see we've reached your corner." He waved a hand up ahead. "I live up in Morningside. Are you going to be in this evening?"

"Yes."

"Very good." He rattled off my address. "I'll have a package couriered round within two hours. It'll tell you all you need to know—along with quite a lot that you don't, but that I'm telling you anyway."

"Why would you do that?"

He stood looking at me, rain slowly drenching his hair and collar.

"You deserve to know. After all this time."

He raised the umbrella again and walked away.

Julie and Gail looked up from the sofa in front of the telly as I walked into the living room. Empty plates, page-shuffled newspapers, and full wine-glasses on the coffee table.

"Lucy, your hair's a *mess*," Gail observed helpfully.

"Got caught in the rain," I said, likewise bearing news.

"There's still some pasta and sauce in the pan," said Julie.

"I've eaten," I said.

All this talk about food brought Hiro bounding in and twining around my ankles, accusations of neglect and starvation going full bore.

"Has anyone fed him?" I asked.

"Yes, I did," Gail and Julie chorused, then looked at each other. "Oh!"

"Now, who's Lucy's lying little bastard?" I said, scratching between his ears. The complaints continued. I straightened up. "No."

Hiro stalked off, too proud to look over his shoulder. I retreated to my room with a mug of coffee and a towel. Hiro soon followed, curling up on the chair I was just about to sit on. I pulled off my damp jeans and sat down at the top of the bed with the pillows behind me and texted Alec. He texted back. This went on for some time.

The door bell buzzed, waking me from a doze.

"I'll get it!" I called through. I flailed into a dressing gown and padded out to the hall and over to the intercom.

"Package for Lucy Stone," it crackled.

"Come on up," I said, buzzing open the outer door lock.

Thump thump thump . . . up the stairwell. I peered through the fisheye. Definitely a courier, helmet politely in one hand, Jiffy bag in the other.

I opened the door on the chain, scribbled on the courier's handheld screen, and accepted the packet. It was much lighter and floppier than I'd expected.

"Thanks," I said.

"Cheers, miss."

Thump thump thump . . . *Slam.*

"What was that?" Julie called out.

"Delivery," I said.

Back in the bedroom, I retrieved my Leatherman Juice from my bag and opened the packet. At first it seemed to be empty and I wondered wildly about some mistake. Then I held the packet upside down and pushed the sides together. A two-gigabyte USB memory stick fell out.

The time was about nine thirty. My toes were cold. I changed into PJs and socks and the dressing gown while running a backup of my laptop. I went through to the kitchen and skooshed a tumbler of Namaqua, then stuck my head around the living-room door to wave goodnight to the girls.

Back in my room I dislodged Hiro from the spot at the top of the bed, and arranged tumbler, cushions, light, laptop, and cables to my satisfaction. I curled my feet under me, inserted the USB stick, and opened the directory.

There was only one file, titled "Dossier.pdf." It had been created and saved at 20:49 that evening.

From the preview, some of the big PDF's contents were pictures; most were scans of handwritten or printed or typed pages. Some of the typed pages were in Russian—I could read them, slowly, but I was relieved to see that each had a parallel page in English, presumably a translation.

The first word that jumped out at me, on the titles of these Russian pages, was "Confession."

And, also as I skimmed these pages, the following names, instantly recognisable to me even in Cyrillic lettering:

Avram Arbatov
Eugenie Montford

On the pages in English:

Amanda Stone
Ross Stewart

One name that I didn't recognise: Yuri Gusayevich. And one more that I did, from the scariest day in my life: Ilya Klebov.

My hand went to my mouth. The scariest day of my life was now inextricably and inarguably part of, and not just associated with, the Other Thing. I slid my hand down and clutched Hiro's side, too hard. He wriggled out and shot away to the foot of the bed.

I jumped to the beginning, to the handwritten pages, and began to read.

4. THE CONFESSIONS DOSSIER

1.

Note by me (Lucy): this part of the dossier was scanned from handwritten notebook pages of unlined A4 paper, presumably Ross Stewart's diary or diaries. Blank spaces, evidently the result of placing another sheet of paper between the page and the plate, are indicated. Other gaps between dates are in the original—Ross was, on this evidence, only an intermittent diary-keeper.

No attempt has been made to reproduce the numerous doodles and scribbles, mostly of a sexual, abstract, or violent nature, that deface the text and its margins.

29/11/79 Trains home to Greenock for Hogmanay. Laden wi presents for Mum, Dad, and the weans. Also washing. Papers full of Afghanistan. All so fucking right-wing and hypocritical I have to fight down reflex to side with Russia. So take a deep fucking breath, Stewart, even the CP has condemned the invasion. Reading more of Conquest's book on train sort of helped to get a perspective.

Anyway...dear future reader (hopefully moi) big news personally is that the other night at party in the Broughton Hilton I met this amazing lassie. Amanda Stone. Yank, with Eng. (?Scottish? does it make any diff?) arist. ancestry. Total knock-out, long reddish (?word? ask sis or poof bro) hair, great figure, bonny bonny face, lovely smile—christ the Yanks have good teeth. Spent half the party talking talking talking, then finally—don't know how, wish I could remember—we went to bed. Spent the last couple days in bed wi her.

Fuck me. So to speak.

Wanted her to come through and see the folks, but she politely backed off that, said she had distant rellies in Ed. to spend NYr with.

Forgot to say, found her opening old brown envelopes from our hall table, cool as cuc. when challenged—impressed. Something to bear in mind for future ref, nudge nudge. Not ready yet to tell her about the Five Cities

Journey. Came close once—blame Cairds for that, spiked my fucking Tennents with vodka.

Will raise with the cdes when I get to know her better. Lkng fwd to that (the getting to know her).

1/1/80 Woke to the new decade about 4 in the afternoon with a humdinger of a hangover. Blame it on the Whyte & Mackay I shared wi the pater when I tottered in abt 5 a. fucking m. last night. He's no taking the redundancy v. well but at 47 he is not exactly in with a shout down the Job Centre. (Even with the Professional Register, him being—having been—a draughtsman.) Nor is he impressed that poof bro (after bailing from the nursing two years in) is now training at Watt Coll. to be fucking makeup artist. I tell Dad the lad'll have a decent chance of a job anyway, better than the yards or factories. Long gloomy discussion abt Maggie, Assembly vote fiasco, et fucking cetera.

Had great time while out tho'. Kicked off after the bells (and the Bells) first footing: Morrisons, Doyles, wee Mrs. McClintock, then hit the serious drinking party's over at Ray's. Talked a bit to Helen, she is well over me and I her but I made a point of mentioning Amanda. Then fell in to long chat wi Cairds. Made point that spiking drinks was something of a no-no esp. considering we were putting him up that night. He laughed & said "Well, it worked on yon American bird," which I thought was out of order but let pass. Cairds then tells me abt new job he has, down in London: driving long-haul container lorries to all over the Continent. As per usual the wee schemie's come up wi a wee scheme all his own, and it's a doozy: hash smuggling from Turkey, using bales of pressed dates or dried fish or the like in the return freight as cover, throw the sniffer dogs off the scent etc. Told him he was fucking mental, asked him if he'd ever seen *Midnight Express*. "Aye," he says, "yon boring one about the gigolo in New York dying of TB or whatever? Sent me to sleep, pal."

Sometimes I think the lad is beyond help.

6/1/80 Back in Ed. Tomorrow, back to the old grindstone chiz chiz as molesworth sa. Flat fucking freezing. Colin back too. Couldn't face cooking (leave aside washing the plates, they're mouldy—note to self: buy Sqezy from paki 1st thing tomorro) so we got in a chinky which we ate from the tins then C. settled down to homework while I hoofed it up to the South-sider for informal mtng of the cdes in the snug.

Presnt: Moira, Jack, Stef, and y.t. Stef has been home (i.e., grandparents') in Gd'k for Xmas and shared his obs on the 2 Gd. towns. Workers in the yards have fried fish and shot of vodka for bkfst! Understandably cagey (Moira being a bit too close to the NUS Euros to be entirely rlbl) but gave us to understand that another big expl is due any time. The 2 K. orgs lflts well rec'd etc. Jack has done the accounts and says funding and docs for nxt 5 Cities run near complete.

I talked abt A. in v. general terms without mentioning her name or ident. dets. Stef said worth cultvtg as long-term contact with regard to as he put it "dropping a package down the shaft of the Death Star." I pointed out also lang. skills v. useful, also in on acad. connections. Noted.

With regard to the Death Star itself, Stef's quite elated about Afghan entanglement bcos: (a) opens people's eyes after years of detente nonsense (good laugh over Carter's speech) and (b) pins down the Galactic Stormtroopers and (he says, tho' I think he's being a bit overoptimistic as usual) makes classic '56 and '68 vintage D.S. response to coming big bang in his homeland v. diff.

AOB: Extra copies of *Labour Focus* and *Critique* to be ordered for stall.

[blank]

16/1/80 Stroll through Meadows to The Links wi Stef, told him about A. Stef wary as usual but said he'd check her out re background, any poss. connec-tions with Imp. Intell (this code has caught on amongs cdes) or for that matter Reb. and/or Jedi. Didn't ask how he'd do this but he's always come up with the goods. S. v. excited re possibilities tho'.

[blank]

2/2/80 Met Stef at Milne's abt. 7:30 last night—had arranged for A. to turn up at 8. She found us app. on 1st pint (actly 2nd) and deep in conv. Stef made to go but she said "take it easy guys" and pounced on latest *L.Focus* which Stef had at his elbow. Quick flick through it, article on Sverdlovsk Helsinki Group appeal got her talking. Then listening to Stef as he did his usual spiel. (I've seen him do this as non-pol chat-up, to the point where was waiting for him to "slip up" and answer q. abt. where he was from with "various places" and it came through right on cue.) After abt half an hour he left us to it. Plan was to give her general outline but no op. details and nothing about personal inv.

A. obviously intrigued but made me bit uneasy wi questions.

Later when she'd gone to sleep I realised what it was made me uneasy. It was like there was something she wanted me to get involved in and didn't want to tell me about just yet. Which is ex. what tune I was playing to her!

Maybe she is a Jedi Knight. hah.

[blank]

10/2/80 Stef said today to pull back from recruitment re A. I told him quite reasonably (in circs.) that I felt I'd been fucked about and A. no doubt would too. S. says that can't be helped, word from on high is that she's got good long-term chance of placement inside D. Star and would be as he put it "wasted on skirmishes with the X-fighters."

Fuck. that leaves me wi a lot of backpedalling and downclimbing.

14/2/80 Dropped slushy V. card in A.'s on way in to Uni. When saw her just after 5 she gave me big smooch and seemed to have forgiven and forgotten recent awkwardness. Stayed off touchy subjects and intend to do so henceforth.

[blank]

8/4/80 Just back from 5 Cities Journey. This time it was Ed., Lond., Amsterdam, Berlin, and W. Fucking hairy. Van was searched more thoroughly than last time (Pg via Vienna). But got through OK. Int. point: instead of journals, main cargo was shrink-wrapped bricks of $$$.

Told A. beforehand was going on impulse Easter trip wi some pals. Tonight told her all except final leg of journey (i.e., to and from W).

27/5/80 Still not decided for def. if going to take Honours. Grant is OK for the year but need more dosh (i.e., I can get by fine on a grant but Mum looking worried abt. need to have more coming in). Also on that side of that balance: got v. favourable reply from Ferranti to off-chance enquiry re job. Well chuffed.

Informal visit set for tomorrow p.m.

28/5/80 Well! Skipped p.m. Biz Stud lecture, dashed to Broughton Hilton, scrambled into suit (Oxfam, just fits) clean shirt and tie, polished shoes. Down to Crewe Toll site for visit. Shown around by Mr. Shaw, mgr in Radar Systems. Great stuff, big projects, liked the guys on the floor, v. pulchritudinous secretarial totty as well it must be said. Shaw says big new def. contracts coming through, lots of opport. for bright young chap like self, laid it on a bit but sincere. Looked over my prov. CV in his office, frowned a bit over Lab. Students on "extracurricular ac" section but I assured him I had no prob. with def. work, not in CND or anything like that, seemed satisfied. Shook hands and said he really hoped I'd cons. ser. app., said no real benefit doing Hons. bcos prac. exp. counts for more in the biz.

Walked out feeling v. heady and stopped out of sight of offices for fly puff to steady the old legs before heading for bus stop. Totally fucking gobsmacked to see Cairds in container lorry turning in thro' gates. He spotted me and jumped out as soon as parked. Said he's still working from Lond., driving for elec. parts co. based in Hayes, Middx next to EMI.

Asked him how his smuggling racket is going (for a laff) and he got v. quiet and ser. and said there's a lot more and safer stuff to do than Turkish blow. Like what? says I. Computer chips, he says. Even defective ones (junked and dumped out back) change hands for good money in W. Germany and Austria, obv. traded on to points East.

Fucking hell. What a bam.

Anyway A. well plsd when I told her abt job offer.

30/5/80 Awkward conv. wi A. Started when for a laff told her abt Cairds and his schemes (obv. not in detail, just general smuggling). She got v. uptight at this point. Told me that smuggling is against the law. I said I was well aware of that but so what. Cue ear-bending abt importance of law.

I pointed out that she smokes blow and how does she think the shit gets into the country and by the way it's illegal too.

Cue further ear-bending from A. whereby she admitted that smoking blow was hypocritical on her part but that it was private (and she wasn't actually buying the stuff, just accepting a toke when offered) whereas smuggling was in the public sphere or some such guff and that what really bothered her was my open contempt and cynicism about the law, which she somehow managed to link to what she called my "deprived background" and "that typical Brit working-class resentful attitude which doesn't actually help anyone, especially those who have it."

That was when I blew it. Told her I'd broken the law loads of times and not just wi smoking blow. Told her abt. 5 Cities Journey. (Still stayed cagey abt. op. details.) She was not as I'd expected all admiring of my bold actions but instead well pissed off I hadn't let her in on it. Esp. re Easter trip, said I'd lied to her.

I said I hadn't, I'd just not told her whole truth. Also, was for her own protection.

Let's just say this last item didn't help matters.

Next step in escalation was when I said I'd wanted to bring her in but Stef had vetoed, for her long-term, "Uh," I said.

"Usefulness?" she asked.

Well you could put it like that I said.

At which point she storms out.

2/6/80. A. still not answering phone.

4/6/80 Angry letter from A, in which she said a lot of very unfair and

[*After a blank, the letter is reproduced, with the address blanked out by a corner of paper. The letter is dated 6-3-80, i.e., in the American format—LS*]

Dear Ross,

Our conversation yesterday has given me a lot to think about. When we met last Xmas we hit it off so well that I really thought you might be the one. (You have never said anything to that effect to me, by the way.) I really, really fell for you and you didn't notice. But what's worse than that is that you seem quite prepared to lie to me "for my own good." We've had lots of good times but for me the issue of trust comes very high on my list of important things in a relationship.

I have put up with your slovenly habits, laddish friends, the casual sexist and racist slang that keeps cropping up in your conversation, your ignorant aspersions on the subject of my studies, and the loudmouthed left-wing rants that you keep inflicting on me. (Believe me, I do understand your sincere belief that your Labour Party brand of socialism is diametrically opposed to Soviet totalitarianism but I can't help but feel a shiver at the naked class hatred you so often see fit to display.)

All of these I can take. What I can't take is that you, behind my back, and evidently in some detail, discuss with your buddy Stefan R. whether or not to let me in on the activities you have also been conducting behind my back. And that he (I guess from what you said) has been checking me out. The issue is not that I don't trust you, it's that you so obviously don't trust me and are quite prepared to look at me in a very cold and instrumental way.

I used to love you so much, Ross.

I'm sorry but that's it. Don't try to contact me. I will be polite if we meet but that is all.

Regards

Amanda S.

[blank]

1/7/80 Started new job at Ferranti.

15/8/80 Ka-boom! Shipyards occupied in Gdansk and Gdynia!

Christ, this could be it. Fucking great to see all our work paying off at last.

[Blank for over three years, going by the dates]

2/12/83 Laid off. You'd think one benefit of having a new Cold War would be reliable work in defence, but seems not. Shit.

2/1/84 Greenock is a total fucking dive these days. Clyde's so clean you can fucking fish in it. Dad's hanging grimly on as a minicab driver. Poof bro is doing well in the great world of Condé Nast glossies but worried sick about AIDS.

Long conversation with Cairds, up from London for Hogmanay. He now has his own business (rents the rigs) and travels as far as Turkey, Yugoslavia, and Hungary. Told me he has a vacancy for a long-distance driver and can sub me for HGV licence course. (As well as put me up on sofa till I find accom.) Got him aside and asked him if he was still doing anything dodgy, esp. in relation to cross-border E. Europe stuff. He said it's a fucking gold mine out there. Forget about drugs, man, you can dae serious time for that, and why take the risk when there's real money in tech and porn one way and caviare the other?

Ah, fuck it. I'm up for it.

Going down to Lond on 15.

10/1/84 Ran into Stef at Milne's. Haven't been on any trips since '80 (job got in the way) but he gave me to understand it's actually easier these days. Dark Side guards just in it for the dosh now, they don't believe in it anymore (if they ever did). Told him abt my new job, suggested we keep in touch. Agreed. Phone numbers exchanged (Cairds' for later, mine for now. Stef has one of the new mobile phones, lugs it around in briefcase).

By sheer fucking coincidence bumped into A. in Rose Street afterwards. Haven't seen her since summer of '80 apart from a couple of frosty encounters in streets or pubs near Uni. She's moved so I don't have her address or phone. This time she gave me a friendly greeting, suggested we nip into Abbotsford for late drink.

A. remarked on my smoking cigarettes—I explained that pipe not too sociable in shared office. Then she asked how/what I was doing and I told her.

She laughed and said she was sorry for having been so uptight about Cairds and his smuggling.

She has graduated with a First and is doing PhD and has scholarship to study/research in Krassnia! Leaving next month.

Agreed to keep in touch. Gave her Cairds' London addr. She promised to write when settled. I said, you never know, I might turn up, Cairds has connections as far as Georgia and Armenia these days. A. laughs. After a bit more chat A. looks at her watch, says she has to go, jumps up, and kisses me on nose before going out.

Left me feeling like there was something I hadn't done or said. I went out to look for her, up and down Rose Street but she'd vanished. Went back inside and had a whisky.

Fuck. It all comes back.

Looking back over this diary, I realise I only write when I'm elated or miserable. Time to draw a line under it.

[Which he literally does. There are no more diary entries. The next section of the PDF file, signed by Ross Stewart and Stefan Rodowski, is (from its appearance) a carbon copy of an original typed on a typewriter.

The signatures on the copy, and the initials "RS" and "SR" at the corner of each page, are original. I have omitted these in the text—Lucy.]

2.

18 November 1984 London

This is a true and complete record of the debriefing of Ross Stewart by Stefan Rodowski, compiled by the latter from contemporaneous notes and tapes and signed and agreed as accurate (though not necessarily verbatim) by both parties. It is agreed that the original will be kept by S.R. and the carbon copy by R.S., that both copies are separately signed at the head and foot and initialled on each page, and that both copies will be treated as equivalent in the event of any appeal.

RS: Stef, are you recording this?

SR: Yes.

RS: We've never done this before. It's a security risk.

SR: We're in a secure place. Swept. This is for you and

me, so that neither of us can use it against the other without—

[crosstalk]

RS: So it's mutual blackmail, then.

SR: If you want to put it like that. I prefer to think of it as mutual insurance.

RS: Aye. So what do you want?

SR: You could begin by explaining a bit of background and context, for the record. You can speak freely—I don't expect we'll ever have to use this, but if we do it needs to be understandable on its own.

RS: OK. My name is Ross Stewart, speaking to Stefan Rodowski. Could you confirm that, Stef?

SR: Confirmed. Go on, please.

RS: I was born in Greenock, Scotland, 1958. I attended Edinburgh University 1976 to 1980, graduating with an ordinary degree in engineering and business studies. From 1980 to 1983 I worked as a Technical Supervisor and subsequently Engineering Project Manager in the Radar Division of Ferranti Defence Systems Limited. I was made redundant in 1983 and am currently a long-distance lorry driver for the haulage company Colin Byrne Associates. Colin Byrne, the owner, nick-named "Cairds," is an old school-friend of mine and, as well as being the owner and operator of a small but highly suc-cessful legitimate business, is a professional smuggler of cigarettes, alcohol, pornography, caviar, and other goods, which to my certain knowledge do not include controlled sub-stances, transport of which he regards as too risky. How-ever, he has no compunction in illegally conveying to Eastern Bloc countries high-technology items embargoed by the Western Alliance's COCOM export control regime, as well as luxury goods and items such as pornography prohibited in these countries by the Communist authorities.

While at Edinburgh University I was an active member of the Labour Club, and through this became acquainted with Stefan Rodowski, here present. He was born in Poznan, Poland, and left at an early age with his parents after the repres-sions of 1968. He recruited me to a clandestine organisation, covertly supported by a number of groups and individuals predominantly of a left-wing character, which exists to deliver literature and material aid to dissidents in the Eastern Bloc. I took part in six journeys for this purpose to Eastern Europe while I was a student, using a variety of forged documents supplied by Stefan. The demands of my work for Ferranti made my participation in any further journeys impracticable, though I continued to support the group with regular small donations of cash.

Shortly after taking up my new job as a long-distance driver I had a conversation with Stefan on the possibility of using Cairds' trucks to transport material to and from dissidents in the Balkans and the southern republics of the Soviet Union. (Hitherto the group had only been able to help dissidents in Central Europe.) I did not, of course, tell Stefan about Cairds' existing illegal activities. Stefan and I agreed that the relatively porous borders and more relaxed internal controls of the southern republics such as Georgia and Armenia, the prevalence of legal and illegal private enterprise, and their proximity to hardline but deeply corrupt Bulgaria and unstable Yugoslavia, make this region the "soft underbelly" of the Soviet Union and the bloc as a whole. A further vulnerability was the known interest of the local KGB and its equivalents elsewhere in the bloc not only in importing embargoed technology but in developing secure undercover export routes into Western Europe, primarily for heroin from Afghanistan but also for firearms and explosives supplied to various armed organisations in the West (which I need not name) currently supported by the Bloc essentially for their nuisance value and as bargaining chips.

My first journey for Cairds was a delivery of stereo players to Hungary, returning with shoes and other leather goods. Apart from a minor consignment of peach brandy, there was no commercial smuggling on this trip. Stefan had set up a liaison whereby I was able to deliver some emigré Magyar-language literature to a dissident group in Budapest, and to return with some documents that from their appearance contained economic data. I delivered these to a contact arranged by Stefan.

Over the next few months similar journeys to Zagreb in

Yugoslavia, to Sofia and again to Budapest took place without untoward incident.

In late October of this year a journey from Turkey to the Georgian province of Krassnia appeared on Cairds' schedule. The cargo container of machine parts for a plastics factory was to be picked up at the Turkish port of Izmir, then driven across Turkey and through Georgia to Krasnod, the provincial capital. Why they didn't simply ship it all the way to the Soviet port of Sochi on the Black Sea I don't know—it may have had something to do with graft or just differences in lading fees. The return cargo was a large consignment of Georgian wine to Istanbul for onward shipment to Greece. The value of both cargoes was such that the shipping company responsible was keen to have a nonlocal driver. I angled for the assignment, because it seemed to hold out possibilities. I informed Stefan, who said that he had a contact in Krasnod. I also had personal reasons for wishing to make this journey.

SR: You have to explain these.

RS: Can that not be left off?

SR: No.

RS: All right. The personal reasons were that I hoped to meet Amanda Stone, a US citizen currently on an exchange scholarship in Krasnod. I'd had a relationship with this woman some years ago, which had ended badly, for reasons not unconnected with my activities for Stefan's group. Early this year I'd seen her again once by chance, and to be blunt have been obsessed with her ever since. She had sent me a postcard from Krasnod, and I'd replied, but she wasn't aware that I was coming.

SR: That'll do. Go on.

RS: OK. I and my co-driver, another of Cairds' employees and quite innocent of any knowledge of my clandestine purpose, flew to Izmir. There we picked up the truck, already loaded at the dock. I myself went into town and picked up the additional cargo—a suitcase full of copies of *The Gulag Archipelago* in the original Russian—from a contact arranged by Stefan, with no difficulty other than that of lugging the case into and out of a taxi. The journey itself was quite eventful, particularly in Eastern Turkey, where the road passes through territory controlled by a Kurdish revolutionary nationalist group with which we—

SR: You can skip that.

RS: Fine by me. Messy business. Anyway . . . after these vicissitudes we crossed the Soviet border into Georgia. The cargo was inspected very thoroughly—dogs, torches, the lot—and passports and manifests double-checked and so on but my contraband passed unnoticed despite a cursory search of the cab. I'd deliberately let the cab get grubby and untidy—fag ash, dirty clothes, food wrappers, and more strewn in the back, where we'd taken turns sleeping. I've found that a little squalor goes a long way to make such searches cursory, Eastern Bloc border guards being somewhat bourgeois about their spick-and-span uniforms.

We drove to Krasnod and made the delivery at KrasNor-PlasKom, the plastics factory. We had a couple of nights to stay in the town, partly to recuperate after the long journey and partly to wait for the wine shipment. The town was pleasant enough: a core of ancient, labyrinthine stone, surrounded by a ring of modern concrete: apartment blocks, shops, schools, the hospital, the university, smaller factories, and the big plastics complex. Our hotel was at the edge of the old town. The first night, as arranged, I left the hotel just as night was falling—it falls fast in these latitudes—and went to where the lorry was parked, several streets away. My co-driver was enjoying a bit of local hospitality in a wine bar. I took the case from the lorry and ostensibly set off back to the hotel, carefully taking a "wrong" turning that led me into a narrow unlit alley in the old town. Halfway down the alley, exactly as planned, I laid down the case and lit a cigarette.

Within a minute or two, a man of about the same height and build as myself walked up the alley in the same direction as I had. He walked past me, turned around, sniffed the air, and asked: "Is that an English cigarette?"

"No," I replied, offering him the pack, "it's a Marlboro."

"Ah," he said, taking one, "what a pity! I prefer a Strand."

"'You're never alone with a Strand,'" I replied.

"But a Strand is alone with you."

"And the band of the Waldorf Astoria," I said.

At this nonsense—which was, of course, the code previously agreed on, which Stef had told me to memorise—the man smiled and lit up, the match-flare showing me his face for a moment—a man younger than me, tense. Without another word, he picked up the case and carried it on down the alley. I walked a few paces behind, turned sharply as the alley gave on to a small square, and turned down the next alley and back to the street. I joined my co-driver in the wine bar, and later helped him back to the hotel.

The following day I rose very early and made my way to the address on Amanda Stone's postcard. Being your typical Soviet small town, there were no available maps (other than the sketch map provided for my meeting, which I had destroyed after use)—but again, being typical, the modern part wasn't hard for me to find my way around. The apartment block had a stairwell without a door. I went up, found the flat, and knocked.

Amanda opened the door. Her expression went from anxious to . . . flabbergasted, I guess, when she saw me. She was wearing a dressing gown and looked as if she'd just got of bed.

"Ross!" she said. "What are you doing here?"

"Well, I said I would come," I said.

She laughed, asked me in, and as soon as the door was closed she threw her arms around me and kissed me, very much to my surprise. Then she broke off, laughed again, and took me into the main room, where she brewed up a samovar of tea. The room was cramped and hot, the concrete sweating. We talked for an hour and . . . one thing led to another and we tumbled into her unmade bed. She told me she was on the Pill.

Around eleven she stirred herself, got up, washed and dressed, and then urged me to do the same. All the hot water was gone, but I complied. She kept glancing at her watch. I assumed she was running late for work at the university. I was just up and at the table and sipping some well-stewed tea while she put together some books in a bag when a knock came on the door.

Amanda answered the door. I heard her say something in Russian. She came back into the room with a man behind her.

"Ross, this is Yuri Gusayevich, a colleague of mine," she said.

He was the man I had delivered the books to the previous evening.

I stood up and shook his hand. Neither of us, as far as I know, gave any hint that we recognised each other.

Gusayevich sat down, and we all had another cup of tea. I told Gusayevich I was a lorry driver, and that I had known Amanda at university. All the time I was watching him and Amanda with intense jealousy. There was nothing obvious, but something about the ease with which he sat, and the way he looked at her, and she at him, suggested an intimacy between them.

My meeting with the wine export agency representative to confirm the lading was scheduled for 12:30 at the hotel. The time was now noon. I said I had to leave. Amanda told me she was giving Gusayevich a lift to the university in a few minutes, but that I should leave first. I rose and shook hands with Gusayevich. Amanda saw me out. She gave me a hug in the hall and said nothing more than, "Keep in touch, Ross, OK?"

I walked back towards the hotel. A minute or two after I'd left I heard a car starting noisily and glanced back to see a Moskvitch estate car head off in the opposite direction in a cloud of dust and exhaust smoke.

Back at the hotel, I saw in reception a slim man of medium height, in a smarter suit and tie than I was used to seeing in the Eastern bloc. He was sitting in a chair near the entrance, reading *Trud* and keeping an eye on the door. There was no one else in the reception area. As I entered he folded the paper, picked up a briefcase, stood up, and stepped in my path with a friendly smile. Good-looking, midtwenties, self-assured, sharp-eyed. I assumed he was from the wine export agency. He introduced himself in fluent, American-accented English as Ilya Klebov, and asked to see my passport and visa. After he'd looked over the documents, he held on to them and said: "I'm going to have to ask you to accompany me to the militia station downtown."

I recoiled, taking a step backward. My arms were grabbed just above my elbows. I looked over my shoulder to see two men with heavier build and shoddier suits than Klebov's. Reflexively, I jerked away. Their thumbs dug in, painfully and expertly—there's a nerve spot there.

"What's going on?" I said. "I haven't done anything."

"There are some irregularities," Klebov said. "I'm sure the matter can be cleared up down at the station."

I realised there was nothing I could do. I wasn't frightened. I had been assured by Stefan and others that as long as they didn't think I was an actual operative of a Western intelligence service, the worst I could expect physically was some roughing up. But to go without protest would have looked suspicious. I stayed in character as a haulier.

"Who are you?" I demanded. "Are you the police?"

Klebov shook his head. "Ministry of State Security," he explained.

"I demand a call to the British Consul!" I said.

"There's no need for that," said Klebov. "Mr. Stewart, the only choice you have at the moment is to come quietly or . . . not. But you *will* come with us. Now, which is it to be?"

"I'll come quietly," I said.

The two burly guys unhanded me at a nod from Klebov. I walked out of the hotel and into a small Lada parked outside, and sat jammed in the back between the two heavies. Klebov sat in the front passenger seat. I didn't see the driver's face even in the mirror.

Needless to say, I wasn't taken to the militia station. The car stopped in a deserted street in the old town. I was hustled through a rusty iron door in the front of a building that looked like it had once been a big shop, with Somebody-ovksi and Sons chiselled in the Latin script of prerevolutionary Krassnia across the frontage. The door clanged behind us. After a few disorienting turns around corners I was left alone with Klebov in a room with nothing but a table and two plastic-seated chairs on opposite sides, overlooked by a flattering colour portrait of Konstantin Chernenko, a black-framed black-and-white photo of Chernenko's recent predecessor Yuri Andropov, and—incongruously enough—a picture calendar of Krassnian mountain scenery. Klebov sat with his back to the wall and motioned me to sit down.

Klebov swung his briefcase up on the table, sprang it open, and slapped down what looked like a dozen or so copies of a magazine, shrink-wrapped in transparent plastic. With his forefinger he swivelled the pack around and pushed it a little towards me. The title of the magazine was *Sadie Stern* and the cover picture was of a woman wearing an SS officer's cap, a pair of shiny black thigh-high boots, and not much else.

"How do you account for this?" Klebov said.

"I've never seen it in my life," I said, truthfully.

"It was found concealed in the cab of your lorry," said Klebov.

"I have no idea how it got there," I said, mentally cursing my co-driver's small-time entrepreneurship. (Cairds, for all that he smuggles porn into some of the Bloc countries, would never have risked smuggling it into the SU. At least, not in such a trivial quantity.)

"Oh, it wasn't . . ." Klebov named my co-driver, and added: "We're quite sure of that."

"Then it's a mystery," I said, looking Klebov in the eye.

"A mystery, eh?" said Klebov. "Nazi-inspired, perverted filth! Is this the type of literature that your group brings to the supposedly deprived Soviet people?"

"Group?" I said. "What group? My employers? They have nothing to do with this."

Klebov cocked an eyebrow. "Your employers? An interesting expression!"

"Colin Byrne Associates," I said. "You've seen the documents."

"Indeed I have," said Klebov, looking amused. "That wasn't the employer I was thinking of."

"That's the only employer I have," I said. "I'm a lorry-driver. Look, Mr. Klebov, if that stuff really was in the cab, it's possible it was some previous driver who left it there. We hired this lorry in Izmir. I can't vouch for some Turkish—"

"Oh, shut up," Klebov said, in a bored tone. He put the packet of magazines back in his briefcase. He then rested his hands, fingers interlaced, on top of the briefcase and spoke straight at me. As far as I can recall, what he said was this:

"Mr. Ross Stewart," he began, "your name is—and your other names are—well known to the Ministry of State Security and to the security services of our allies. We know about your activities at Edinburgh University. We know about the Five Cities Journeys. We know about your meetings with members of Charter 77, the KOS-KOR, the so-called Solidarity union, the Leipzig pastors, and all the rest."

"I'm sorry, Mr. Klebov," I said. "I haven't a clue what you're talking about."

Klebov then proceeded to list my journeys over the years, from memory. There was no way he could've gotten these off my passport—I'd used different passports. For each journey, he mockingly rattled off some code phrase or password I'd used (probably—of course I'd forgotten which code was used on which journey, but they all sounded about right). He named my contacts—their code names and (he said) their real names, some of which are quite well known in the West. He listed the false names and IDs I'd used on my passports. These, I remembered all right.

I listened to all this with a fixed expression of baffled resentment, and a growing feeling of dismay. I wouldn't be surprised if I was turning pale as he spoke. I tried to conceal it by tightening my belly muscles and arse sphincter to force blood to my face. It was abundantly clear that our entire operation was compromised from within, and had been for years. And it wasn't exactly difficult for me to work out just who had compromised it—any more than it is for you, Stefan, you weaselly Polack [redacted]. But what terrified me was that Klebov was telling me this, as if it didn't matter that I knew. It seemed to mean he didn't expect me to go home any time soon, if at all. Unless of course the KGB had decided to roll up the whole thing and the culprit was already home clear, in which case my likely intended role was to star in a gloating press conference if not a show trial.

Klebov finished up by listing my visits this year to Budapest and Sofia though not, interestingly, to Zagreb. He leaned back, tipping his chair against the wall, and looked at me.

"Well?" he said.

I shook my head. "I went to Hungary and Bulgaria, sure, on deliveries for Mr. Byrne. But these others, no."

"Ross, Ross, Ross," Klebov said, in a patient, friendly voice. "If you will insist on wasting my time, I'll have no alternative but to turn you over to the two citizens who accompanied us here. If you don't talk to them, they will call on specialists-colleagues with recent experience in Afghanistan, Ethiopia, Syria, Iraq . . ." He shook his head. "Need I go on?"

I asked, as if in disbelief and indignation, if he was threatening me. He said that he was trying to spare me a great deal of needless distress. I repeated my demand to see the British Consul, and my ignorance of what the hell Klebov was talking about. At this he changed tack.

"Come on, Ross," he said, leaning forward again with his elbows on his briefcase, hands apart. "There's no shame, no dishonour, nothing to betray. You've been betrayed already, lock, stock, and barrel. We know all the names-you've heard them. All I'm asking is that you come clean and admit what you've done. And you *will* admit it. Your only choice is to admit it now, or later."

I knew he was right. I was still clinging to the straw that they were unlikely to torture me in the manner of their third world allies, but in all honesty I don't think I'd have stood up for long to the less gruesome but no less effective techniques of coercive interrogation used in the Bloc itself-and in the West, come to that. And none of the bullshit cover stories we'd all had prepared for the old Five Cities Journeys would be of any use here. (The first-level cover was that we were innocent students who'd been offered a free driving holiday in exchange for leaving the van overnight at some agreed-upon location, and that we had no knowledge at all of the hidden compartments.)

It was as the thought of all the cover stories flashed through my mind that I came up with a plan.

I put my hands up and said: "Mr. Klebov, you're right. OK, I do admit it. But there's two things I don't understand. One is why you've told me all this, because *you* know and *I* know that what you've told me points to exactly who the agent of your side is who was basically running the Five Cities Journeys. The other is why you've chosen to bust my current employer's operation, seeing as how you must know how helpful he's being to *your* employer's operations."

"In what way has he been helpful?" Klebov asked.

"He smuggles embargoed technology to the Warsaw Pact countries," I said.

"So you know about that?" Klebov said.

"Yes," I said.

"Well, that saves me a lot of wearisome explanation," Klebov said.

He rocked his chair back again, and looked at me in a more respectful way than he had hitherto. "You've dropped the pretence. So will I. The answer to your two questions is the same. I don't know who the agent of the Socialist camp is in your group, but I certainly knew that you could identify him or her. The reason I told you enough to do that, and the reason I busted your current employer's current operation, as you put it, is this." He took a deep breath. "I want you personally to have a hold over the Socialist camp's plant in the Five Cities operation, and I personally want in on your employer's operation."

"What?" I said. It must have come out as a yelp.

Klebov told me to keep my voice down, and explained, somewhat as follows:

"Ross," he said, "the only organisation better informed than people like yourself about the state of our country is the Ministry that employs me. We know how dire it is. The ascent to power of Brezhnev's mineral-water-bottle-opener is the last wheezy gasp of the old guard. That geriatric dodderer is not long for this world. A change at the top is imminent. From that, greater changes will follow. I have every intention of being well placed to survive these changes. And that means getting in on the ground floor in such operations as those of"—it was like he paused to consult a mental note—"Colin Byrne Associates. The possibilities are vast—far vaster, indeed, than you realise. You and I, my friend, could become rich."

I said that it was just as likely that a new hardliner like Andropov could come to power after Chernenko shuffled off—and then where would we be? Klebov just laughed at that.

"I happen to know," he said, "that there are no new hardliners with anything like Andropov's ability, but plenty of reformers with ability. Besides, I know personally that the entire Soviet system is based on a gigantic lie—not a lie about Lenin, or Stalin, or the production statistics, but something far more fundamental than that."

I asked him what it was.

"Materialism," he said, to my surprise. "I know—I *know*—that there is, if not a God, then an order of things higher than the order the scientists talk about. Don't ask me how I know."

I didn't. I assume he was talking about some spiritual or mystical experience, albeit one that has clearly not made him in any way saintly. Instead, I asked him why the Eastern bloc security service whose initials I knew but avoided mentioning had been running the Five Cities Journeys all along, and why that hadn't resulted in the arrests of the dissident contacts.

Klebov shrugged and said he had no inside information on the thinking of the top levels of the Ministry, let alone those of its allied services, but assumed that it was considered desirable to have the operations continue monitored so that the internal networks could be tracked, and presumably further infiltrated and suborned. He then explained exactly how I could make use of the agent concerned—which you, you little scumbag, are about to find out. He also explained how he—Klebov—and I could cooperate to our mutual profit.

Which, Stefan, you are not about to find out.

But there was one condition. One thing I had to do for him, first, right now.

"I need a name," he said. "Just one name, to take to my superiors. The name of your contact."

"How come," I asked, "you don't have it already?"

"Presumably," Klebov said, "even the agent knows the contact only by a pseudonym."

"If I name someone," I said, "what will happen to . . . that person?"

"I can give no guarantees," Klebov said. "But I would quite seriously expect no more than a maximum sentence of five years. More likely, two. No psychiatric hospital, no prosecution for espionage, terrorism, or any such nonsense."

I gave him a name: Yuri Gusayevich.

We shook on the deal, and I walked out and made my way back to the hotel.

3.

[Note by Lucy: I'll give my own reactions to the above later. For now, I'll just say that some parts of it made me actually gasp. The next two pieces are from PDFs of typed English translations from handwritten Russian originals which are also reproduced as PDFs (from photocopies) in the dossier. The note that immediately follows this is from a PDF of a page typed on a word processor, printed off, and scanned in.]

Note: These two documents are from the archives of the Krassnian NKVD, and were posted to me by Y. G. from Moscow in 1992. I have never asked how he obtained them but I have no reason to doubt their authenticity. R. S.

Personal Confession of A. ARBATOV
2 November 1937

In this confession I wish to lay bare the political basis of the views that led to my errors and subsequently to my crimes. As is known I joined the party of Socialists-Revolutionaries in 1912. It can be said that I was strongly infected by that party's peasant-populist orientation and likewise by their glorification of terrorism, which together make up the notorious theory of "heroes" and "masses." At different times in my political life one or other of these only superficially opposed orientations–viz., peasant-populism and terrorism–rose to prominence in my mind and it is evident that they obtained their final so-to-speak synthesis in my criminal participation in the counterrevolutionary Right-Trotskyite bloc.

At the outbreak of the imperialist war I was temporarily swept away by the patriotic tide and sincerely and enthusiastically volunteered for military service. In my later application to join the Bolshevik Party I claimed that I had joined the army in order to carry out revolutionary work within the ranks but this was at best an exaggeration in retrospect. However I can say quite honestly that my experiences at the front shattered my illusions and by 1916 I was giving an attentive ear to such distant echoes of the genuine revolutionary position as reached me. After the February revolution I joined the Bolsheviks and broke decisively with the S-Rs in terms of politics though not in terms of my fundamental orientation. However I categorically deny that I was in any way involved in or sympathetic to the "Left" S-R counterrevolutionary uprising of 1918 and in fact I took part in its suppression. I served honourably in the Red Army during the civil war. I furthermore categorically deny that my contacts with L. D. TROTSKY all of which took place in my capacity as an officer and as a Party member during the civil war were in any way a cover for participation in his counterrevolutionary or anti-Party activities, of which no one had the smallest inkling at the time.

If during my Red Army service the "left" side of my political character was dominant I must admit that the experiences of the war, famine, peasant uprisings, and it must be added occasional excesses that I witnessed had a profoundly disturbing effect on me and in my civilian work it was the right-populist side that again came to the fore. My research in ethnology and folklore bears strong marks of both a "peasant" (in reality, kulak) orientation and also of a bending towards Krassnian "nationalism," likewise a covert sympathy for the Krassnian "legend of the returning hero" and the so-called Krassnian truth. In a similar manner, I strongly sympathised with the NEP and later with N. BUKHARIN's Right deviation, at the same time retaining a personal admiration of L. D. TROTSKY while disagreeing with his "Left" political line.

It was that stubborn "hero"-worship that led me to refuse to accept the decision of the overwhelming majority of the Party to expel L. D. TROTSKY and his supporters after their provocation of November 1927. For this I was justly expelled from the Party. However I remained politically close to the position of the Rights and of N. BUKHARIN. During my exile in Kazakhstan [several lines blacked out in original] in short, the intensity of the class struggle around collectivisation and denomadisation shattered my morale and drove me to seek out some contact with the Rights inside the Party. On this basis I spoke to A. SLEPKOV during his visit to Alma Ata in late 1932 or early 1933. He appraised me of the contents of the Riutin Platform and I agreed with it, notably in respect of its call for the sharpest struggle against the leadership of J. V. STALIN, a "return to the New Economic Policy," an end to collectivisation, etc. He told me that on the basis of this platform a fighting agreement had been reached by the Rights with the followers of L. D. TROTSKY allied with those of G. E. ZINOVIEV and L. B. KAMENEV such that the former "Left" and Right were in complete accord with respect to not only the "removal" of STALIN but also economic policy and the policy towards the peasantry and collectivisation, which at that time weighed very heavily on my mind. He urged me to pretend to capitulate, recant, and make every effort to worm my way back into the Party, which I did. However I was unable to maintain contact and this conversation was my sole participation in the organisation of the Rights.

In Krassnia I completed the writing of my former "academic" work, giving it a particularly pernicious slant and even inserting into it oblique references to the notorious so-called secret of the Vrai or Krassnian truth into which I had been initiated as a boy by (as was normal in such cases) an elderly goat-herd. So subtle was I that this work succeeded in being published and even proclaimed as a triumph of Soviet ethnography by the University of Krasnod. I should say at this point that all those formally responsible for this publication were cruelly deceived by me and were not complicit in the bourgeois and feudal-tribal "national" distortions that I had smuggled into the work.

I should also say that once I had got back into the Party I became so caught up in the great work of socialist construction that for long periods my counterrevolutionary inclinations were far from the forefront of my mind. Nevertheless they caught up with me. In 1934 I was assigned to negotiate purchases of mining equipment with a British trade delegation, which included representatives of the former capitalist owners of the Krassnian copper mines, the Ural Caucasian Mineral Company. Under the influence of a morally and politically corrupt relationship with one such representative, a young woman named EUGENIE MONTFORD, I approved the purchase for the State Mining Trust of a mining-shaft hoist that I knew did not meet the requirements of shock-working and the Stakhanovite movement, counting on my continued covert opposition to Stakhanovite methods of work to keep the use of the hoist within what I considered safe limits. I also gave away to the aforementioned E. MONTFORD state secrets pertaining to the copper industry. I firmly deny that I knew at the time that E. MONTFORD was connected to the Intelligence Service of British imperialism and that the Ural Caucasian Mineral Company was notorious for financing Whiteguard conspiracies.

The new hoist was delivered a few months later. On the adoption despite my opposition of Stakhanovite methods of work in the mine, the hoist failed in operation with tragic consequences. If I had had the moral courage to admit right away at the meeting adopting the new method of shock-work that I had speculated on the continued success of my opposition to Stakhanovism for the safe use of the hoist, the appalling loss of life and limb and the grievous cost to the national economy would not have taken place. In the light of my grave responsibility I admit to the charge of wrecking, as well as to participation in the counterrevolutionary organisation of the Rights and, in the case of my published thesis, to wrecking in the sphere of nationalities. I however deny that my wrecking activity was directed by the Rights or the Trotskyites or was conducted in the interests of hostile foreign powers.

Addendum
10 November 1937

After further reflection and interrogation I withdraw my evasive statement in the concluding paragraph of my above confession and fully admit that my wrecking both economic and academic was carried out on the direct instigation of A. SLEPKOV under the direction of Y. L. PYATAKOV and with the collusion of N. BUKHARIN and that it was directly aimed at undermining the defence capabilities of the country in the interests of British imperialism's long-standing aims in the Caucasus region. I further admit that I was fully aware from early in my acquaintance with her of the connections of E.

MONTFORD with the British Intelligence Service and that she
maintained clandestine contact with me through coded letters
in the form of letters of a personal nature.
   [Signed] A. Arbatov
   Witnessed: [signed]
   V. Beryozkin, NKVD, Krassnia.

4.

*Note by me (Lucy): After reading the above—the last written words of a man whose
name I'd known for years, and who was connected to me in a way I'll make clear in
a minute—I felt severely shaken. I got off the bed, padded through to the kitchen, and
refilled my tumbler of red wine. Back on the bed, I took a few quick sips, then scrolled
on to the next set of pages. It was the confession of the man who'd witnessed—and, no
doubt, extracted—the confession I'd just read.*

Transcript of interrogation of former NKVD officer V.
BERYOZKIN

   15 May 1940

The accused began by spitting out vituperative slanders
against the organs of State security, the Party, etc. and by
offering to sign any confession set before him on the alleged
grounds that as he was accused of having beaten confessions
out of innocent people he had no intention of any confession
being beaten out of him. He was assured that the investigation commission had no intention of applying methods of physical pressure and that nothing less than a full and sincere
confession from his own lips or by his own hand would be
accepted.
   After being given some time to think this over, the
accused BERYOZKIN reconsidered his position and began to talk
freely. He stated:
   "I don't give a shit what YEZHOV has or has not confessed
to. If he, the late chief of the NKVD, is a hidden enemy and
has been all along then your glorious leaders are even bigger

fools than I have always thought. Speaking for myself I have been a hidden enemy from the very first day, from 1921. Before that, I was an open enemy. I fought in the Great War, I fought in the Southern White Army of Deniken and after its rout returned to Krassnia, which at that time was part of Menshevik-ruled Georgia. I was one of the Krassnian so-called bourgeois-national intelligentsia, or truthkeepers as we call ourselves. We considered that our best hope was to align with the enemies of Georgian nationalism, which at that time were the Bolsheviks, despite the fact that in all other respects I sympathised with the policies of the Menshevik government of Georgia, particularly their repression of the Ossetes and other such peasant scum. I concealed my past, falsified my class origin, joined the Bolshevik underground, and took part in the Red Army's liberation of Georgia from the Mensheviks. At that time I had the great satisfaction of shooting Georgians, Ossetes, Mingrelians, and Chechens. Steeled by that experience I was given a responsible position in the Krassnian division of the Cheka of the new, Bolshevik Georgia. I used my position to eradicate Georgian influence from our national culture. I built up within the Party and Cheka a close-knit association of loyal Krassnian truth-keepers, whose names I need not mention because you have already rooted them out."

The accused was pressed on this point but gave no names other than those already known to the investigation. He further elaborated on his group's bourgeois-nationalist orientation and relations with the Rights throughout the last two decades. With regard to his recent counterrevolutionary activities he said:

"Yezhov's directive, and the circular of the Central Committee dated [blacked out in original] with regard to quotas for [blacked out in original] of suspect categories of the population were a godsend to us. It was like being given a hunting licence. Naturally we had speculated on the possible victory of the Rights but as the saying goes 'a bird in the hand is worth two in the bush.' We immediately set about finding 'hidden enemies' within the ranks of the Party, the Soviet *aktiv*, the technical intelligentsia, the collective farmers, Stakhanovites, and so forth. We rapidly over-fulfilled the

quota for [blanked out in original] based on what you now call
'confessions extracted using impermissible means.'"

Questioned about the case of former Academician A.
ARBATOV, the accused BERYOZKIN said:

"I knew of ARBATOV from before the War as a dedicated revolutionary and naturally as an enemy of the Krassnian nation
and of the Empire. I had no knowledge of his activities until
his return to Krassnia in 1934. When I read his book *Life
and Legends of the Krassnar* I was shocked to the bone. He
had dared to hint at matters of Krassnian truth which are
not for public discussion."

The accused stubbornly refused to specify what these matters were and continued:

"Our method of disposing of ARBATOV was, so to say,
'straightforward.' Certain members of our group implanted in
the trade-union apparat of the State Mining Trust posed as
militants and Stakhanovites and accused him of virtual
wrecking through his opposition to increasing fivefold the
regular load carried by the pitshaft hoists. By this and
other methods we succeeded in getting our 'Stakhanovite'
motion passed at a meeting of the works collective. This had
the expected result of causing a mining disaster when the
overloaded hoists gave way. ARBATOV had opposed the motion
and written a protest to the Trust management and to the
oblast Party committee but nevertheless felt he bore a heavy
responsibility for not taking more decisive measures. This
and not 'impermissible methods,' is what led him to confess
to wrecking.

"As for the rest, what had he done? He had hero-worshipped
the yid leader of the Red Army. He had exchanged some bitter
words years ago with a representative of the so-called Rights
in Kazakhstan, at a moment when your great STALIN's policies
had led to [blacked out in original]. He had become infatu-
ated with a young British lady who by nature of what you call
her class position was bound to have some connection or other
with the Intelligence Service. That was quite sufficient for
us to get an indictment and confession in the atmosphere of
two years ago. Apart from that, he was sincerely devoted if
not to your STALIN then to what you call 'socialist construction' and 'the defence of the Motherland.'"

Asked what he called these, the accused spat.

He went on to say:

"I know exactly what is in store for me. I have no illusions about that. I have no fear of death. I know the truth and with my Vrai forefathers I laugh at the lies of the priests about Hell, and with my brothers I spit on the lies of your Red professors about annihilation. I know there is a better world beyond death. The joke is that you too will go to that better world, and perhaps sooner than you think. Hitler will in a year or two have all of you Bolshevik swine hanging from telegraph poles, just as we did with your kind under Deniken."

In this final sortie the accused thus added direct counterrevolutionary agitation and agitation against the Soviet-German Non-Aggression Treaty to his admitted crimes against the Party and State and, no further evidence being required, the sentence of death by shooting was applied forthwith.

[signed] A. I. Klebov, NKVD Special Commission of Investigation into the crimes of the Yezhov gang, Krassnia AR.

5.

The time on my laptop showed 11:15. My knees quivered inside the dressing gown.

I scrolled up and down, almost giddy at the weirdness of seeing my great-grandmother's name on the same page as names I'd hitherto only seen in history books. Bukharin and Trotsky, Stalin and Yezhov, now, quite suddenly, stood out in my mind as vividly as my image of Great-Grandmother Eugenie as a slip of a girl, in her pirate days. I knew of Stalin, Trotsky, and Bukharin from high school in the US (and not, you may be surprised to learn, from elementary school in the USSR, where none of them were mentioned in front of children) and as for Yezhov . . . I knew about Yezhov through having read a sensational paperback about Beria, his successor as head of the secret police and (some say) his executioner, just as Yezhov had himself executed his predecessor, Yagoda, who himself was widely suspected of and had indeed confessed to murdering *his* predecessor, Menzhinsky. . . . Killing your predecessor and getting killed by your successor went with the job, as did—if the successive successors were to be believed—being an agent of several imperialist secret services and a sworn enemy of Soviet power.

The mentality that had produced all that, and so much more and worse, was all over the confessions like the smell of blood. But in the midst of all that sinister stuff, it was the last signature that had rattled me the most. I had sat gazing at it for at least ten minutes. I found myself thinking in the paranoid style of the confessions.

A. I. Klebov. Could he by any chance be related to one I. A. Klebov, Ilya Andreievich Klebov, the same Klebov whom Ross Stewart had met and who had a few years later told me to remember his name, on the most terrifying day of my life?

Yes, I thought, he could. A. I. Klebov could quite easily be I. A. Klebov's father. The elder Klebov might even still be alive, though I didn't fancy his chances.

It's about time I told you about the most terrifying day of my life. But first I have to tell you what it was that had given me some sharp intakes of breath as I read Ross Stewart's diary and debriefing, and then again as I'd read Avram Arbatov's confession.

As I read them I'd remembered another confession: the one I'd heard from Great-Grandma Eugenie, Eugenie Montford herself, that Saturday evening in Boston when I'd gone to visit her after finding out that my mother was a spook.

So . . . we turn again to teenage Lucy, way back in the nineties, that age of innocence, after the Wall and before the Towers. You see me sitting on a Greyhound bus. Black jumper dress over white T-shirt and black-and-white striped tights. Hair just two days ago dyed electric blue. Cassette player on lap, earphones in, book in one hand, the other hand over my shoulder bag on the seat beside me. I rode the Greyhound to Boston and the T to Harvard Square and came out of the station into a bright late-summer late afternoon of open-air chess and ice cream drips and walked through familiar streets to the old brownstone where Eugenie had (and has) an upstairs flat. She's lived there since Great-Grandpa Bart died.

Eugenie didn't comment on my hair or clothes. She just greeted me with a big hug and hauled me in. Her flat was small, and full of artfully placed old furniture, perilous stacks of books, big plants growing out of pots, and the smells of cooking and of the little black liquorice-papered cigarettes Eugenie chain-smoked. These smells were on good days mitigated by fresh air from a tall door-window opening onto a small balcony with window boxes on its curvy wrought-iron railing. Eugenie had us sitting on wrought-iron chairs on opposite sides of a round wrought-iron table within about five whirly seconds. Somehow she had managed to get a fresh pot of coffee ready just in time for my arrival.

"Now, dear," she said, pouring while lighting up, "you simply must tell me *all* about it."

I did.

"Well, well, well," she said, puffing away. "How very, very interesting!"

"Didn't you know about Mom?" I said.

"Of course I did, dear. *Far* more than she's told you, actually. That's what's so interesting."

"There's *more*?" I cried. "What more?"

Eugenie crushed out her cigarette. "You must be hungry," she said.

"But—"

"The time for long reminiscences is *after* dinner, my dear."

I knew better than to object, or to help. I mooched about the flat and flipped through books, discovering to my amazement that I could still read Russian, while Eugenie busied herself in the kitchen. Within about half an hour she'd rustled up chicken blinis and boiled potatoes, with side dishes of rollmop herrings and chopped liver. We ate on the balcony, looking out over the back gardens of the brownstones and exchanging remarks on what people and cats and dogs were doing in them. Too soon, the meal was over and we were back on the coffee and (in Eugenie's case) the cigarettes. She took a hard first drag, blew smoke out of the side of her mouth, propped her chin, and gave me an earnest look.

"Now, my dear," she said, "the truth."

That's how I heard all about her years as a wild young thing, including her trip to the USSR and her brief, intense affair with Avram Arbatov. She told me something she'd never admitted to my mother.

"Don't repeat this to anyone, dear, but it's the truth: your grandma Gillian was Avram's daughter."

At the time I was quite thrilled at having such a romantic character for a great-grandfather. I asked what had happened to him, and she told me the sad story. She showed me her own copy of Avram Arbatov's book, talking to me as I flicked through it.

"I told most of this to Amanda, years ago, when she first got interested in anthropology. And I made her a photocopy of Avram's book. Naturally enough, the story of Avram and his book got her fascinated with Krassnia, Georgia, and the Soviet Union in general. It was when she applied to go to Edinburgh University, though, that things started to get *really* interesting. She was quite excited about finding places that had been in the family, tracing distant relatives, and so on. Just before she left, she told me she'd been approached by someone from the CIA, asking her to report on anything . . . interesting . . . she got wind of in the world of Soviet studies, of any students or academics with contacts in the East, that sort of thing. She asked me for advice. About whether it was a good idea to work with the spooks, you know? And of course I told her to go right ahead, but to keep her eyes open, because I'd once been a spook myself."

"What?" I cried. "You?"

Eugenie leaned back and looked at me defiantly. "Yes, I was, and why shouldn't I be? King and country and all that. I wasn't even paid. I was just asked by a nice old gentleman and friend of my father's to keep him informed of anything interesting I learned at the company—the Ural Caucasian Mineral Company, that is. There were all kinds of intrigues going on there, you know—Whites, Reds, Whites who were secretly working for the Reds—which as a secretary I got wind of quite a lot, and I passed on anything I could to the old gentleman. He may have pulled strings to get me on the trade delegation, and before I went he impressed on me how important it was to keep a very sharp eye on everything I saw in the Soviet Union, and to write it all up for him the moment I got back. And I did, of course. Including some tiny snippets of information about the mines that Avram had mentioned in passing. *He* certainly didn't know I was going to report it!"

Eugenie looked down for a moment, and sighed. "I may even have mentioned Avram's name. I don't remember. I suppose I must have. I feel very guilty about that, now."

"Why?" I asked.

"Because it could have got back to the Soviets. I don't know if you know this, Lucy, but even in the thirties the Intelligence Service was positively *riddled* with Soviet spies."

"Philby and those guys?" I said, trying to sound knowledgeable.

"It might have been a little early for the Cambridge spies, but yes, chaps like that. Anyway, my dear, I wasn't to know any of that at the time, more's the pity. After my flight to the States . . . it seems the old gentleman had been quite impressed with my work for the Service, and put in a word for me somewhere, because in 1940—long before Pearl Harbor—I was contacted by someone from Washington, DC, who wanted me to work for what became the Office of Strategic Services—the OSS. I worked for the OSS throughout the War. Started off translating cables from Russian into English, then later worked in Switzerland with East European refugees and resistance people."

"Wow!" I said. "That must have been exciting."

Eugenie sighed again. "It was. But it all got very messy. Some of the people we worked with were Communists. We all had the same enemy, the Nazis of course, but we knew that the Soviets and the West were going to have some little differences of opinion once the War was over—or rather, *some* of us knew, that was the problem. We had people in the OSS who were starry-eyed about the Soviets, and some of the Communists were starry-eyed about *us*. Or at least about the possibilities of East and West keeping the alliance after the war. And of course, each side had its own people in the other's side, actual secret agents, you know? And some of *them* were double agents. . . . The upshot was, it got hard to tell which was which."

"Like the White and Red Russians you met at the company?" I said.

"Yes, exactly!" said Eugenie. "That's the trouble, you see, with the whole business. All it takes is one person working for the other side to turn everyone reporting to them—at least—into unwitting enemy agents. Now, of course, there are ways to spot that, very subtle ways, and on the other hand there are ways to *play* that—by planting in the other side's mind the suspicion that one of their people is secretly working for you. And if that person is *already* a double agent—apparently working for you, secretly working for them— well, you can see how it gets complicated, can't you?"

"Ye-es," I said.

"Well! As I said, it got messy. After the war . . . there were people in the

Eastern bloc who'd been in the Swiss refugee camps, Spanish Civil War vet-
erans mostly, about whom I'd always had a shrewd suspicion they were
Russian agents. And lo and behold, they popped up in the puppet govern-
ments of the Soviet satellite states, the quote-unquote People's Democracies.
Aha! I thought. And then, in the late forties, some of them confessed in show
trials that all along they'd been working for us, having been recruited in the
camps by people like me."

"And were they?" I asked.

Eugenie shook her head. "Not these ones. There's long been a suspicion
floating around that the Russians got *played* by Dulles—the head of the CIA,
as it became—who very cleverly planted the suspicion that one of their
agents, or dupes, a man named Noel Fields—had been working for us at a
deeper level than he seemed, and had recruited a network which happened to
include just about every leading Communist in the satellite states who had
an ounce of credibility in his own country because he'd been in the resistance
and hadn't spent the war behind a microphone in Moscow."

"Why would Dulles . . . Oh! I get it! To get rid of the least unpopular
Communists?"

"Yes," said Eugenie, with an approving look. "Leaving the least popular
ones in charge, and thus giving the populations no choice but to revolt. Hungary '56 might be seen as a success for that strategy, if that's what it was."

She fiddled with her cigarettes and lighter for a moment, brushed something from her eyelid, and lit up.

"Some of my contacts," she said, "were shot in the East in '47. I still don't
know why, because soon after that I fell under suspicion myself, and had to
leave the Agency."

"Suspicion of what?" I asked.

She doodled a trail of smoke in the air between us. "Nothing was ever
said. Later I picked up some scuttlebutt to the effect that someone high up
thought *I* was a Red . . . either because I'd got on too well with the real Reds
during the war, or because I was suspected of having betrayed the fake ones
afterwards. Maybe it was the British connection."

"That's awful!" I said.

"Oh, it's all water under the bridge. I'm just thankful I live in a country
where suspicion alone can't get you shot."

"Uh-huh."

"Anyway . . . you might think after all that I would be well out of the spook business. Not quite! In 1952 I got a visit from a pair of "—she smiled wryly—"CIA agents disguised as FBI agents. Smart suits and shoulder holsters, you know? Goodness knows what the neighbours thought—McCarthy was running wild at the time. It turned out they wanted to talk about Krassnia. They kept going on about some mountain, which I knew nothing about. Now why . . . ?" She frowned, as if trying to recall. "Oh yes. They wanted to know if I knew whether there was uranium there."

The mountain . . . uranium . . . I felt some niggle in my mind.

"Oh!" I said. "1952! That was when Mount Krasny glowed for a week! When Beria came to Krasnod!"

Eugenie gave me a very odd look.

"What do *you* know about Beria?" she asked.

"Not much," I said. "Only what Nana-in-Krassnia told me. He'd been the head of the secret police and . . ." I closed my eyes, thinking back. "'A Mingrellian, with cruel eyes,'" I finished, in a rush.

"He was all of that," Eugenie said, wryly. "And in 1952, he was the head of the project to build the Soviet atomic bomb, and then the hydrogen bomb."

"So that fits!" I said. "That must have been what they were asking you about. Some kind of nuclear accident . . . ?"

Eugenie looked disappointingly wary. "Maybe, maybe. It's a hypothesis. Now, tell me more about what your Nana told you. . . ."

So I told her about the daytime stories. She listened intently, half smiling, chain-smoking, as the summer evening darkened to twilight. And at the end, all she would say was: "That was very interesting, Lucy, very interesting indeed."

At the time I didn't have the wit to notice, in what she told me, all that she *hadn't* told me. Now, as I sat on the bed scrolling back through the texts, I did notice. She hadn't said, for one thing, whether her 1952 visit had been her last contact with the Agency. And she hadn't said, either, whether any of her "contacts in the East" from her refugee-camp OSS work *hadn't* been shot. Nor, indeed, had she said anything about whether, and if so when, she'd ever stopped working for *British* intelligence.

All these thoughts, however, were a sort of penumbra to the big dark shadow cast by two realisations I'd had while reading the dossier.

First, Eugenie had been identified, correctly, by the NKVD—the Soviet secret police, back in the day—as a British agent.

Second, during all the time when my mother, Amanda, was being oh-so-hurt about Ross's secret activities and his going behind her back, *she* was almost certainly reporting on him to her handler in the CIA.

Oh! And speaking of Ross . . . make that *three* realisations. From what Ross had written, it was entirely possible that he wasn't my father at all, and that Yuri Gusayevich, the dissident he'd betrayed to Klebov, was.

Talk about not knowing your father. I didn't know my fucking mother.

(That epithet, dear reader, is considered, and deserved.)

And now I really must tell you about the scariest day of my life.

5. THE SCARIEST DAY OF MY LIFE

1.

The scariest day of my life was Wednesday, September 4, 1991. Just a couple of days after I'd started my second year at primary school in Krasnod. The second-year classroom looked just like the first-year classroom, except that the pictures and maps looked a little more grown-up. And the lessons and exercises in the textbooks were more difficult.

But lots of things had changed over the summer. It had been a strange, unsettling summer: days when jet fighters flashed around the flank of the mountain and streaked low overhead to vanish in the sky to the south; a day when a tank had idled at a corner of the main street, then squeaked and clanked away; nights when my mother and Nana had sat together in front of the television watching very boring pictures of men behind desks droning out long sentences, as if they were reading from a book they didn't find exciting. In all the classrooms a Georgian flag hung on the wall in the place where the portrait of Lenin had hung the year before. Few of the children wore a red Pioneer scarf anymore. The teacher, Miss Yesiyeva, wasn't kind and attentive and cheerful like our first-year teacher, Mrs. Tushurashvili, had been. Each morning Miss Yesiyeva looked like she'd been crying the previous night, and sometimes she didn't notice what one of us said even in answer to a question she'd just asked, and several times a day she'd raise her voice or sound all snippy with us. At breaks, when we ran around in the playground, fights were more frequent and seemed to have children from different nationalities on different sides. Just in my class of twenty, five children were Russian, three were Georgian (in a different way from how we were all "Georgian"), two were Jewish, and there were other odd little lots and cliques that I didn't know the names for.

We were just starting the third lesson of the day around about ten o'clock when I was distracted from Miss Yesiyeva's telling us which page to turn to by a commotion in the corridor. I looked up. Miss Yesiyeva stopped, and looked at the door. There was a sound of tramping boots, then the door opened. In marched a squad of five men in militia uniforms (that's police, not the sort of militia the Caucasian peoples got to know so well later) headed up by a man in a very sharp suit. A thin briefcase was tucked under his elbow. I didn't think in these terms at the time (in my world there were: children; big boys and girls; grown-ups; and old people) but looking back I'd say he was about thirty. I was sitting in the front row so I got a good look at him, and also at the teacher's face, as her startlement gave way to alarm. In my memory I see him loom above me, though another memory snapshot from a few moments later shows him no taller than the other men in the room. I could even smell him, a sharp tang of an unfamilar scent. For some years after, I would flinch at a whiff of Old Spice.

Two of the militiamen stood just inside the door, blocking it. The other three strode one to each front corner and one to beside the teacher's podium. All three looked very young, pale, and nervous, their gaze twitching about the room. Not the man in the suit, though. He smiled at us all and whispered something to Miss Yesiyeva. She didn't look reassured at all. Her hand went to her throat and she took a step backwards, then nodded at the man.

"Good morning, pupils," he said. "Please don't be frightened. I'm from the Ministry of State Security. Some of you have to leave the school for a day or two, because there are some bad people on the streets who might want to harm you. If you come with us, you'll be quite safe. The rest of you have nothing at all to worry about."

Meanwhile Miss Yesiyeva had passed him a sheet of paper, which I recognised as the class register. The man looked intently at us, held up one finger, and glanced down at the paper. His upraised finger rapped down on the sheet, several times, skipping down it. He looked up, and started reading out names.

"Klidiashvili Levan Nugzarovich, Gogolidze Mariya Ivanovna, Lifshitz Sofya Abraamovna, Barbakadze Giorgi Kakhaberovich, Stone Lucinda Erikovna, Sherling David Yakobovich . . ."

Me, the two Jewish kids, the three Georgians. And then two more: "Melyukhin Andrei Vladimirovich and Zemskova Irina Ilyinichna."

Behind me someone sobbed. I didn't look around. I looked up at Miss Yesiyeva and said, very firmly: "I want to go home to my mother."

At that, lots of kids started wailing.

The man banged his fist down on the podium. The bang rang in my ears. "Stop!" he said. "Listen!"

His voice was quieter than when he'd read out the list. For some reason, that made the kids who were bawling shut up and sniffle.

"You have to be brave," he went on, still quietly. "We only have a few minutes. You must leave with me and the boys from the militia. Just pick up your satchels, and walk with us to the bus outside."

Miss Yesiyeva was nodding vigorously. "Yes, yes, children, you must do as the man says. You'll be safe with him."

She then looked straight at all of us who'd been named—I guess she must have, because I remember her red-rimmed blue eyes staring straight at me—and added: "Really and truly. From my heart. You must go. You'll be back very soon."

Now I don't know how I'd picked up an apprehension about lists of names and buses and going away with militiamen, but I had, and I wasn't the only one in the class who felt the same. I could see Sofya Lifshitz out of the corner of my eye, in the same row a couple of desks away, and under her curly black hair her face was white as paper. So what Miss Yesiyeva said made a big difference. She wasn't as motherly as Mrs. Tushurashvili, for sure, but we all trusted her implicitly. If she hadn't backed up the man, we might very well have had to be dragged out kicking and screaming.

As it was we all got up and filed out behind the man in the suit, with the two militiamen who'd stood at the door in front and the other three bringing up the rear. Just before the door closed behind us I heard one of my classmates say something in a jeering tone, and Miss Yesiyeva utter a sharp reproof.

Out in the playground, among the slides and swings and carved painted logs, it became evident that matters hadn't gone quite so smoothly in other classrooms. Militiamen were chasing small children and grabbing them, one teacher waddled towards the bus with a child under each arm, and screams and yells echoed off the front of the school building.

The man led us straight to the bus and we piled on. I ended up sharing a hard seat with Sofya Lifshitz, who said nothing and just sat with a fist at her mouth and her shoulder shaking. A pair of militiamen stood at the door, hauling kids on and blocking the few who tried to get off. After what seemed a long time, the bus was full. The militiamen stepped inside and sat down. The man in the suit jumped on and stood beside the driver's seat, facing back along the bus. The door closed, the engine coughed into life, and the bus lurched forward. I clung with one hand to the back of the seat in front of me and with the other arm clutched my satchel to my chest. We were swayed back and forth as the bus made a couple of sharp turns, into a street lined with apartment blocks and heading north out of town. The bus moved slowly through light midmorning traffic and after a couple of blocks stopped at a red light.

By this time the sobbing and shouting had stopped. I had stopped feeling scared and even begun to feel a little butterfly of excitement and novelty, and it was as if all or most of the other pupils on the bus felt the same way all at once. Even Sofya had turned to look out of the window, and then back along the bus. I saw her cast a wan, fleeting smile at someone behind us.

The light changed. The driver engaged the gears and the bus began to move. I saw out of the front window a line of men in civilian clothes but carrying rifles running across the intersection in front of us. At the same moment I heard a loud clang on the roof, then out of the corner of my eye I glimpsed something black hurtling towards my side of the bus. I ducked, just as a loud thump came from the window. Sofya yelled. I looked up as more thuds and clangs resounded through the bus.

The man in the suit had whipped around to look out the front. He bent over and said to the driver: "Step on it, man!"

I rocked back as the bus accelerated. The men with rifles stood for a moment on the road, then leapt to the sides. I saw their faces, mouths open, yelling, as we passed them. They were thumping the sides of the bus.

Then we were moving very fast up the street, overtaking, weaving in and out of, traffic. Sofya clung to me and I clung to the seat in front. A small child tumbled down the aisle, then picked herself up, howling, and returned to her seat.

I watched her go, and just as she reached her seat I saw the back window go all cloudy with a hole in the middle. Something went *spang* off the inside of the top of the bus. At that everyone except me started screaming. The only reason I didn't was that I had no idea what had just happened.

The man in the suit leaned towards the two militiamen and said something, then cocked his ear to a reply. He made an impatient gesture and held out his hand. A militiaman, with reluctance, handed over a pistol.

The man in the suit stuck the pistol in his waistband. Very carefully, but quickly, he paced to the back of the bus, steadying himself hand over hand on the seatbacks. As he passed me he glanced down, smiled, and said: "Don't worry, Lucy, I'll take care of you."

He said it in English. He said something else to Sofya, in a language I didn't know, but I knew he didn't use her name. I wondered how he knew mine. I watched his back as he went up the bus. He knelt on the rear seat and looked back at us over his shoulder.

"Heads down!" he shouted.

I ducked, but peeked out around the seatback. The man hit the damaged rear window with his elbow and the glass all fell away like ice from eaves in the thaw. From the angle I was looking I couldn't see anything but sky, treetops, the upper floors of buildings. The noise of air and traffic got louder. Sweet wrappers and cigarette butts moved on the floor in the sudden draught. The man reached down in front of himself, then raised both arms, together, out in front of him—I could see that from the set of his shoulders.

There were a couple of very loud bangs. A pause, then another.

The man stayed kneeling on the back seat for a few more seconds. Then he turned around, moved a thumb on the pistol, and stuck the weapon back in his waistband. He brushed the knees of his trousers and the elbow of his jacket, frowned at the palm of the hand he'd used for this, and walked back to the front of the bus. He smelled of fireworks and, quite sharply, of armpit sweat. He returned the pistol to the militiaman, with a sort of bow from the waist, and resumed his position beside the driver, with his back to the windshield.

I looked around again and saw that we'd passed the town's outer ring of buildings. Far away to our left I could see the blocks of the university. That made me think about my mother. I began to cry. Sofya put her arm around me.

About twenty minutes out of town, the bus turned sharply off the north road and bumped along a narrow track through scrub. A wall topped with barbed wire filled the view ahead. A Soviet flag hung from a pole at one end of the wall. The bus stopped.

"Everybody out," said the man in the suit. He opened the door. "It's all right, it's a Russian army base."

Believe it or not, every kid on the bus cheered. I couldn't have said why, but I whooped too.

We stood up and began to file out. As I edged past him the man in the suit gripped my shoulders and squatted down in front of me.

"Lucy," he said, "my name is Ilya Klebov. Remember my name. What's my name?"

"Ilya Klebov," I said.

"Ilya Klebov," he repeated. "Remember that!"

He let go of my shoulders and stood up. I hopped down off the bus and walked after the other children, through a door in the wall. Beyond it was a big square of tarmac and some low wooden buildings. A few tanks were lined up in front of the main gate, away on the other side of the square. Young soldiers lounged around the perimeter, smoking. Half a dozen women in white uniforms hurried up to us and took the hands of the younger ones and led us into a big room with lots of tables and a smell of cigarette smoke and boiled fish.

We were all given tea and bread with vile, metallic-tasting jam, which we devoured. Afterwards we queued up to deliver our plates and mugs back to the serving-hatch. That was when an odd event happened which in any other context would have seemed innocuous (if, to me at the time, inexplicable) but which frightened me even more than the shooting. One of the nurses stood at the top of the queue and called out three names: "Andrei Melyukhin, Irina Zemskova, Lucy Stone." Even if we hadn't answered, I'm sure she'd have identified us all from the way we flinched.

She beckoned. We followed. She led us into a small room where a man in a white coat with a stethoscope around his neck sat behind a table. He wore round glasses over his bright, cold eyes—features that reminded me, quite unreasonably, of Nana's descriptions of Beria. With the nurse's help, he gave us each a brusque physical examination. Height. Weight. The stethoscope was cold on my chest. He yanked a single hair from each of our heads, and put each hair into a clear glass tube, stoppered with a little rubber bung. It was while he was doing this that I noticed the only thing we seemed to have in common: all three of us had red or ginger hair.

The doctor wrote our names on labels and stuck them to the tubes. Then he asked us, one by one, to open our mouths. He stuck a fresh cotton bud into each child's mouth, rubbed it against the inside of cheeks, and popped each cotton bud into a little plastic bag, which he labelled. He smiled at us and told us to go. The nurse led us out, back to the other children.

We stayed in the canteen for a few hours, increasingly bored and fractious. As the afternoon shadows lengthened, the nurses led us out, and onto another bus. It went past the tanks, and out the main gate, back to Krasnod. Our parents met us at the school.

And that was that. The scariest day of my life. It was terrifying at the time, and even more in the nightmares I had afterwards, and nobody ever explained it to me, not even who the bad men on the street had been. But that day's violence, such as it was, was the only day when things got scary in Krasnod. Nothing untoward happened for the rest of my time in Krassnia, until the day my mother took me away to the big aeroplane.

I never forgot the name of Ilya Klebov.

6. PROBLEM NUMBER ONE

1.

The day after I met Ross Stewart was Friday, April 18. I woke at 6:45 to a red wine hangover and the afterimages of bad dreams. A shower helped. I sat, with a towel around my hair, over a breakfast of generic crunch and repeated applications of black coffee and orange juice. Julie and Gail came and went to the bathroom and finally rushed in all made up and neatly dressed for work, grabbing a sip of coffee and a bite of berry-bar before rushing out. At that point I got dressed. Flared jeans, high-heeled boots, and the soft leather jacket improved my morale. Two ibuprofen and a brisk walk to work finished the job. By the time I bounded up the stairs to unlock the Digital Damage door at 8:30 I was back to feeling almost bright.

Around 10:30 an email from Small Worlds hit my inbox. As we'd agreed on Wednesday, they'd sought out studio spaces in Edinburgh. They'd found one with a slot available at two that afternoon. Would I take it? I checked my schedule, to-do list, and the nearest wall's Post-It foliage, consulted Sean, and agreed. Small Worlds responded with an address and a Google Map attachment.

The studio was in one of the commercial estates around South Gyle, two train stops west of Waverley. I printed off the map and my own Krassnian translation of the game's dialogue and prompts. For the next hour or so I went through it with a highlighter, marking the female voices. After lunch I stuffed the sheaf of paper and a 4G memory stick into a laptop bag, slung it in parallel with my shoulder bag, and set off.

The studio was on the third floor of a block of red brick and brown glass. No reception, entryphone at the door. I pressed one of those unmoving button things labelled "Sound & Around"—it looked like a good guess—and tipped my ear to the speaker. Sounds came forth. All I could make out was the question mark.

"Lucy Stone," I said.

The buzzer sounded. I pushed the glass doors open and stepped into a narrow atrium that smelled of whitewash and hessian. It had a stairwell, lit by fluorescent poles and tall windows, and a lift. I took the lift. Sound & Around had a pair of solid swing doors with tiny wire-meshed windows. I pushed through. Man-size framed posters of rockstars, felt-tip signed; framed silver discs, a plant pot, and a Kona and an Eden Springs water cooler. Behind a reception desk sat a guy in a Stereophonics T-shirt and blond dreads. He spared me a glance from his computer screen and nodded me towards a door with a light above it.

The door closed behind me with a rubbery smooch. The room contained a swivel chair in front of a table with what looked like a window with one-way glass behind it and metre of fluorescent tube above it. A big swing mike and earphones took their cabling from a hole in the middle. A jug of water and a transparent plastic cup sat to one side. Thick, worn carpet, and walls of egg-box goose-pimple deadened the sounds I made stepping forward, hanging my jacket on the chairback, sitting down, and unpacking my script. The memory stick, forgotten, fell out as I unzipped the bag. I picked it up from the carpet and fidgeted with it for a moment. Then I pulled the head-phones on and tugged the mike towards my mouth. There was no static hiss or crackle, but some aural tension told me the system was live. I gave the mike an experimental tap.

"Finally," said a sarcastic male voice, in stereo in my ears. "Ready to record, Miss Stone." The accent was English posh with a faint Slavic overlay.

"I can't see a USB port," I said.

"That won't be necessary," said the voice. "I'll burn a disc and give it to you when we've finished. You can take a copy to the memory stick then if you like." A pause. "Ready when you are."

"OK, thanks."

I turned to page 13, cleared my throat, took a sip of water, and—in Krassnian, and in the slyest and slinkiest tone I could conjure—said: "Wel-come, stranger, to our dark land."

It could have been tedious and annoying, but it was fun. I let my mind sink back into childhood memory, and there trawled for voices: the wise woman was Nana, the wench was the girl in the meat shop, the crone was Miss Yesiyeva, the prompts were Mrs. Tushurashvili at her most maternally didactic, and the femme fatale was (to my surprise, but that was how the voice came out) Amanda. The warrior princess—every orc army needs a warrior princess—and on the other side the elven queen were, you will not be surprised to learn, me.

"When you see a single crow, beware."

"Hasten, warrior, to yonder gorge, where much wisdom will be imparted."

"Come with me to the inn."

"Wouldst thou take some amusement before thou retirest, big boy?"

"Forward, the host!"

"Slaughter the vile rebels!"

"To escape from this maze at any time, press Esc."

And so on, for about an hour and a half (some of which was rerecording lines I'd muffed with coughs, sips, throat-clearing noises, or giggles).

"That's it," I said.

"Very good, Miss Stone. A moment, please."

The mike and earphones went dead. I took the phones off, pushed the mike away, and spun the seat around, leaning back and reaching sideways for the water. Despite my frequent sipping, my throat felt raw. The silence in the room, and the way the walls and floor absorbed sound, became suddenly oppressive. More than ever the tinted window seemed like a one-way mirror. I had the feeling of being watched.

There was a light rap on the door. For all that I was expecting it, I jumped, almost spilling the water, and my reply was a yelp. The door opened and a man put his head around it, smiled, and then stepped inside, leaving the door ajar.

For a moment, strangely enough, he reminded me of Alec: tall, with a beard. But this man's beard was a stiff spade of grey, and his sharp blue eyes were magnified by thick glasses and enfolded by wrinkles. His tweed jacket, check shirt, and ancient corduroys completed the Russian-professor look. I retrospectively placed his accent: Krassnian, well educated.

His left hand clutched a cased CD, the other he stuck out, smiling.

"Yuri Gusayevich," he said.

Another man who might be my father. This was getting embarrassing.

"Pleased to meet you," I managed to say, shaking hands and not knowing where to look.

Gusayevich pressed the CD into my hand.

"Take this if you need a backup," he said. "Already I have sent the sound file down the line to Small Worlds."

"Uh, do you work for . . . ?" I waved a hand around.

"The studio company? No, no," said Gusayevich. "I work for Mr. Ross Stewart. I am here because I did some of the male voice acting on this game. Also, I am here to meet you."

"Oh!" I said. "Just a moment."

I was glad the door was open. I turned away, swept up the loose script sheets and the USB stick, and zipped them and the CD into the laptop bag. I shrugged into my jacket, slung the bags, and stepped past Gusayevich, out into the reception lobby. I nodded to the dreads and T-shirt guy and headed for the stairs. I was in no mood to share a lift. Gusayevich hurried after me. I sped down the stairs, swinging around corners with one hand on the balustrade. The main doors opened to a push-button. Gusayevich, a few steps behind, had to wait for them to reopen. This gave me time to get to the edge of the road before I turned and waited for him to catch up.

Midafternoon, scudding white clouds, raw wind funnelled by the buildings, which stood in discordant styles among the green mounds and long barrows of turf-over-rubble landscaping. Container lorries rumbled past. People dotted the surrounding pavements like figures in an architect's presentation drawing. Not far overhead, an EasyJet screamed out of Turnhouse.

Gusayevich halted, facing me, a little out of breath.

"What's the matter?" he said.

"I'll tell you what's the matter, Mr. Gusayevich," I said. "I didn't expect to meet an employee of Ross Stewart. Is Small Worlds one of his companies?"

"No, no," said Gusayevich, shaking his head as if to clear it. "You misunderstand. Small Worlds is indeed a front company, but not for Mr. Stewart. I am one of those doing the male voices because only very, very reliable people can be employed on this. I am one, and so are you."

I laughed. "*I'm* reliable?"

"Oh, yes." Gusayevich pulled a packet of Marlboros from his pocket and lit up, staring at me all the while. He took a deep draw and glanced around. "This is as good a place as any. Lucy—I may call you Lucy?—you can have no idea—how could you?—of how devilishly difficult it is to find exiles

fluent in Krassnian who are completely above suspicion of collaboration with
the Russian or the Krassnian secret services."

I held his gaze, wondering if he was winding me up. And wondering,
too, if he might really be my father. The man whom the other man who
might be my father had betrayed. Wondering if Gusayevich knew that Ross
Stewart had betrayed him.

"I do have some idea," I said. "And as I understand it, the problem is
running an op like this without having someone working for you inside the
security services, and that leads to the problem of double agents and all the
rest. You can never know who's going to betray you, can you?"

That was me winding *him* up.

"Indeed you can't," said Gusayevich, without a trace of irony.

"That's why you and I are needed for this. As for using elements inside
the . . . other side . . . I'm familiar with the problems, yes."

"Ah," I said. "I see. So . . . uh, why were you sent to meet me?"

"Mr. Stewart has asked me to accompany you to meet him for dinner."

"Bit early for that," I said. "Besides—"

"He has booked a table for six o'clock," said Gusayevich. "Harvey
Nichols, St. Andrew's Square."

"Very kind," I said. "But I'm seeing my boyfriend this evening."

Alec and I had planned to meet in the Doctors', after work.

"You can still see him," said Gusayevich. "We'll be finished by eight."

I thought about it. "OK."

Alec was already on the train when I called. He didn't sound put out
when I suggested we meet up at the Auld Hoose at 8:30. Neither did Sean
when I told him I wouldn't be back for the usual Friday evening after-work
pint.

I put the phone back in my belt pouch and nodded to Gusayevich.

"Let's go," I said. "Do I have time to go home and change?"

"No need," said Gusayevich, after giving my appearance a critical up-
and-down. "Smart casual is acceptable. And there are some things that Mr.
Stewart wished me to discuss with you before we reach Harvey Nick's.
Things it is better not to talk about in a restaurant."

"Fine," I said. "Where do you want to go?"

He cocked an eye skyward.

"The weather is fine," he said. "We go to Harvey Nick's."

"But didn't you just—?"

"We walk."

2.

We walked, through the Gyle estates, over the railway bridge, through a ramble of residential back streets, then along St. John's Road and Corstor-phine Road and other stretches of the A8, the main drag into town, all the way to Princes Street.

"You have questions," Gusayevich ventured, as we set off.

"Yeah," I said.

I couldn't ask him the most pressing question, so instead I said: "Uh, Ross Stewart, uh, mentioned your name, or at least—I mean, you *are* Yuri Gusayevich the Krassnian dissident, right?"

Yuri—that was when I began to think of him by his first name—laughed.

"It's some time since I have been called a Krassnian dissident! But yes, I am the man Mr. Stewart met in Krasnod, all those years ago."

"And were you imprisoned?"

"Imprisoned?" He sounded startled, then gave a leaning-forward head-shake and sidelong glance. "Hah! So you know my friend Ross better than he has thought to let on. And you only met him yesterday, isn't that so?"

"Yes, but—"

"Doubtless he showed you some documents, eh?"

"Yes, but—"

"That simplifies matters. So, Lucy, to answer your question. No, I was not imprisoned. I was not even arrested. The first I knew about this possi-bility was in 1992, when out of the blue I received a letter of grovelling apology from one Ross Stewart, whose name I struggled to recall. I was living in Moscow at the time—working at the university, in fact. That was how he found my name, and knew who I was. He offered me employment, which was very welcome, given the condition of the economy in those years. I told him the truth by return post. I had not been arrested and had no idea that he had betrayed me. What had happened was that in 1984 I received a warning from a friend, to leave the group and concentrate on my studies.

Which I did. My relationship with your mother broke up some time after, in January '85, if I remember that miserable month correctly."

"So—"

"Yes, I may be your natural father. As may Ross. Do you have any more questions?"

"Well—"

"Good! Then I have a question for you. What do you think this Krassnia business is all about?"

"The game's going to be used as cover for organising . . . the Maple Revolution, that's what Ross called it."

"Yes, yes," said Yuri, impatiently. "Of course the revolution. But why? Why has your mother's employer turned its attention to our godforsaken birthplace?"

"It's all about the pipeline," I said.

"The pipeline?" he said. "In President Saakashvili the Americans already have a friend to guard it."

"But not the pass around Mount Krasny. That puts Russia in striking distance of the pipeline."

"Even if the Russians lost Krassnia, they'd still have South Ossetia and the Roki Tunnel. There are no great military advantages in using the Krasny pass—rather the reverse. No, Lucy, you have the right idea in postulating a material motivation for America's new enthusiasm for liberty in Krassnia, but the pipeline has nothing to do with it. Nor is it the territorial integrity of Georgia—in relation to that, Krassnia is a pinprick compared to South Ossetia, which has actual Russian troops deployed on the territory, or even Abkhazia, a rich coastal region of which Georgians have, let's say, *warm* memories."

He chuckled at his own pun, and continued: "So the question remains—why is the CIA interested in Krassnia?"

"That's just what I asked myself," I told him, "as soon as my mother proposed the game. I thought—well, apart from the pipeline, that's a constant—there's an election coming up in September, and that might seem a good chance to help the Liberal Democrats against the Social Democrats—isn't that what the former Communists call themselves?"

Yuri snorted. "Liberal Democrats, Social Democrats, National Democrats, and all the other democrats—they're all former Communists. Except the young people, obviously. Yes, you're right, the election is a chance, and will be the pretext. The SDs don't need to rig the election to win, but they will be accused of that regardless. No, it is about something much more significant than a friendly regime or a pipeline."

"So what *is* it about?"

We were standing at an intersection, waiting to cross, so Yuri had a moment to turn and give me a solemn look, and speak in a low, portentous voice.

"It is about the secret of the Vrai."

I almost giggled.

The lights changed. We crossed the road and turned left, into an identical residential street of former-Communist (well, that's how I tend to think of it) housing. I didn't know if Yuri knew the area really well, of if he was navigating by the polarisation of light in the sky or some inner magnetic sense, like a migrating bird.

"What's the secret of the Vrai?" I asked.

"What do you know of it?"

"I saw it mentioned in the documents Ross sent me last night."

"The confessions?"

"Yes."

"In which mention is made of 'the secret of the Vrai,' also known as 'the Krassnian truth.' Do you know what that is?"

"No," I said.

"That's a pity," said Yuri. "I had rather hoped you might."

I nearly stumbled.

"Why?" I cried. "How the—how on earth would I know that?"

"Oh, from your mother's side of the family, perhaps, or from some old woman who your mother introduced you to, a servant or a nurse."

"No, nothing like that. There was an old—well, she wasn't very old— there was a woman in her fifties, I guess, who remembered something that happened in 1952."

I didn't explain further, waiting to see how Yuri would react. He gave a yelp of delight.

"Yes! Yes! The Mount Krasny incident! It is very relevant, but it is not the secret."

"So what *is* the secret?"

"I wish I knew."

"So how do you know that the 1952 incident is relevant? I thought it had something to do with Beria and the Bomb."

"Ah," said Yuri. "I know because it happened on or around Mount Krasny. That is the heart of the Vrai secret. You must know this from the legends, from the folktales and even the rumours."

"Oh, yeah, the magical inscription in a cave. That was the secret of the power of the Vrai, right?"

I must have sounded scornful. Yuri gave me a sharp look.

"The Vrai secret is no joke, and more than a magical inscription. There is something on or in that mountain which was a source or guarantor of power for the Vrai. Its secret was passed down within the ruling tribes for centuries—strangely enough, not always from parents to children, but to children from someone of the lower classes: herdsmen, hunters of animals too lowly to count as game, nursemaids. If you look at old memoirs, time and again you come across statements like 'and in my tenth year I learned that of which I need not speak' or 'so the mountaineer took me to a certain place, and my eyes were opened.'"

"Sure they weren't talking about sex?"

"Yes, I'm sure," said Yuri, sounding irritated for a moment. "But yes, I admit, it does sound like that story by Borges. . . ."

"Yes," I said, as if I knew what he was talking about (I didn't, but I looked it up later), "but who initiates the initiators? And if it's a secret of the ruling tribe, why does it get passed on by people outside it?"

"Good questions," said Yuri. "I have long puzzled about them myself. Possibly the older person of the common people acted merely as a guide to—let's say—the entrance to a cave, or chasm, and the young person of the Vrai made his or her own way in to witness the marvel, whatever it was."

"But if this secret has been passed down for *centuries*," I continued, as we turned on to the main road, "*somebody* would have given away what the secret is, surely."

"You would certainly expect so," said Yuri. "However, I've found no record of such."

"Why can't someone just go to Krassnia and *ask?*"

"I've tried that," said Yuri. "No one will talk, even if you can get close enough to them in the first place. The very few people who may readily be suspected of having Vrai blood are well inside the oligarchy, protected by everything from unhelpful secretaries to goons, not all of them in police uniform. I soon concluded that this was not a subject healthy for me to pursue." He sighed. "It's even possible that no one alive knows the secret—the Terror and the War may have swept them all away."

"Like that secret-police guy whose confession . . . ?"

Yuri glanced sharply at me. "Beryozkin? Yes, that's the one. He may have been typical. When Colonel Aleksey Klebov blew out Beryozkin's brains, he may have destroyed the last—"

"Oh!" I cried.

"I apologise," said Yuri. "I shouldn't have—"

"No, no, it isn't that," I said. "You just reminded me, about Klebov."

"In what connection?"

"You've read Ross's, uh, confession?"

Yuri chuckled darkly. "The blackmail document? Indeed I have."

"Well, was that Klebov—Aleksey—connected to Ilya Klebov, the KGB man who Ross did a deal with?"

"He was his father," said Yuri.

"Yesss!" I said. "I *knew* it!"

"What's so exciting about that?" Yuri asked.

"Klebov—Ilya—told Ross that he knew materialism was false, right? Sounds to me a bit like what Beryozkin said just before they shot him— about another world beyond death. What if Ilya Klebov knew the secret? Maybe learned it from his father—maybe his father got it out of Beryozkin? Or was he in on it himself—was he one of the Vrai?"

Yuri snorted. "The opposite, entirely. The Klebov clan is Krasnar through and through. That may be one reason why Aleksey Klebov was chosen for the job of wiping out the Vrai clique inside the local NKVD. He may have enjoyed it."

"I've always thought *Ilya* Klebov was a decent man," I said.

"What do you mean, always thought?"

"Well, I met Ilya Klebov when—"

"*You? Met? Klebov?*" Yuri said, each word emphatic and interrogatory and disbelieving.

I told him, briefly, about the scariest day of my life, as we walked out of Corstorphine and past the zoo. As we walked Yuri occasionally stopped to look in shop windows. Once, he stopped and stooped to tie a bootlace, and I noticed him checking the wing mirror of a parked car just before he stood up.

"A moment," he said, when I'd finished my story. He stepped into an empty bus shelter, and stood facing me as I stopped too.

"Are you sure," he said, looking me alarmingly in the eyes, "about the swabs? And the hair samples?"

"Yes," I said, puzzled at this particular question. "Positive."

He lidded his eyes and nodded slowly. "Very interesting," he said. "Very puzzling." He stroked his beard with thumb and forefinger. "Today that would obviously be seen as DNA sampling, but in 1991 . . . I wonder."

Yuri turned and resumed his walk with a swifter stride, making me hurry to catch up.

"DNA?" I said. "Hair?" I laughed. "You mean there's something special about *red hair*, like in something by Marian Zimmer Bradley?"

"I know nothing of this Marian Zimmer Bradley," said Yuri, in a deadpan tone that reminded me of Slartibartfast talking about sitcoms, "but yes, in this context red hair is special. It is not diagnostic in itself, but in Krassnia it is a sex-typed genetic marker indicative of Vrai ancestry on the female line."

"Oh."

"Indeed," he said. "You must tell Ross Stewart all of this. But not tonight. Write it up and email it to him—he will give you a secure email address. And if you remember the names of the other children who were sampled, that might be of use to him as well."

"Of use—why?" I asked, above the din of the increasingly rush-hour traffic.

Yuri stuck his hands in his jacket pockets and walked more closely beside me. When he replied his voice was so low, and so aimed at the ground in front of us rather than at me, that I strained to make him out.

"It is to do with the nature of the business. Whatever the secret may be, there is no chance of finding it as long as the slopes and summit of Mount

Krasny remain guarded, as they are to this day. It's still a Zone, you know that? So to have access to it, one must have control or influence over the Krassnian state. After the Maple Revolution, the CIA—or whatever other agency, the NSA perhaps—will have that. Fine. But not enough. One point that the legends are consistent on is that only those of Vrai blood may safely approach the actual site of the secret—though they may be guided there by others, as I've said."

By now I was quite thrilled. "So the children that Klebov took away from the school—you think those who were tested might have been Vrai?"

"I think that Klebov may have thought so," said Yuri. "In any case, the time may come when it would be of interest to ask any who can be traced."

"*I* was tested," I objected. "And he must have known that *I* wasn't—oh."

Yuri laughed, and quite unexpectedly patted me between the shoulder blades, in an odd, quick gesture that ended with his hands rammed once more in his pockets.

"You know you have some Vrai blood at least," he said. "And perhaps some Krassnar, too."

I felt a little embarrassed. It wasn't that I didn't like him. I did. I thought he was *really cool*. An actual dissident! It was almost as cool as my other putative father's being an actual criminal. Either of these was *way* more cool than an academic like Eric. But the thing was, Eric very much occupied the "father" address in my mind and heart, and always had done, even though I'd long known he wasn't my actual father. What made me uncomfortable was the reminder that I might have a blood relationship with this new stranger, cool though he was.

Awkwardly, I changed the subject.

"What's Klebov doing now—is he—?"

"Running the RSB—Krassnia's local version of the FSB? The local *branch* of the FSB, I would say! No, he is now the wealthy businessman he always wanted to be. He made a fortune in importing cars, in good time to buy most of the shares in the copper mine when it was privatised by his former colleagues."

"I meant, is he still working with Ross?"

Yuri frowned.

"Not a good question, Lucy. Let's say they liaise on commercial matters.

About the Maple Revolution—no. He is against it, obviously, and doesn't know at all the extent of Ross's involvement."

"Is Ross going to be involved enough to need the names of the other kids, after the Maple Revolution?"

"It doesn't matter," said "Yuri. "He will liaise with your mother. Much depends on circumstances at the time. The window of opportunity may be short."

"How d'you mean?"

"Oh, the Russians will do what they can to prevent the Americans getting to the secret. They will after all retain many friends in Krassnia, especially in the apparat, even after the fall of the current regime. Klebov, for instance. And they will not hesitate to intervene directly—"

"Invade?" I said. "That seems a bit . . . extreme."

"They could use special forces," said Yuri. "Parachute troops, for example."

"If this secret's so big," I said, "why don't they do that already? Just go in and get it?"

"They? The Russians?"

"Yes."

"They have done it already," said Yuri. "They got very badly burned. That was the 1952 incident. Bear in mind, anything to do with uranium and the atomic bomb was a closely guarded state secret at the time. Even the existence of the atomic gulags was secret. And yet, those in Krassnia who were old enough to remember always associated the Mount Krasny incident with Beria and the Bomb. Always one would be confidently"—he tapped the side of his nose, theatrically—"and confidentially told that Beria came to Krasnod to supervise some experimental uranium extraction process in the mountains, and that it blew up in his face. It is very consistent. That is what you heard, as a child, yes?"

"Uh-huh," I said. "More or less."

"You see?" he said. "It is more than a rumour. It is so consistent it has to have been a cover story, planted by the KGB. And if that was the *cover story*, what was the truth?"

"But—if the story's so consistent, that might be evidence that it's true," I said.

"No!" Yuri said, angrily. "You don't understand. If the story was true, nobody would have heard it, or dared to repeat it. The Soviet Union was a state that kept its secrets, and tenfold so in Stalin's time. And in Krasnod in 1952 people prattled about Beria and the Bomb? About the most feared man in the country, and the top military secret? No. If people spoke of such things, it's because the authorities wanted them to talk of such things. That story was planted, Lucy, it was disinformation."

"You're saying the truth must have been something that had to be kept even more—"

"Yes! Exactly! Something quite shocking—shattering."

"*How* shocking?" I demanded. "An alien spaceship? A stargate? An angel? The Ark of the Covenant?"

"The Ark of the Covenant," said Yuri in a serious tone, "is in Ethiopia. So that is ruled out. An angel would tend to confirm religious belief, which does not seem to have been the effect. An alien spaceship is a possibility, but it wouldn't undermine materialism. Now, a stargate or some such space-time anomaly—there you may be close to the mark. It's certainly the sort of thing I find myself speculating on when I think of Beryozkin's confidence that there is a better world beyond this one. Perhaps he literally *saw* that better world. And I think the secret is something that can be seen, because . . . now here we are in the realm of rumour, Lucy, and in my country that is a wide and treacherous realm, where rumours enter history all the time. But for whatever it may be worth, here is the rumour. I heard it from a friend in Moscow in 1990, who had a friend who worked in the archives—the same friend, by the way, who later, at some risk to himself, obtained for me the confessions of Arbatov and of Beryozkin. This friend of a friend had heard from yet another friend a story which, needless to say, was itself a tale whispered in shadowy aisles between dusty filing shelves, year upon year.

"The tale was this: Beria really was involved in the 1952 Mount Krasny incident—perhaps not personally on the scene, but involved—Beria was after all in charge of the State Committee on Problem Number One, the atomic bomb program, and its successor, the hydrogen bomb program. And the incident may initially have had something to do with prospecting for uranium or some other radioactive element. Beria knew the legends, of course—he was a Mingrelian, a people who have a long acquaintance with the Krassnians, an acquaintance shall we say intimate, or as the Americans put it, 'up close and personal.'"

He chuckled darkly again, and mimed a knife thrust.

"Like that. But being a convinced dialectical materialist, and an ambitious and driven man to boot, Lavrenti Beria sniffed a hopeful possibility in these legends. He wondered if the legendary mysterious glow in the mountainside might indicate a rich deposit of radioactive material, if the fabled grotesque consequences for normal people of approaching the site of the Vrai secret might be some kind of mutation or radiation sickness, and if the power of the Vrai might be itself a mutation that perhaps protected against the radiation that had originally given rise to it. Or he may have suspected that all except the strange glow were legendary accretions—to the benefit of the local aristocracy, no doubt—around an outcrop of radioactive ore. In any case—radioactive ore! Just what he needed!

"But how to find it? Beria knew well—from the records of such interrogations as that of Beryozkin, if not from his own recollections—that the location of the site could not be extracted from the supposed Krassnian truth-keepers by any means. Even assuming that any one of them could be found to have survived the work of the likes of NKVD Colonel Klebov. Being a man of some experience in these matters, our Lavrenti reckoned that folk from among the stalwart working class and peasantry were more susceptible than the degenerate national intelligentsia to bribery, flattery, persuasion, intimidation, and what the NKVD called 'methods of physical pressure' and what the security agencies of your own motherland and your adopted country call 'repeated application of legitimate force'—and what more honest criminals call 'beating the living shit out of them.'

"So—a small army of NKVD men descends on the goat-herding collectives of Krassnia, and starts knocking on doors, banging on tables, and knocking out teeth. By one means or another they eventually get an old herdsman to agree to guide them to a place from where they can proceed to the spot—nothing they can do, he tells them, can make him go all the way himself. Naturally, the NKVD men don't go charging off up the mountain. They report back. Beria gets a team together, a dozen or so men, including a physicist with a Geiger counter, a geologist, and even a man with a handheld cine camera to record this triumph—or not, if it's a wild goose chase. In great secrecy, they arrive in Krasnod, rendezvous with the old man, and follow him up the mountain, into forests, through screes and gullies, across treacherous snowfields. . . . Eventually the old man stops within sight of the entrance to some cave or gorge—the tales vary, naturally—and tells them he's not going a step further. Our intrepid explorers press on, leaving only one NKVD man behind with the old man.

"An hour passes. The old man is increasingly nervous. Suddenly, an eerie light shines from where the party have gone. Out of it, moments later, stumbles the cameraman—blinded, by some accounts; burned, by others. He does not survive, or is speechless, or mad. But his cine camera is still with him, and he gives it to the NKVD guard, perhaps with the last of his strength or his sanity. The guard makes to rush to the aid of his comrades, but is hauled back by the old man and the cameraman. Together, or apart, the three survivors stagger back to Krasnod. Nothing is said of what happened to them. But it is said that the reel of film was sent under heavy guard to Moscow, where it was watched in Stalin's private cinema in the Kremlin—Beria himself taking the place of the projectionist, Stalin alone the audience.

"No one else saw it. Someone—again, from hearsay—saw Stalin and Beria emerge from the cinema looking severely shaken—'as if they'd seen a ghost,' as it is of course said, in that kind of story.

"That would be in late 1952. In March 1953, Stalin is dead, the dread Beria is the new boss. Strangely enough, he begins to initiate liberal reforms —half emptying the Gulag, banning torture, discrediting the 'Doctors' Plot,' urging change on the East German hardliners, and so on. In June he is arrested, in July denounced, in December executed. And the reel of film?"

Yuri had timed this pause to arrive while we stood at a pedestrian crossing.

"Yes?" I said.

"Recycled for the silver in the emulsion," said Yuri, and stepped out on the crossing.

3.

"That isn't a rumour," I said, indignantly catching up on the other side of the street. "It's a fucking shaggy dog story!"

"Such things happened in Soviet times," said Yuri.

He said it like it was the final explanation.

"I'm not buying that," I said. "Come on! This film *just happened* to be destroyed?"

"Yes," said Yuri. "The same was blindly and stupidly and unforgivably done to priceless footage of the early Soviet space programme—its triumphs and disasters alike. As I said, such things happened. Normally the loss of the only physical evidence would for me suggest that there was nothing behind the story. In this case, it inclines me to think the story is more than a rumour."

He glanced around.

"We are nearing Haymarket," he said. "Let us talk no more of these things."

I couldn't think of anything else to talk about. Yuri regaled me with stories as we walked, up Shandwick Place and around Charlotte Square and along George Street. They weren't tales of his life in the Soviet Union—they were scurrilous, eye-opening, unrepeatable snippets about what went on behind the sandstone and granite walls of Scotland's imposing institutions: Bute House and the law firms and learned societies and brokerages and the small nation's mighty, world-straddling banks.

We reached the side door of Harvey Nichols a few minutes before six.

"A moment," Yuri said. He lit up, and stood watching the rush-hour homeward flow of people through the mall. He said nothing, but I noticed on his face a pensive and almost sad expression, which after a few moments I recognised as compassion. The look made me feel vaguely uneasy. Yuri stubbed his cigarette on the wall, looked around for somewhere to put it, then dropped it. We stepped through the glass doors and took the lift to the top of the store, stepping out into a broad space of polished wood, white tablecloths, dim lighting, and bright windows. Ross Stewart was sitting on a stool at the small bar on the way to the restaurant area. He saw us, smiled, knocked back a shot, and swung his feet to the floor.

"Good to see you, Lucy. Hi, Yuri. Let's get dinner."

We had a table near the window overlooking St. Andrew's Square. The sun was still high enough not to be a nuisance. I had a G&T, Ross had another whisky, Yuri chose vodka.

Time to order.

"And how would you like your venison?" the waiter asked Ross.

"Very rare. Just caught in the headlights."

Over my seared salmon and Ross's startled deer and Yuri's roasted chicken we talked about everything except what I wanted to talk about. It was frustrating. Ross, in waistcoat and shirtsleeves (complete with stretchy silver armbands to keep his cuffs from slipping too low), jacket over the back of the chair, was in relaxed and expansive mood. Yuri (sleeves rolled up) was sombre. I could have done with picking the brains of both of them—about Amanda, about Krassnia, about the Maple Revolution and "the business," but they instantly cut out any such allusion. Not that there was anything secretive about their manner—Ross surprised a Polish waitress with a few fluent sentences, Yuri nodded to a young Slovenian waiter as if they were old pals, and now and again some person of substance dining out said hello in passing. I recognised a byline photo here, a television face there.

By the time the coffee came round I had found a way in to what I wanted to talk about.

"What happened in 1937?" I asked.

Both men looked at me funny.

"You don't know?" said Ross. "About the Great Terror?"

"I know about it," I said. "I just don't know why it happened."

"Ah," said Yuri. "The big question. Why did it happen? Everything else, we know why it happened. The Red terror in the Civil War, the de-kulakisation, the famine, the deportations of suspect nationalities. . . . In the early thirties, the late forties, and the early fifties the camps and prisons and exile settlements were full of people who knew why they were there. They either hated the system or knew why the system hated them. In '37, the camps and the cells are full to bursting—or I should say, to *crushing*—with people who have *no idea* why they are there. Party members, active citizens, and ordinary nonpolitical people, ninety or more percent of whom have never raised a finger against the system. Of the seven hundred thousand executions, three hundred and fifty thousand were of supposed 'class enemies'—priests, kulaks, former Whites, former members of the possessing classes, and so on. A further two hundred and fifty thousand were of supposed suspect national-ities, from Koreans to Germans via Persians. Let us grant some perverted rationality to these slaughters—though even in those cases there were ten times as many victims as had been fingered in the original quota. That leaves another hundred thousand who, with very few exceptions, can have had no idea why—" He made a pistol with his fingers and thumb. "That's the problem, yes?"

"Yes," I said.

"It's simple," said Ross. "Stalin wanted to cut down anyone who might conceivably be a threat, and started up a chainsaw that even he found hard to stop."

"It is not so simple," said Yuri.

Ross gave me a wry smile. "Our dissident is a quixotic upholder of Stalin's honour," he said.

"What!" I said, shocked.

Yuri scowled.

"Again, it is not so simple. Let me explain. Look."

He waved a hand towards the window. The sun hadn't set, but clouds had darkened the sky, and the west was red; Arthur's Seat, the Castle, the spire of the Scott Monument, black. The rectilinear reflections of the restaurant's overhead lighting hung above the city like an alien invasion fleet.

"What?"

"The people out there," Yuri said, "what do they have? Nothing!"

I looked at him, puzzled. "Well," I said, "I suppose it makes a difference whether it's the West End or Wester Hailes we're talking about, but I'd say apart from the homeless most people have a great deal more than nothing. They have better housing and food and entertainment and so on than—"

"Yes, yes, yes," said Yuri. "I know what it is to be compared with, thank you very much. In terms of having their own culture, their own politics, they have nothing. In those respects the working classes of the West are little better than slaves."

"Now wait a minute," I said. "That's—"

"Look at yourself, Lucy. You do not have nothing. What you got from your mother was a tradition, a knowledge, a culture that came from . . . her mother and her grandparents. A certain confidence, a set of reflexes—I can see it in the way you move, the way you think, the way you hold your head. You may be a very uncertain young woman, you may be in a lowly occupation—though still well-off, in a way—but you have it in you to rise, and when you do, you will find that life is not strange but somehow what you were born to. You may not know this now, and you may disagree with me now, but you will see."

"Disagree with you?" I said. "Why should I? I'm flattered."

Yuri flashed his bushy brows at Ross. "You see?"

Ross shrugged, and sipped his double espresso.

"What's that got to do with—oh!" I said. "I see! They wanted to wipe out people like me!"

"There was a great deal of that—as I have just said. But for the rest, the other hundred thousand, I mean something quite different. The possessing classes, the classes from which you come, have a culture of their own, and great political experience. Experience acquired over centuries—over millennia! Their schoolboys did not study the classics of antiquity for nothing! But it is not learned from books. The lower classes, the working classes, no matter what their standard of living may be at any given time, have nothing of that kind."

"That's ridiculous!" I said. "Look at any big bookshop—Waterstone's in Princes Street—they have *walls* of classics, in cheap editions. The working classes can read Aristotle if they want."

Not that they want to, I forbore to add.

"Ah, now Aristotle—" Ross began, but I hadn't finished.

"Not to mention all the other education and culture ordinary people have access to, that they never did in the past, that's far more than slaves or serfs ever—"

"Exactly!" said Yuri. "The working classes have *access* to culture—we can argue about how real that access is, but yes. The fact remains that the only culture they have is that of the classes above them—because they have none of their own. Likewise in politics."

"What about the Labour Party?" Ross demanded.

Yuri joined in my hollow laugh.

Ross made a face. "All right."

"Now," Yuri went on, "let us imagine that in some particular country, the working classes acquire first a party, then a state, then a culture. We are speaking of a revolution, of course, but imagine—armies, universities, secret police, diplomats, millions of people who all have to at least pretend to believe that they are in the service of the working class. You can imagine it, yes?"

"Kind of," I said, grudgingly. "It sounds scary."

"Precisely!" cried Yuri, finger upraised. "Now—imagine what it would take to destroy that." He brought the finger slicing down. *"That* was 1937."

"Just as I've always said." Ross's voice had the tone of someone slipping into the deep, comfortable ruts of an old argument. "Stalin destroyed the Party."

"The Party was destroyed, yes, but that was not Stalin's doing," said Yuri. "It was Yezhov's."

"Ah, of course, Yezhov," said Ross, sarcastically. "Stalin's loyal executioner!"

*"Dis*loyal," said Yuri, making it sound like a pedantic correction. "Or so he confessed."

Ross snorted. "He confessed to the secret police that he was a traitor who had, as head of the secret police, had the secret police beat and torture countless innocent people until they confessed to being traitors . . . you see the problem?"

"Of course I see the problem. The evidence is thin, I agree, and tainted, but . . ." He shrugged, and spread his hands. "It's what we have."

"But Yuri," I said, "I thought the people whom this guy Yezhov slaughtered were supposed to be part of a conspiracy to overthrow Stalin and restore capitalism."

"They were supposed to be, yes. Some of them were, at least to the extent that they hoped to remove Stalin forcibly from office and return to a market economy—like Deng Xiaoping did in China, though in his case the revolutionary tyrant was removed by natural causes. Anyway—Yezhov was part of the conspiracy, or of an overlapping or rival conspiracy. He killed many innocent people, as well as rival conspirators, to cover for the conspiracy and to advance *his own* aims. Stalin started the Terror, but it ran out of his control, and struck down far more people than he had intended—which number was, God knows, large enough."

"But that's—" I shook my head. "It's like saying Hitler didn't know about the Holocaust."

Yuri stood up. "I need some fresh air," he said, taking his cigarette pack and lighter from his jacket pocket as he left.

"Now you've pissed him off," said Ross. "Don't worry, it'll blow over."

"Is he really a Stalinist?"

Ross laughed. "Not in the least. He just has a bee in his bonnet about his conspiracy theory. And you're right, it's—" He shrugged one shoulder. "I mean, who could imagine Soviet secret policemen and veteran Party members and Western leftwingers and Western intelligence services getting all tangled up together in a plot to restore capitalism?"

I glared at him. "Are you having a laugh?"

"No," said Ross. "I have no idea at all why Yuri could think that was even a little bit plausible."

He stretched, sighed, and signalled a waiter for same-again coffee.

"Christ," he said, "I could do with a smoke myself. That pipe got me back on the old nicotine treadmill. Maybe I'll bum a fag off Yuri when we leave."

Yuri returned just as the second round of coffees arrived.

"Anyway," said Ross, settling back into the argument as Yuri settled in his seat, "you're wrong, Yuri, about the working class having no culture of its own." He jabbed a self-mocking thumb on his waistcoated chest. "*I'm* from the working class, mate, and we bloody well do have a culture. And politics. And traditions—ah!" He smiled. "When you mentioned Aristotle, Lucy, I remembered a lovely example. When I lived in London back in the eighties I shared a squat in Camden with a few people, one of them a nurse. Cockney born and bred, she was. One night I was mouthing off about Aristotle, as one does, and she said she had an old book by Aristotle. I was well impressed to hear this. Off she goes to her room and brings back the book. It was a reprint of some seventeenth- or eighteenth-century work on gynecology. Illustrated with the most grotesque woodcuts—you can imagine. And it's supposedly by Aristotle. His name's right there on the title page. So I say to Lynne, that was her name, look, this can't possibly be by Aristotle. He never wrote a work on gynecology. It's *obviously* written with seventeenth-century knowledge. And so on.

"She wasn't having any of it. Aristotle was a very clever man, she said, knew lots of things, wrote about everything. He could *easily* have written this book."

Ross leaned back, with a self-satisfied smile.

"I don't get it," I said.

"My point," said Ross, tipping himself forward again and jabbing a fore-finger, "is that if my friend the Cockney nurse was anything to go by, some-where in the working class of inner London there was a tradition handed on by word of mouth, quite independent of official education and so on, about *Aristotle*. The universal genius and the great philosopher. Handed down for centuries—maybe longer, maybe since the *Romans*! So don't tell me the working classes don't have an independent culture."

To my surprise, Yuri didn't seem to think, as I did, that this was a bit of a stretch.

"They may remember Aristotle," he said sadly. "They don't remember Spartacus."

This mention of the Romans and Spartacus reminded me of something and I was about to chip in and divert the discussion to a subject less depressing than (and yet in a frustrating tip-of-my-tongue way obscurely *con-nected with*) dead bloody Russians when Ross glanced at his Rolex and called for the bill.

4.

What I'd been reminded of was the first time I'd walked into the Auld Hoose, one Wednesday night in July 2006. I didn't know anyone there, but it wasn't difficult to identify the SF fans from the way they all *talked in italics*. The pre-vious Saturday I'd spent exploring the Grassmarket. I'd bought the black-net-over-red-satin skirt and the spangly top I was wearing in a vintage store, Arm-strong's, and almost next door to that shop had found Transreal, an SF book-shop where I picked up a paperback of the latest Ellen Kushner and from the friendly owner a few pointers to the haunts of SF fans in Edinburgh.

And to one of those haunts, that Wednesday evening in July 2006, I went.

I checked out the vast range of unfamiliar beers and settled for a bottle of Miller Lite, then sidled to the periphery of a conversation going on around a couple of adjacent tables. Some people were standing, others sitting. A guy with a ponytail was sitting behind the table beside a woman whose long hair brushed the threads and busy needle of a beadwork project in her hands. Two guys—one with dark curly hair, the other with a blond buzz-cut of hair and beard—standing at the corner of the table were in conversation with this couple, or at least listening with the others around the table while the pony-tailed guy held forth.

". . . so we looked for some way to get Romans on Mars," he was saying, "and we came up with Spartacus, who was—"

Cue ragged chorus of: "I am Spartacus!" with one voice saying: "I am Neil Kinnock!" followed by a yell of "Splitter!" and then a short round of *Life of Brian* jokes.

Ponytailed guy sat out the flurry and continued: "Spartacus gives us a time-line where there wouldn't have fucking *been* a People's Front of Judea, and where there would have been Romans on Mars. Here's how. Suppose the armies of Spartacus take Rome, and there's a general slave uprising as the news spreads. The empire collapses. There's no barbarian threat at this point, the migrations haven't started. But the work still has to be done. A lot of the economy just goes to peasant farming. No doubt they get screwed by taxes and moneylenders, but that's all. The sort of proto-feudal stuff that got fastened on them after the fall in our time-line hasn't had time to develop. But what about the urban slaves? Well, the former gladiators and soldiers who are now in charge are already familiar with a way of getting people to work without directly forcing them: pay them. Salary, *salarium*, get it?"

The long-haired woman said something about soldiers being paid in salt, and someone chipped in with the derivation of *sarariman*, and on the edge of the ensuing fannish digression I stood clutching my Miller Lite and flicking through my mental thesaurus for something on the tip of my tongue, some word that *salarium* reminded me of and that seemed important, like a fragment of a dream recalled in the middle of the day, but before I could retrieve it the ponytailed guy managed to get a word in to the interruption.

"My *point is*," he said, "that paying wages already exists, even if it's peripheral. And the Roman world already has loads of knowledge and technology that it's never been profitable to implement in a slave-labour economy—look at Hero of Alexandria's steam engine—OK, a toy, but the principle's there—and the Antikythera mechanism. There are even some factories employing waged workers in very narrow specialised areas—perfume-making, I think it was. So—what happens if all these come together, and wage labour takes off in a big way? You get to capitalism without going through feudalism, you jump from Antiquity to the Industrial Revolution without a Dark Age or the Middle Ages in between, you don't lose all the books the Christians burned, you get history with fifteen hundred years of misery left out!"

"How does Christianity drop out of the picture?" someone asked.

"Slave religion," said the cuter (the curly-haired one) of the two guys standing at the table. Somebody laughed.

"No, seriously," said the ponytailed guy. "We worked it all out. Judea drops off the Roman map. No Hasmoneans or Herodians or whatever. And anyway, no decline and fall, no hopelessness, no transfer of hope to the after-life. . . ." He waved a hand. "Look, give us a fucking break, OK? It's just a premise, it doesn't have to be rigorous. The upshot is you get the Industrial Revolution about AD 300 instead of AD 1800, except there's no AD of course, and space flight AD 500 at the earliest, but realistically ha-ha a bit later and anyway even on worst-case assumptions you can *easily* have Roman astronauts fighting rogue AIs on Mars in what would be our sixteenth century. Hence our game, Olympus, ta-dah! *Except* . . ."

At this point he leaned forward and buried his face in his hands, and his presumed girlfriend looked up from her beading project and grinned around and said: "Having done all that—spread-sheeted the economics, Googled up history details, heaved their arses to the library and cracked a book or two *and* adapted the fucking physics engine *and* sketched the artwork—the poor fuckers haven't got a story!"

For some reason this got everyone within earshot roaring with laughter, as people will at tales of misfortune.

The curly haired guy noticed me looking puzzled on the sidelines, and brought me up to speed a bit, and that was how I got to meet Sean, Joe, and Matt, as well as Sean's girlfriend, Janine. It was how I started flirting with Matt.

It was while I was listening to Joe explaining at great length how the whole gameplay scenario of Olympus had gotten bogged down in the sands of Mars that I found a thought bugging away at the back of my mind, a thought that had—maddeningly—some connection with that word I couldn't recall, and I blurted out of nowhere into a sudden moment of silence: "Why don't you turn it around and set it back on Earth?"

Heads turned and looked at me with the characteristic vague fannish new-person-meeting expression that suggests they can't place who you are but can't quite bring themselves to ask because for all they know they might have met you before.

Joe blinked. Sean cocked his head. "Explain."

"You're basically trying to fit dark fantasy into an alternate history space-opera setting," I said. "It's one twist too many. That's why you keep tripping over yourselves. Like finding a rationale for swordplay. Why not just drop the space-opera angle, and rejig it all as basically dark fantasy? Turn the AI lab into, I don't know, a fucking magic castle or something, turn the desert into a mountain, make the rogue AI program the Holy Grail or whatever—just be honest about what you're doing, and everything falls into place, because you don't have to keep twisting it sideways to fit."

"Bor-ing," said Sean. "Sorry, been there, done that, got the chain mail."

He looked about to make sure this witticism was fully appreciated, got a well-deserved cuffing around the head from Janine, and went on: "There's any amount of games like that—we need something original."

"Well," I began, "why not make it have lots of players, each of whom starts off in the attacking horde—or the defending guard, if they want—and make it so the defenders have powers that get transferred to an attacker who kills them, and make it endlessly replayable by—"

"You mean make it an MMORPG?"

I had no idea what this meant, so I nodded firmly. "Yeah, and make it sort of cycle because when you get to the top of the game you have to turn around and defend yourself from the horde, which is of course all the new players—"

"*Genius!*" Sean shouted. "Joe, what d'you think?"

Joe looked at Sean then at me and blinked very rapidly.

"I'll have to go out and think about it over a smoke," he said.

"Code's doable," said Matt, the curly-haired cute one. "Lotta work though. I wouldn't have time for all the admin."

"Admin?" I said.

"Matt's the prettiest so we made him the secretary," Sean explained. (Janine jabbed a needle in his thigh.)

"Like, spreadsheets?" I persisted. (Excel being the one office skill I'd mastered.)

"You looking for a job, American lady?" Sean said, with a fake accent and a real leer.

"You bet I am, mister," I shot back.

"Can you handle Open Office?"

I thought he meant, you know, *an open-plan office*, so I said yes. After I'd worked my notice at Starbucks and started at Digital Damage I learned better, but the guys were kind about that.

The memory of that first evening at the Auld Hoose stayed in my mind after I said goodbye to Ross and Yuri. As I walked briskly along one side of St. Andrew's Square and down West Register Street and across Princes Street and up the bridges and down West Crosscauseway and around the corner and through the cloud of smokers around the entrance and into the Auld Hoose where Alec leaned at the bar with a hand on his pint and an eye on the door and a big range-finding rangy smile for me as I walked in I was thinking about that first time I'd been in that pub and had met the guys and that nagging half-caught memory of some word I had been reminded of by hearing Sean say salarium and that had slipped away like a fish through my fingers got . . .

—hooked, as Alec gave me a hug and whiskery kiss and set me back on my feet—

—and I smiled back and remembered where I'd seen that word and how its half-recollection had brought the Krassnian template for the new game from my childhood memories—

—because I had seen it in the Vrai glossary at the back of Avram Arbatov's book in Eugenie's apartment in Boston.

I stood grinning at Alec and I heard myself say, in a puzzled tone, "SIMULACRUM."

"What?" said Alec.

"Nothing," I said.

PART TWO: RENDERING

7. OVERTURE WITH STALIN ORGAN AND VOX *HUMANA*

1.

The stretch limo was the exact shade of lilac made by black-currant juice dripped into melting vanilla ice cream, and so was my dress. I stepped out of the one, hitched up the skirt of the other, and ducked under an upraised golf umbrella through a skirl of bagpipes and a smirr of rain into the doorway of the Orroco Pier hotel. As I clicked my high-heeled way across the wet pavement I distinctly heard a hard-bitten old woman's voice say, "Aye, yon's another poor soul getting married."

The wedding had been in the local Episcopal church, down by the shore of the Firth of Forth. A blink of sun had arrived just in time for the photos on the step and the later photos on the Binks—a grassy bank with a granite monument to Queen Margaret of Scotland—and on the quays of Queensferry Harbour. For both photo-ops we'd practically had to form an orderly queue, what with all the other bridal parties posing against the backdrop of the Forth Bridge and making the whole foreshore a fashion-shoot for kilts and satin meringues.

Most of the guests walked around the corner to the hotel, and I was quite willing to risk my heels on the cobblestones, but Suze insisted on squeezing every full contractual drop of juice out of the limos and dragged her groom, her parents, and me and the other bridesmaid back to the parking lot at the Binks. Just as well, because that was when the drizzle started. So, after a journey of one hundred yards and (no doubt) a mile-long contribution to the carbon footprint, here we all were.

And among the people who'd been invited for the reception but not the ceremony was Alec. I could see him, awkward in a suit, at the far side of the hotel lounge, beyond the dresses and hats and handshakes, smiling at me over all the headgear foliage with a look of surprise and delight, catching my eye.

I smiled back across ten metres of crowded room and dreaded speaking to him.

Two days earlier, my future had been bright and shiny and happy. I had been really looking forward to seeing Alec at Suze's wedding, on Saturday, August 9.

I sat curled up on the sofa in front of the television, watching the Olympic opening ceremony. Julie sat at the opposite end and Gail leaned against the middle on an arrangement of cushions.

All of us had reached the comfortable stage of having recovered enough from the previous night's hangover to be ready for a small G&T or glass of wine before bedtime. It was the night of Thursday, August 7. On Wednesday evening we'd all been out for a post-hen-party (Suze's, the previous weekend) getting-straight-back-in-the-saddle-after-a-fall-sort-of-thing session in the Brauhaus next door, and had slightly—well, to be honest, greatly—underestimated the potency of a succession of Belgian beers, particularly as chased by an interesting experimental range of special-offer brandies made from fruits other than grape.

Gail yawned. "Time for bed."

"Uh-huh," I said.

Julie, currently in charge of the zapper, flicked to text and brought up the news headlines. All Olympics, Beijing, fireworks, local news, and—

Georgia enclave town under fire.

"Hey!" I said. "Go to 116."

Heavy shelling and rocket fire is reported from the town of Tskhinvali, capital of the breakaway Georgian region of South Ossetia. . . .

"Uh-oh," I said. Or maybe: "Shit!"

Gail and Julie looked at me curiously. "What?"

"This is *huge*," I said.

"Why should—oh, is that the place where you were born?"

"It's close," I said. "Shit, shit, shit."

Facepalm.

"You're really upset about this," Julie said. "Uh—do you still have people there?"

I looked at my flatmates' concerned, puzzled faces and felt a bit bad that

I couldn't tell them the real reasons why I was worried, or indeed just how I knew that this was big news.

"No, no, nothing like that," I hastened to assure the girls. "It's just—I mean I do feel for the people there, even if they're . . ."

I stopped, confused: I'd been about to say "even if they're Ossetes." You can take the girl out of Krassnia but . . .

"Uh, I mean, even if there's fault on both sides, you know? But what I'm actually worried about is that this means that *right now* there's Russian and American troops on opposite sides of a *shooting war*."

"Americans?" Gail looked even more confused.

"Advisers in the Georgian army," I told her. "And of course the Russians have soldiers in South Ossetia."

"Oh, don't worry about that," said Julie. "Bush and . . . the Russian guy will sort it all out at the Olympics."

And with that we all wandered off to our beds. I sat up for a while looking at news on my laptop. Updates came in with frustrating slowness, even on the Russian TV online services. My last thought before I went to sleep was *I have a bad feeling about this*.

Not bad enough, as it turned out.

Up until that night in August, everything had gone quite smoothly. We'd finished the Krassnian version of Dark Britannia in the second week in June, bang on schedule. It was very much a beta release, lacking some of the finer points and details that we were rushing to include in the official version, but it was robust and playable. We had an automatic system set up to send updates and bug fixes to anyone who had the game on their system. Small Worlds had taken delivery of a set of master disks; Ross Stewart, in the only communication I'd had with him since that evening in Harvey Nick's (other than emailing him an account of the scariest day of my life), had sent me a secure email of thanks for unspecified services; Amanda had called to tell me she was pleased with how well I was doing these days; £50,000 had been deposited in Digital Damage's bank account; and we'd all had a £500 bonus and a meal in the Kampong Ah Lee Malaysian Delight; and the morning after that, Sean had cracked the whip over us about how much harder we were all going to have to work to meet Dark Britannia's release date in September.

Well, the lads all had to work harder, but (despite Sean's "Everybody drops! Everybody fights!") I didn't. I'd taken to going online to check out news from the Caucasus on sources like *Antiwar.com* and *the eXile* (and after that site got shut down in June, *the eXiled*) and Radio Free Europe and *Pravda.ru*. Krassnia came up rarely—a small demo here, an arrest there, the occasional word of concern about the fairness of the upcoming elections from Human Rights Watch or the International Crisis Group or the OSCE—but the escalating exchanges of fire between Georgian and South Ossetian forces had pushed their way far enough up the news agenda (of the sites I was following, I mean, not of the BBC, ITV, or CNN) for me not to be surprised this Thursday night, but not far enough for most people in the UK to have so much as heard of Ossetia.

Looking out for advance tremors of Krassnia's coming colour revolution was nowhere near the top of my agenda. I'd firewalled the Other Thing. The mysterious "Krassnian truth" intrigued rather than obsessed me—it was something I'd find out more about in due course, or that I'd someday have to regretfully file under "Forget." The same was true of finding out which (if either) of the two men I'd met in April was my real father. Neither of them had shown any interest in having a closer relationship with me, or indeed in finding out himself what that relationship was.

No, what I was interested in that summer was Alec. Alec, and the build-up to Suze's wedding.

Alec first. He and I had fallen for each other, and that was that. We no longer spent every minute of every weekend together, but that was because we didn't have to. And although the research grant for Alec's project was about to run out, he was seriously considering staying on in Scotland for at least another year rather than go back to New Zealand. Secretly, I was considering going to New Zealand—two of the girls I'd met at Starbucks and whose Facebook pages I still followed had gone out there (one of them returning home, the other checking out the place to see if she liked it enough to emigrate) and both of them wrote glowingly of the country and of how easy it was to find work, what with Australia's open-cast mining boom luring people out of middle-class jobs and into driving hundred-ton dump trucks and the like, thus creating vacancies for Kiwis, whose flight across the Tasman Sea to fill the missing places in nursing and teaching and programming and office admin in turn created vacancies for incomers to NZ.

Alec had introduced me to hill-walking, in the Pentlands—the hills south of Edinburgh, and not too challenging, but he'd insisted that I bought proper hill-walking boots, trousers, fleece, and waterproof jacket in Tiso's on Rose Street, and that I got the hang of using a Silva compass and an Ordnance Survey map. It was a better way to spend the out-of-bed parts of weekends than in shops and pubs, and it gave me a whole third circle of friends to add to the other two, of normal people and SF/F fans. And, by way of return, it had made sure Alec got included in these two circles.

I'd even managed to wangle Alec an invite to Suze's wedding reception. He was pleased. Without either of us saying anything, we both knew—well, *I* knew and I assumed Alec did—that one or other of us would announce some kind of decision about the next step of our future at this auspicious occasion.

Thursday, August 7, the morning after the bombardment of Tskhinvali, the front pages were all fireworks and acrobats.

My mind was all rockets and corpses. I walked briskly up Lauriston Place in sunshine on rain-shiny pavement and grabbed a banana and a *Grauniad* on the way. At the corner of Forrest Road I almost collided with the heart-breakingly pretty girl in the headscarf and long skirt who sold the *The Big Issue* there every Thursday and Friday.

"Oh! Sorry!" I said, fumbling with the paper and the banana while opening my bag for change.

"You go," she said. "Now."

"What?" I said.

Black eyebrows, untidied. Little wrinkles forming between them.

"Mr. Stewart see you at top of Chambers Street."

Eyebrow flash and quick glance in that direction.

"What?" I said again.

Deep wrinkles.

"You go! Now! Mr. Stewart waits to see you. Now!"

She thrust a copy of *The Big Issue* under my thumb, smiled, and stepped back, making quick, surreptitious little go-go-go flicks with her free hand.

I turned away, shaken, hoping she hadn't seen or hadn't taken in how I felt. This young woman had been spying on me! It felt like a personal betrayal of all the smiles and encouraging words and one-pound-fifty-pences I'd so graciously bestowed on her. A moment later I was ashamed of that thought. But I was still shaken. How many other unseen eyes did Ross Stewart have on me?

I hurried past our office door, almost turned then and there to go in, and then crossed carefully at the lights at the junction of Forrest Road and Bristo Place in front of the Traverse, waiting each time for the green man. Walked beside the smooth sandstone cliff of the National Museum and around the corner into Chambers Street. I glanced all around and saw no sign of Ross. I dawdled on a few paces towards the steps of the museum, and was overtaken by a tall man in blue one-piece overall and a pulled-down baseball cap.

"*There* you are," he said, as if I were half an hour late already.

It was Ross—I realised I'd looked right through him while he stood on the corner bowed over a red-top and clutching a Subway paper bag.

"This way," he continued, nodding diagonally across the street at a parked white van.

"Good morning to you, too," I said, walking faster to keep up. "I'm due to start five minutes ago, and if you think I'm just going to hop into—"

"Oh, don't be a child, Lucy," he said. "You know what this is about. There's no time to waste. The tanks are rolling *as we speak*."

"Tanks?"

Ross sighed theatrically as he stopped on the edge of the pavement to look both ways for a gap in the slow rush-hour traffic down Chambers Street.

"There's a huge Russian armoured column pouring through the Roki Tunnel. Beats me why the Georgians didn't think to blow up the exit, but there you go. The first engagements should be happening any minute now."

We dodged and skipped between bumpers.

"Holy shit!" I said as I leapt onto the opposite pavement. "What about our troops?"

"'Our'?" Ross shot me a puzzled look from under the peak of his cap. "Oh, the Americans. Don't worry, they're well out of it. Poolside in Tbilisi."

"Well, that's—"

"Yes, yes. Fuck knows how long that'll hold. Putin's royally pissed off."

He stopped by the side of the white van, unlocked the door, and hauled it open.

"Hop in," he said, with a wave of his paper bag.

I balked, not because the setup was so ludicrously reminiscent of what every parent warns every child against.

"Where are we going?"

"Nowhere," Ross snapped. "Not right now, anyway. The van's a good place to talk. Nobody looks twice at a van."

He walked around the front and climbed in on the driver's side. I hesitated a moment, then climbed to the passenger seat and slid the door shut after a couple of inadequate tugs. Ross was already pouring black coffee from a thermos into two unwashed mugs. He slid one across the windshield shelf and cracked his Subway bag and its contents in half and passed me one portion of what turned out to be pork sausages with Worcester sauce in a baguette.

"I've had breakfast," I said.

"Consider it an early lunch," Ross mumbled around a mouthful of crust. He barely looked at me—he had the *Daily Record* open across the steering wheel.

As the baguette actually smelled very appetising all of a sudden (my breakfast having been a quick muesli and already twenty minutes ago) I tore into it and sipped hot black coffee with some gusto.

"What's all this about?" I said, after we'd both settled to a politer rhythm of chomping. "Why all the—"

"Oh, yeah," said Ross, gaze still on the sports pages. "That. Sorry about the drama. Quick uptake re the gypsy lass, by the way. Good for you. Anyway." *Chomp chomp, slurp.* "Bottom line is, you have to go to Krassnia."

"*What?*" I cried, through a cloud of crumbs. "Why? When?"

"Krassnia," Ross repeated, as if clarifying. "Because, um . . . that'll take a bit of explaining. When . . . well, ASA fucking P. Now is good."

For a moment I had the crazy thought that he was about to turn the ignition key and we'd be off and I almost reached into my bag to check that I had my passport in it.

"Wait!" I said. "Uh, I mean—why do I have to go to Krassnia?"

As I asked the question I had a sinking feeling that I knew the answer. I wasn't far wrong.

"Lucy," Ross said, frowning over the racing results, "the Russians have just let the world, and more especially the US, know that they are not going to be messed about with in their own backyard. The tanks are rolling and we don't know where they'll stop. They could roll all the way to fucking Tbilisi and string that smarmy bastard Saakashvili up from a lamppost. I don't think they'll go quite that far, myself, but—"

He shrugged, and turned a page noisily.

"Thing is," he went on, "given that they're willing to do *this*, there is no fucking way they are going to sit idly by and watch a US-sponsored colour revolution take out one of their client statelets in Georgia. So, come September and assuming the whole fucking situation hasn't gone tits-up by then and we aren't in a guns of August scenario in which case all bets are off . . . we can expect the Maple Revolution to face a severe crackdown from the local security forces and/or Russian tanks on the streets of Krasnod. In terms of what's likely to be going on by then even if the worst doesn't happen, it'll be a sideshow to Ossetia and Abkhazia."

"Abkhazia?" I hadn't yet heard anything about that region.

"Yeah, they're moving there too. Naval forces, Kodori Gorge, you name it."

"So . . ." I said. "I guess the, uh, Agency is just gonna have to call the revolution off, right?"

Ross spluttered coffee.

"Call it off? The CIA couldn't even if it wanted to—which I doubt it does, given the chance to poke another sharp stick in Putin's eye, regardless of whether they expect the regime to give way. It's not like blood on the streets isn't a win, in terms of making the Russians look bad. But in any case . . ." He sighed, this time not theatrically but from the bottom of his chest. "It's unstoppable. We've got the Liberal Democrats, the unions, the NGOs, some fucking bunch of Enver Hoxha idolators—fuck knows where *they* crawled out from— all wound up and agitating their little hearts out about how the elections are going to be rigged or cancelled by the Social Democrats."

"Did the game thing work?" I asked, momentarily diverted from my own worries.

"Did it ever fucking work," said Ross. "It's not just turned out to be a safe space for organising, the whole legend and folklore stuff is bleeding into the nationalist mood on the streets. I've been sent mobile-phone pics of posters with what's-his-face, the once and future hero guy—"

"Duram," I said.

"Yeah, that's the one." Ross pulled an iPhone out of his pocket and thumbed through pictures. "Look."

Sunny street, dusty trees, low-rise apartment buildings; couple dozen young people, possibly students, holding up A4 sheets, most with black-printed slogans in Krassnian and six with a blocky woodcut-type portrait of a bearded barbarian in a helmet with a nosepiece—

"Hey!" I said. "That's our *cover art*!"

(Joe had been quite proud of it. He'd based it on a photo, from someone's holiday-snaps Flickr set, of the statue of Duram in Krasnod's main square.)

Ross took back the phone. He drained his mug and set it down above the dash.

"So you see why you have to go to Krassnia," he said.

"I don't see anything of the kind!" I said, though as I've mentioned I had a shrewd suspicion. Ross just looked at me.

"You do see," he said. "But if you insist . . ."

He peered out and upward through the windshield for a moment, as if checking the sky, and then leaned back shaking his head.

"Christ," he said. "I'm getting fucking paranoid about all this. I keep thinking about *camera drones* . . ."

He closed his eyes for a moment and shook his head again.

"All right," he said. "Time to level with you, Lucy—"

"Can I just say that I instantly distrust someone who says that?"

Ross laughed. "So would I. But hear me out. Yuri told you what this thing is about, right? Not democracy, not the fucking pipeline, not even sticking it to the Russians. It's about getting our hands on—or to begin with, getting a *look* at—whatever's up there on Mount Krasny."

"'The secret of the Vrai,'" I said, mimicking Yuri's accent.

"Please don't use that phrase," Ross said. "But yes, that's what this is about. The idea was, we get a friendly regime in place, one that isn't watched over by the RSB—a security apparat inherited from Soviet times and still joined at the hip to the Russian FSB, who are basically still the same bloody chekists, the same fucking institution as the KBG and the NKVD and the OGPU and all the way back to the Cheka, and whose power—apart from anything else—is pretty blatantly flaunted by a former dyed-in-the-wool

KGB man's having been president and now prime minister of Russia. Now, the top people in the Krassnian RSB may or may not know what the secret is, but they do know that there's something very dangerous there and that it has to be *kept* secret—the Zone is still in place, still guarded."

"Guarded?" I said. "Who by?"

"A small contingent of former MVD border troops. The story is that there's an area of radioactive contamination, and for all I know everyone involved believes that. It might even be true. Anyway, uh . . . Well. Now what the plan was, was that after the Maple Revolution the new regime— which, in the nature of the case, will include certain people who are, let's say, *obliged* to the Agency—would be willing to let us send someone in to have a look. Someone who has enough Vrai blood to be safe, and who is totally and completely reliably one of us. "That person"—he looked away for a moment, as though embarrassed, as he damn well should have been—"is you."

Like I said, the suspicion that this was the case had begun to darken my mind, but having the suspicion confirmed still took my breath away. And what came rushing in, like the air after I'd got my breath back, was fury.

"How long have you planned this? And who's 'us'? And just when were you figuring on *telling* me?"

"Your mother and I—"

"My *mother*?" I cried. "*She* was in on it? Oh, fuck! This is just so, so sick."

Sick was how I felt. It was as if the Other Thing had all along been lurking right in my own family, and was now right here in the cab of the lorry, somewhere behind Ross's shoulder. I pulled away, huddling against the door. I knew I was scowling at Ross with the exact outraged sulky expression of the Cheerleader in *Heroes* confronting the latest lie or betrayal from Horn-Rimmed Glasses Guy.

"Your mother and I," Ross repeated, rolling over my outcry like a tank over plasterboard, "agreed to a request to this effect a long time ago."

"How long ago?"

Again with the looking away. "A few years ago."

"What? When I was just—"

"Yeah, yeah, when you were just an annoying teenager."

"Wait, wait, wait! A request? From the CIA?"

"Well, not exactly," said Ross. "From . . . another agency of the US government. One that has . . . well, let's just say one that has a legitimate and pressing interest in unusual phenomena with military potential, even if the phenomenon is just, uh, an anomalous deposit of radioactive ore. Especially a phenomenon that's currently in the Russian near abroad, and that Russia can keep us from finding out anything about, and that Russia might someday figure out a way to find out about. And maybe use, you know? I mean, if this thing is as powerful or as significant as *some* of the stories imply, like, say, a stargate as Yuri sometimes thinks, then—it's the sort of thing you do *not* want to risk the other guy getting his hands on first. So the idea came up of using a US citizen who has enough Vrai blood—or the right genes, to state the case properly—to go in and have a look. And you were the only one who fitted the bill. Believe me, they checked. There are only a handful of Krassnian US citizens, and none of them have both Vrai ancestry and political reliability. You're unique. Of course the actual mechanics of the insertion hadn't been decided then. That was only finalised—we thought—when the Maple Revolution was pencilled in."

"'The actual mechanics of the insertion!'" I said, this time in jeering mimicry of Ross. "Gee, thanks. Why can't Amanda do it? She fits the spec just as well as I do, or better."

"She's far too well known and traceable to get in, even with a false ID. You aren't."

"Well," I said, "maybe I would have done what you want, if you'd asked nicely. But what's the urgency of doing it now?"

"You mean, doing it before the Russians clamp their grip on all of Georgia's breakaway border provinces?" said Ross. "I would have thought that's—"

"No, no," I said. "I get *that*. But what I don't understand—well, there's several things I don't understand. You say the Russians might find out what's there, but they've had over half a century to come up with something and they haven't yet? Why not? And why don't *they* just send in some loyal person with this mysterious Vrai gene or blood or magic red hair or whatever the fuck it is? And why don't you, I mean our side, send in, I don't know, a drone or something?"

"That last one's easily answered," said Ross. "There are no such drones as can fly into a narrow ravine and report back, especially without being spotted."

"There's those bomb-disposal robots they use in Iraq—"

"Which need nearby real-time operators. No, I think you slightly over-estimate the state of the art in robotics. As for why the Russians haven't tried it—who says they haven't? Those kids who were tested along with you—thanks for telling me about that, by the way, very interesting—may have been kept track of by the FSB. Who knows? Or if research was done on the genetics of the thing, maybe someone has found what the gene does and found a way to replicate its function. Or perhaps the Russian army can send in a camera on a crawler. Again, who knows? Point is, whether or not any of these things might happen in the future, or may have already happened, the next few weeks may be our last chance to get someone in to have a look before the region comes under complete Russian control. Right?"

"Uh-huh."

"So you see why you have to go to Krassnia," Ross repeated, by way of conclusion.

All I could see was the Other Thing like a black cloud and in front of it Ross's patient, perseverant face, that of a middle-aged man who still had the callow guile and crass insensitivity of the youth whose diaries I'd read. Someone who thought that all you needed to do to persuade was to explain. I could feel myself getting worn down by him already, leaving aside the obvious big objections in principle and coming up with a couple of small ones in implementation, like a TV talking head interviewing a politician.

"How do you know all this stuff about Vrai blood or genes making it safe to go there isn't just nonsense?"

"We don't, really," said Ross. "Apart from the legends and rumours being so damn consistent on this very point, no matter how much they're contradictory on others."

I was not reassured, but I let that go and moved to my next item.

"And how would I—anyone who did go in, I mean—know the way to the secret place? Yuri said there might be no one left alive who can act as a guide."

Ross wiped his greasy fingertips unsatisfactorily on shiny paper, and his lips on the back of his hand.

"Now, there we do have something to go on," he said, cheerfully. "We know the route—well, the likely route. Your mother worked it out . . . some years ago, after I sent her copies of Arbatov's and Beryozkin's confessions. You know, where Arbatov mentions having alluded to the Vrai secret? And how Beryozkin confirms this?"

"Yes," I said.

"Amanda looked again at Arbatov's book, *Life and Legends of the Krassnar*. She looked for references to places, landmarks, and directions, and pencilled them all on a map. The marks were, well, all over the map until she narrowed her search down to references that seemed a bit more specific than the context called for, or than she would expect in a folktale of a given type, or that used a later form of the dialect than the body of the tale, and so on—lots of subtle clues, difficult for anyone but an expert like herself to spot. And when she mapped *them*—aha!"

Ross flung out a hand.

"She found a route?" I asked, disbelieving.

"Yes," said Ross. "A path right up the side of the mountain, to a deep, narrow ravine."

"Just like in that story Yuri heard?"

"Mmh-hmh," Ross nodded. "Exciting, eh?"

"Yes," I admitted.

Something nagged me from the back of my mind. "Uh, was this before or after she wrote *The Krassniad*?"

"*The Krassniad*?" Ross frowned. "That came out when?"

"'94 or '95," I said.

"Oh!" Ross said, brow clearing. "It was after that. Well after."

"Shit!" I said.

"What?"

"Have you read it?"

"Glanced at it," said Ross. "Not my horn of mead, so to speak. Why?"

"*The Krassniad*'s littered with details about places. I thought it was, like, local colour. Like, you know, every time we meet a new warrior we get his father and grandfather's name and his mother's nickname? Same with places, including places along the way Duram and his men took up to the Vrai fastness. The cave of the magic inscription, the spells, yeah?"

"I'll take your word for it," said Ross. "What are you—?" His eyebrows shot up. "Wait—you think the route's spelled out for all to see in the fucking *Krassniad*?"

"There's *a* route," I said. "I don't know if it's the right one, obviously."

"Probably not," said Ross, sounding unsure of himself. "I mean, this was written before Amanda studied Arbatov's book with this in mind."

"Yeah," I said. "But not before she'd spent years studying it in depth, checking every source and footnote and gathering even more Krassnian folklore in her fieldwork. And if some of these details were the sort of thing that she could pick out as salient, maybe even without realising it . . ."

"I suppose," said Ross. "Anyhow, water over the dam now, eh? Book's out of print, and it was always banned in Krassnia. . . ."

"Banned, huh? And that means no one read it? Come on! You were a book smuggler!"

"So?" Ross shrugged. "A few copies may have circulated. A lot of copies, even. It's hardly a bestseller—I don't think it's even been pirated."

"Maybe not," I said. "But I know something that has been. The game."

"The game? Why would that—oh, Jesus H fucking Christ, you didn't! Did you?"

"Of course I did," I said. "I based the map in the game on *The Krassniad*. What else would I have based it on?"

Ross looked back hard at me and said: "So you see why you have to go to Krassnia."

"All right," I said. Maybe he really had worn me down. "All right. But—"

"Tomorrow," said Ross.

"No *way*!" I yelled. "I have a wedding to go to."

"A *wedding*?" Ross sounded like he didn't believe anyone would think that was important. It was like I'd said "a picnic."

"I'm a bridesmaid," I said.

"Well, in that case . . ." He frowned, considering. "We can delay until Sunday."

I seriously thought he was joking. Then I saw he wasn't.

"And how d'you expect me to get to Krassnia?"

"In one of my artics," he said.

"Artics?"

"Container trucks."

I stared at him. "*Container trucks?* What the fuck's wrong with flying? There must still be flights in to Batumi, or even just to Istanbul, it'd still be quicker than a truck."

Ross shook his head. "Even without the likelihood that the airspace around Georgia might be a wee bit contested, or the airports closed, or whatever . . . I don't trust flying for this kind of thing. Too controlled. You're in a plane, you get clocked, end of story. Nowhere to run. Whereas in a lorry . . ." He smiled into the middle distance. "You have options, know what I mean?"

"And how long will I be away?"

"Allow a week and a half to get there, a few days to reach the place—call it a fortnight, and double that for complications." He shrugged. "Allow a month, tops. Any longer we're into September, and one way or another the place will have blown by then anyway."

"What about getting back?"

"Oh, the exit's easy enough," he said. "You can fly out, maybe not from Georgia but at least from Turkey."

He didn't sound like he'd given this aspect of the matter much thought. I gave him a suspicious look.

"I *am* supposed to get out, right? To come back? That is part of the plan, yeah?"

To my surprise, he didn't brush off my misgivings. He looked me straight in the eye.

"Lucy," he said, "I know what I'm asking of you. I'm not going to try to kid you that it's not dangerous. Leaving aside the little problem of the ex-MVD guys patrolling the mountainside, whatever is in the secret place it's something bloody dangerous. You heard Yuri's story about 1952, right?"

"Uh-huh."

"OK. Whatever is there, just seeing a film of it left two of the scariest guys who ever walked the earth shaking in their boots. So . . ."

"It didn't scare the Vrai," I said.

I felt a strange thrill of pride in these mysterious ancestors of mine, and I added: "And it doesn't scare me."

Ross slapped my knee. "That's the spirit!"

But as soon as I'd somehow talked my way into saying I was brave enough to face something that had made Stalin and Beria quail, a more sensible part of my brain popped up with practical objections.

"What about my *job?*"

"Are you the only person in the whole wide world who can do your job?"

"Well, not exactly—"

"Right then," he said. "You're the only person in the whole wide world who can do *this* job."

"But what about notice, and—"

Ross leaned across me and slid the door open.

"You'll sort something out," he said.

It sounded the same whether it was a prediction or an instruction. I made to leave.

"Oh, and do something about your hair," he said.

"What?"

He waved a hand above his head. "The colour. For the passport photo."

I was down on the street again, looking up. He was still leaning over, holding the door handle.

"I *have* a passport," I said. "In fact, I have two."

"You'll need another."

"How do I—"

"I'll be in touch," he said.

The door slid shut.

2.

I tucked my lilac satin clutch bag under my left elbow, wedged the stem of my champagne flute between two spare fingers of the hand already holding a side plate of cucumber-and-tuna white bread triangles and tikka chicken wings, and with the lilac-polished fingernails of the other hand raked some flakes of sausage-roll pastry out of Alec's beard.

"Thanksh," he said, around a mouthful of aforesaid sausage roll. He washed it down with a swallow of beer. "Mmm. Well."

He looked around the reception-crowded lounge bar, then back at me. "You look absolutely fantastic, Lucy," he told me, for the third time.

"Thank you," I said. I risked a nibble of tikka, kissed the sticky sauce off my fingertips, reshuffled the plate and glass. "Uh, Alec—"

"Yeah," he said. "Music is a bit loud in here."

"What?"

He tipped his head to indicate the balcony. I threaded after him as he sidled out. The MC was tooling up to bully everyone into another complicated Scottish dance. The balcony was hardly less crowded than the room, but Alec had found a spare white-enamel wobbly round table in the corner. No seats, but it gave me somewhere to put down my plate and bag. Below us, smokers in suits or kilts or long dresses stood or teetered on wet pebbles in the lowering sun. Little white triangular sails scudded on the Firth. A long train rumbled over the bridge.

"So," I said, around nibbling on a fishy sail of damp bread, "you'll admit now that modern wedding dresses look good?"

"Oh, sure," said Alec. "Suze is beautiful." He gulped beer. "You too," he added.

"I know," I said, posing (palm upraised at raised shoulder, one heel kicked up) though a fourth reminder seemed a little excessive. Another awkward silence. This was getting like our first conversation, at Suze's flat-warming all those months ago.

"Uh, Alec—"

"One, two, three BACK, now TURN your partner THREE times ending with your LEFT arms CROSSED," the MC boomed.

"Oh, fuck," said Alec. He put down his pint and made his way to the balcony's double-glazed patio door and slid it shut, returning to our table in a spatter of applause. He brushed pastry flakes and grease from his fingers and dipped into his suit jacket's inside pocket, from whence he withdrew a long white envelope.

"Uh, Lucy," he said, "this is, uh, something I wanted to give you here, I mean don't take it the wrong . . . Anyway. Here it is."

With that he handed me the envelope. I gave him the quizzical eye-brow—for a heart-sinking moment I'd thought he was about to give me a "Dear John" letter, but his expression was more worried-but-eager-to-please than expecting-a-goodkicking—and thumb-nailed the envelope open. What was inside was leaves and leaves of flimsy and carbon-copy and took me a moment to figure out: an Air New Zealand open return ticket. I didn't know how much the New Zealand dollar was in pounds but there was an eye-watering four-digit number of them printed in a box at the bottom corner.

I looked up, blinking. "Alec," I said. "You shouldn't'—I flung my arms around his neck—"have."

"Shouldn't at *all*," I added, disengaging arms and lips about a minute later. "This is crazy. This is like—a car, or your tuition, or—I don't know."

Alec shifted and shrugged. "I can afford it. My folks own a *sheep farm*."

He said this like it was *oil well*.

"All the same," I said.

"The thing is," Alec said, looking even more awkward, "I'm going back."

He must have mistaken my stunned expression for incomprehension. "To NZ," he explained.

"But—"

"I'm sorry, Lucy, it's just—I'm homesick, I miss NZ a lot and—uh, well, like I said I can afford that ticket but I can't afford another year in Scotland, no way, and my folks deserve a bit of help on the farm to cover my studies, the old man's getting on a bit, and I love you and I want you to come out to, uh, like be with me—when you can, I mean, but that's why it's an open return so, what I mean is, no pressure."

I stood listening to this babbling stream of talk with my mouth open.

"Wait, wait, wait," I said. "When are you going?"

"Next Friday," he said.

"Oh," I said, with a lift-shaft feeling in the pit of my stomach. "Like that."

"Well, I already had that flight booked," he said. "All along. The only question was whether to postpone it. So." Big smile. "The money I saved from not taking the penalty for that went straight to your open ticket."

"Alec," I said, "I love you too, but . . . well, this is all a bit . . . fast."

He took his pipe from his pocket, turned it over several times in his hands, and rattled the stem between his teeth.

"Like I said. No pressure."

"Jeez," I said. "No pressure."

I slithered the flimsies and carbons back into the envelope, and thumbed the tacky strips to an inadequate reseal. My name was written on the front, in nerdy Rotring tech-pen ink, the lines all the same width like in a diagram.

I could just see Alec, labouring for a minute or two over the lettering, tongue-tip protruding, like a small boy inking his first Valentine card. SWALK. This wasn't a goodbye note, as I'd momentarily feared—it was practically a marriage proposal.

"Oh, Alec," I said. "You're wonderful."

He smiled back in such a relieved way that I hugged and kissed him all over again.

I disengaged, still holding the envelope. I didn't want to fold it in half, so I curved it around the inside of one end of the clutch bag, and clicked the clasp shut.

"There's something I want to tell you, too," I said.

"Yes?" He looked nervous again.

"I'm not pregnant or anything," I assured him.

"Oh," he said. "Good."

"Let's step down on the shore," I said. "I can see you want to light that pipe."

Alec laughed, in a caught-out way. "OK."

He went to the foot of the steps and held out a hand to help me down. With my other arm I did the elbow thing with the clutch bag and the hem-hitch with the hand, and descended step by step. On the shore (or beach, as I seemed to recall its being grandly called in the ads) I was able to hold the purse in one hand and the loose fistful of fabric in the other, and thus keep my balance while finding places to plant a heel that weren't sand, slippery stone, or seaweed. We didn't go far. Alec crunched along in his sensible black boots (polished, I'd noted, as a gesture to the occasion) and then turned about and lit his pipe while waiting for me to catch up.

I located two adjacent patches of acceptable ground to put my feet on and stood pigeon-toed on them, facing Alec while holding my purse in my crossed hands in front of me. I must have been trying for a sort of girlish guilty-but-innocent owning-up look, but from the way Alec eyed me, wary and puzzled even through his first puffs on the pipe, it didn't seem to be working.

"So," he said. "What do you have to tell me?"

"I have to go away," I said, as if confessing to something.

"Away? Where?"

"Ah—" I hadn't thought this through. It was on the tip of my tongue to lie; to invent some elderly great-aunt in the South of France or a girlfriend with a sudden spare holiday ticket to the Caribbean; but I couldn't.

"I can't say," I blurted.

"What?"

"I just can't," I said, digging myself in deeper and wishing fervently I'd had the wit and guts to lie a second ago.

"When?" he said.

"Tomorrow."

Alec exaggerated a blink. "That's sudden. Everything all right?"

"Oh, sure," I said. "Everything's fine."

"And when are you coming back?"

I got lipstick from my lower lip on my upper teeth. I could taste it.

"I don't know."

"You don't know? What sort of—?" He cocked his head, narrowing his eyes against the sun. "Is this some . . . confidential business trip or something?"

"Something like that, yeah."

"You got some, what is it, *ballpark figure*? Days? Weeks?"

"No idea," I said.

Alec ducked his head, shaded his eyes and peered all around, then leaned forward, hand cupped to a conspiratorial ear. "Come on. You can tell me. Nobody's listening."

"I can't," I said, miserably. "Sorry, Alec."

He straightened up.

"That's a bit—look, is it something to do with your work?"

I shook my head, then temporised. "Sort of."

I found myself blushing, not because this wasn't true (it was, though just as evasive as it sounded), but because mention of work brought back a cascade of uncomfortable memories of Sean criticising me at some length and depth and volume in the office the previous day, basically losing it—a phrase that could also be applied to my current employment status.

Alec of course saw the blush and interpreted it the obvious way.

"Are you in some kind of trouble?"

"What's this, twenty questions?"

"Hey!" He sounded stung. "No, just wondering if it's anything I can help with."

"Oh!" I said, relieved. "No, it isn't."

"And you don't trust me enough to tell me about it?"

"It's not like that!"

"What is it like, then? Hey, come on, Lucy."

He stepped closer. Rough-skinned palm gentle on my bare shoulder, moving slowly. I felt tiny, tickly vibrations from the chiffon frill snagging on the hairs on the back of his hand.

"Tell me."

I so wanted to tell him everything, to throw on him the burden of the Other Thing, but the thought of that made me physically jolt, and Alec withdrew his hand, looking hurt.

"I do want to," I said. "But I can't. I just can't."

"Why the hell not?" he said. "I don't mean to pry, or anything, but—" He rubbed his hand backward across the top of his hair. "It's nothing personal, right?"

"No," I said. "It's not fucking personal."

Alec took a step back. Shells crunched. Somebody opened the door on the balcony and a jaunty fiddly tune skipped out, then got slammed again.

"I don't get it," Alec said. "It's not really business, it's not personal, and you can't tell me anything about it, not even how long you're going to be away."

"I don't know how long," I said.

"If you've joined the bloody army and you're flying out to Afghanistan, now might be a good time to tell me," he said.

"Well . . ."

"Well, what?"

"It's sort of like that. More like that than the other things."

"Jesus!" Alec stooped, and tapped out the contents of his pipe on a stone, then straightened up, not taking his eyes off me all the while. "You are messing with my head, girl."

He said this in a forced, light tone I'd seldom heard in his voice before, and never in anything addressed to me. The few times I'd heard it, it had meant he was really angry and not showing it, like with bad service or a railway fuck-up.

"That's not what I meant," I said, "to do."

"OK," he said. "OK." He let out a long sigh. "So I won't be seeing you again before I go?"

In all this fraught conversation I'd almost forgotten he was leaving too, in a week. I caught myself doing that annoying nerdy visible wheels-turning-over mental calculation, just blatantly standing there thinking about things instead of answering right off the bat like normal people, and closed my eyes and gave my head a little shake, to stop it.

"No," I said.

He looked out at the Firth for a moment, then back at me, and smiled. "Well," he said, "there's always tonight."

I'll say this for guys: they'll forgive a lot if there's sex in prospect.

"I'm sorry," I said. "I can't."

"Can't what?"

"Have you over tonight. I've got a million and one things to do, really late, and get up really early, and—oh shit! I have to do my *hair*."

He just looked at me.

"That is so fucking lame, Lucy," he said. "You'll have to learn to do better than that."

"What do you mean?"

"Take it any way you want," he said. "Oh well. Enjoy the rest of the evening."

"Wait, what—"

He leaned forward, caught my shoulders, and kissed my forehead, quickly.

"See you in New Zealand," he said. "If that's what you want. I don't know if you do anymore."

And with that he turned and ran across the sand and shingle.

"Alec!" I cried.

I took a couple of paces after him and sank a heel into sand. By the time I'd extricated it he was gone, up a slipway on to the pier and around a corner to the alleyway that led to the street.

I dithered for a moment, then opened my purse and took my iPhone out. I almost dropped it as I thumbed his number. After a couple of rings I got the message service.

Fuck, fuck, fuck.

Asshole.

I tramped back across the stepping-pebbles and up to the balcony in very bad dudgeon indeed.

3.

"Lie like a rug," Ross advised me.

I looked at him across the cab. We were hurtling down the A1 in a big container-truck. I'd just poured out my troubles to him.

"What?" I was getting tired of hearing myself say that.

"That's what you gotta do, in this business," he said, overtaking a Sunday driver as if crushing a bug underfoot. "Lie like a rug. To your nearest and dearest. First time I went to the East, I phoned my mother as usual on the Saturday evening from some pit-stop outside Dortmund and nearly told her where I was going, and mangled it at the last second to 'East Anglia.' I'd never lied to her before." He laughed. "The guilt wears off with practice. Didn't your mother ever tell you that?"

"No," I said. "I guess because she was too busy lying like a rug to me."

"Didn't you get it?" said Ross. "She was teaching by example."

I had to laugh.

This is how I'd got there.

After a few more futile attempts to contact Alec on his turned-off mobile, including leaving a couple of weepy messages on the answering service, I went to the Ladies, blew my nose, dried my eyes, splashed my face, reapplied makeup, and marched out, making a bold face on it. I joined in the Scottish country dances, and bopped to the disco beat when these mercifully stopped, and joined hands and sang "Auld Lang Syne" about ten o'clock, drank too many flutes of cava and tall glasses of vodka and cranberry juice, and did all the bridesmaidy things for Suze and saw the newlyweds off and fell into a black cab and slept all the way from South Queensferry to Lauriston Place and fell out of it and gave the driver thirty quid or so in a completely wasted (in both senses) grand gesture and toppled up the stairs to the flat.

That was about midnight.

I woke with a thumping headache and a full bladder and the clock at 03:25, wondered why (a) I was sleeping on top of the duvet with the light on and (b) where I'd got this long posh pale lilac nightie. For a blissful but brief moment I snuggled into a warm thought that maybe Alec had bought it for me and by the way where was he?

Memory restore.

Enter panic mode.

It was kind of like the *fuck fuck fuckitty fuck* scene at the opening of *Four Weddings and a Funeral*, except satanically played in reverse: I had to scramble out of my bridesmaid dress and shoes and jewellery and makeup and underwear and (via a shower and a hair-dying episode involving a stolen bottle of Julie's Clairol, for which I left a guilty fiver, and a twenty-minute wait with wet hair, and another shower and an impatient session with Gail's hair-dryer) into jeans and Kickers and top and the soft leather jacket, and, in the various interludes of that, stuff a week's worth of casual wear and one pair of oxblood pixie boots and my walking boots and trousers and fleece and waterproof and compass and a week's supply of indiscriminate knickers and bras and paperbacks and toiletries into a big black bag with a pair of carrying handles and a shoulder strap; empty the contents of the lilac satin purse into my everyday mini-backpack, remembering (as instructed) to pack my US and UK passports, and to leave behind my laptop; while the red numbers on the clock incremented ever closer to 05:15, the time for leaving the flat on the timetable so very helpfully texted to me by Ross Stewart on Friday evening.

At 05:05, as per timetable, I called a minicab on a number included in Ross's text. At 05:10 I scribbled a note claiming a family emergency for Julie and Gail, clipped it to a couple of fifties to cover my share of next month's rent, and left it weighted with a dirty coffee mug on the breakfast table. I gave a reproachful Hiro a tearful hug, hoisted the black bag, hastily rethought my reading requirements, dumped a stack of fantasy and space-opera paperback bricks, remembered to pick up my everyday mini-backpack in the nick of time, and saw myself out.

I waited at the corner beside the Brauhaus. In the early August morning my mood brightened with the sky. After five minutes a minicab pulled up, with the right phone number on its door and nothing else to recommend it. I climbed over my misgivings, and into the backseat.

"Waverley?" said the driver, facing straight ahead.

"Yes, please."

At Waverley I lugged the bag to the photo booth and got a passport photo. As the damp quadruple picture dried in my fingers I waited for the colour of my hair to match that of the supermodel's on the Clairol carton. This didn't happen.

I rode the shiny steel escalator to the top of the station, trudged up the steps to Princes Street, and caught a bus to Leith and then another bus out towards Seafield. At a long mile or so of carpet emporia and car dealerships I spotted my stop, scrambled off, and waited by the roadside.

A surprising number of heavy trucks rumbled by. Gulls cried, on the same wind that rearranged my hair. Steel rollers rattled up at the dealership doorways. A container truck passed me, honked, and pulled in just past the bus stop, emergency lights flashing. I stared at it for a moment, then ran to the cab as the passenger-side door swung open and impatient horns sounded behind me.

"You look like shit," Ross told me.

If he'd looked different in his white van man gear, he looked different yet again now, in plaid shirt, padded olive-green gillet, and aviator shades; his swept-back, gentlemanly grey hair gone, buzzcut to a five-millimetre fuzz; gold sovereign ring and weighty gold neck chain; hands and fingernails and knuckle-wrinkles like he'd worked for decades with wet cement. He took my big bag and slung it behind the seats.

"You didn't say you'd be the driver," I said, buckling in. "Isn't that a bit risky?"

"Not half as risky as sending Amanda's little girl across Europe with another driver," he said, as he went through the mirror, signal, obscene gesture out the window, manoeuvre routine.

"You can't trust your drivers?" I asked.

"I don't mean risky to you," he said. "Risky to me."

"Ah."

"Got your passport pics?"

I patted my jacket above the deep inside pocket. "Yes."

He glanced sideways.

"You look like shit," he said again. "That's good, by the way. What happened?"

So I told him.

I dozed, to wake with a jolt to a glimpse of a sign for Newcastle.

Ross glanced sideways. "Coffee?"

"And breakfast."

"Rough night you must have had."

"Don't remind me."

Ross swung the big rig off the motorway an exit or two later and stopped at a service station.

I made to get out.

"A mo," Ross said. "Your passport photos."

I handed them over. Ross snipped them apart with Swiss Army knife scissors, and fished a trucking trade mag from the door pocket.

"Got a black ballpoint pen?"

I rummaged a Fisher space-pen bullet from the depths of my mini-backpack.

"Sign on the back of two of them," Ross said, passing me the photos and the mag to lean on. "Use the name 'Emma Taylor.'"

"'Emma Taylor'?"

"T-A-Y," Ross confirmed.

"Doesn't sound like me," I said.

He gave me a look.

"That," he said, "is what we old hands in the business refer to by the technical term: The. Fucking. Point."

"Oh!" I said. "I see."

I scribbled on the back of the mag to dislodge the inevitable unused space-pen initial blob, and awkwardly signed the unfamiliar name in the square inches of white card. When I'd finished, Ross slid the signed and unsigned photos inside the mag.

Before we reached the cafeteria Ross led me up some stairs and across the bridge to the mirror-image building on the other side.

"Going for a slash," he said, and disappeared into the Gents. He didn't have the mag in his hand when he came out. He wandered into the W H Smith's and bought a Sunday middle-class tabloid. The front page showed a middle-aged, smoke-blackened woman keening in helpless grief, arms out, amid ruins. The headline read: "Victim of the Pipeline War." In the queue Ross scanned the main section, and—as if absentmindedly—passed me the women's glossy supplement.

We got our trays—coffee and chocolate croissant for me, black tea and bacon roll for him—and sat down at a table near the counter queue. Ross ate and drank while reading the paper as if decoding hidden messages. Seething a little, I peoplewatched in between turning over pages of winter fashion and autumn makeup and yummy mummies' problems. I was halfway down my coffee when I noticed the trucking mag lying on the table at Ross's elbow. A moment later it had vanished inside Ross's Sunday paper as he folded pages back. When we'd finished Ross wiped his mouth with a paper napkin and said under it: "Would you mind sticking the papers in your bag?"

I did so as Ross gathered our empties and litter onto the trays. The bulk and breadth was such that the zips wouldn't close all the way, so the papers and mag stuck half out and I had to carry the lot in my hands. Back we went, across the bridge to the truck.

"That wasn't exactly an inconspicuous way of carrying it," I complained, as I clambered in.

"The point was so nothing fell out," said Ross. "Have a look in the mag."

I pulled out the wodge of newsprint and rummaged out the trucking magazine. Inside were a passport and an Edinburgh University student ID card, both in the name of Emma Taylor and with my photo, not stuck on but reproduced and laminated over. The passport gave me a different 1985 birthday and a 2005 holiday in Lanzarote.

"Good, eh?"

"How the fuck?" I said.

Ross laid a finger to his nose.

"What about the passport number?" I asked. "Don't they scan for numbers?"

"Taken care of," said Ross. "Don't ask."

So I didn't.

"And you've got your real passports?"

I took them from the bag.

"Anything else to identify you?"

I rummaged out the little plastic wallet with my credit and debit cards, and a pink Moleskine notebook with my name and address on the front page.

Ross leaned back and reached up to an open, hollow space in the top of the cab, just behind the sunshade. He tugged out a thin, rubber-buffered aluminium case, about the size of a thick hardback book, like a handbag-version Samsonite. He twiddled a combination lock, raised the lid a couple of inches, took my passports and cards and notebook, and slid them inside. Then he clicked the case shut, spun the lock wheels, and stashed the case somewhere in the space behind the seats—I guessed it was in the floor, but the bulk of his body concealed from me the exact location.

"Oh, and here's a Visa and a Switch," said Ross, sitting back in the seat and taking an envelope from his inside pocket. "Name of Emma Taylor. PINs included. Try and get the signature right."

I didn't ask about that, either. I did ask about what we were going to do when we got to Krasnod.

"Better you don't know the details until we get there," said Ross. "On the possibility that we don't get there, and you get, ah, asked."

I shivered. "If that happens, I'll need *something* to say."

"Say we were going to meet an old man, whose name and address you don't know, and that he lives outside of town." Ross chuckled grimly. "That'll narrow it down."

After that the journey is something of a blur in my memory, or rather a series of blurs. We travelled through England, the Channel Tunnel, Belgium, Germany, Austria, Slovenia, Croatia, Serbia, and Bulgaria to Turkey. I know that because the Emma Taylor passport has the stamps. Several times, we changed containers. The final load, hauled along the coastal roads over two days from Istanbul to the muggy plain just beyond Kobuleti, and then up through mountain roads and passes to Krasnod, was of cigarettes. Ross explained that it wasn't smuggling, exactly, more of a tax scam. He seemed to have a lot of explaining to do at the border post between Turkey and Georgia at Sapri, and I don't think that was the explanation he gave.

Sometimes we slept in truck-stop motels. Wherever there was Internet access, Ross would buy some time, call up Google Earth images of Krassnia, and stand behind me while he pointed out the route to the secret site and the landmarks along the way. He seemed to have it in his memory, and he burned it into mine.

Increasingly, as the journey continued, we slept in the narrow shelves at the back of the cab. Ross hadn't driven a truck himself for several years. His own false passport, in the name of Hamish MacDonald, was one of the new biometric ones, and a fresh ID, not renewed from any he'd used before. He told me he enjoyed being back behind the wheel, and as far as I could see, he did. For every hardship and inconvenience, he had a tale of worse. Every so often he'd use a payphone to call his business, or home. His mobile—it wasn't the iPhone I'd seen earlier, just a thin blue-anodised tinny flashy slidy one like a kids's first—didn't ring once. I learned that he had a wife, two teenage sons, and a younger daughter, and that they thought he was on holiday, or had at least been told that. The only people who knew where he was really going were Amanda (and whoever she reported to, presumably) and his business partner, still Colin Byrne, aka Cairds. Ross never let slip any other name, of anyone in his business or in his family. Though I inquired curiously after my possible half-siblings, he told me just enough to get a notion of their personalities (quite unlike mine, I have to say) and nothing by which I could have identified them.

Apart from that, I thought I got to know him reasonably well. You can't live in a confined space with someone for over a week without getting to know them at some level. The thing that struck me about Ross Stewart was that he was mature and deliberate: a very self-controlled, self-possessed guy. He never lost his temper, even when I whinged (which was more often than I like to remember). In the whole awkward everyday business of climbing over and stepping around and averting eyes from each other inside a space of about four cubic metres, like astronauts with the added drag of gravity, he treated me like a rather distant father might an adult daughter: considerate, confiding rather than intimate, correct.

While driving, though, whether going far too fast along an autobahn or far too slowly up a mountain road, he talked to me like . . . well, not like any man had talked to me before, with cheerful cynicism and open uncertainty. It was like I was a girl he wasn't trying to impress. At less reflective moments he'd point out sights, sometimes connecting them to an event in history or an adventure or misadventure of his own; then he'd listen to what I had to say, even if it had no connection with what he'd been talking about, or answer questions I came up with. We followed the progress of the Georgia–Russia war and the uneasy, fragile peace on conflicting shortwaves, and bristled into wariness at what distant glimpses we had of it: a jet fighter flashing past us about ten metres above the road, a grey irregularity of naval vessels on the sea's horizon, a tank nosing through conifers on the other side of a valley, a column of tractors with trailers stacked with furniture and lined with impassive, sun-cracked faces.

We had become so used to the long drive that it came almost as a surprise when on the evening of Tuesday, August 19, we topped a low rise at the end of an ascending series of foothills and there before and below us was a plain, patchworked with fields and meadows and vineyards, with beyond it a snow-capped peak standing a little away from the great mountain range, and, in the middle of the plain, Krasnod. Straight in front of us, a hundred metres down the road, was the border post. It looked like a little flying saucer done in white concrete and plate glass, said UFO being held to the ground by a somewhat larger, wedge-shaped space freighter made from grey concrete and corrugated asbestos. Shadowy humanoid shapes sat looking out from behind the little saucer's big windows. Two container trucks and a dozen or so cars queued in front of it, beside a bullet-riddled billboard with the same message in Latin, Cyrillic, and Georgian script.

"'Welcome to Krassnia,'" Ross read: "'Forgotten jewel of the Caucasus.' Hah! Forgotten pimple on the arse-end of nowhere, more like."

We continued in this vein, joking over our tension, and I'd reached "Forgotten bogey in the nostril of democracy" by the time there was just one truck and one car in front of us and we could see the border guards: a couple of guys searching the vehicle at the front, three more casually covering the driver and passengers with hip-slung AKs.

"Uh-oh," said Ross.

The guards weren't wearing uniforms.

You haven't lived, really, in the wonderful world of the twenty-first century until you've had your passport and possessions examined by a nervy, spotty kid in black bandana, scuffed white trainers, a NATO-surplus camo jacket with an internationally unrecognised flag patch stitched to it by his proud mother and a pewter skull badge on the lapel, a Motörhead T-shirt and Russian army combat pants, with a Russian assault rifle waving toward your waistline to further accessorise the look. It's an experience I can't recommend, but it builds character.

That last is what Ross told me, as we drove down the slope towards Krasnod, our cargo of cigarettes a pallet or ten lighter.

"I couldn't take my eyes off the AK muzzle," I said. "Blackest hole I've ever looked into."

"Stop fretting," said Ross. "You get used to it."

He steered one-handed for a moment, dangerously on the cracked and pot-holed tarmac, to punch the air.

"And anyway," he said, the low sun lighting his face as he turned to grin at me, "we *got through*."

"Yay!" I cried, entering into the spirit of the occasion.

"That was the high point," Ross warned. "It's all downhill from here."

"That's a bit discouraging."

Ross waved a hand towards the windshield. "The *road*, I mean."

If he hadn't been driving I would have clouted him.

8 . THE PERSISTENT WORLD

1.

The thing that surprised and disconcerted me about Krasnod, I realised as I ambled through the ventricles of its old and stony heart the following morning, was that it had gone on changing while I'd been away. Places from our childhood aren't supposed to do that (we childishly assume). We expect them to stay the same, to match our memories, and we feel vaguely betrayed when they don't, as if they were an old school friend (I'm speaking hypothetically here, you understand, the hypothesis being that I had school friends instead of school enemies, allies, and neutrals) who has not only had the ill grace to grow up but has completely forgotten you in the meantime.

The first shock of nonrecognition had hit me when we arrived the previous evening. Off the main road into town from the south, unpatriotically but unchangeably called Tbilisi Road, and just outside the ring of Soviet-era apartment buildings and inside the more spread-out ring of post-Soviet villas, was a broad flat patch of rough grass about five hundred metres square. In the '80s it had been an unofficial park—I definitely remember playing there, in among weeds and long grass and the rusting wreck of a bus. Officially the field was the site for a brave new Western-style shopping complex, planned in the '70s, proudly displayed on billboards in the '80s, and never built.

Now, it was a vast marshalling yard for commercial road traffic. This use had made it a churned-up waste of mud—dry at the moment, with half-metre-deep ruts and a nasty taste in the nostrils as the evening wind came in off the mountain—on which were parked scores of container trucks and articulated lorries, all massive and modern and Western, among which tractor-trailers, Moskvitch flatbeds, Lada pickups, taxis, and minibuses bumped about. Ross hadn't been in Krassnia since the late '90s, and this place was new to him, but he seemed to know his way around. He eased our truck onto what looked like and could well have been a wooden barn door laid across the roadside ditch. I could feel the bounce and hear the creak as each pair of wheels passed over the makeshift bridge. About twenty metres of broad dirt track farther, past a file of waiting taxis, a post hammered into the mud on either side of the road marked the entrance. A man in a peaked cap and neat, pressed militia uniform rose from a plastic bucket seat by the lefthand post as we rolled up, and crossed the path to face the driver's side.

Ross rolled down the window, cocked his ear to a sentence in Krassnian, called back in confidently mangled Russian, and handed over eight Georgian twenty-lari notes topped with a five-dollar bill, and was waved through. We bumped forward, and were directed around corners and into a vacant space by uniformed cops, and in one case an army corporal.

"No uniforms at the border," Ross remarked. "Looks like this is where they all went."

"The guys at the border took a bigger cut," I said.

"Noted," said Ross. "Worrying. Not good."

He took a bulging plastic wallet of customs-related (etc.) documents from the glove box, and leaned over the back of the seat for his bag, swinging that bulky weight around and into his lap with one long strong arm like a chimp bowling a coconut.

"Time to go," he said. "Don't leave anything, OK?"

"Won't the truck be safe?"

"Oh, it'll be safe," said Ross. "But you know how it is."

I didn't know how it was at all, but I took him at his word. As I heaved my bag (by now, the pillowcase of unwashed clothing filled about half of it) into the front, he recovered the small aluminium case from some cubbyhole which (again) I didn't see, and slid it into a side pocket of his bag, which he zipped shut.

"Got everything?"

I patted my big bag and lifted my small one.

"Toothbrush? Cloth?"

"Ah, shit."

I rummaged and stuffed.

"Definitely ready?"

"Definitely," I said, shoving recalcitrant zipper teeth into the slider, more or less one by one.

"Hot meals, hot showers, and cool beds beckon," said Ross.

That thought kept me going as I lugged my bags along the lumpy aisles between the trucks, and scowled away the urchins who offered to help for "Fifty tetri, only fifty tetri to the taxis."

"Yeah, and ten lari to get it back once you're there," Ross grunted. He said something I didn't catch in a stream of fluent and well-accented Russian that scattered the kids, their rebuffed faces giving me a momentary pang of sentimental guilt.

Around us, the huge parking lot was going like a fair, which as the swift dusk descended it was beginning to resemble, with hawkers and hookers, stalls and fires, and everywhere money moving and deals being done, between truckers and traders from all over the Caucasus and Central Asia. The air stank of diesel exhaust, tobacco smoke, roasting shashliks, and heated sugar. Ross ignored all temptations and attractions, and glared at any guy who ogled me. We slogged through the gate with a nod to the cop, and took a taxi into the centre.

The hotel was just behind the main drag, a five-storey Soviet-era concrete building freshened by French ownership, Croatian management, and Georgian staff. Grubby and sweaty as we were, we got dirty looks at the reception desk. Ross changed that with a ten-euro note and a sheaf of lari for two adjacent single rooms with en-suite. The lift worked.

"Twenty minutes," Ross said, unlocking his door.

I flicked my hair. "Forty."

"Half an hour," Ross conceded.

The room was clean, neat, and had drawn inspiration from (I guessed) the cheap end of the Scandinavian market and the better efforts of the late GDR. After the days in the cab and in motels, it felt like luxury. I showered, changed, and tapped Ross's door two minutes under budget. Ross appeared in polo shirt, green cords, and brown deck shoes, and still with his sovereign ring and gold neck chain, as if aiming to look more like a businessman on holiday than a trucker and then ruining the effect with bling. He beckoned me in.

"Are you *trying* to get noticed?" he asked.

My one sparkly top and my last clean pair of jeans. It didn't seem fair.

"This isn't the Soviet Union anymore," I said.

"Ach, it'll do," he said. "For the restaurant, anyway."

"Good," I said. "I'm starving."

"Business," he said. "Then we eat."

He sat down on the bed. "Pull up a chair."

When I did so he had the little aluminium case across his knees. His thumbs flickered over a combination lock, and turned the open case around. On top were my American and British real passports, and my cards and notebook. Ross nodded. I took these out, and found underneath a plain-covered paperback book that turned out to be a bound volume of reduced photocopied pages of Avram Arbatov's thesis, a folded map, and what looked like a slightly oversized mobile phone.

I took out the map. It unfolded to over a metre square, much larger than it had looked folded up. The material was as thin as balloon foil but stiffer and tougher, like something recovered from a flying saucer wreck. One side was a fine-detail map of the supposed route, from the main road up onto the mountain. The other was a high-res satellite image of the final kilometre or so.

I looked around the room. "Can we talk?"

"Like you said," Ross told me, "this isn't the Soviet Union anymore. But yeah, as it happens, I've swept the room."

"What with?"

He patted his shirt pocket. "A handy gadget."

"Very James Bond."

"Chinese, actually," said Ross. "Bought it on eBay."

He lifted the phone from the case and held it up as if weighing it in his hand. "This thing, however, really is James Bond, or maybe Jack Bauer. It's a satellite phone, state of the art, Agency bespoke this year, Special Forces standard issue by about 2010, I guess. Built-in GPS accurate to a metre, video camera with live streaming uplink, battery life of about twelve hours' talk time and two hours' video time, solar recharging, Internet access, and for all I know a word processor and iTunes. Oh, and a very intuitive interface."

He pressed his thumbnail to a switch in the side, then handed the phone to me. "Take a look."

The thing wasn't much bigger than one of the chunkier mobiles, like last year's Sony Ericsson, but it weighed about a pound. It was like holding a bar of lead, a theme continued by the colour scheme of the case, a patternless dapple of shades of grey that I guessed was camouflage. The lens cover was flush with the back and slid without a click. The face was all screen, like an iPhone, the display sharp even before I touched the backlight's virtual toggle.

I played about with the phone for a minute or so. The interface was indeed intuitive, and also like the iPhone's, but with less fat and more muscle.

"Three numbers," I remarked, looking up. "In Calls."

"The first one's for this," said Ross. He flipped out his cheap-looking mobile. "Hmm, better tab that to your iPhone while I'm at it." He did, then put his phone away again. "The second—that's like 911, it's your helpline for emergencies. Matters of life and death. It's like a scream. You don't even have to say anything, just ring it. The GPS will tell them where you are, and the fact that you're using it will let them know you're in serious trouble. The other, the long number . . . that's for the video uplink. Might not be a good idea to use it for anything else, given that you'd be talking to a chip on a geo-synchronous satellite, as far as I know."

"Hang on," I said.

I gave each number a contact name: ROS, 911, and SKY, just so I'd never get them mixed up.

"OK," I said. "And as for what I'm supposed to do with this—it seems pretty obvious."

"Yes?"

"Use the GPS and the map to get to the place, the camera to video it and uplink to the satellite, and the call to you to say mission accomplished—or the scream call if something's gone badly wrong."

"Near enough," said Ross. "Only, not the call to me. You can do that after you get out, not after you've done your job on the mountain. I don't need to know and I couldn't do anything even if I did."

"How not?"

"Well, for one thing, I'll be in Turkey or Bulgaria by then."

"What?"

"Sure." He looked like he wanted to say *duh*. "I'm heading back on the return trip tomorrow morning."

"*Tomorrow?*"

"Yup," he said. "I have a container load of Chinese coming in tonight for Germany. Can't leave them hanging around for days on end, they'll go off."

"Off where?"

"What I mean is, they'll die."

"Oh," I said.

"I check the exporters very thoroughly," he said, still as if talking about ethically sourcing free range eggs. "The passengers have perfectly adequate supplies. But there isn't much margin for error."

"OK, OK," I said, shaking my head to dislodge the images overcrowding it. "But when I saw you were driving me all the way here, I thought—"

"That you'd have the benefit of my on-the-spot experience and advice? Sorry, no can do. That's exactly why I'm the wrong person to have around you here. I can't go into the underside of this place because too many people there know me. And for all that I'm a master of disguise . . ."

He smiled and shrugged. "Klebov would at least do a double take, and that might be enough. So, even besides that this trip is business, I'd best be off ASAP, for your sake."

I boggled. "So I'm supposed to do it all myself?"

"Oh, no." Ross looked taken aback at the suggestion. "No, no. There's an Agency contact, obviously. He's expecting you. I'll give you the details before I leave."

"All right," I said. "And what about *my* return journey?"

Ross sighed, standing up and sidling away from between my knees and the end of the bed.

"Bus to Batumi," he said, pacing the room. "Or on to Trabzon, if Batumi's shut. Plane to Istanbul, then Edinburgh via London. Whatever. You have five thousand pounds cash on that Switch card, twenty thousand dollars credit on the Visa. You don't need to worry about being able to afford a last-minute booking, that's for sure."

"But what if—I don't know, the revolution's started or the Russians move in or—"

Ross sighed again. "Use your initiative, Lucy. You're your mother's daughter. How hard can it be?"

2.

So, here I was about eleven in the morning of Wednesday, August 20, dawdling along Krasnod's main drag, still called Kommunisticheskii

Prospekt and dotted rather than lined with (mostly) trendy modern shops: five cafés, ten wine bars, three boutiques, one hardware store; the relict Soviet-era department store Krasnorglav; an ill-advised direct retail outlet for the plastics factory, KrasNorPlasKom, with a window full of U-bends and dust; an HSBC branch, one supermarket, and a secondhand bookshop, Anti-kwariat, that doubled as a newsagent. This last sold week-old editions of *USA Today*, the *FT*, and *Das Bild*, as well as the alarmingly named Turkish paper *Fanatik* (entirely devoted to soccer), yesterday's Georgian daily news-papers *24 Sati* and (in English) *The Messenger*, and the current editions of Krassnia's: *Respublika Krassnya*, which backed (and was backed by) the gov-ernment, and *Novaya Krassnya*, for the oppo.

The Western front pages, of course, were all screaming headlines about the Russian invasion of "Georgia proper," as the rather self-negating catch-phrase had gone, and might as well have been history books by now (and inaccurate or at least tendentious history at that, as Ross and I had sussed while it was happening, just from listening to different radio stations in the cab). That didn't surprise me. What did surprise me, as I shelled out a couple of lari for each of the local rags, was that the opposition paper had finer paper and sharper print than the government paper. A moment later, I realised I shouldn't have been surprised. This was Colour Revolution 101: covert financing of the opposition. At the next café along I dropped a fifty-rouble note for a coffee and sat down at a table on the sidewalk outside to read.

The air was warm, but not humid—Krasnod's about a kilometre above sea level—and with an occasional breath of refreshing chill from the moun-tains carrying the smell of trees, which made a welcome change from the all-pervasive acetone tang from the plastics factory and the brown haze from the copper mine that had always hung over Krasnod in my childhood. As both factory and mine were still operating, I guessed this was due to better anti-pollution equipment having been installed since they were privatised. Strange to think that Ilya Klebov was now involved in running, or at least owning, the mine. (A mine which, now that I came to think of it, my mother's side of my family had once partly owned. I wondered idly if Eugenie or Amanda still kept the share certificates, and whether anyone was still pur-suing the Ural Caspian Mineral Company's claim for compensation. A fine sort of counterrevolution it had been, I thought, that had left the former

Communists *still* owning the property their predecessors had stolen from the legitimate owners all those decades ago! A fine restoration of capitalism, that didn't restore any actual capital to the capitalists! The notion nagged away at me, but I couldn't see its relevance, and dismissed it to the back of my mind.)

From this low vantage—I could just see the white peak of Mount Krasny above the rooftops if I craned my neck—Kommunisticheskii Prospekt looked almost normal for a post-Communist provincial capital. Well-dressed people walked briskly with hard-shell briefcases or designer handbags, or tapped at laptops and PDAs over tiny cups of coffee and tall glasses of water at the pavement tables of the cafés. Old men sat smoking at the long, awning-shaded tables outside the wine bars. Old women trudged about with laden plastic shopping bags. The flow of traffic was sparse, but the cars were mostly German or Japanese. Even the tractors were new, the trailers full of fresh produce or plump animals, and the old ladies sitting at the backs of the trailers wore bright headscarves, clean black dresses, and black stockings without holes. The businesses along the street could have been anywhere—except most British small-town high streets, what with the lack of charity shops and estate agents.

It was only when you noticed odd little things like the traffic cop's shoulder-slung AK-47, and the squad of six or so likewise armed irregulars strolling down the other side of the street systematically ripping down entirely legal-looking election posters, and spray-painting over spray-painted stencils, on street furniture and walls, of an innocuous-looking maple leaf, that the seasoned observer might get the subtle impression that Krassnia's internal affairs weren't quite as relaxed as they seemed.

Likewise with sounds: traffic noises, the thump or click of feet, voices. But every so often, from the people around those sidewalk tables, I heard raised angry voices, and among the footsteps I heard running feet, and in the traffic hum I heard a deeper note that made me look up from my cup and page to see a six-wheeled armoured personnel carrier cruise by.

From the papers, I didn't learn much: there was, of course, a lot of coverage of the aftermath of the Georgia–Russia War (to me a tedious rehash of the kind of claim and counterclaim and conspiracy theory that I'd heard and read over the past ten days) with the government paper taking the Russian POV, and the opposition the Georgian. I didn't know enough about the local politicians to disentangle the domestic coverage: the contested political issues were taken as read, or to be inferred between the lines, and the reported arguments consisted of mutual, indistinguishable, and (from my POV) undecidable accusations of dirty tricks with the electoral roll or the ballot-counting arrangements, made by and against individuals whose names, let alone affiliations, I had great difficulty keeping in the correct columns of the score-sheet.

So far, so familiar, for an outsider like me: I'd had much the same experience several times in the past few years, trying to follow the ins and outs of Georgia's Rose Revolution, Ukraine's Orange Revolution, and all the rest. It was while I sat pondering all that and thinking it was about time I made contact with the Maple Revolution—or at least with the guy whose name Ross had given me—that an anomaly-detecting switch in my head tripped and I started consciously noticing a phenomenon whose separate instances I'd seen but not summed. Lots of women here had red hair. Young women, mostly, but also some middle-aged and (my guess, based on clothes and bearing) middle-class women. It wasn't what I thought of as natural red hair, at least not the carroty gingery colour I'd covered with Julie's Clairol dye. It was more Natural Bright Auburn red, Giselle in *Enchanted* red, Bree in *Desperate Housewives* red, like there'd been a run on henna.

Now that I came to notice it, the colour was so common among women my age and general look (I wished I'd thought to pull on my denim skirt and purple leggings and pixie boots this morning instead of the jeans and Kickers) that it was my mousey-brown cover-up hair colour that stood out. I felt suddenly noticeable, as if a badge I'd thoughtlessly stuck on to accessorise a jacket had turned out to be making a strong political statement. (That sort of thing in my case usually goes the other way—over the years I've had lots of channel interrupts with people wearing vintage Soviet badges.) I rather suspected all this unnatural red hair was a political statement, but I couldn't parse it.

There was only one way to find out.

I stood up, left the papers and a one-lari tip, and headed for a side street I'd already walked past and glanced down, above one café which bore a sign in three scripts and one language: Internet.

In case you're wondering about Ross Stewart: we'd gone over a few more details—how to meet my local contact, the URL for the local version of the game, the lock combination for the aluminium case, the route on the map, how to hire a car and not get robbed, and so on—before we went out for stuffed vine leaves, mint yoghurt, and sticky wine in a dark restaurant. I'd almost fallen asleep over my plate. Ross had seen me to my room, carried off my pillowcase of manky clothes, and returned them laundered when I woke bleary-eyed to his knock on the door at eight that morning.

"Thank you," I'd mumbled, all foul breath and gummy lips.

He'd stood in the passageway for a moment, back in his trucker gear, out of place.

"You'll be all right?" he'd asked, just as if the whole thing of leaving me to fend for myself was my idea and not his.

"I'll be fine," I'd told him.

He'd looked at me as if trying to read some small print on my face, stuck out an abrupt hand to shake, and left. I'd heard his boots thump on the steps and the plastic buckle of a stray strap on his black bag tick against the bannisters as he hurried down the stairs.

I'd closed the door, locked it, and thrown myself back on the bed and stared at the ceiling for about a quarter of an hour.

3.

The Internet café was a real café, with coffee. And cigarette smoke, which metaphorically took me back and literally almost sent me back, out the door. I blinked hard a few times and recovered, but not before my missed step at the threshold had turned a dozen pairs of eyes from two sides of a long table lined with recent-looking flat screens and keyboards and tangled with cable in between cups and cola cans and ashtrays. I hadn't even summoned a glare before all the heads jerked quickly back to the screens. I walked to the counter and asked, in Krassnian, for a cup of black coffee and a half hour on one of the machines.

The guy behind the counter looked as if he'd have been much more in his element working in a butcher's shop, though no self-respecting butcher would have allowed a white apron to get that dirty. He gave me a look of pitying suspicion and rattled off a phrase far too quickly for my out-of-practice conversational Krassnian.

"Sorry?"

"Filter coffee or Nes Coffay?" he said slowly.

"Uh, filter, thank you."

Again with the pitying look. I glanced at the board and realised that instant, that is, Nes Coffay (sic), was the more expensive and doubtless stylish option. After I'd taken the mug to the machine whose number matched my chit, I discovered that the plus side of the Nes Coffay might very well be that instant coffee, however vile, can't be simmered.

It was as well that I hadn't been expecting the Internet café to be full of fresh-faced young democrats plotting insurrection in the safe spaces of Dark Krassnia, because if I had I'd have been disappointed. The twenty or so people there all looked like *elitny* spoiled brats, and—from my sidelong glances at the screens as I walked from the counter to my seat—the handful playing Dark Krassnia were too busy slaughtering orcs to do any plotting, and everyone else was lost in World of Warcraft or updating their Livejournals.

I fought the temptation to check my Google Mail account and my friends' Livejournals and went straight to the game. The opening screen at dark-krassnia.ru gave me a pang of nostalgia for Edinburgh and Digital Damage and the lads. I resisted another temptation to get back in contact with everyone and signed in, using a string from my months of testing that gave me command-level privileges, and an avatar that placed me as a low-level grunt in the barbarian horde. I swivelled the avatar's head, in the hindmost ranks of the welter. Suresh's algorithm was being worked hard. In the café's low bandwidth every avatar was a wire sketch and the scenery was blocky monochrome.

I teleported to a secure location, the privy at the back of the Inn of Unrighteousness, and scribbled a message on the wall. More literally, I typed a message and it appeared on the wall, while my avatar's arm gestured a scrawl. Almost at once, another avatar appeared beside mine, facing the wall. This proximity gave me the oddest feeling, like I suppose guys get when they stand side by side pissing. My writing faded and a new message came up while the other grunt handwaved at the blank partition in front of us: *Gemarov St off Freedom Sq 10 min?*

OK, I wrote back.

The other avatar vanished and I did likewise, backing out of the game with (I noticed) two experience points for just turning up.

"Where the fuck is Freedom Square?" I wondered frantically, and was on the point of Google-Earthing it when I remembered that it was what I'd always known as Revolution Square, in front of the offices of the regional Soviet—formerly of the Zemstvo, and now of the Krassnian parliament—at the far end of Kommunisticheskii Prospekt.

I logged out, took the almost-full mug of almost-cool coffee back to the counter for safe disposal, and left.

Freedom Square turned out to be where it was all happening.

It's a pleasant, open space, about a hundred metres by fifty. Along one side there's an Orthodox church. At the top there's the parliament, a still impressive Tsarist pile, crusted with Soviet add-ons and scarred by democratic deletions. At the bottom there's the end of the Prospekt, and the final side is lined with low buildings with pillared frontages. Within its perimeter of road it's more like a park than a square. Scrubby patches of grass alternate with cracked expanses of paving shaded by century-old trees.

As I entered the square I passed a statue at one corner of a barbarian warrior, dated 1992 and nameless, but bearing a suspicious resemblance to the traditional depiction of Duram. That statue was diametrically opposite the one I was familiar with, in the corner beside the parliament. A small group of people stood holding a huge pictorial banner beneath a clump of red flags around the farther statue's plinth: Stalin, still there. (It's a Georgian pride thing, even in Krassnia.) The pictorial banner showed Stalin too, in a row of overlapping profiles: Marx, Engels, Lenin, Stalin, and a dapper chap I guessed was Enver Hoxha. It looked like an illustration from a history of shaving.

Rather aptly, the space between Duram and Stalin was occupied by the revolution. Hundreds of people, mostly young, and a disproportionate number red-haired, milled around a camp of small and large tents, some collapsible tables stacked with leaflets, and a speaker's podium empty at the moment but whose PA system was bouncing Krassnian patriotic songs set to rock music off all sides of the square. Krassnian flags and plastic maple-leaf cutouts on sticks wagged above the crowd here and there or lay in metre-high heaps for any coming demonstration. A few militiamen (the cops, that is, not the scary guys I'd seen at the border or ripping down posters) hung around the periphery, sitting on low parapets, talking on mobile phones and smoking, like bored teenage boys in uniform, which most of them were.

I walked along the side of the square, keeping out of things, smiling and accepting every leaflet offered. Gemarov Street was so narrow its whole width was in shade under the noon sun, and my eyes took a moment to adjust. About ten metres ahead of me the road was occupied by a small bus. Three cops with visored helmets leaned against the front, their heavy shields of curved Perspex and long wooden batons propped beside them. More riot police sat inside the bus. For a moment I almost turned back, but decided that would look suspicious, and in any case my contact had specified this street.

I held my head high and walked forward. As I passed the three cops at the front of the bus the nearest one stuck his truncheon across my path at waist level. I stopped and looked up at my reflection in the visor, and tried to smile. The cop pointed to my mini-backpack with his left hand. I unhitched it from my shoulder and unzipped it, feeling very glad that, after some swithering, I'd decided to leave the aluminium case and its incriminating contents in the hotel room safe.

The cop lowered his impromptu barrier and grabbed the bag, then began to poke around inside it. He found my false passport and took it out, and dangled the bag by one of its straps on his wrist while flicking through the pages. He peered at the passport photo, then at me.

"English?" he said.

"Yes," I said, in Russian.

"Journalist?" he asked.

For a frantic moment I forgot what the passport showed as my occupation. I shook my head.

"Student," I said. "Tourist."

He dropped the passport into the bag and handed the bag back. "You go."

I went, sidling along the half-metre gap between the side of the bus and the wall. The cops inside the bus watched my every step, heads turning one by one as I went past. The rest of the narrow street had only two shops. The window of one was stacked with pyramids of tins circled in faded pictures of fruit. The other had layers of fresh blue jeans. Music thumped from a Sony speaker over the door. I glanced inside and saw a young woman doing her nails amid shelves and shelves of yet more blue jeans. No customers. I walked on. After a few paces I heard footsteps behind me. I stepped onto the cobbled and empty road. A young man overtook me on the sidewalk, then turned and smiled.

He wore a nylon sports jacket over T-shirt and jeans. I guessed he was about my age, with darker skin and naturally redder hair. Friendly, open face behind rimless glasses.

"Ah, it's you!" he said, in American-accented English. "I almost didn't recognise you."

"I've recovered from the flu," I said, feeling very silly.

"Then it's safe to shake hands," he said, and did.

"I'm Emma," I said.

"My name is Fyodor," he said, I guessed probably as truthfully.

We walked on down the street and turned into an even narrower alleyway, which opened out on a much wider street. Fyodor led the way, one step ahead, until he reached a wine bar with round tables outside. No one sat at them. Fyodor gestured.

"Take a seat," he said. "Would you like a drink?"

"I'd kill for a decent coffee," I said.

He looked at me, puzzled. "You would kill?"

"British idiom," I said.

"Ah! Very good. Please wait."

He disappeared inside. I sat down. The table was metal, and wobbled. I found a beer mat and wedged it under the offending leg. While doing so I cast a quick glance up and down the street. Still very quiet. Fyodor returned with a coffee and a bottle of beer.

He raised the bottle to me. "Welcome to Krasnod!"

"Thank you. Is it safe to talk here?"

"I wouldn't have chosen this place if it wasn't."

"Yeah, but . . ." I glanced around.

"The RSB's budget doesn't stretch to directional mikes," Fydor said. "There is no one inside but the owner, who is reliable. You can see for yourself whether anyone is near."

All the same, it didn't seem right to ask the question that had been on the tip of my tongue: are you really with the Agency? I wondered for a moment why that question had risen unbidden in my mind, and realised I'd been half-consciously worrying away at the odd thought that had struck me at the pavement cafe, about the ownership of the copper mine. And then I realised: I'd been about to ask Fyodor if he was with the CIA because I *didn't know*.

The only evidence I had that the CIA was involved in my mission *at all* was what Amanda, Ross, and Yuri had told me. Apart from the saucer-wreck look and feel of the map—and what the hell did I know of current paper and plastics technology, let alone of commercially available satellite and aerial imaging?—I didn't have a shred of physical evidence. I couldn't even be sure that the Agency had a direct hand in the Maple Revolution—the money and strategy behind it could have come from some philanthropic foundation or from some NGO (yeah, I know, but . . .) or indeed from some private business interest, and one which didn't need to be particularly wealthy, at that. The whole op—the game development and distribution, and the evident subsidy to the oppo press, and all the leaflets and flags and maple-leaf symbols, and my journey itself—could all have come in at well under a million dollars. Was it possible that what was really going on was that Amanda, and maybe someone with big money behind Amanda, was trying to get the mine *back*, out of the hands of the local ex-commie oligarchs like Klebov and into the hands of whatever or whoever had inherited the claims of the Ural Caspian Mineral Company?

And if that was the case, what was my mission supposed to accomplish?

"Shit," I said, out loud.

"I beg your pardon?" said Fyodor.

"Sorry." I shook my head. "Just . . . remembered something I hadn't done before I left home. It's trivial."

I smiled reassuringly, leaned back, and sipped the coffee. Missing out on coffee earlier, what with the undrinkable muck in the Internet café, had left me with acute caffeine deprivation. I tried to think of a more innocuous question than the one I'd almost asked.

"What's with all the red-heads?" I said.

"The Hoxhaists?" Fyodor frowned. "They're insignificant. Completely mad. They huddle around the Stalin statue and sing Soviet Krassnian anthems."

"No, no," I said. "I meant, all the people with dyed red hair. What's that about?"

"Ah," Fyodor said. "It's for the colour, you see, of maple leaves in autumn."

"Really?" I said. "Nothing to do with the legendary flame-haired Vrai?"

"Nothing at all." Fyodor ran a hand backward over his own red hair. "Well, possibly it has something to do with the game that has become so popular. The Vrai were the rulers long ago. Perhaps having red hair is a way of claiming the people should rule? I don't know."

"Oh!" I said. "I get it! It is because of *The Krassniad*! Amanda was so clever . . ."

"Amanda?"

"Amanda Stone," I said. "She wrote the book. Before she wrote the book, there were just folktales and traditions, but by tying them together into one story, she made it a story that both the Krassnar and the Vrai could take pride in. Of course she got the idea from Avram Arbatov's thesis, so it was really Arbatov who had that idea, and that must have been what he was trying to do. . . ."

I fell into a place where I could see things falling into place.

"You know about Arbatov?" Fyodor said. "The academician who was killed in the Terror? He is quite obscure, even in Krassnia."

"Oh, he's well known in the West," I said.

"Really?"

"Yes."

An awkward pause.

"I know why you're here," Fyodor said.

"Yes?" I said, uncertainly. Of course he knew why I was here.

"The mountain and its secret. Hence your interest in the flame-haired Vrai." He passed his hand over his hair again. "In case you are wondering, I am not one. I'm not a native Krassnian. My parents came here from Russia in the sixties."

Why was he telling me this?

"Anyway," he said, "are you ready to go?"

"Yes, when—"

"I mean today. Now."

I nearly spilled my coffee. "Now? It's what, twelve thirty now? I wouldn't have time."

"The mountain is only ten kilometres away. Half an hour's drive."

"But the climb!" I said. "The place is above the snowline."

"Another couple of hours, three at the most. Plenty of time to return before sunset."

"Not counting evading the guards, apart from anything else."

Fyodor looked impatient. "I have spent days observing them through binoculars, from a safe house in one of the villages. Their patrols are regular. The soldiers are of low morale. We can time your ascent to avoid them."

"But—I need to acclimatise, to—I don't know, I just didn't expect—"

Fyodor leaned forward. "Listen," he said, his voice low and fierce. "Every day you remain here is another day in which you could be picked up. This evening there is a rally of thousands in Freedom Square. That could be the occasion for a crackdown. The sooner your job is done, the better."

What he said made sense. But I still felt rushed and disoriented. I'd expected more time.

"I'll have to get my walking boots," I said. "And the map and so on, from the hotel."

Fyodor sighed, exasperated, as if I'd said I had to wash my hair and choose an outfit.

"Which hotel is it?"

"The Metro," I said.

"Two minutes' walk from here," he said. He tipped the bottle to his mouth, drained it, and stood up. "I will be in a car outside it in ten."

4.

Simkin Street, off the Prospekt, has two hotels on opposite sides of the road: the Kosmo and the Metro. I went into the Kosmo and up to my room. Changed into my big, lightweight walking boots and my warm trousers, grabbed my fleece and waterproof jacket, stuffed a pair of gloves and the contents of the aluminium case into my mini-backpack, checked that my torch and compass and Leatherman Juice were in its zipped side pockets, and left.

Down in the lobby I waited beside the glass sliding doors and watched the entrance to the Metro. A small yellow car drew up and parked, the driver's side to the sidewalk. No one got out. More to the point, no one went into the Metro, and particularly not the cops I'd half expected. I waited five minutes, took a deep breath, and went out and crossed the road. I leaned down at the front passenger window and tapped. Fyodor's head jerked around. He was wearing shades, so I couldn't see his eyes. I saw a frown, then a nod.

"Sorry I'm late," I said, as I got in.

"You said you were in the Metro," Fyodor said, turning the ignition key.

"Did I? Sorry." I threw my stuff on the back seat, beside a litre bottle of water and a pack of fruit-and-nut bars—for me, I guessed—and buckled up.

"An easy mistake," Fyodor said.

By now I was feeling a small pang of guilt about having mistrusted him so much.

"I guess it's safer to talk here than on the street," I said.

"I should hope so," said Fyodor, keeping his gaze on the road.

"Are you really working for the CIA?" I said.

"That's a very improper question," said Fyodor. "Why do you ask?"

"Well," I said, "I *think* I'm working for the CIA, but I'm not sure."

Fyodor laughed. "This is a common experience!"

He took the opportunity of a turn off the Prospekt to glance sideways at me, and smile.

"You are having the cold feet," he said, looking back at the road. "This too is a common experience."

He turned again, onto a street parallel to the Prospekt which led north out of town. Apartment blocks, painted up and freshened; more small shops than I remembered from—oh! This was, of course, the same main road north-ward out of town that the bus had driven up on the scariest day of my life.

I made a weak little "Uh!" sound.

"Yes," said Fyodor, apparently taking my pathetic mew as an inarticulate reply, "it *is* frightening. You come to a strange country, you have a false identity, you tell lies about yourself, you know you are at risk of discovery, you are in what we call *konspiratsia*, which is a little broader than 'conspiracy.' And you naturally come to see *konspiratsia* everywhere, you become a little bit paranoid. It is normal."

"How do you know it's normal? Have you done this yourself?"

"No," said Fyodor. "I haven't worked abroad, not even 'near abroad.' But I was taught this by men with experience of such matters."

"Men you won't say were your Agency handlers?"

"Exactly, I will say no such thing. And you shouldn't ask!"

"Sorry," I said, abashed.

"You needn't apologise," he said, in Krassnian. "It merely confirms who you are—a young English woman whose inexperience in the business is compensated by her local knowledge and fluent Krassnian."

"That's what you were told about me?" I asked, replying in Krassnian by reflex.

"And it's true, as you've just again demonstrated. So you need not worry about me, Lucy, I know who you are."

"How the—?" I said, in English. My hand went to my mouth, too late.

Then I saw, or thought I saw, what had happened.

"Oh! Fuck, I get it. If you were told just that about me, you could find out my name."

We passed the edge of town. On either side now were the well-spaced villas of the new rich.

"How so?" said Fyodor, his voice cool. "Let us treat this as an exercise. See how you would do, in the business."

"Well," I said, "there's really only one way to be fluent in Krassnian, and that's to have spoken it in childhood. So I would look for records in the local Soviet—the municipality, I mean—of someone English and now living in the West who was born here about twenty-odd years ago and/or who lived here for a few years after that. As far as I know, there's only me." "Very good," said Fyodor. "That's what I would have done, if I'd had to. As it happens, I didn't."

He took a hand off the wheel and gestured at the road ahead, towards the Caucasus range and Mount Krasny.

"You are familiar with this road, yes?"

"Oh, yes," I said. I couldn't keep a grim tone out of my voice.

"I was on that bus with you, Lucy Stone," he said. "My name is Andrei Melyukhin."

You might think I'd have been delighted and amazed at how screamingly unlikely this was—though it wasn't, as I shortly found out—but in fact the big shock was that I remembered his name from much more recently than the scariest day of my life. I remembered it from almost exactly five months earlier, from the time I'd dredged the names of Andrei Melyukhin and Irina Zemskova from my memory, to include them in my email to Ross Stewart giving him an account of the event. These names had recurred to my mind even more recently when Ross had thanked me for that account, when he'd been persuading me to go to Krassnia.

He'd said the FSB might still be keeping track of these names.

"The moment our teacher—Miss Yesiyeva, you remember her? Drank herself to death by '95, the bitch—gave that man with the militiamen the class register, I became a revolutionary. I knew then that nobody in this system could be trusted, not even the 'nice' ones. When she helped him to pick us out and assured us we would be all right, my new conviction was confirmed. Ever since that day, I've wanted to see a clean sweep of the people who were in power then. Which hasn't happened, and won't happen with the Maple Revolution. Do you think I don't know what is going on? Until I was pulled from the job a few days ago to prepare for this one, I was full-time on the revolution's finances. But the Maple Revolution is necessary. When the Liberal Democrats reveal themselves to be as corrupt and useless and Communist as the Social Democrats, the way to get rid of them will at least be obvious."

"That's worked so well in Georgia and Ukraine."

"Patience. Anyway, Lucy, it is no accident that the CIA's man in Krasnod should once have been a boy in that classroom with you. As I sat on the bus on this road, I was sorry that Hitler was dead, because that meant I couldn't help him fight these bastards. Then I remembered the other great demons we were always being warned about, and I swore to myself that one day I would join the CIA or the Zionists. I had no more idea of what these names stood for than I did that of Hitler. I had no idea what Zionists were, except that they were enemies of Russia and of the nomenklatura that ruled us and still does. As I grew older and learned more, I discovered I was not, shall we say, well qualified to be a Zionist. But the CIA, ah! It still exists and is open to all! What joy!"

"I can see that, but—"

He ignored me, and waved a hand to indicate a dirt road going off to the right. "You remember we passed down that road, to the Russian army base? And what happened to us there?"

"Of course I remember," I said. "That's what I was about to say. Nothing bad happened to us. OK, it was terrifying at the time, we didn't know what was going on, and I always think of it as the scariest day of my life. But the fact remains that Klebov and the militia pulled the Georgian and Jewish kids and, uh, us out of the way of a Krassnar ethnic attack. It felt like we were being singled out, but it was the very opposite, wasn't it?"

Andrei said nothing for a moment. Then he said: "Klebov? Klebov the mine owner? What did he have to do with it?"

I looked at him with new surprise. "You don't know? He was KGB then."

"Of course he was KGB, that is well known."

"He was the man in the suit."

The car swerved, veered, recovered.

"I didn't know that," said Andrei.

9 . THE PHYSICS ENGINE

1.

At the top of a steep dry gully I stopped for breath, and looked back. Far below was the road from Krasnod, curving now around the side of the mountain towards the pass a few kilometres to the west. A kilometre or so in that direction, half hidden in a clump of olive trees, was Andrei's yellow car. He himself was, if all had gone to plan, sitting at a roadside refreshment stall, sipping lemon tea, flipping over pages of a guide to bird life of the Caucasus, and occasionally scanning the mountainside through binoculars. He had my mobile number on his phone, and he was ready to warn me if he espied any patrols in the vicinity.

A couple of kilometres in the opposite direction, back towards the city, a spur from the road led through scrub and trees to the bare rectangle of the former Soviet military base, within whose stockade stood long barracks buildings and above which I could just make out as a tiny green-and-yellow dot the bicolour of the Krassnian flag. Armoured vehicles and squads of drilling soldiers moved about like blocky pixels.

I turned back to my climb. Just up ahead of me and to the right stood a mobile-phone mast, but that wasn't the landmark I was looking for. It should be—ah, yes, there it was: a twisted, ancient oak tree, with a stand of more recent stunted birch and maple covering a few hundred metres of the slope behind it. I emerged from the lip of the gully that had been my staircase and cover for most of the ascent, and scrambled upward across a steep slope of scree, feeling very exposed. Stones rolled and rattled behind and below me. At one point, my boot slipped and I fell on the stones, slithering back a couple of metres until a boulder stopped me. I made up the distance crawling, then resumed my crouched clamber.

At last I arrived at a lip of firm soil and grass. I reached for an exposed root of the oak tree, hauled myself up and over, and darted behind the tree. Another pause for breath, for a swig of water, and to look back—this time, I couldn't see the road, and barely the base, just the sweep of the plain with its neat squares and columns of ranked vines and olive trees and its more complex geometry of field and meadow, bisected by the main road and crisscrossed by small roads and meandering streams, and the city hazy in the distance. The landscape was busy with the crawling dots of tractors, trucks, and trailers, gathering in the harvest or transporting it to town.

Through this sloping woods before me there was supposed to be a path, leading to a large boulder of arguably artificial placement, at which my directions indicated that I should strike off diagonally to the left and up, across the side of the mountain, and into a further declivity which—if I arrived at the correct spot—I could cross easily to climb the other side and find another landmark, a spring that rose straight from a crack in the rock. I unfolded my map, checked my compass, and proceeded into the woods.

Branches above me, bracken and moss-furred roots at my feet. Nothing in sight looked remotely like a path. I stopped and checked map and compass again, and the GPS. I was going in the right direction, no doubt about that, but not on a path. The GPS gave my location more exactly than the scale of the map warranted—I could be twenty metres out on either side. I took out the copy of Arbatov's book, the original source of *The Krassniad*, and flicked through its pages, looking for lines that Amanda (I presumed) had marked in fluorescent yellows and pinks.

> *In the wood of the oak stood Duram*
> *by a cleft cliff three-men high*
> *Forward he urged his valiants*
> *onward to the altar of sacrifice*
> *from where heathen smoke rises. . . .*

A cleft cliff three-men high? I peered around in the green gloom. The ground to my left seemed a bit higher. I moved cautiously in that direction, stopping every few paces to look back the way I'd come. Five metres, ten, fifteen. . . . There was a clearing ahead. My foot sank into undergrowth and leaf litter, and I banged my shin on a sharp obstacle. Recovering my balance, I found I'd almost tripped headlong on to a flat expanse of partially grass-covered rock that rose about a metre above the ground. I heaved myself onto it and walked forward on this firmer footing, and then almost stepped into a deep, foot-wide gap between it and a similar flat outcrop of the same size. The gap, now that I saw it, ran clean across the rocky platform.

A cleft. The word came to my mind and stopped me in my tracks.

Was this what a thousand years of worms working the leaf mould could do to a cliff three-men high?

I walked along the side of the cleft, and found at its end, beyond the far edge of the rocky platform, cutting clean through the undergrowth, a stony path. Clear, well-trodden, and narrow, it didn't look like it had been made by human feet. Here and there I noticed cloven hoof-marks in patches where a seep of water had muddied the ground. They might have been the tracks of sheep, or goats, or even deer for all I knew. By now, I knew, I was well into the Zone, and had good reason to think no or few people had walked this way for years.

After about ten minutes I reached another clearing, within which lay an approximately cuboid boulder about three metres by one by two, through a crack in which a lone tree had forced its way over many decades, if not centuries. Triumphant, I paused there, spread my map on this lichen-crusted natural table, checked my direction, and headed off. The woods ended a little beyond the edge of the clearing, and the ground rose sharply. I climbed amid ankle-high, heathery scrub and tough grass, up and across a hillside that sloped at (I reckoned) exactly forty-five degrees.

Up and up, and then down. In the declivity the path I'd followed in the woods seemed renewed, this time as a fortuitous—perhaps—alignment of stones across the scree-covered slopes and floor. I reached the spring, just beyond the far lip of the declivity, about 3:30. I had been on the mountain almost two hours, and had ascended about eight hundred metres. I stooped to scoop water from the spring to my mouth.

Behind me, and out of my sight, I heard scree-stones slip and chime, rattling down the slope I'd just come up. I froze for a moment, then flattened to the ground and crawled on knees and elbows to a shrub at the lip of the rise. Very slowly, I raised my head to look over, and in doing so disturbed a branch above me. The low bush rustled and shook. I heard swift footsteps racing away, in a crunching of gravel and clashing of stones. I rolled sideways from the shrub and raised myself higher. I saw a dark figure just as it reached the top of the far side before it disappeared into the shadows under the trees. The figure was running on two legs and had two arms, and looked about the right size for a small human being. I couldn't be sure it was human, or even whether it was covered in clothing or hair.

I crouched there for what seemed a long while but was actually just a couple of minutes, somewhat shaken. Of course I'd heard (from Nana Krassnia, for a start) about the *almas*, the alleged relict hominid of the Caucasus. At that moment I thought I'd seen one, and that its kind had tramped the paths I'd followed. Looking back, I don't know. I may have seen an adventurous and athletic child, if there are people living on the mountain who evade the soldiers. It's a possibility. In Siberia there are groups in the forest so elusive—they sometimes trade for matches, fish-hooks, and salt—that the Soviet state and the entire bloody twentieth century came and went without touching their lives at all. Some are rumoured not to have heard of the Revolution, and to think the Tsar still rules.

After another bushy incline of a hundred metres or so the mountainside sloped sharply upward again. My path led across a snowfield on that slope to its top, beyond which—according to the map—lay a short walk to the ravine with the secret. It was in a very thoughtful mood that I pressed on.

What I was thinking about, though, wasn't which species of primate—my own or another—I'd just observed, but about what Andrei Melyukhin, aka Fyodor, had told me as he drove me to the mountain. And what I hadn't told him. I hadn't told him that I'd told Ross Stewart about him and the others, mainly because I was fairly sure he had no idea who Ross Stewart was, and because it seemed pretty clear that Ross had said nothing about any of this to the Agency—otherwise, they'd have made sure that my contact in Krassnia wasn't someone who already knew me. (But surely they knew that I'd been at school here, and that Andrei had been at the same school? Perhaps not—putting two and two together like that, or at least putting all the relevant information on the same page or even in the same dossier, has never struck me as one of the Agency's strong points.)

Just before Andrei had dropped me off at the foot of that steep dry gully, we'd talked about what had happened to us in the military base, and neither of us could come up with an explanation—other than that someone in the then-Soviet nomenklatura was interested in the DNA of the Vrai. Andrei was as certain as before that, whatever the gene was, he didn't have it—his parents were from Russia.

"You can't be sure," I'd told him. "What about your grandparents? People moved around a lot in the thirties, and some falsified their backgrounds, especially if their backgrounds were suspect to the Party."

He'd just grinned. "Maybe so. I don't want to find out whether or not I have Vrai blood by coming with you."

So he too believed that story. He might not be Vrai, but he sure was a Krassnian.

I shivered, unknotted the sleeves of my fleece and light jacket from around my waist, and put them on. I shoved my hands in the jacket pockets, found my gloves there, and put them on. Then I set out across the snowfield. There was no way to avoid it: my next landmark was a notch in the skyline, between two prominent rocks, and the snowfield covered the slope below it.

The snow was half a year old, the surface hard and slick from daily melts and nightly freezes. The slope was another erosion pile, forty-five degrees. I made progress by kicking my feet (and sometimes punching my fists) through the ice and into the packed snow beneath, and hauling myself up. It took twenty minutes to climb eighty metres. I remembered the story Yuri had told, about the NKVD expedition, and imagined doing this with a cine camera on my back. I was exhausted when I reached the top. From there I could see some of the way down the mountain—the stony vale, the woods— but not the road and only a part of the plain. The sun seemed to my northerner eyes still high, but it was far on its way down the sky to my right, to the west. The time now was 4:05.

I beat the snow off my gloves and kicked it from my feet. The ground here was dry and stony, sloping gently to a cliff a hundred metres away and about fifteen metres high that barred further progress on this route up the mountain, at least for me. Somewhere ahead of me, in the lower part of that cliff, was the entrance to a ravine, and my destination. It wasn't, now, the cold that was making me shiver.

I climbed that last slope in less than two minutes. The slope was steeper near the cliff face, the stones larger. I hopped onto a boulder beside the cliff and looked around. No opening or gap was obvious. The GPS and map indicated that I'd come to the right place, but as before I could be tens of metres out in either direction. I tossed a mental coin, and headed left and to the west.

The cliff face was irregular, with great buttresses of rock alternating with places where the cliff had eroded farther back. As I worked my way around one such buttress, a flash of light from the rock caught my eye. I stopped, stepped back, and moved my head back and forth until I caught the gleam again. It came from the sunlight shining through a crack in the rock. I tracked the crack upwards, and saw that five metres up it merged with a cleft about a metre wide. I stepped away from the cliff and saw what I had been too close to see before: a series of shelves and ledges that formed natural steps up to that cleft. I didn't stop to consult Arbatov's work and Duram's lays. I climbed.

Hugging the rock, I stepped around the corner from the ledge to the crevice, and then took a step inside. I looked up, and could see the blue sky maybe ten metres above me. Ahead, when my eyes adjusted, I could see a fainter vertical band of sunlight on rock. The floor of rock was solid, except for that tiny crack. An entire wall of rock, it seemed, had become separated from the cliff face. Its sides weren't straight: a few metres ahead the strip of rock floor, and both facing walls, angled to the right. I walked forward, and around that angle. The gap between the rock walls now widened to two metres, then three. I could see a broad band of sky between them, about a hundred metres ahead. Being in this gap was indeed like being in a ravine: a few steps later, I was walking on pale grass that had taken root on the thin accumulation of dust and gravel on the rock. My toe snagged on something, and I almost tripped. Looking down, I saw what looked like a thick insulated electrical cable snaking along in the grass. It emerged from the dirt a few steps behind me, and continued on the surface before me, occasionally disappearing for half a metre or so. The walls went on widening. Ten metres on, they were a good five metres apart. The light from the westering sun struck almost straight into the gap—dim, but quite adequate to see by. I walked along, step by step, looking up and down the walls on either side for anything that might seem unnatural or out of place.

And then I saw, on the outermost of the two walls—on the rock, not the cliff—just ahead of me, what seemed to be an inscription. I hurried forward, keeping to the cliff side of the crevice, partly so that I could see the inscription clearly and partly because I wanted to keep well clear of it. The walls around here were darker and more cracked than elsewhere. I could imagine sacrifices being burned here, and Beria's men caught in the glow.

The inscription began far above my head, and continued all the way down to the floor. Its letters appeared freshly carved and about a foot high. The lines of the text were up to three metres long, and seemed to be in Latin. A typical chunk of it looked like this:

SIC
LOGINQVITAS MINOR QVAM QINQVE STADIA
TVNC
OPEROR COMPVTVS VNVS
ALITER
OPEROR COMPVTVS DVOS
VT PRAECESSI MAIRIBVS QVAM VNVS
OPEROR INSQVEQVO TERMINVS

I read something like that, my eye tracking the lines down to the foot of the rock face. The lowest line was half hidden in the ground. I looked along it and almost idly tried to work out what the letters were whose tops I was seeing. Then I looked back, and noticed that I could see less of the letters. I thought it was a matter of the light, of a shadow deepening. I glanced to left and right, just to see that nothing and no one was casting an unexpected shadow. When I looked back, the half-sunk line had almost disappeared. I blinked, and stepped forward, peering closer.

What had been the second-lowest line of the inscription was now the lowest, and apparently sinking into the floor, at a rate of about one centimetre every two seconds. I watched for the disbelieving minute it took for that line, too, to disappear.

My first thought, and one that almost threw me into panic flight back the way I'd come, was that the entire wall of rock in front of me was slipping downward—that I had by the most freakish ill-luck chosen to come here the moment when, after centuries or millenia, the great wall of rock finally crashed away from the cliff. I pressed myself as close as my backpack would allow against the cliff wall, and reached out on both sides and scrabbled my gloved fingers to grip the rock behind me, as if that would do any good.

As I looked wildly about at the rock face opposite, I saw that its other features and irregularities weren't moving at all.

I fixed my eye on a distinctive protrusion of rock right in front of me, and it wasn't moving. The line of text beside it, however, was.

It was sinking at the same inexorable rate of one foot per minute. All the lines were.

The entire inscription was *scrolling*.

For a moment, relief at knowing I wasn't about to be killed by hurtling rocks washed away the high weirdness of the sight. Then, just as a rational explanation comes to you after you've been briefly baffled and thrilled by a strange light in the sky (well, it does to me) I thought I knew exactly what was going on. A flicker of memory of the story of the NKVD film, and the puzzle of the cable along the floor, made me think of the obvious explanation: that the scrolling lines of capitals were a projection; that somewhere in the cliff behind me a film was running through a cunningly angled projector; that what I was looking at was a hoax.

I let go of the cliff and walked across the floor of the chasm, waving my hand in front of me to see if it would intercept the projector's beam. It didn't. I leaned forward and laid a gloved finger on a "V" at eye level. My finger poked right into the incision in the rock. Two parings of thermal-lined Goretex fell from the tip of the glove, one on each side, where the seams brushed the groove's edges.

So what did I do? I did what any sensible, red-blooded American geek girl would do. I tugged the glove off, peered at the smooth damage, and then touched the letter with my bare fingertip, prodding into the groove and then touching its edge, rather like someone stupid enough to test a blade on their thumb. I felt a sharp pain and saw blood well.

"Ow!" I yelped, jumping back and sticking my cut fingertip in my mouth. I stood for a minute sucking at the cut and staring at sharply carved lines of Latin scrolling down a surface of solid rock.

"The blood of the Vrai," said a calm, amused voice behind me.

My spine seemed to contract as I reflexively jumped and ducked at the same moment. My feet jarred back on the ground, hurting my hunched neck. I spun around, to see a man standing by the cliff and aiming a pistol at me. For the second time in two days I stared into that blackest of black holes, and then I looked at the man's face.

"Tastes just the same, doesn't it?" said Ilya Klebov.

2.

In his late forties now, stouter around the middle, clad in ski jacket and trousers, thin gloves, and thick-soled boots, he was still instantly recognisable to me as the man I'd last seen seventeen years earlier. He held the weapon in his right hand, steadied on his left forearm, and looked at me with the same earnest, urgent expression as he'd had when he'd beseeched me to remember his name. I stared at him, speechless.

"My dear Lucy Stone," he said. He didn't say it sarcastically, but with warmth and affection. "It's good to see you."

My breath came out in something between a grunt and a laugh.

"Mr. Klebov," I said, "how did you get here, and what are you doing?"

Which, looking back, strikes me as quite the most rational thing I could have said in the circumstances. Klebov seemed to think so.

"Good questions," he said. "I got here along much the same route as you did, but rather more directly, because I've come here many times. As for what I'm doing here—I've come to meet you, to stop you from carrying out your mission, and to rescue you, as you may remember I once did before."

"I've never forgotten it," I said. I knew he could tell from the way I said it that this was my thanks. "Rescue me from what?"

"Lucy," he said, "what are you seeing?"

"I'm seeing a man pointing a gun at me," I said.

He smiled, as if he had to smile. "Very good," he said. He made a flicking motion with the pistol barrel. "I mean on the wall behind you. Look at it."

I turned away—neck already a little stiff—and looked again at the scrolling stone text.

"What do you see, Lucy?"

"Lines of Latin, I think, scrolling down the rock. It's . . . something impossible."

"Forget impossible," Klebov said. "It exists; therefore it's possible.

Look at what you see, Lucy! Some of the 'V's are 'U's, if that helps. But don't try to read every word on the lines—look at the whole thing. What are you seeing?"

"Sic, something, tunc, operor computus treos, aliter, operor computus quadrus . . ." I laboriously read aloud.

Computus? I thought. The Romans had a word for *compute?* Wait a fucking minute. . . .

I gazed at the patterns the lines made, at how they were indented, how lines got repeated and how they varied, how certain words like SIC and TUNC and ALITER always appeared on a line by themselves, and always in that sequence.

I whirled around again to face Klebov.

"Sic—tunc—aliter!" I shouted. "If—then—else! It's *code!*"

"Yes," said Klebov.

"It's high-level computer code written in Latin!" I squealed, as if he doubted it.

"In *bad* Latin," said Klebov. "Nevertheless. Yes, that's what it is. You are looking at a programme, written in Latin, that has been scrolling down this rock for centuries. That is *remembered* to have been here before there was a computer in the world. If"—he sighed, as though over a hopeless wish—"it were merely carved in the rock, that would be a most remarkable and surprising fact, but not beyond the wit of man to explain away. That it is scrolling down the rock in complete defiance of physics and common sense—you'll notice that, though seemingly cut deep in the rock, the letters leave no trace in it of their passing—is rather compelling evidence that the world is not what we think it is."

"Or at least that that rock face isn't," I said.

"What?" said Klebov, sounding taken aback. "What do you think it is? Silly Putty?"

"Something like that," I said. "But a lot more advanced. Material that can behave like this is supposed to be possible with nanotechnology—smart matter, utility fog, you know? A swarm of programmed lock-and-release micro-machines?"

"I'm aware of the concept," said Klebov. "Are you telling me the *Romans* had nanotechnology?"

"Not in the world where Spartacus lost," I said, much too flippantly. (I was a little light-headed at this point.)

"What?"

"Nothing," I said, shaking my head and smiling. "Just a joke to myself, sorry. The point is, this exists in our world so it must follow our world's physics. Even if it comes from outside our world. Wow!"

Klebov still had me covered, but he was looking at me very oddly indeed.

"This thing doesn't disturb you?"

"No," I said. "Not now that I've seen it as code. It's amazing. It's wonderful, it's like we're seeing—maybe we *are* seeing—the physics engine of the world."

"The physics engine?"

"You know, the programme that controls the movements and so on of objects in a computer game?"

"Ah yes," said Klebov. "As in the game you have so craftily written for our little country. And who do you think wrote the game of the world? What programmer wrote that?"

"I don't know," I said. "Maybe we're living in a simulation—you know, like in *The Matrix*?—or maybe that rock is some kind of alien message that got placed here way back in Roman times and something got lost in transla-tion, or—"

Klebov, still keeping the pistol pointed straight at me, took his left arm away from under his right wrist and raised his hand.

"Enough," he said. "Curious speculations, no doubt, and interesting in their way. You are a more consistent materialist than I am, or than anyone else who has looked upon this sight, Lucy, I'll tell you that."

"What do *you* think it is?" I asked.

He shrugged. "I still incline to the view that the Vrai always took: that it was written by God, and that it was written in Latin because Latin was the language of the Church. By writing—in a rock, no less!—this endless and meaningless text, instead of, let us say, the Scriptures, God is telling us that all other writings and commandments attributed to Him are false. It tells us that He exists, indeed, but has left us no instructions. We are free."

From the tone of his voice I guessed that some of what he said was a quotation, a formula, perhaps a creed.

"And that's the secret of the Vrai?" I said. "The Krassnian truth?"

Klebov nodded. "Yes."

"What a beautiful message!" I said. "Why did they keep it secret? Why didn't they preach it to the world?"

Klebov's laugh echoed in the canyon. "They took from it the message of God's indifference and Man's freedom. And you ask me why they didn't preach that to their serfs?"

"Oh," I said. "Point. But if that's all there is to it, how come the serfs—the Krassnar—couldn't come near it safely?"

"A lie, as you see," Klebov said. "I have come here safely for years. In feudal times, when they were the rulers, the Vrai made sure to murder or mutilate any Krassnar who dared to come to this place. They cut out tongues. They gouged eyes. They hammered heads and damaged brains. After some centuries of this, the legend grew that the secret place guarded itself in horrible ways. In time, the legend itself was enough."

I shuddered. And then, as before, my mind came up with another question, another objection.

"That doesn't explain what happened in 1952," I said.

Klebov jumped as if stung. He almost dropped the heavy pistol. If I'd been trained in martial arts, I could probably have taken him down in that moment. He steadied his gun hand again over his left wrist, and took an involuntary step forward.

"What do you know about that?" he demanded.

"Only what my Nana told me," I said, and as I said so I realised I now knew—or could guess—a lot more than that. So I added, as if casually: "And that was just a tale I heard in childhood, Ilya Alekseyevich."

Klebov stood stock-still, breathing heavily.

"What are you saying?"

I took a deep breath myself, as if about to dive into water. Water whose depth and rocks I didn't know.

"Your father, Aleksey I. Klebov, blew out the brains of the last keeper of the Vrai truth—Beryozkin, that was his name, wasn't it? A man who despised the Krassnar and who would have loved to restore the Vrai to their ancient glory. A restorationist, working away inside the Party and the Cheka to undermine the State from within. A man who had framed and killed many loyal Party members, including one who was himself a Vrai and who had almost given away the secret to the grandchildren of those despised serfs.

"Your father knew this place—he was from one of the families or trades who guided the young Vrai to within sight of it. How pleased he must have been to have got rid of the old oppressors at last! And how shocked he must have been when Beria sent his men to find the secret. Of course your father knew something like that was going on—he was in the NKVD himself. He may not have known what the secret was, but he did know it had been used to oppress his people for generations, and that knowing it had made the Vrai confident and fearless enemies of the Soviet state.

"So he ambushed Beria's men, from the top of that cliff behind you. He hurled down grenades and followed that with firebombs. In such a narrow space, that should have been enough. But one man survived, perhaps because he was standing back and filming. He staggered out with the camera, and the film. The film that made Stalin and Beria quake in their boots, because they too saw it as God's writing on the wall."

Klebov listened to all this without expression, until the end, at which point he smiled.

"So you have heard that rumour too," he said. "A pretty story. A legend, that ends with a point, as all good legends must. You identify a legend by the fact that it *has* a point, Lucy. Your mother should have taught you that."

"What about the rest?" I cried. "What about your father?"

"What you said is . . . not quite how it was, but close enough. My late father was more superstitious than you imagine—he felt it his duty to guard, not the secret, but Stalin and Beria and the people *from* the secret. He really believed it could do terrible things to people who were not of the Vrai. Oh, and you are wrong about the grenades. He used explosives from the copper mine, and petrol. Enough petrol, it would seem, to start a brush fire on the mountain that burned for a week. A pity he didn't think to bring more explosives."

He glanced around, and down at his watch, and up at me.

"But I did," he said.

3.

I just stared at him, feeling stupid after having felt clever.

"Did what?"

"I have brought enough explosives here," he said in a patient, explaining voice, "to bring down that rock wall. They are planted along the crack. They are wired to this cable." He indicated, with his toe. "I have done this over many months, in readiness for this day."

"But why?" I cried. I closed my eyes and shook my head. "It's a wonder of the world! It's the most significant thing in the world! Maybe in the universe! Every scientist on earth would love to see this!"

He looked unmoved.

"If this thing reveals some deep truth, as you think, science will someday find that truth by itself."

I thought of another plea.

"That would be the best revenge on the Vrai," I said, "to give their secret to the world."

This time, he looked pitying.

"How wrong you are," he said. "It is the Vrai—and their like—who want the world to know this. Why do you think you are here?"

I said nothing.

"Come, come, Lucy," he said. "Don't be stubborn. I know you were sent here. And I don't know, but I can assume, that you have some recording and communications equipment in that bag on your back."

"Well, all right," I said. "There's not much point my denying it. But what has that got to do with the Vrai? There aren't any Vrai anymore, except . . ."

"Except distant descendants," said Klebov. "Quite. Descendants like you, and, more to the point, your mother. Your mother, Amanda, who has a claim to a piece of property that I own, and who has some reason to think that everyone knowing what's here will help her to get it back."

"That's not it at all," I said. "I'm doing this for the US government, which wants to know what's here before the Russians come in or the revolution is crushed."

Klebov shook his head. "The US government and the CIA have a hand in this, yes, but what is essentially going on is a family quarrel over property, fought with armies and secret services."

A *family* quarrel? I thought.

"You're saying Amanda is *using* the CIA? To get the mine back?"

"Exactly."

This was so close to my own earlier suspicions that I was a little shaken.

"But why should she want the secret to be known?"

"Because it would make Krassnia the centre of world attention. At present, this country is so obscure that any crackdown or even a Russian incursion would be seen as a minor mopping-up operation between Ossetia and Abkhazia. If this comes out—it's just as you say, every scientist in the world would want a look. It would indeed be a wonder of the world."

"And you would destroy it, to hang on to a bloody copper mine?"

"Not for that, no," said Klebov. "It's not about *a bloody copper mine.* It's about the blood of the Vrai. I will destroy this rock to prevent the Vrai raising their heads, claiming their obscure bloodlines, and basking in the prestige of having guarded this wonder for centuries."

"If you hate the Vrai so much," I said, "why did you rescue us?"

"I don't hate the Vrai," Klebov said. "I hate what they did to our people, not just in ancient times but in Stalin's time. I hate their traditions, their sense of superiority, their 'truth' and their 'blood.'" He laughed bitterly. "There is no *truth* in the story of the *blood* of the Vrai. There is not even a genetic difference between Vrai and Krassnar. There is a gene for red hair, yes, but generations of rape and bastardy spread it among the Krassnar, usually unexpressed, as in my case, because it's recessive. Apart from that, nothing. That's what I asked that doctor to find out. And when he did—or rather, when the results from those DNA samples came back from a very dilapidated Institute of Physical Ethnography in Moscow, years later—I knew it was safe to come here."

He motioned briskly to his left with the weapon. "So, Lucy, enough talk. Place your bag on the ground and walk away. Wait for me, if you wish, at the bottom of the last slope you climbed, and I'll join you at a run in a few minutes. I'll see you safely off the mountain and back to your CIA pal Andrei Milyukhin before the sun sets."

I reached for my shoulder strap, moving slowly, thinking fast.

"You knew about him?" I asked.

Klebov snorted. "It was because he disappeared from the revolution that I knew to expect you."

"You've been expecting me since before I was born," I said. "You knew what would someday be asked of Amanda's child. The only person of Vrai ancestry the CIA could rely on. One of their own. And yet you saved me, when you could have abandoned me to the pogrom."

I laid the bag slowly on the ground. "You saved me for the same reason you're not going to shoot me now. Because you're my father."

After having all those guys (well, OK, two, but I was beginning to feel a bit like the girl in *Mamma Mia!*) claiming they might be my father, I felt a small triumph in batting this ball the other way for a change. Small consolation, because if what I'd said was true . . .

Klebov stuck the pistol in a side pocket of his jacket, and wiped his nose on the back of his wrist. This might have indicated a sentimental moment, or that his nasal septum had an itch or a drip that had been bothering him for some time while he'd been keeping me covered.

"I've committed a lot of crimes," he said, "but you were my only sin. The only thing I did not because I had to, but because I could. It wasn't rape, you understand. Your mother and I came to . . . an understanding."

"One in which you had the power."

"Yes." He looked uncomfortable. "A favour, in exchange for Gusayevich's freedom, and . . . other considerations."

"*What* other considerations?"

"Her area of study was more sensitive than the fools in Moscow knew when they approved her stay, or than we in Krassnia could tell them. I had real concerns about so-called ethnic tensions, the nationality question as we called it, to say nothing of her poking into the business of Arbatov and the whole legend. She was travelling around Krassnia, talking to people—old folk, mostly—and uncovering some very interesting information about how they and others really felt. I suspected she was reporting—by what channels, I didn't know, but could have found out—to the US embassy in Moscow. I told her that I wouldn't have her slung out of the country, if she would share her reports with me—at least, those that concerned certain individuals who were, as we put it, speculating on difficulties in the nationality question. My superiors were far more satisfied with that success than they would have been with Gusayevich's name."

"You got *Amanda* to work for the KGB?"

"I never turned her, if that's what you mean."

"Great," I said. "But she did spy for you on, what, Krassnian nationalists?"

"Krassnar chauvinists—the same people who later, in 1991 when they had their chance, tried to launch a pogrom against ethnic Georgians, Jews, and supposed Vrai. Thanks to Amanda's information, I and my men had enough advance warning to crush that pogrom before it could get off the ground."

"You're saying that somehow justifies what you did? That it's all square?"

"I don't think in those terms," said Klebov. He grimaced. "You're right, I won't shoot you. But I can hurt you, very painfully, and quicker than you think. You would be unable to move for several minutes, which is all the time I need. After that we could leave, though not as fast as I would like. Let's spare ourselves the embarrassment. Step well away from the bag."

I did. Klebov snatched it up, and fished out the satellite phone. He gave it a curious look and thoughtful heft, then put it somewhere inside his jacket. He zipped the bag up and tossed it back to the ground at my feet. I crouched to pick it up, not taking my eye off Klebov.

"You're relieved you still have your own phone," Klebov said, as I stood up. "Too bad for you there's no network coverage up here."

I must have still looked smug instead of crestfallen, because he added: "I don't care about pictures. Take as many as you want."

He gave me a dismissive wave and walked away, disappearing around the side of the ravine. I fumbled out my iPhone and videoed the scrolling text until Klebov came back, at a run.

"Fifteen minutes," he said. He motioned ahead. "After you."

I ran for the end of the ravine, scrambled down the rock steps, and hared down the slope. Klebov caught up with me as I teetered on the edge of the snowfield. He stuck his legs over and slid down on his back and elbows, heels dug in. I did the same. Down we went like toboggans. At the bottom we both got up and ran, our long shadows pacing us to our left. Up the shorter, scrubby slope on the other side and over into the scree-covered declivity where I'd seen what might have been an *almas*. Down and up the sides we crashed, feet slithering on the stones. Just as we reached the top and were about to plunge down the longer scrub-covered slope, I felt a shudder in the ground under my feet.

I turned as the air thumped my ears. We must have been about a kilometre from the cliff face. Its detail stood out sharply in the slanting sunlight. The rock face in front of the ravine was quite distinct. Dust clouds bloomed above it, then from two vertical cracks about a hundred metres apart. For a moment nothing more seemed to happen. Then, with a crash that shook the ground again, the entire rock face slipped down about ten metres. Its top began to move forward, then the whole rectangle of rock toppled forward with another groundshaking crash. Curtains of dust obscured the raw new cliff face for a minute, then began to dissipate and settle.

"For a moment there," Klebov said, "I was afraid the text column would hold the cliff, or stay standing like a pillar." He clapped me on the shoulder. "So much for nanotechnology and smart matter, eh?"

I shook with reaction and exertion. Sweat chilled on my brow and back.

"It's not funny," I said. "You've done something . . ." I shook my head. "I don't know, it's like . . . sacrilege. Like the Taliban blowing up those Buddhas in Afghanistan, only worse, because that thing was *real*."

"Best thing the Taliban ever did," said Klebov. "Iconoclasm is progressive."

He reached inside his jacket and handed back the satellite phone.

"I suppose you have calls to make."

He took a few steps away, as if to give me privacy. I glared after him, then looked down at the phone. No point in using the SKY number—I had no streaming video on *this* phone to uplink. I could have kicked myself for not having whipped the satellite phone out and hit Record the second I saw the stone text, instead of wasting a precious minute or two gawping at it and cutting my finger and letting Klebov sneak up on me. For a vengeful moment I considered hitting the number I'd labelled 911—the scream for help. What would happen, I wondered—parachutes or hang gliders suddenly blossoming in the sky, Special Forces snake-eaters jumping out of the undergrowth, ready to snatch Klebov away to some ghost prison or black site? Hah! That'd larn him!

My finger moved to the number tagged ROS. I hated the thought of telling him how the mission had turned out. Just as I was about to press it I saw a bright flash. I looked up, startled, and saw another, and another, light up the newly exposed cliff face. As the third went off I heard a bang and a peculiar screaming sound, which was repeated at one-second intervals. White-hot splashes erupted along the line where the ravine had been: *flash-flash-flash-flash* . . .

After about ten flashes there was a momentary pause, in which the bangs and screams continued and echoed, like thunder after lightning. Then I saw another flash, on the slope beside the fallen rock face, then another, closer to us. A moment later, a splash of red and white erupted steaming from the snowfield. The flashes were tracking the exact route we'd taken. A phrase rose to the top of my mind: *creeping barrage*.

Then another: *GPS*.

I hurled the satellite phone as far as I could across the vale of scree.

"Run!" I shouted.

Klebov, who'd been as transfixed as I was, jolted out of his open-mouthed rigor and fled downhill. I threw myself after him, helter-skelter. A flash-bang-scream behind us and a blast of heat was followed seconds later by a hissing shower of stones and red-hot debris that made the scrub smoulder. None hit us. At the foot of the slope we blundered in among the trees. I shielded my eyes with my arm as branches lashed my face.

By the time we reached the clearing we knew that the bombardment had stopped. We continued by sheer momentum until we collapsed from the waist across the sacrifice stone. Klebov was saying something in Krassnian that sounded like a prayer, but not to God. After a few gasps I recognised his words as lines spoken by Duram at this very stone.

We heaved our chests from the stone and turned around, leaning against the rock, hands on our knees, still breathing hard. Klebov looked sidelong at me.

"I thought if I was going to die here I might as well have a word with the gods of our fathers first," he said. "What the devil were these things?"

He sounded as bewildered as the characters in *Lost* fleeing from the black smoke thing in the forest.

"Kinetic-energy weapon," I said. "Metal shafts, dropped from orbit or very high altitude. Rods from God."

Klebov took a few more deep breaths. "I've heard of that project," he said. "It hasn't been built yet."

"Looks like it has," I said. "Black-budget job, I guess."

"You assume they were American?" Klebov said. "With such precision? More likely your aliens."

"If they'd been aimed by aliens they'd have hit us," I said. "These were striking the places where the phone had been—along where the ravine was, then along our path. That last one probably hit the phone."

"I'm not going back to find out," said Klebov. "Or stay around, for any more magic weapons—or the patrols coming to investigate."

He shoved himself upright. "Let's go."

We got off the mountain about 6:30. Klebov confidently followed a different route from the one I'd taken, a route with better concealment: thicker woods, deeper gullies, fewer scree slopes. All the time I felt exposed, not to the patrols (we saw one, of two men toiling up a hillside far away), but to whatever had aimed and hurled the strange shafts from above. The feeling of being watched never left the back of my neck.

Nor did the feeling of betrayal from my gut.

I kept thinking about what might have happened if I'd succeeded in using the sat-phone to take and uplink a video of the ravine's secret—to a geosynchronous satellite, Ross had speculated. Would the phone, and I holding it, have been obliterated as soon as its job was done? I couldn't believe that Ross, let alone Amanda, could have countenanced such a plan. But I was in no mood, now, to phone either of them. Ross wasn't expecting a call from me anyway, not until I'd got out of the country. When I did, I intended to give him a piece of my mind. As for Amanda, I would make her ears burn.

We climbed down to the road through a copse of conifers about a mile farther west than I'd ascended, and walked along its side a few hundred metres to the farmhouse with a refreshment stall where Andrei waited. Anxiously scanning the mountainside and checking his phone for messages, he didn't see us coming until we crunched across the gravel in front of the corrugated-iron canopy that shaded the benches and tables.

He sprang up. "Emma! Are you all right?"

"I'm fine," I said wearily. "Forget 'Emma.'" I jerked my thumb over my shoulder. "He knows. Andrei, meet Ilya."

We sat down opposite Andrei. Klebov waved to a woman sitting by a table in the room back of the veranda and asked for more tea. Andrei took the opportunity of this distraction to lean across the table and speak quietly and urgently in my ear.

"What does he know?"

"Everything," I said. "He recognised me, and he knows about you."

"How did you recognise her?" Andrei asked Klebov.

"She recognised me," Klebov said truthfully enough, and smoothly added the lie: "And from that, of course, I knew she could only be the American girl from all those years ago. The events of that day were just as memorable for me, you know."

The two men regarded each other warily, silent until the tea had been brought.

"Well," said Klebov, passing a cup to me, "this is a little awkward. Shall we declare a truce?"

Andrei frowned, then gave a reluctant nod.

"I heard explosions," he said. "I was very worried."

"Not worried enough to phone," I said.

"Too worried," Andrei said. "I didn't want to make things worse, if you'd been captured."

He looked hurt.

"Sorry," I said. "I didn't think of it that way."

"What happened?" Andrei asked. He lowered his voice. "Did you find the famous secret?"

Klebov and I looked at each other. The first sips of tea, and the relief of getting off the mountain, went to my head. I giggled. Klebov gave me a severe look that only made things worse.

"I'm sorry," I said, spluttering. "This is all so—"

I took out my iPhone, selected the video I'd made, and handed the phone across to Andrei.

"This is what I found," I said. "Press Play."

Andrei watched the recording, and passed the phone back.

"This is an illusion of some kind?" he asked. "A projection?"

"Well done," I said. "That was my first thought, too, until I cut my finger on one of the letters."

Andrei stared at the little scar on my fingertip as if it might hold some clue. Evidently not. He shook his head.

"I don't understand," he said.

"Neither do I," I said. "But take it from me, there was a totally bizarre phenomenon up there, and Mr. Klebov can assure you that it had been there for many years."

"Was?" said Andrei, suspiciously.

"This is where our story becomes truly incredible," said Klebov, sounding sincerely apologetic. "Those explosions you heard were in fact a bombardment, which utterly destroyed the ravine of the stone text mere minutes after we had left it."

"'We'?" said Andrei. "You were there too, were you?"

"I was," said Klebov, still with the smooth assurance. "Through certain . . . old and trusted acquaintances of mine, I had in recent days learned a number of disturbing facts." He began ticking these off on his fingers. "One: the online game which has become so popular among our excitable youth has in its landscape a route and other clues to what certain experts in such matters considered to be the likely location of the so-called secret place of the Vrai, and some of the young players were becoming interested in this. Two: it was considered necessary, in the interests of public safety, to prevent unauthorised access to this site, which was after all a very dangerous place. Tragic, almost inexplicable events have occurred there within living memory. Given the inadequacy of the patrols on the mountain, any wide-scale exercise of public curiosity about this place of grim repute would sadly stretch the resources of the State. Consequently, a decision was made to ask a friendly neighbouring power to destroy the site by aerial bombardment. Three: a certain young activist in the self-styled democratic opposition had been pulled from his leading position in the movement by his, let us say, paymasters and had taken up bird-watching, training his binoculars on this very mountainside.

"I had the young man placed under discreet observation. Imagine my horror when this afternoon I learned that he had sent a young foreign woman up the mountain on an apparent foray to the site! The regular RSB forces were fully occupied with keeping watch on the antics of the so-called democrats. The mountain's guards were impossible to reach. There was not a moment to lose. I took my car to a spot not far from here and hastened up the mountain myself. What terrible fate—whether from the unknown but severe dangers of the site itself, or from its imminent destruction—might await her? What awful consequences might this have for our country's reputation? Such thoughts preyed on my mind as I hurried to the scene. Imagine my relief when I found the young lady! Imagine my amazement when I saw that the site actually was the location of a most mysterious phenomenon! Imagine, if you can, my dismay when this fascinating site was utterly annihilated by a precision strike not ten minutes after we had reluctantly dragged ourselves away from marvelling at it!"

He told this bullshit story in such a smooth tone I could almost have believed it myself, and finished with a smile at me. "However, all's well that ends well, eh?"

I didn't know what to say. How he could pull off such a performance so soon after what had happened was beyond me. I had to remind myself that the two biggest shocks I'd had this afternoon—that the world was a very different place from what I'd always thought, and, oh yes, quite apart from that little piece of empirical metaphysics, that Klebov was my father—were old news to him.

"I'm very grateful to you, Mr. Klebov," I said. "Not for the first time."

Andrei scowled. "I suppose I should say the same."

Klebov bowed from the neck. "It was only business, both times."

"I'm . . . surprised . . . you didn't think to phone someone and call off the air strike," Andrei said. "Especially once you'd seen this marvel."

"I have less influence than you might think," said Klebov. "Besides, there's no coverage up there. Now that you mention it, I had switched my phone off."

He took his phone from his pocket, checked for messages, and rang his voicemail. He pressed the phone to his ear in intent silence for a minute, his lips compressing more and more. When he'd finished he gazed at the phone in his hand for a moment as if it were some shiny toy he was going to have to part with. He slipped it back in his pocket and stood up.

"I have to get back to Krasnod immediately," he said. "Andrei, could I trouble you for a lift?"

"Certainly," said Andrei. He laid a few notes on the table under a saucer.

As I too rose to leave I said to Klebov: "Didn't you say you'd left your own car somewhere nearby?"

Klebov and Andrei laughed.

"My dear Lucy," Klebov explained, "a man in my position does not *drive his own car*."

Klebov insisted, in what I thought an odd reversal of the usual courtesy, that he take the front passenger seat and I sit in the back. As soon as Andrei pulled out, Klebov told him to drive fast.

"Why?" asked Andrei.

"There's trouble in the town," said Klebov. "The troops are being readied to move out of barracks. I'd rather be ahead of the column than behind."

Andrei stepped on it, overtaking a bus and avoiding an oncoming truck. Ahead lay the spur of road to the military base. I leaned forward to look between the men's heads through the windshield. Dust was rising from behind the scrub and trees that shielded the base from view. Around the long bend towards town, traffic looked heavier than normal. Buses, trucks, cars . . . it might be just the local rush hour, but I doubted it.

"Stop," I said.

"What?" said Andrei, catching my eye in the rearview mirror.

"Please," I said. "Just let me out, now."

Klebov looked over his shoulder. "This is a bad idea, Lucy."

"Sorry, Ilya Alekseyevich," I said, "but I am not going into Krasnod if the troops are about to go in. I am just—fucking—not."

Klebov turned away and looked straight ahead.

"Drive," he said. Then, still looking ahead: "Lucy, I will not let you become a refugee."

"Fuck you!" I screamed. "Andrei, stop!"

"Sorry," said Andrei, "but I agree with him. If you think the troops are dangerous, wait till you see the militias."

"I've *seen* the militias!" I said. "On the border on the way in."

"Yes," said Klebov. "You don't want to meet them on the way out. You'll be safe in the city even if the troops do come in. Stay in your hotel, stay away from Freedom Square, and leave the country when the government has proper control of the border again."

My panic began to subside.

"All right," I said, with ill grace. "Why doesn't the government have proper border guards, anyway?"

"Because it needs all its available security forces to keep the opposition down," said Klebov.

"Now there at least we are in agreement," said Andrei.

The two men chuckled in the complicity of mutual respect. I sat back in sullen silence for the rest of the journey. Andrei, with a wry smile, dropped me outside the Metro. Klebov looked at me with the same odd expression as he'd shown when he'd met me at the ravine, and at our previous parting. It was like he was trying to memorise my face, and hoped I would remember his.

"Goodbye, Lucy Stone," he said, leaning over to the back for an awkward handshake.

"See you in another life, Father," I said.

Andrei shot me a startled look.

"A private joke," said Klebov.

I watched the yellow car out of the street, then crossed the road and entered the Kosmo.

10. THE SIMULATION ARGUMENT

1.

The room had been made up. Like all European hotel rooms, it was far too warm. I shrugged off my jacket and fleece and turned up the aircon. I boiled water in the kettle, made Nescafé, and devoured the complimentary biscuits. All that did was stack a shaky sugar and caffeine rush on top of my hunger. I hadn't eaten since breakfast. Thinking about food and the morning reminded me of Ross. The time now was 7:30. Knowing Ross's habits, he was probably stopped somewhere, having a bite. I called his number, which he'd so thoughtfully tabbed to my iPhone the previous night.

"Hi, Lucy." Sound of chewing and swallowing. "How's things?"

"Mission accomplished," I said.

"Oh, brilliant! Well done!"

"Uh, not exactly," I said.

Wary voice: "How so?"

I gave him a fast-forward account of how so.

"Jesus!" he said, not for the first time, when I'd finished. "Klebov . . . ? And then . . . ? Fuck."

"They were trying to kill me," I said.

"Or maybe just destroy the sat-phone."

"Don't make excuses for them," I said.

"No, no, I'm just . . . trying to figure out where their minds are at. Look, it must have been triggered by not getting the uplink, before you—I mean, the GPS trace—started heading back down the mountain. Maybe they thought you or more likely someone else, the Russians or whoever, had made the video and was making off with it, to sell or use or take back to Moscow."

"So the rods from God weren't aimed at me? Just the phone I was carrying? I'm feeling safer already."

Actually, I was, but I wasn't going to give him the satisfaction of my admitting it.

"You have to let them know the Russians don't have it," said Ross.

"Let who?" I asked. "Even *you* don't know which three-letter agency we're working for."

"I'll tell your mother," said Ross. "Right away. She has the contact. And I'll let her know you're safe."

"Yes, you do that," I said. "And while you're at it, tell her to hang on to her shares in the Ural Caspian Mineral Company."

Long pause.

"That isn't what this is about," said Ross.

"Klebov thinks it is."

"Klebov's an old commie. For him, everything's got to have a materialist explanation."

"You know as well as I do, that's kind of the opposite of the truth."

"Yeah, I suppose I do. Shit. What a maroon."

"That's a bit racist."

"Is it? Fuck me. These days . . . it's like you're not supposed to put salt on your language. Anyway. I wish to fuck he hadn't blown the fucking thing up."

"So do I," I said. "Still, at least it means the Russians won't get it."

"There is that," said Ross. "There is that."

I thought about room service, looked at the menu, then thought again. I remembered Klebov's advice to stay in the hotel, and bristled. No way, I thought, no fucking way was I going to cower in my room through a revolution, if that was what was about to happen. I considered changing, and again thought, the hell with it. I'd changed once already today, the hill-walking trousers would keep the evening chill off, and if I had to run, the boots were as good as any footwear I had. I wouldn't need the fleece, or the gloves. As I took the light but bulky gloves from my bag (and wondered again at the two enigmatic surfaces left by the two smooth slices taken from one fingertip) I thought to empty out other stuff I wouldn't have to lug around. Might as well keep the two real passports: though they'd be embarrassing in a search, I didn't want to leave them, even in a hotel safe. And the cards . . . I'd need the cards for cash and credit. The pink Moleskine . . . I physically swithered over that, tugging it out, hefting the bag to see how much difference that made to the weight, and sliding it back. As I did so, the notebook's stiff cover snagged on something.

A long white envelope, bent into a curve around the inside of the little backpack. Just as it had been in the lilac satin bag I'd emptied into this one, ten days ago when I'd been setting off. My amazing, knee-shaking gift from Alec, the open return airline ticket to New Zealand. Suddenly I missed Alec so much that I threw myself face-first on the bed and cried.

The funny thing was, up until now I hadn't missed him. The journey was in a different world than Alec. I'd tried texting him, on the first few days of the journey. After getting no replies, I'd stopped. My guess was that Alec wanted to hear me saying I was coming out to NZ, before he'd respond, because anything less than that would have meant that all of a sudden we were just friends. Something like that. I was cross with him. In the first days of trucking, my thinking was muddled. I hadn't missed him anything like as much as I'd missed Hiro, the girls, the lads, even my job. These were in a part of my mind labelled "things I do every day"—and, every day for the past ten days, these were all things I hadn't been doing. And it wasn't like a holiday. I couldn't think "wish you were here," which (unserious though that sentiment usually is) does stop us missing people while we're away, and stops us feeling bad about not missing them.

So right now I felt guilty about not having missed Alec. On top of missing him enough to make me cry.

I rolled over and sat up, sniffling. I went into the en-suite, wiped my nose and splashed my face, and put on some makeup, just as I'd done the night of Suze's wedding, when Alec had gone away. Suitably freshened-up, I pushed the white envelope back in the bag, zipped up the bag and slung it over my shoulder, and stepped more cheerfully to the door. I'd get a good hot dinner inside me, have a look at the fringes of what was going on at Revolution Square, and—assuming the tanks didn't roll tonight—get the bus to Batumi in the morning. From there I could see about flying back to Edinburgh.

Hand on the doorknob, I stopped, struck by a thought.

Why should I go back to Edinburgh? I didn't have my job anymore. My flatmates weren't expecting me back in less than a month. Hiro . . . yeah, yeah, the little bundle of fur and hunting reflexes would come over all snooty and accusing after my absence, but he did that whenever I went out, and I didn't kid myself the cat missed me anything like I missed him.

Whereas Alec must be . . . Oh, God. My eyes welled again. Don't waste all that hard work in front of the mirror, Lucy! Sniff. Wipe. There.

Out I went. I took a stroll down to the corner of the Prospekt, glanced left and right, and saw nothing untoward—lots of lights and loud music from Freedom Square, lots of people heading in its direction, that was all. I turned and walked back up Simkin Street, away from the Prospekt and towards the nearby bar-restaurant where Ross and I had eaten the previous night. The menu hadn't been outstanding, but I was far more hungry than fussy and in any case I didn't fancy wandering about looking for somewhere else.

I ate shashliks and rice with salad, on my own at a table for two. The place was about half empty, dim-lit, fast. I drank only water, and a coffee at the end. As I ate I thought. In the short term at least, I had serious trust issues with everyone involved in my mission. Ross and Amanda had, I couldn't help thinking, shown a less than parental regard for my safety, and—if Klebov was right, and Ross was lying—were using me and a lot of other people in a pretty instrumental manner, all things considered. As for the shadowy backers of these two . . . well, if I was going to report back to representatives of the agency that'd launched the rods from God at me, I wanted to set that up very carefully indeed. Flying to New Zealand looked more and more like a good option.

That settled, my mind turned to other worries. While waiting for the coffee I replayed the video of the scrolling text. Klebov had been so right not to bother about my making this recording. With the moving text itself destroyed, what did moving pictures of it matter? They weren't evidence that could convince anyone. Not much could even be learned from the statements themselves: as far as I could see they were all banal, along the lines of "If distance greater than so and so, apply calculation number one; if not, apply calculation number two." Which, given that you didn't know what the calculations were, was not a whole lot of help. If this was a sample of the physics engine of the universe, it told us nothing about the physics.

What did it tell us? Only that if we were living in a simulation, the programmers of that simulation spoke (or at least coded in) something like Latin.

Which was, now that I came to think of it, useful information.

Lots of people are familiar with the simulation idea, if only because so many people have seen *The Matrix*. Not so many are familiar with the simulation argument. The mere *idea* that we might be living in some kind of simulation or illusion is as old as Plato's Cave. There's the veil of *maya* in religion, Descartes' demon, the more recent puzzle of how you can be sure you're not a brain in a vat being electrically stimulated by some mad scientist, Nozick's experience machine, Boltzmann brains . . . the list goes on. The simulation *argument* is something else.

Here's how it goes.

There's no reason known to us, in principle, why we shouldn't someday invent an artificial intelligence, and (given that) why said AI shouldn't itself invent a better AI, and so on. There's (likewise) no reason why all the experiences of a human life couldn't be simulated in (or by) such an AI. So, a bit down that road, we have vastly powerful AIs with the capacity to simulate not just one human life, but many billions of human lives. Why should they do that? Well, a machine civilisation that had come out of our civilisation might well be interested in its origins, and could test various hypotheses about what made us tick by, well, making us tick. Given that the future for thinking machines (if not, alas, for us) is indefinitely long, this experiment is likely to be done many, many times in the future history of the universe . . . whereas, you know, the original history of real flesh-and-blood human beings happened at most once.

So, what are the odds? How much do you fancy your chances that you're in the *one true real world* and not in one of countless simulations of it in all the billions of years to come?

(Turns out the odds are only one in three that we *are* in a simulation, because several of the premises of the argument are questionable, and you can put numbers on just how questionable they are.)

What I'd just thought of was a very small variant on this: that there's no reason why every simulated history should turn out the same, and in particular, no reason why it should turn out the same as the original. If something like Sean's Romanson-Mars scenario of a Rome where the slaves had won and gone in for capitalism instead of Christianity was the original history, then they'd be centuries ahead of us technologically, centuries ago. Might that civilisation's AIs be programmed in something like Latin (in the same way as ours are programmed in something like English)?

The more I thought about it, the more plausible that seemed. After all, it was unlikely that Latin would become again a *lingua franca* in our future, and vanishingly less likely that it'd be used by aliens in our time—and if aliens had left the message in the era Latin was widely spoken, how likely was it that they'd chosen the form of computer code? Not very, it seemed to me—contrary to my initial speculation to Klebov.

All of which raised a very troubling thought indeed, quite apart from the sheer wackiness of the postulate.

How likely was it to be a coincidence that Sean and the lads had been struggling with a game—Olympus—whose scenario had turned out to be a possible explanation for something in the real-world equivalent of the game that I'd come up with to replace that one? (And I remembered remembering the word from Arbatov's book, the word that had been on the tip of my tongue, the word that had come back to me in the Auld Hoose: *simulacrum*.)

Was whoever had written the Stone Text tweaking our brains? And if so, why? It seemed a very small intervention, almost undetectable, as if they didn't want to be noticed. In which case . . . uh-oh. But the *really* disturbing thought was that the writers of the code might be aware of, and interested in, whatever happened around it. The feeling of being watched returned to the back of my neck.

It left, along with any chance of my taking all this simulation speculation seriously, when the waiter came with the bill. I paid in cash—roubles were good, I gathered—and left. Outside I looked at my watch. 8:45. Time I had a look at the revolution.

2.

I cut through a couple of side streets on to the Prospekt, and strolled to Freedom Square. As I approached the square the sidewalks became busier, the crowd spilling over onto the roadway and forcing cars to crawl. Though hardly packed, the square itself was far more crowded than it had been in the morning, with the proportion of young people a lot lower. The majority was now people in their twenties or thirties. There were old people and parents with kids here and there. The faces reminded me of the sort of faces I used to see in this very square on the first of May and the seventh of November. The most visible difference between now and then was in their clothes: still made under Communism, but in China. Bright maple-tinted lights hung from cables strung between trees and lampposts. From the sound systems, songs alternated with speeches. Most of the flags and maple-leaf cutout placards had been picked up and were being waved about or used as sticks to lean on. The tables of leaflets were bare, and the leaflets now in hands or littering the ground. I saw a lot of those A4 woodcuts of Duram pirated from our cover art, some on the ground, some being held high. Someone had turned on, dyed, and illuminated a fountain in the middle, so that it now spouted and bubbled and splashed pinkish-red water, a colour not so much maple in autumn as blood in rain.

The mood I caught from faces and voices was enthusiastic and hopeful. Even the speeches denouncing the governing party's preelection shenanigans sounded scornful rather than angry. I paced the fringe of the crowd, alert to who was around me and to where I was in relation to the square's entrances and exits. Gemarov Street, the alley in which I'd met "Fyodor," looked at first completely dark, and then as I saw it from a better angle, black with riot police like an insect infestation, all visored eyes and transparent shields and waving antennae.

At nine, they swarmed. They emerged from Gemarov Street and four other streets adjoining the square, and spread out along three sides, leaving the Prospekt clear. The sound system suddenly cut out. Above yells from the crowd, a bullhorn announcement told us that the permit for the demonstration in the square was only until nine o'clock. Everyone should now go home.

Quite a lot of people did, especially the old and those with young children. From where I was, up near the front, I could just make them out streaming away down the Prospekt. The PA system came back on. A Krassnian patriotic song boomed out for a couple of minutes, then a man in a light-coloured jacket took the podium and urged everyone to leave, and to return tomorrow.

Boos from the crowd. I elbowed my way to the steps of the parliament building, stepped between two riot cops—there were one-metre gaps between them at this stage, and they were letting people through—and looked back. The man in the light-coloured jacket walked away from the podium, and a man in a leather jacket took his place at the mike. I couldn't make out what he said, but I did hear an answering roar from all across the now more compact—and again younger—crowd. People in ones and twos passed between the cops, and unlike me didn't hang around on the parliament steps but walked across the corner and down to the street and away.

The previous speaker glanced over his shoulder, shook his head, and bounded up the broad shallow steps towards a gap in the line of cops. I remember his rueful smile as he approached, and the indignation on his face as a cop stuck out an arm and planted a thick-gloved hand on his chest. He took one step down and back, grimaced at the smudge the black glove had left on his open-neck white shirt, and reached inside his jacket. I distinctly saw he had two fingers curled back, two stretched out, the way you do when fishing a card or something out of a thin pocket.

At this the cop next to the one who'd stuck his hand out brought a baton, longer and thicker than a baseball bat, down hard on the top of the man's head. The sound of that crack gives me a flinch and a chill even now. The man sagged to the steps, stood up, staggered for a moment, and toppled backwards. The back of his head hit the paving at the foot of the steps with another crack I'll never forget.

The leather-jacketed guy at the podium was still ranting on, his words remixed by echoes from the surrounding buildings. Even above all that noise, I heard a collective gasp from the front of the crowd, followed by yells. Arms were outstretched, fingers pointing forward. The speaker stopped and turned around. At that point all the cops that I could see, and I guessed others I couldn't, strode forward and closer together at the same time. From where I stood, just by a pillar of the parliament's portico, their backs made a black wall.

A wall that moved away from me, down the steps, past or over the guy on the ground, and on. I recovered from my frozen shock enough to run down the steps and crouch beside the felled man. Maybe if I'd been better prepared I could have done something for him, but I doubt it. Someone with an armband and a case rushed up, knelt, leaned forward, and then rocked back, as helpless as I was.

Next thing I knew, I was back up the steps. The cops were wading in, batons flailing. People in the front of the crowd pushed back, and jabbed or

swiped with the flimsy sticks of their flags and placards. Almost no one was running away down the Prospekt. At first I thought this was because the riot cops
weren't getting the best of it—there were maybe three hundred of them, and
thousands in the crowd. Then I stood on tiptoe and gazed down the Prospekt
and saw why: a column of trucks and tanks was about two hundred metres away,
oily green under the yellow streetlights, and getting closer by the second.

The vehicles halted. Soldiers jumped out from the sides and ran into for-
mation. Moments later they marched forward, on the double. *Thump thump
thump* of their boots up the street.

The front ranks of the soldiers suddenly and raggedly stopped. The still-
marching ranks collided with them from behind, in an almost comical con-
fusion. I heard the angry shouts of officers. Then a hush rippled from the
Prospekt and through the square like a noise. Everyone was looking towards
the front of the square, it seemed at first—I looked around for some imposing
presence, and saw only faces as puzzled as my own—and then I saw the backward tilt of the heads.

They were looking at something behind the parliament building. Something to the north.

I dashed across the corner of the pediment and down the steps to the
street back of the square and clear of the crowd, and looked in the same direction. Even through the streetlights, I could see in the distance, above and in
front of Mount Krasny, a glow that shone straight up into the sky, a glow the
colour of maple leaves in autumn, the colour of auburn hair.

Later, it was claimed that the glow was from a heath fire on the mountain's
slope, and when the absence of vast areas of blackened hillside became embarrassing, that it was an unusual—indeed, unique—southerly auroral display.
My own instant explanation was that the Stone Text must have had its own
energy source, and that the glow came as the last of its energies dissipated,
ionising the air as they bled off into space.

The main thing I knew, the moment I saw it, was what was going to
happen next. That was why I ran for the hotel and, when I got there, locked
myself in my room.

All through the night I heard shouts, sirens, shots, the crash of glass in
the distance, now and then the rush of running feet in the street outside, and

the full-throated drunken singing of the songs that had boomed from the PA system in Freedom Square. I slept fitfully. In the morning I checked that the power was still on—it was—and had a shower. After breakfast in a front room of the hotel with its windows shuttered, I ventured out.

Broken glass on the street, a burned-out car at the corner. A roving militiaman reeled across the nearest junction, a bottle in one hand and a rifle in the other. From not far away, a shot echoed. I retreated hurriedly inside. Every terminal in the hotel's Internet room was taken, most of them by young backpackers who looked like they spoke English and with whom I'd no wish to speak. But the place had free wifi, and I remembered my iPhone. I sat at an empty table with a pot of coffee and went online.

. . . to find no news of the night's events in Krasnod, except a brief account on Russia Today TV. It stated that the Krassnian authorities had completely lost control of their own capital. The precipitating incident was said to be the unfortunate death of Edward Tuzmukhamedov, a Liberal Democrat MP. The report didn't mention the glow over Mount Krasny, but I could easily guess what had happened. The troops and cops had been shaken by the phenomenon, and the crowds enthused, all seeing it as some portent.

This hadn't been supposed to happen. It wasn't in the Colour Revolution script. What was supposed to happen was that the government would concede massive invigilation of the elections by the opposition and the NGOs, or, after narrowly and contestably winning, bow out with ill grace under the pressure of massive, peaceful demonstrations claiming (perhaps correctly) that the elections had been rigged. Nobody wanted this chaos. I expected the Russians to come in at any moment, probably from Abkhazia: their troops were roaming around there at will.

I finger-pecked awkwardly at the on-screen keyboard, searching for local travel information. The nearest I could find, going by the map reference, was in Georgian, a script I couldn't read. I went offline and phoned Andrei.

"You're still *here*?" he squawked.

"Yes," I said, somewhat defensively, "but I'm trying to get out. Are the buses running?"

"I'll call you back," he said.

A few anxious minutes later, he did. "There's a bus at ten for Nal'chik, in Kabardino–Balkaria," he said.

"That's in fucking Russia!"

"Yes," snapped Andrei, like I'd given him an insultingly needless geography lesson, rather than raised an objection, "but that's a better bet than Georgia, at the moment. Nothing's flying out of Nal'chik, but from there you can get to Sochi. Do you know where the bus station is?"

"Is it still back of the Opera House?"

He laughed. "As was. Yes. You can get a . . . Fuck it. I'll take you there. See you outside in half an hour. The Metro, yes?"

"Yes."

I packed, checked out, and waited, and the yellow car arrived outside the opposite hotel. I lugged my bag across the road and jumped in.

"Why did you keep doing that?" Andrei asked.

"I didn't trust you," I said. I strapped in. "I trust you now."

Everything happened just as I thought it would, working itself out like destiny, like machine code. Andrei dropped me at the bus station. The bus to Nal'chik, and every other bus across any of Krassnia's borders, was crowded with people who'd had the same idea as I'd had. I barely had time to wedge myself in a seat with my bags on my lap before we were off, on the road to the north. Looking back, I saw several separate pillars of smoke in the air above Krasnod.

Before long, the city was out of sight, as the road curved around the sides of the mountains. There was a junction where the road divided, the pass to Russia to the north, the road to Abkhazia going west. Along the road to the north, after another little while, we stopped. All the traffic stopped. An hour passed. Dull thuds up ahead, smoke. A tank and truck column, Russian tricolours flying, came out of the north, going past us at speed. The traffic moved forward. A couple of kilometres farther on, the Krassnia–Russia border was marked with a tank half off the side of the road, its turret like a hat askew; a couple of trucks twisted open, like aerosol cans on the ashes of a bonfire; and the gnarled and blackened meat of men smouldering by the road. The border post had been ground flat by tank treads.

There is no such place as Krassnia.

11. THE EXPLOIT

1.

And that, dear reader, is how I came to be in New Zealand.

(Remember, at the start? Queenstown airport? The Remarkables? The sinister note? We're getting there.)

When I reached Sochi, after three twelve-hour bus rides, I looked and no doubt smelled like a refugee. This had helped, at the border. I used the Emma Taylor cards for cash and credit, cleaned up, and booked a flight to Frankfurt via Istanbul in the name of Lucy Stone. I used my US passport at Sochi airport. The official frowned, tapped at the page with the entry stamp for Russia that I'd got at the Kabardino–Balkaria border, then stamped my passport and nodded me through. At Frankfurt I used my open return to New Zealand to get on a flight to Auckland, via Singapore, and time-travelled into Wednesday, August 25.

As I trudged the long queues from the time machine to the portal of normality at Auckland, the bag straining my shoulder more than usual, I passed several bins pointedly placed beneath notices warning of the dire consequences of taking undeclared biological materials into the country. Mud and grass on walking boots counted. I thought frantically of binning my boots, thought better of it, and became increasingly paranoid about the forged passport and dodgy cards stashed in a zipped inner pocket of my little backpack. Nothing happened.

At the first ATM after Arrivals I took out a wad of NZ$, real funny money made of waterproof paper with a little leaf-shaped transparent panel, on Emma Taylor's account. Feeling as if I'd gotten away with something, I walked with shaking knees into a spring dawn and found the taxi rank.

"Where to?"

The driver was dark-skinned with tattoos dotted over his cheekbones and had an indistinguishable Kiwi accent and manner. I'd thought the UK was racially relaxed but this was something else.

241

"Uh . . ." I knew exactly one address in Auckland, from an evening of idle browsing of fashion sites (with New Zealand floating at the back of my mind) in the buildup to Suze's wedding. "Trelise Cooper, Princes Wharf."

The driver gave me an appraising look, as if to check whether I was an actress or model travelling incognito. With depressing alacrity he clocked that I wasn't.

"Hop in then, miss."

Didn't even offer to take my bag.

From the fast road into town the place looked like England. I nearly cried. Only the roadkill was different. Long-tailed furry animals, flattened except for their teeth.

"Possums," said the driver, noticing. "Bloody pests. Even the eco people tell us to run them over."

Half an hour later I found myself standing on a sidewalk near a development the general size and shape of a cruise liner, looking in the window of a boutique full of floaty dresses on snooty mannequins, and wondering what to do next. A sudden pang inside reminded me that airline meals don't actually nourish. I checked Google Maps on my iPhone, and lugged my bag a few hundred metres to a café near the Maritime Museum, where I sat at an outdoor table on a floating deck and ordered up a full English breakfast served by a small Irish waitress. After leaving a few crumbs for the plump sparrows, I felt fortified enough to call Alec.

"Lucy!" he said. "Wow! Great to hear from you! Are you back?"

"Back where?"

"Back from your trip."

"I'm in Auckland," I told him.

He was silent long enough for me to get worried.

"Wow!" he said again, at last. "That is so great! I'm, I'm . . . Jeez. I'm overwhelmed, Lucy."

"So am I," I said, shakily. "Uh, why didn't you reply to my texts?"

"I'm sorry," he said. "I was angry. There didn't seem much to reply to."

I took a breath deep enough for him to hear. "OK. OK. Well. Maybe you're right. Where are you and when can I see you?"

"Driving around on the South Island, running errands for the old family business. I can fly to Auckland from Queenstown tomorrow."

"You can? That's fantastic!"

We made arrangements to meet.

"I love you," I said.

"I love you too," he said. "See you tomorrow."

I lugged my big bag along until I happened to pass a luggage shop, where I (well, Emma) bought a strong-shelled rolling case, into which I stuffed the bag as it was. Happening to pass a chemist's shop resulted in a similar happy thought, and I came out with a box of a hair colour approximating what mine had been like before. I booked in for one night to the Mercure on off-season rates that looked reasonable in NZ$ and cheap in pounds. There I showered, changed my hair colour, changed my clothes, repacked, and set out about eleven to see the sights of Auckland. The hotel was more or less in the CBD, the Sky Tower struck me as an experience I'd want to share with someone, for example, Alec, and I hadn't a clue where to go. I shuffled tourist information leaflets in the lobby and decided on Devonport, a small touristy town just across the water. I remembered seeing ferries at the wharf near where I'd had breakfast, so I ambled along East Customs Street, feeling very light and jaunty with just my little backpack, and around the corner to the quay area. By the time I got there I'd almost, but not quite, overcome the startle reflex at the loud, chivvying chatter made by the noisy gadget in the pedestrian crossing lights. I found Fuller's Ferries and bought a return ticket.

On the way across I sat out front. The breeze and spray dispelled my jet-lag. The lightness I felt stayed when I sat. It came from more than having less to carry, more even than having touched base again with Alec. It came, I realised, from the sense of being free of it all. Free from the Other Thing. As the boat butted the waves I marvelled that I was facing north, at nearly noon, and the sun was in front of me. I was on a whole other side of the planet. The Other Thing had never been destiny. It had never been some occult emanation from the Stone Text. The whole time, all the way back along the mother-lines to Lord Hugh Montford himself over a century earlier, the inveiglement of my family with the dark affairs of Krassnia had been the by-product of the machinations of intelligence services, of imperial and business interests, of Communist and capitalist conspiracies. Here, almost half a world away from Krassnia, I was well shot of the lot of them.

I skipped down the gangplank and found to my delight that the shopping started even before you'd got out of the pier's long shed. I picked up a Stewart & Cohen at a bookstall, plunged into a stall for a vintage clothes shop called Enygma, and bought a pretty skirt made from thin orange satin with vertical orange lace panels, like something recycled from a bridesmaid's dress that had traipsed down the aisle in the decades that taste forgot. It went very well with a rust-brown top with a boat-shaped cowl neck, which I bought too.

"Eat your heart out, Trelise Cooper!" I said to the girl at the stall as she folded them neatly into the bag. She smirked complicitly, then put her hand to her mouth.

"Actually," she said, "I'm trying to get a job there."

"Your secret's safe," I said.

I walked out grinning and swinging the fat plastic bag. Above the shore streets rose a low hill, maybe a hundred metres high, called Mount Victoria. Diverted through two more secondhand bookshops and another clothes shop in Victoria Road, my ascent of Mount Victoria was longer and more laden than I'd expected. It was about two o'clock before I'd wended to its grassy summit, and stood amid the grooved steel circles of gun emplacements that had once guarded Auckland from the Imperial Russian Navy. In its spectacular obsolescence, as much as in its shape, the site resembled a hillfort or a henge. If our civilisation were to fall, I'd reckon on little more than a millennium until antiquaries and tomb robbers would be speculating on what great king lay buried here.

I sat on a stubby concrete obelisk and gazed across the choppy water at the Auckland CBD skyline. No crashing airliners could topple that front rank. Threats that loomed large now would pass, and perhaps more quickly than we thought—just as the Tsar's reach had, so soon after this fortification had been built. The city and the earth seemed alike solid.

And yet, and yet . . . there was another world beyond this, perhaps even a better world beyond death, as the death-defying Beryozkin had told his executioners. This world that seems so real is contained within another more real, which in its turn may be contained within a world that is more real still. I now knew that for sure, or at least to a high probability. I didn't know much else. Where does it end? Is it simulations all the way down?

Maybe it was that reverie of simulations within simulations that gave me the idea. At one level, it was an idea so cheeky, so snook-cocking, that it made me giggle. It would let me say to the unknown gods: *I know you're there! I'm on to you!*

At another level, it was as improbable a method of making contact with another world as a cargo-cult tower is of making contact with passing aircraft.

I remembered seeing a sign for an Internet café in Victoria Road. There was no need to wait. I could do it now. I jumped up, picked up my shopping bags of books and clothes, and followed the zigzag path back down the grassy slope of Mount Victoria.

I contemplated using my command-level access to set up the implementation of my idea directly, but quickly decided that it was beyond my coding skills. Instead, I compiled a careful email, with several attachments, for Matt at Digital Damage. I knew he'd jump at the suggestion: he'd go for it first thing, when he came into work in a few hours, on the opposite side of the planet. When the email was complete I hesitated a moment. If I was right, this would change the world in ways I couldn't predict. The hell with it, I thought. The gods had dicked me about long enough. This was payback time.

And anyway, it almost certainly wouldn't do anything, beyond making Matt and a crowd of gamers smile: a little injoke, an Easter egg as the programmers call it, though I'm surprised they don't call that kind of code a Kinder Surprise egg, a chocolate egg the whole point of which is the snap-together plastic toy inside. (Particularly as so many programmers have a row of Kinder Surprise toys lined up on their desks.)

I hit Send, tilted back the plastic bucket chair, apologised to the guy behind me whose dreads I'd leaned into, rocked forward, and stared at the screen for a minute or two. At ten New Zealand cents a minute, this could have become expensive. I shook myself out of my contemplative trance and was about to log off when it occurred to me that I hadn't been properly online for almost a fortnight. I went back to my Google Mail account and found about five hundred messages in my inbox. I cleared the spam and other crud with a few keystrokes and set about ploughing through those that needed answers—starting with one from Sean, dated Monday, August 11, climbing down from his high horse and saying that of course I wasn't sacked and would be welcome back.

And a dozen that didn't need answers—long, chatty emails from Alec, describing his wrap-up research, his leaving do, his flight to NZ, what he'd been doing since he'd got back, his folks, the dogs, the horse . . . my ears burned as I thought how I'd complained about his not replying to my texts. I fired off one embarrassed reply, hoping he'd see it before he saw me tomorrow, and then set about catching up with my friends' LJs and blogs—mainly, I think, to stop myself from banging my head on the table.

I dropped a ten-dollar note and two dollar coins on my way out, about five. I couldn't believe I'd spent two hours of this sunny, breezy afternoon indoors and online. When I arrived back at the foot of Victoria Road I saw the ferry leaving the pier. Too bad. I'd just have to have a chardonnay and a grilled fish at this bar-restaurant I'd just passed. . . .

A glass or two later the sun had set. Darkness fell within fifteen minutes. The moon was upside down and too high in the sky. On the ferry back I stayed inside, but still looked out at the front at the lights of the CBD skyline and the winking warning beacon at the top of the Sky Tower.

I got back to the hotel about eight, dropped into bed, and slept for eleven hours. I was wakened by a text message from Alec. He said he couldn't get away from Queenstown for another couple of days, so why didn't I just fly there and he'd meet me off the flight at one?

I thought a few impolite things, and texted back to say I'd love to and was on my way.

Cue scramble. But booking was actually a doddle, and the trip to the airport and the flight itself uneventful (apart from my gawping at the mountains and the lake as the plane came in to land.) Alec wasn't there to meet me at Arrivals, but he hadn't texted again, so I expected to see him outside, probably (knowing him) just pulling in to the parking lot. I walked out of Arrivals at Queenstown with my head high, my hair down around the cowl collar of my new top, and the pretty skirt fluttering above my ankles.

That was when I heard the PA system paging Lucy Stone, and got the note:

Please tell Lucy Stone that Alexander Hamilton has been unavoidably detained with friends from the East.

That, and a mobile phone number that wasn't Alec's.

2.

There were several things I could do. One was to call Alec's number. I crossed that off the good ideas list. The next was to call the police. I filed that one under "last resort." I could call Amanda and/or Ross. But neither of these could do anything unless they knew who was holding Alec and what they wanted.

Was it possible, was it possible at all, that the message was innocuous and that Alec was merely deep in a meeting with a bunch of Chinese or Japanese wool importers, and that the negotiations were so delicate or the negotiators so touchy that Alec couldn't possibly take time out from the meeting to text me?

Stop kidding yourself, Lucy.

My fingers trembled as I punched the numbers on my iPhone's screen keypad. The phone rang for so long that I expected it any second to go to voicemail. But it just went on ringing. I was on the point of checking that I hadn't rung the wrong number when the phone was picked up.

"Hello?" I said.

"Lucy Stone?" Male voice, Russian accent. I almost dropped the phone.

"Yes," I said.

"You have something we want. We have something you want."

"Yes," I said, faintly. "Yes. What do you want?"

"We want what you found, Miss Stone. *All* of it. If you give us that, you will get *all* of what you want. If you do not, you will not get *all* of what you want. You will get only part, or parts, of what you want. Do you understand?"

I was sure he could hear my teeth rattle, but I was not as terrified as I had been.

"Y-y-yes," I said. "How do I give it to you?"

"You meet us, and answer every question, and give us everything we ask for."

It sounded like he expected some objection from me.

"Oh," I said, my voice squeaking with relief, "I'm quite happy to do that. Where do you want to meet?"

"The café at the wharf. As soon as possible."

"How will I recognise you?"

"*We* will recognise you."

"Oh."

"Yes. One more thing. If you attempt to use your phone, or otherwise contact anyone, we will know. If that happens, you will never get what you want. Not any of it. If anything untoward happens at our meeting—the same. Do you understand?"

"Yes," I said, more firmly this time. I felt I had their measure.

"See you very soon, Miss Stone."

End of call.

I tugged my rolling case to the taxi rank and took a cab into town.

Queenstown's basically a resort, on the shore of a deep, narrow, long, fresh-water lake, surrounded by high and jagged mountains.

The most impressive range is called the Remarkables, as if the first Euro-peans had staggered down here from the *Lord of the Rings* landscape of the Cook Mountains with nothing left but a mouthful of surprise in their last barrel of adjectives. The harbour is a U-shaped bay between the main shore and a small, wooded headland which is now a public garden, and behind which lies a minor arm of the lake.

The wheels of my case went bump-bump-bump over the timbers of the quay. Small boats and speedboats and jet-skis bobbed at their moorings or cut across the lake. A steamship, gleaming with polished brass and hardwood, lay hard by an adjacent pier. I headed for a corner of awnings and tables. Not many people were around—off-season, midweek. A young couple in cagoules, sipping tea, heads together over a map. A middle-aged man, staring into the distance through the smoke of his cigarette. A woman arguing with a six-year-old. I walked to the counter, watching out for men in suits, men in black, men like Mormon missionaries with shoulder holsters.

I ordered a coffee and carried it out in a yawing saucer. As I passed the cagoule couple's table, the young woman looked up from the map and said, "Oh, hi, Lucy!" in such a friendly tone that for a blank moment, as I turned so fast that the coffee slopped and stung on the back of my hand, I thought she might be one of the Russian or Polish girls from my old Starbucks crew.

"Please, come and join us," the man said, in just as friendly a tone, and as Russian an accent.

At the same moment as I recognised his voice as the voice on the phone, I recognised the mountains on the map. They weren't the Remarkables. They were the Caucasus.

I laid the cup and saucer on the table, and sat down opposite the couple.

"Ask anything you want," I said.

The man smiled. "No, Lucy. You tell us what you know."

"I'll tell you something I know," I said. "You're not from the *Mafiya*. You're not from the FSB or the RSB."

"And if we are not?" the man said.

"You're bluffing about what you threatened to do."

"Really?" said the woman. "You may underestimate us."

I glared back. "I don't underestimate you," I said. "I know there's an agency darker and scarier than the one my mother used to work for."

"And you're less scared of it than of Russian gangsters or spies?" The young man's Russian accent thickened with his sarcasm. "The black sites are such that the threat of them can terrify gangsters and spies. You wouldn't wish for anyone to be a ghost prisoner." He jerked his head to the left, in the general direction of the airport. "There is an aircraft fuelled, cleared for takeoff, waiting."

"Now you're talking," I said. "I can believe that." I leaned forward. "Look, there's no need for any of this. Like I said, I'm quite happy to tell you anything. You could have just *asked*."

"Why did you flee, then?" the woman asked.

"I didn't want to have this discussion except in a safe place," I said. "I mean, you're the guys who tried to hit me with rods from God."

"It was thought at the time that the recording had fallen into enemy hands," the man said.

"The only recording is on my phone," I said. "You're welcome to it."

"It is not the only recording," the woman said. "You emailed it yesterday, to an IP address in England."

"Scotland," I corrected, automatically. "To the games company I work— used to work—for."

"Yes, Lucy, we know that," the woman said. "What we don't know is, why?"

"I thought it would be amusing," I said, "to have the actual Krassnian secret in the virtual secret place that's the goal of the Krassnian game."

"Amusing?" the woman snapped. "*Amusing?*"

The man frowned. "How would it get in the game?"

"It would get included in the daily updates that go out to beta versions of the game," I said. "That one would have gone out about, oh, over twelve hours ago."

They both looked shocked.

"You mean it's already out there?" the man said.

"Yes," I said. "But don't worry, nobody who sees it is going to take it seriously, and nobody who takes it seriously is going to look for it there. It's hidden in plain sight."

"'In plain sight,'" the woman said savagely, "for you to reveal at your whim or discretion—or when you're told to."

"Told to?"

"By whoever you're working for. Such as, for instance, those Russians you mentioned."

There's only one right response to that, and it's the one I made. I laughed in their faces.

"Do you know who I am?" I said. "Do you know who you are dicking about with?"

"Yes," the man said. "Lucy Stone, daughter of Amanda Stone, great-grand-daughter of Eugenie Finn, née Montford. We know. Don't try to wave your family's old Agency connections at us. We don't work for that Agency."

I nodded. "Yes, I'm Amanda's daughter, and all the rest."

I waved a dismissive hand and took a deep gulp of cooled coffee.

"Let me tell you what you don't know," I went on. "I'm the natural daughter of Ilya Klebov, the richest man in Krassnia—"

The guy snickered. "That's like saying, 'the richest man in the South Bronx.'"

"—who is," I went on, "the man who back in the eighties turned a CIA op into a KGB op, then turned them both into his own op—in order to become, yes, the richest man in Krassnia. The man who destroyed the thing that I recorded—you can check that, I'm sure you have the satellite pics—and do you know *why* he destroyed it? This unique, irreplaceable, amazing thing? Because he wants to go *on* being the richest man in Krassnia. The man who—I have no doubt—called in the Russian troops last week, for the same reason. But there's more to him than that. He's a man who knows more about this thing than anyone else alive, because he's been observing it for years. He's also a man who knows exactly how capitalism got restored, going all the way back to the fifties—hell, the thirties—because his father was there, and told him, and he was there himself at the end, and helped to bring it about. He's a man who knows, literally, where all the bodies are buried.

"And you know what else? He's a man who cares about me. He took a great risk to save me, personally, when I was a little kid. You can ask Amanda about that. She'll confirm it. He took another risk to save me, just last week. You can check that on your fucking satellite pics, too.

"So my advice to you is, don't mess with Ilya Klebov. Don't harm a hair on the head of Ilya Klebov's little girl—or her boyfriend's. Let me tell you how it's going to be. You're going to release Alec, unharmed. You're going to tell my goddamn mother that she can settle this dispute over the copper mine by coming to an amicable arrangement with Klebov: he'll bequeath his shares in the mine to me, so it comes back into our family when he dies, and at the same time there's no acceptance of the old Ural Caspian Mineral Company's claims against Russia. On her side, if he does that, she stops trying to stir colour revolutions against him."

I was, of course, winging it. I was guessing that there were long and murky conspiracies in play, that they had at least an uneasy awareness of as matters best kept in the dark. Fundamentally, I was lying like a rug.

"And if we don't do all this?" the woman said.

At that point I knew I'd won.

"Klebov will blow the whole thing wide open," I said. "And if he doesn't hear from me, before this day is out, or if anything happens to me after that, he'll come after you, personally, to say nothing of what he'll do politically." I shrugged. "We've just stepped back from the brink of war over Georgia. Think what a mess it would make if it came out that the US had used kinetic-energy weapons on a territory claimed by Russia."

"Take a walk," said the man.

"What?" I said. "You're not—"

"I meant literally," he said. "To the end of the pier, and back." I left my case—theft was the least of my worries, at that point—and in as casual and confident a manner as I could manage, took a stroll. The Remarkables really are remarkable. I returned about five minutes later.

"One condition," the man said. "You must say nothing of this to anyone, not a hint, for the rest of your life. If you do—"

He drew his finger across his throat. I thought this was being a little too dramatic, but I nodded.

"OK. There's nothing I want more than to forget it."

They stood up.

"Your friend will be here in half an hour," the woman said.

"And you will call Klebov today, yes?"

"Yes," I said, wondering how. I'd find a way.

"One thing," she said, folding the map. "How did you know we were not, as you might have thought, Russian gangsters or such?"

"The Russians don't make threats with one eye on the possibility, however remote, that they might one day have to answer for them," I said.

"That's still the difference between us and them, you know," the woman said.

I decided this was a good time to say nothing.

Half an hour later, Alec walked around the corner of a building, onto the pier, and ran to me, and stayed with me, and I with him, and that was that.

I kept my promised silence for a long time. I'm only breaking it now, all these years later, because it no longer matters. I knew that someday I would, because in the half hour that I waited for Alec, another person came to see me.

MUNDUS IN MACHINA: MARS, 2248 A.U.C.; EARTH, AD 2008

You position your avatar precisely, calibrate the sensorium input jacks, give a thumbs-up to your teammates, and hit the switch.

And *wham*, you're there. You stagger for a moment in the higher gravity—you've got used to Mars—and then your muscle feedback adjusts. A chemical and fecal stench assails your sinuses. Dim light, a narrow stall with partial walls. You're in some kind of human waste recycling facility.

You tug the unlocked swing door open, and step out, past mirrors and washstands. Another woman, washing her hands under running water, doesn't give you a glance.

Outside, you take a few steps to get away from the waste facility and stand still for a full minute or so to breathe deeply and to absorb the sights and sounds of the mountains and the lake and the people. You can feel the air expand your chest, the fresh smells hit your nose, but this air isn't filling your real lungs. This sunlight, UV-rich (overrich, as it happens) isn't warming your real skin. But the illusion that it is is gratifying, and induces an intense homesickness for Earth.

Enough self-indulgence. You don't have long. You stride across the wooden decking and approach the red-haired girl who sits alone working with her thumbs on her handheld comms device. She hears your footsteps and looks up, startled, wary.

You rest your hand lightly on the back of a wooden chair opposite her.

"May I join you, Lucy?" you say.

The translation software is working: she seems to understand.

"Go ahead," she says. Still wary.

You pick up the chair, swing it behind you, and sit down on it in one smooth, fluid motion. Lucy looks surprised.

"That was neat," she says.

You realise that isn't how they do things, here. They aren't very athletic.

"I didn't mean to show off," you say.

"Who are you?" Lucy says. "Do I know you?"

You lean across the table and hold out a hand.

"My name is Daphne Pontifex," you say.

Lucy clutches your hand feebly, lets go, and flinches away a little.

"Who are you?" she repeats. She glances around, and over her shoulder. "Are you from the Agency, or . . . ?"

Her voice trails off on an unvoiced phrase of the question.

You decide to cut to the chase. She understands, she must understand, she can take it.

"No," you tell her. "I'm from the real world."

Her face pales. Her mouth works.

"No," she says. "No. This can't be happening."

"It's what you tried to make happen," you say. "Yesterday, in Auckland."

She smiles as if she suddenly understands.

"You *are* from the Agency, or from . . ." Again the trail-off, as if there's a name she doesn't dare pronounce, of some power that watches and listens and must not be carelessly invoked. "You're here to warn me off."

She waves her hands crosswise in front of her face. "OK, OK," she goes on. "I won't do it again. I *said* I wouldn't, to the other two. You don't need to do this. *They* didn't need to do this. They could just have asked nicely."

She looks as if she is about to cry.

"We could do with some coffee," you say.

She blinks. Her mouth begins to form a word—

You back out, jarringly, scan the local environment, and do a quick double copy-and-paste of some coffee and pastry. You drop back, into the machine world.

Lucy looks at the steaming, fragrant cup and tasty snack in front of her as if they were snakes. Her face, when it eventually tilts up, is even paler than before.

"How did you do that?" she says.

"You know how I did it," you say. "We *know* you understand."

She lays the fingers of one hand across her mouth.

"All right," she says. "All right."

Shakily, she picks up the cup, inhales through her nose, blows on the coffee, and sips.

"Tastes real," she says, with an experimental smile.

"It's all real," you say, after sipping and nibbling from your own copy-and-pasted coffee-and-pastry, and for a moment, as you enjoy the taste and heat and smell, it is all real to you, even though the caffeine won't stimulate your neurons and the carbohydrate and sugar won't go into your blood.

"Why are you here?" Lucy asks.

"Because you made contact. You let us know you knew. No one else has ever done that, at least none that we know of. We want to warn you not to do that again."

"Why not?"

"It's destabilising. If people become prematurely aware of what's going on, the feedback becomes chaotic."

"What *is* going on?" Lucy asks. "Do you people . . . intervene?"

"Not intentionally," you say, smiling. "The code you saw was what you would call a patch, to help us to observe without having to track millions of individuals. It was placed in an obscure location. Not obscure enough, as it turned out. The effects of its discovery by the Vrai weren't intentional on our part, but as it turned out—again—they were benign, in the long run. But with deliberate interventions, we have to be very, very cautious."

"But you're the programmers!" she says. "You can do anything!"

You recoil slightly.

"No!" you say. "We're not the programmers! We wouldn't do something as horrible as this!"

She gazes around at the milieu. "This isn't horrible."

"Not here, no, for a postcatastrophe civilisation in recovery. The catastrophe itself, and all the other places and times that you know about—these were and are horrible."

"Then who did set it up?"

You tell her.

"Oh, God," she says, almost groaning. "So we're a history experiment set up by amoral AIs."

"Synthetic Psyches, we call them. Yes."

"There must be a reason," she says, "why I thought of the Krassnia game just after I'd heard about another game about Romans on Mars and Spartacus winning and all that."

"Spartacus?" you say. "Never heard of him."

"He led a slave uprising."

You shrug. "In our history, there were a lot of slave uprisings."

"But still," she insists. "It wasn't a coincidence."

Oh, poor Lucy. She must never know. Never have the spell of her life broken. Never know of the fine-grained tweaks and fixes that have been made to the code that runs her mind. Else she will never trust her mind again.

Just as she must never know that Colin Byrne, aka Cairds, is an avatar of your comrade Hector O'Donnell, and that he has been on the case since before he opened the door of Ross's flat to Amanda, back in 1979 AD. Because if she knew that, she would have an even lower opinion of destiny.

And that would never do, because she still has a destiny.

You give her your most persuasive smile.

"In this world," you tell her, earnestly, "there are connections that are not quite causal within the physics of the world. There are what we call affinities. We don't fully understand them, but we suspect they are a result of efficiency savings and data compression. The same code is run in different contexts. There was an affinity between the legend and the real—so to speak—effect of the code running in Krassnia, and there may have been a like affinity between it and our level of reality. Hence, a game that echoed our reality, however distantly."

Lucy is still suspicious, unconvinced.

"You mean, like Sheldrake's morphic resonance?"

You have no idea what she's talking about.

"Something like that," you agree, confidently.

"I might buy that," she says.

(It's a strange usage they have. It means something to do with their equivalent of points.)

"It's the best explanation I can give," you say, truthfully enough.

"I'm going to look for explanations," she says. "You can't stop me doing that."

You restrain yourself from sighing with relief.

"We don't want you to stop, Lucy," you tell her. "We want your world to find out the truth for itself, in its own time. People alive at that time could even, we hope, come out of this world and into the real world. There are certain areas of physics where a concentration on anomalies would be a fertile line of investigation."

"But I don't know anything about physics."

"You don't have to," you tell her. "Someday, you'll be rich. When you are, you can put money into these lines of research."

"Which lines?"

You tell her.

She shakes her head with a sad smile, as if you are the one who is naive.

"Not even the shares in a copper mine could pay for that."

"I'm not talking about getting rich that way," you say.

You give her some hot tips for sound investments.

"But they'll only pay off in the long run," you caution her. "Meanwhile, work hard and stay well."

You know her lover is almost in sight. You rise to leave. Lucy stands too, looking you straight in the eye.

"I understand," she says, "I think, how knowing about the Stone Text affected the Vrai, and how the Vrai and people they affected brought down communism. But what about the West? Doesn't capitalism have its destructive consequences too? What are you going to do about that?"

You wish you could tell her about how the fall of communism led to an overweening overconfidence which is about to lead to another fall, from which something quite different from either of the old rival systems will arise.

But you don't have time. You don't have a minute.

"It's in hand," you tell her, and walk away without saying goodbye. You feel a pang. You liked her. You hope she succeeds in the task you've set her. If she does . . .

You'll see her again, in a better world, in another life.